EVELYN CROWLEY

A HARRY BECKER MYSTERY

GORDON REID

Printed in Australia

First Printing: March 2021

Shawline Publishing Group Pty Ltd
www.shawlinepublishing.com.au

Paperback ISBN- 9781922444585

Ebook ISBN- 9781922444592

For Lesley and Lisa

CHAPTER 1

It was a simple enough job. All he had to do was return a woman's handbag to an address not far out of town and hope she'd be at home. He found the place, stopped the car and got out, dangling the bag from one finger to avoid spoiling any prints. It was a black Gucci. There might be a small reward, or there might not. It didn't matter. He was just doing someone a good turn. Virtue, they said, was its own reward. He didn't think much about virtue these days. Staying alive was his main concern. Some days, he wondered why he bothered.

His name was Harry Becker, and he was feeling a bit stupid carrying a handbag, but this was a quiet street, Empire Circuit. And the suburb was Forrest. Anyone who could afford to live in Forrest was sure to be worth a packet. The street was heavily treed, spotted gums and cedars and elms, he thought. Across the road was a park, Collins Park. To one side was a group of oaks, turning red. Among the oaks was an old seat, wooden. It looked forlorn, as if hoping someone would come along and sit on it, make it feel wanted.

The house was a long, low Californian bungalow of the late twenties or early thirties, which had probably been converted and refurbished more than once over the years. A place like that in Forrest could have been worth half a million back then, back in 1995. This was well before Canberra house prices really took off. A small, dark-blue BMW sedan was standing on the bricked apron before the double garage at one end of the house. No doubt a bigger one was locked away inside. Or if there wasn't, there would be when the joker who owned this fancy joint showed up. It looked the sort of place where they would have a His and Hers.

Becker tended to limp because of arthritis, which went back to his football days. That was long ago, long before Whitford had tried to kill him. He was still carrying a damaged shoulder, hit by a .38 calibre bullet. The damned thing had never been fully reconstructed. No orthopaedic surgeon could work miracles. It was his right shoulder, and he was right-handed. He wasn't sure how fast he could react if he ever had to pull a gun to save his life. Probably not fast enough.

He climbed a few steps onto a porch, one of those big porches that went with big houses of that time. The porch had two trim pillars and the front door was set well back, so that when you reached it, you felt that you were already in the house. There was a heavy metal screen door and behind it, a heavy timber door. The windows, he noticed, were firmly screened, as if barred. Lights covered every square metre of the garden. Pointing at him from a high corner of the porch was a camera. No doubt it was linked to a recorder. This place was locked up fast, as tight as a bank.

On a window, he noticed a sticker he knew well: Guarded by Stanton Security. In this suburb, residents took intruders seriously. They had more to lose than handbags. You were always being watched, not necessarily by human eyes. He didn't like his chances. He wasn't in uniform, didn't carry even a Stanton card, but he did have the air of a tradesman, so maybe that would help.

He pushed a button on a wall and stepped back a respectful distance. A bell had rung inside, but there was no immediate response. After a while he pushed it again— still nothing. Two vehicles went past, a Land Rover and a Lexus four-wheel drive, both driven by women. One contained three girls, all in Canberra Grammar uniforms. No one in this kind of area sent their kids to a state school—and the kids never walked. You never knew when someone might grab them.

Out of the corners of his eyes he saw something move, a vertical slat at one of the windows. He knew he'd been observed, but had not been quick enough to see a face. These days he couldn't turn quickly, not even his head. If he tried, pain would shoot up his neck and into his skull. A doctor had said it was a pinched nerve. He'd given him injections, but they hadn't helped. Some days it was like a knife going into his brain.

He waited, thinking he'd better leave the handbag on the doorstep and depart. But some passer-by might nick it. There was nothing much in it, just some makeup and a linen handkerchief with the imprint of lips on it. And of course, the letter. But no purse and no keys. He lingered, unsure what to do. And unsure what to do about his life, now he'd got this far. Things weren't looking good. If he were called before the royal commission down in Sydney, he did not know what he'd do—spill the beans and risk another bullet? Or just shut up and say nothing on the grounds that anything he said might incriminate him? Either way, he'd look bad—even worse than he did now.

His job at Stanton was on the line. Three nights ago, someone had got into one of the big auto dealers in Lonsdale Street, opened the doors and made off with four late-model sedans, each worth more than thirty grand. According to the police, one man could have taken the lot, one after the other. It would have taken him some time to hide each car, come back and take another, at least two hours. Becker had called three times during the period, and the roll-up doors had been locked. It must have been an inside job, someone who had a key, probably a key copied at lunchtime and returned without being detected. With that kind of caper, how could a mere security guard know the place was being robbed blind? Stanton had lost the contract and Becker had almost lost his job. His boss had not been impressed.

'You should think about retirement, Harry.'

'I've got an ex-wife and three kids to support.'

'For an ex-copper, you're not too smart.'

'If I'd been smart, I'd be rich now.'

'What do you mean?'

'If you were in the force, you'd know.'

'You watch it, Harry. We can't afford to lose another client.'

'Yeah, I know...'

CHAPTER 2

A door opened—not the screen door, but the inner door. A woman stood behind the steel mesh. The hall was dark, so he could barely see her, just a collection of dots with a womanly shape. She could have been anybody, except that, when it came, her voice wasn't just anybody's. It was a rich voice, full of perfect vowels, but slow and sleepy as if she'd been dozing—or drinking, maybe a pick me up. Perhaps she'd had a bad day. Immediately he thought her a woman more aware of the past than the present. 'Oh, I apologise for keeping you waiting.'

'Good afternoon, ma'am. Are you Mrs Crowley?'

'Yes, I am.'

'I think I have something of yours.' He held up the bag.

'Oh, so you have.' She moved to open the outer door but hesitated, no doubt wary of a strange man. He could be anyone, perhaps an opportunist who'd seen her address and decided to take his chances on pushing his way in. 'I found it in a bin in Civic.'

'In a bin?'

'Yes, in Garema Place.'

'Did you indeed? Oh, yes, I had just reached my car, when a fellow came up behind me and snatched it.'

'A mugger?'

'Yes, in fact—,' she sighed. 'He knocked me aside. I fell against another car. He was off like a rabbit, dashing across Bunda Street and into Garema Place.' She paused, her voice trailing off. It was the kind of voice that habitually trailed off. Obviously, she was not going to open the screen door. He made to depart. 'I'll leave it on the porch.'

'Oh, thank you.'

'I wouldn't touch it too much if I were you. He probably left prints.'

'Prints?'

'Yes, just in case the police have them on file.'

She seemed puzzled. 'Police?'

'If you report it.'

'Oh, I see.' She didn't seem to care about catching the thief.

'Lucky I spotted it.'

'Yes, it was. How kind of you to bring it.'

'It just caught my eye as I was passing.'

'Yes, of course.' She took a deep breath, brightening now. 'How did you know where to find me?'

'There was a letter inside.'

'Oh, yes, so there was.'

'No purse.'

'No, I suppose not.' She didn't seem to be a woman who would miss a few dollars.

'Any cards, Mrs Crowley?'

'What's that?'

'Credit cards. You should notify the bank immediately.'

'Oh, yes, of course. I will.'

'You have the numbers? Of the cards?'

'I think so, somewhere.' She looked around, as if trying to spot them, at the same time pushing back her hair. It was very dark hair, almost black like dark chocolate. It was parted in the middle and hung down on both sides, showing only a triangle of pale forehead. And below that was the kind of face you see in movies of a woman staring from a narrow window in some back street on the other side of the world, where you wouldn't want to walk alone. Not if you valued your life. 'My husband made a note of them, I think. Yes, he did.'

'You should cancel them immediately.'

'Yes, I suppose—' Her voice trailed off again. She seemed unable to think clearly. Perhaps she was on medication. A few times during the conversation she had rubbed her eyes and then her forehead, not with a hand but just the fingertips. He set the bag down and began, again, to depart. 'Good afternoon, Mrs Crowley.'

'Yes, thank you, Mr—'

'Becker.'

'Becker?'

'Yes, Harry Becker. I work for Stanton Security. I see you're one of our clients.'

She did not seem to understand. 'Oh?'

'The lights and the cameras.'

'Oh, yes. Stanton? Is that the name?'

'Yes,' he said, thinking: This woman is stupid. She must see the sticker every day. He went down the few steps without looking back. It didn't matter about a reward. He'd long given up expecting rewards in this life and didn't expect any in the next. He'd done the decent thing by returning the bag. Now he could get on with the rest of his life, waiting for someone to kill him. To finish the job.

He heard a click behind his back. She'd opened the screen door. He was far enough away for her to take a chance. Quickly, she picked up the bag and glanced inside. 'Oh, Mr Becker?'

'Yes?'

'Did you read it?'

'The letter? No, I didn't.'

'It's just that I'd opened it.'

'Yes, I noticed.'

'You didn't look at it?'

Becker was mildly offended. 'Ma'am, I just said—'

'Yes, you did. I'm so sorry. I shouldn't have doubted—' She sighed, again running a hand through her hair. It was long, curly hair, almost frizzy, the tips of which reached just below her collarbones. And it was not as dark as he'd first thought. Rather, it was a rich brown, reminding him of fruit cake or something just as luscious. She was, he saw, neither young nor old, perhaps his own age, which was thirty-eight. Her face was strained, her eyes a little puffy. Perhaps she'd been crying, although her cheeks were dry. That may have been why she'd taken so long to answer the door, checking her hair, dabbing her eyes, trying to make herself look reasonably presentable—even for a tradesman.

She stepped out of the shade of the porch and into the sunlight—a tall woman, not a string bean but not plump. Statuesque, you might say. One day she would be heavy, even matronly. Already she was probably a bit heavier in the breasts, belly and hips than she would have liked. She must have been a beauty in her youth. As yet, she was far from faded. There was a Mediterranean look about her. She could have been

Italian but had no noticeable accent. She was wearing a soft, milky white blouse and a black skirt, the blouse not being tucked in but hanging loosely, possibly to hide her waistline. An over blouse, his wife had once called it. That was when she was pregnant. 'Good afternoon, Mrs Crowley.'

Once more, he headed for his car. To her, he was probably nobody, just a man who delivered the groceries or the mail, a functionary in an orderly world in which every little thing had its place. She stood on the porch, holding the bag. 'Stanton Security, you said?'

'Yes, that's right.'

'Did you install the...?'

He looked at the warning light on the fascia boards above her head. If anyone broke into the house, the light would flash, a siren would sound, and a panel would buzz back at base. The police would be notified immediately. In no time, a patrol car would be on its way, so would a car from Stanton. Probably the thief would be well away by then. The neighbours would try to ignore the alarm, gritting their teeth and hoping someone would switch it off. Only the rich cared about theft. The poor did not. For them, it was part of the price you paid for being alive. 'System? No, I'm not a technician.'

'What do you do, may I ask?'

'I rattle doors in the night, check windows.'

'You mean a watchman?'

'That sort of thing.'

She took one or two more steps, as though tempted to follow. He had almost reached his car. It was a strange experience, something that had never happened to him—being followed by a good-looking woman trying to make conversation, as if he mattered. As if he could do something for her, something that no other man could do. As if she'd be grateful if he'd do it, whatever it was.

'Mr Becker, I can't let you go without...' She seemed lost for her next words. 'You know, giving you something for your trouble.'

'No trouble, Mrs Crowley. Just remember me in your prayers.' He'd intended the answer to be flippant, but she took it seriously. 'You pray, Mr Becker?'

'I used to—'

'What did you pray for?'

'A better job than this.'

'It doesn't pay well?'

'The pay's all right, the hours are the killer.'

'What hours do you work?'

He was about to open the Holden. It was a bit of a wreck, but it still fired when he turned the key. 'Eight until eight.'

'Eight at night until eight next morning?'

'That's right.'

'That's twelve hours a day.' He nodded.

'Five days a week.'

'Sixty hours a week? Oh, that's...' Again, she had to think. 'That's awful.' She'd stepped into the garden, moving in her absent-minded way, glancing about as though she'd lost something. Or perhaps she just wanted to talk. There wasn't much in the garden, just an immaculate lawn on which stood three silver birches, not the kind of trees anyone could hide behind. Nothing big and dense anywhere, just low gardenia bushes against the walls and roses against the fences. Honeysuckle along the top of one, probably the neighbour's vine. It was all perfectly trim, like her. 'Have you always been a... security guard?'

'I used to be a cop.'

She was startled. 'A policeman?' She gazed at him, slightly frowning, as if surprised to find herself talking to a policeman and did not know what to do about it—get rid of him as soon as possible or ask for his help. Her eyes, he could now see, were heavy lidded and her eyebrows arched. Her expression was remote and vaguely defeated, as though she'd lost something she knew would never come again. He lingered. You didn't meet a woman like Evelyn Crowley every day. Not a man like him.

He nodded again. 'Twelve years in the force.'

'In Canberra?'

'Mainly in Sydney.'

'Were you really?'

'Rose to the dizzy heights of Senior Constable.'

'And you quit?'

'I was told to resign.'

'Really? Why was that?' What did it matter if he told her?

'I knew too much.'

She tensed. In her small world, where everything went like clockwork, she probably knew nothing of police corruption. 'I'm sorry.'

'That's how it goes, Mrs Crowley.'

'Yes—' She spoke as if she did know after all. 'Mr Becker?'

'Yes?'

'If you were in the police force—'

'They call it the police service now, Mrs Crowley. They want people to think they're all public servants, who wouldn't hurt a fly. Force is bad for the image.'

'Yes—' She took a deep breath, a hand to her breast without actually touching it. 'I was wondering whether you do private work?'

He didn't, not with his horrible hours, but he was intrigued. 'What sort of work?'

'Well, I...' She looked around, as though afraid of prying neighbours. Nothing moved in the street, neither a car nor a bird. It was mid-April, the sun was shining and there was very little wind. A good autumn day, but it would not last long. The first leaves had begun to fall.

'I'd just put on some coffee, when I heard the bell. Would you care for a cup?' He was surprised. Coffee with a woman like her would be a treat for a man like him, a lost soul in baggy jeans, lifeless joggers and a shapeless old jacket. If he'd known he was going to be invited into a place like this, he'd have done something about it. But it was too late now. She was waiting for a reply. 'If you have to be on your way...'

'No, not at all. Coffee would be fine, Mrs Crowley.'

CHAPTER 3

She showed him into the house. She tended to saunter like a guide in a gallery full of famous pictures. Or a woman in no hurry to go anywhere, just filling in time. The hall was wide and from the ceiling hung an electric chandelier. On each side hung Canaletto prints of Venice, tastefully framed. The house had a distinctive odour, beeswax. And there was a perfume, although not hers. On a small table by the door stood a large brandy goblet, peacock blue. In it were dozens of crumpled petals, no doubt from her own garden, perhaps the last roses of summer. Beside the goblet was a small bottle in a ceramic dish, labelled Attar of Roses. 'If you'll just go into the—' She waved a hand.

'Thank you.'

'I won't be long.'

The sitting room was simply and yet expensively furnished. Everything looked old-fashioned, but too clean and too neat to be used. A large Bokhara rug graced the shiny jarrah flooring. To one side was a sofa with cabriolet legs and, facing it, two chairs in the same suite. It looked like a suite he'd seen in a famous old house in Vaucluse, which was open on special days to visitors. There had been a break-in, a priceless painting stolen. That one, according to the guide, was a genuine Queen Anne. This one, however, looked brand-new, probably a reproduction. On the walls were paintings and drawings, at first sight too many. They filled his gaze to the point of distraction so he could not fix upon any particular one. Then, as he looked, they seemed to form themselves into a geometric pattern, which might have been the whole point of their being there, rather than any artistic value.

Above the marble fireplace was fixed a huge mirror, in which he saw himself reflected as a scruffy man in a large room full of rich trappings, a man surprised to find himself there—an intruder in a private museum. He strolled from object to object, wishing he had the knowledge to appreciate them. He'd never seen such wealth except years ago, when he'd been called to house break-ins in Elizabeth Bay and Point Piper in Sydney. In those days, he'd had to focus on the job. Now he could take his time. If things got any worse at Stanton, he'd have all the time in the world.

He was examining a carved ebony head of an African woman on the marble mantelpiece, when she returned bearing a silver tray. She had combed her hair, he noticed. Not a hair out of place now. A well-groomed woman, who knew how to look and walk and talk to strangers. When he offered to help, she said, 'If you'd just move that newspaper—' The paper was open at the financial pages. There was a headline, against which someone had put a cross: 'Canberra man tipped for World—' He didn't have time to read the rest, but he did glimpse a photo of a thin man with black eyebrows and intense eyes, just like hers. Otherwise there was no resemblance.

She placed the tray on a low table, fashioned in the same style as the suite. As she did, she bobbed rather than stooped. The top button of her blouse, he noticed, had not been undone. Nor, as far as he could detect, had she dabbed on more perfume. Nothing sexy about her. Not overtly sexy anyway.

'Oh, please be seated. I'd been resting and thought I must have some coffee to—' He sat at one end of the sofa, while she sat on one of the chairs, facing him. He watched as she poured. The low table was more or less between them. She was leaning forward, her knees pressed together so correctly that she had to lean to one side. Women in high heels, he had noticed, tended to do that. Her shoes were black, no doubt to go with the bag, or the other way around. She was sure to have a handbag to go with every outfit.

'I know I should offer you a reward, but, you see, without my purse... My cheque book was in that bag too.'

He had not seen a cheque book. The thief might have taken it, or it might have fallen out as he'd run. 'I don't want any money.'

'I feel so embarrassed.'

'You've reported the loss?'

'Of the bag? No, I hadn't got around to that.'

'And the purse?'

'Well, you see...' She thought about it as she poured. Or, more likely, she thought about her next words. 'I was so upset at being knocked down that, when I got home, I just flopped on my bed and—' She must have realised this was a feeble excuse. 'I know

I should have, but I was so rattled.' The pot shook as she poured the second cup, so she had to steady it with the other hand, just the fingertips against a wrist. 'Thank goodness I had my keys in my hand when that fellow—I don't know how I would have returned home without money.' She shrugged slightly. 'Do you take sugar, Mr Becker? Milk?'

'Just sugar, thank you. One spoon.'

'I take saccharine.' She opened a silver pillbox on the tray, selected one. Becker watched it fizz in her coffee. She sat back and took a sip, one hand holding the cup and the other holding the saucer, as if she feared spilling a drop. As she'd sat back, she'd begun to cross her legs. The skirt was calf-length and wouldn't have shown her knees. Even so, she changed her mind, as though thinking it improper to cross her legs in front of a strange man. A real lady, she knew how to behave.

Mrs Crowley cleared her throat. 'As a matter of fact, Mr Becker—' Even before she said it, he knew what she was going to say. 'I had a reason for not reporting the loss—of the bag, I mean.'

'The letter?'

Mrs Crowley flinched, rattling the cup. It had been obvious it was the letter. She didn't want the letter to fall into the wrong hands, not even the police. She sipped the coffee once again, taking her time. This woman appeared to think out every little move down to the last detail—like a jumbo captain lining up the massive metal beast for the runway and a perfect touchdown.

'Yes, the letter.' Mrs Crowley licked her bottom lip, delicately. Then, just as delicately, she ran a fingertip along the lip. He'd seen all these tricks before, many times. He might have been a failed cop, but he wasn't stupid. 'You see, well, it's a bit embarrassing—' She coughed delicately. 'Before I married, I had an affair with a man in Melbourne. As a result, I had a child, a girl.'

'Out of wedlock?'

'Yes.'

'And you had to give her up? For adoption?'

'Yes.'

'The man was not your husband?'

'No.'

'Does he know about the child?'

'My husband? Oh, no, I didn't dare tell him.'

'Why not?'

'Well, I... No, I just couldn't. I was ashamed of that part of my life.'

'What do you want me to do about it, Mrs Crowley?'

He waited while she thought about her next words. Mrs Crowley spoke very correctly. You could hear the punctuation in her voice, every full stop and comma. He was prepared to wait all day. He could have been in a cinema, watching a woman sitting on an elegantly carved chair, elegantly drinking coffee and modestly displaying her elegantly carved legs.

Some time ago, on one of his lonely nights off-duty, he'd gone to the Canberra Playhouse to see a play. He didn't recall much about the play, largely because it was apparently very modern and he'd not understood it—something about totalitarianism and probably set somewhere in Eastern Europe, but that was not clear at all. He did, however, remember the last scene. A woman sat alone on a chair reading a book beside a small table, on which was a telephone. She too had gorgeous legs. The phone rang. She picked it up, listened for a few seconds and said, 'Yes.' She listened some more and again said, 'Yes.' Once more she listened and said, 'Yes.' Then she said, 'Thank you for letting me know,' in exactly the same tone each time. At last, she put down the phone and picked up the book as the curtain came slowly down. Perhaps that was the whole point of the play. Life was like waiting for a call, which ultimately changed nothing.

'Do you think you could find her—for an appropriate fee, of course.'

'Find her?'

'Do you think you could?'

He watched her, a well-heeled woman who hated to beg. 'Well, I can't say I'm a man of the world, Mrs Crowley, but it seems these things happen. No need to be ashamed of it.' She did not reply. 'How old is she now?'

'Oh, she'd be seventeen. Yes, seventeen. I would so much love to see her, find out where she is, who she is with, how she is getting on. I—' She appeared to run out of ideas.

'You've tried to contact her?'

'No, I can't.'

'The adoption agency won't tell you anything?'

'Not a word. It's against the rules, they said. They cannot give me any details without the adoptive parents' permission.'

'And they won't identify the parents?'

'No.' She sighed, raised a hand as if to push back her hair again, but left it hanging in the air. She had lovely hands, broad at the base with long tapering fingers, which ended in perfectly manicured nails, not coloured but highly polished. Hands too precious to be touched by just anybody.

'I thought the law had been changed so you could ask the adoptive parents whether they would permit you to contact the girl. I think you have to go through the agency.'

'Yes, yes, I suppose that's it.'

'Why don't you do that?'

'Oh, I don't know—What if they refuse?'

'Well, I guess that's that.'

'If I could just see her—'

'How are you going to see her without meeting her?'

'Oh, I thought perhaps you could find out where she lives and perhaps—'

'You could take a private peep?'

'What? Oh, I see what you mean. No, well, I suppose that would be possible, wouldn't it?'

'You know it is illegal to make contact without permission?'

'It wouldn't be actual contact, would it? I just want to see her, if only for a few minutes.' She was waving a hand around, hopelessly.

'You want me to make enquiries?'

'Could you?' Again she pushed back her hair, just a touch with her fingertips. Perhaps it was a habitual gesture, although he guessed she never did anything habitually. Everything was worked out in advance, even the dainty licking of her lips and the precise angle of her gaze. She was looking straight at him, pleading. Her eyes were not black as he'd thought at first glance, but mid-brown flecked with gold. But, as he looked, he got a shock. Something, he realised, behind those eyes was watching him carefully.

She was a beautiful woman. Or, if not exactly beautiful, she had once been beautiful. Probably a passionate woman, who'd got herself pregnant. Now, seventeen years later, she wanted to see the child. It seemed a simple enough story, perhaps too simple. After all, where did the letter come into this? 'You could go to an enquiry agent, you know. Or a lawyer.'

'Yes, my lawyer said she could write to the adoption agency on my behalf, but—' She shrugged, perhaps flustered, embarrassed. 'I do not want to meet my daughter, I just want to know that she is safe.' Safe? Safe from whom? Mrs Crowley, it seemed, wanted to know about her daughter but did not want the girl to know about her.

'If you have been a policeman—'

'I might know how to get around the rules?'

'Could you really?' She brightened, almost smiling—at the same time leaning forward and running a hand down one leg. Scheming females did that in all the movies, to draw attention to their legs—and what was between them. Was she offering a reward in bed? She didn't seem to be the type at all. Anyway, why would any woman try that trick just to get someone to find a missing daughter? At this stage, he should have stood up and said, 'Listen, sweetheart, don't try to pull no funny business, okay?' But he didn't. He enjoyed looking at Mrs Crowley, listening to her, being with her. 'Might be possible.'

'I'd be so grateful.'

'I'll check around.'

'Really?' She was excited. Her eyes were smiling, and her hands were fidgeting, her feet too. She had beautiful feet, he noticed—at least beautiful shoes, Italian no doubt, most likely crafted in Milan. He wondered whether she really was Italian. She had all the colouring, if not the voice. That was purely Australian, but well-trained, professional. She probably sounded great on the phone. It was a womanly voice, mature, soft and easy with a slightly earthy edge to it. He'd noticed that Italians, some Italians, perhaps only those from the south, tended to have such voices. Not exactly husky or gritty, but earthy. People of the soil who ate nothing but cheese and olives and drank rough red wine. He finished the coffee, began to rise.

'Would you care for another cup?'

'I drink too much coffee, Mrs Crowley.' He'd had coffee with his lunch and had walked to a bin to throw in the paper cup, when he'd spotted the bag. He'd have another coffee before he began his shift this evening and another about midnight. It was the only thing that kept him awake on the job—that and the fear of death. A bullet in the cold, empty night. She rose too. 'You're working again tonight?'

'For my sins.'

Again, she took it seriously. 'Your sins?'

'Being too stupid.' He walked towards the front door. 'Someone took a shot at me three years ago in Sydney—wanted me dead.'

'Oh!'

He wasn't sure why he'd said that. It just came out.

'Lucky I moved just in time. I took it here.' He tapped his right shoulder.

'I'm sorry.' She did sound genuinely concerned, following in her casual way, arms folded. 'Mr Becker, why did they do it?'

'As I said, I knew too much.'

'May I ask why you knew too much?'

'I was one of them.'

'You mean you were—'

'Corrupt? Yeah, I took money from crims, we all did. All of us in a certain little group at the Cross.'

'The Cross?'

'King's Cross.'

'Oh?'

'So we'd turn a blind eye.'

'But you were shot?'

'I saw a bloke almost beaten to death, because he wasn't paying up. That was the end, I was fed up. I decided to go to the top, tell the Commissioner all about it. Unfortunately, I told a few friends.'

'And someone tried to stop you?'

'Correct.'

'I'm so sorry.'

He paused at the door, a hand on the handle. She was standing close, so close that he could have touched her. She was giving him something of herself—her nearness, her shape, her grace, her deep-brown eyes and her perfume. Not exactly perfume but all those things that women used—makeup and hand cream and oils and even the shampoo redolent of almonds she'd used on her hair that morning. He could smell it now. It was part of her, like the heat of her body. 'And you, Mrs Crowley?'

'What's that?'

'The letter, it's not about your daughter, is it?'

She jumped. At first, she was going to disagree. 'No, I mean—' He waited. She wanted to tell him, he sensed. But she did not.

'It's none of my business,' he said.

He opened the door and stepped out. She followed, arms still folded, then leaned against the brickwork of the porch, head down, eyes shut. He had felt he should help her, whatever it was she was hiding. But, if she were not going to tell the truth, why should he get involved? He walked to the gate. There was no real gate, just an entrance with a brick pillar on each side. In one was a brass letter box, and above it a brass street number. On the other was a brass lamp. A coach lamp, he thought. When he reached the Holden, he saw she had stepped well out, her eyes downcast, her expression disappointed. He felt sorry, so he came back just a few paces. 'What was your maiden name, Mrs Crowley?' He didn't know why he was doing this. Already he'd decided he should be quit of her. She straightened. 'What was that?'

'Your maiden name?'

'My—? Oh, it was—' She had to think. There was something seriously wrong with her, he could see. It was drink or drugs or just a bad conscience, or all three. 'Scarafini.'

'Evelyn Scarafini?'

'Yes... no. It's Evalina Scarafini, but I've always been called Evelyn.'

'Evalina?'

She spelled it. 'It means Little Eva. My mother's name was Eva, you see.'

'And the date of birth?'

'Mine?'

'The child's.'

'Oh, yes, the fourth of January 1978.'

'Place of birth?'

'The Women's Hospital, Melbourne.'

'That should do it.'

'Oh, thank you, Mr Becker.'

He was pleased. You could say he was hooked already. The warmth in her voice did it, the earthiness and the quality. If he found the girl, she might be grateful, not with money or even a kiss on the cheek but just friendship. Something might come of it. Who knows? Even if she were strange and perhaps dangerous to know, just to stand close to her again, that would be enough.

'Thank you, Mrs Crowley.'

CHAPTER 4

He had nothing better to do, so he drove across the border to Queanbeyan and saw Bob Fricker, the only honest cop he knew. Or at least, the only cop he could still call a friend. Not that Fricker was all that friendly—he couldn't afford to be seen too close to a man who had been kicked out of the force for taking bribes. Fricker had urged him to go to the top and tell what he knew about Sergeant Whitford, even if doing that would implicate him in the whole scam. He'd taken the advice and gone to the top, spilled the beans. For his pains, he was told to shut up, not say a thing about it—not do anything that would give the force a bad name.

At that time, in the early nineties, the New South Wales police already had the worst reputation in the country. Now it was all coming out, slowly but surely, under the grilling they got from the royal commission headed by Mr Justice James Wood. His investigators were producing recordings of secret meetings. Videotapes of deals done in cars, money changing hands. And it had all been leading to Senior Sergeant Dickie Whitford, the man who ran things at the Cross.

When he walked into the Queanbeyan station and asked to see Fricker, the young constable at the desk simply stared at him.

'You want to see Sergeant Fricker?'

'That's what I said.'

'Got an appointment?'

'I don't need an appointment. We go back a long way.'

'What name?'

'Becker.' The young bloke still stared at him. 'Harry Becker,' he said, the way James Bond said James Bond. When James Bond said James Bond, people reacted. When Harry Becker said Harry Becker, people just stared.

'Yeah?' The constable continued to stare at him. In some circles, Becker was a legend, a man who'd taken money for years from Whitford and then had tried to roll over, wanting to tell all. He hadn't been given the chance. One night he'd been shot as he'd stepped out with his garbage can—nearly killed him. If a car had not driven up, the assassin would have taken another shot, finished the job. Most cops in New South

Wales had heard about it soon after—and learned the lesson. You don't squeal on your mates.

Becker stared back. 'You going to tell him?'

'I'll see if he's in.' Becker followed him. Fricker was not pleased to see him. On the other hand, he had a moral duty. If he hadn't advised Becker to go up the line and tell all, he wouldn't have been shot. As for Fricker himself, he'd been transferred to Broken Hill, where he'd languished until six months ago. Now he was in Queanbeyan, twiddling his thumbs in a desk job. After more than thirty years in the force, he was still a sergeant. He never would be promoted. Someone would see to that. Now he was just hanging on, waiting to retire.

When Becker told him what he wanted, Fricker was surprised. 'You've turned private eye?'

'I need to do her a favour. She wants to know what happened to her daughter.'

'Is this a police matter?'

'She's afraid her husband will find out.'

'What's this got to do with the police?'

'Nothing at all, but I said I'd try to help.'

'This is against the rules, you know.'

'I know.' Fricker sat back, studied Becker.

'You've heard about Whitford?'

'Whitford?'

'Someone bashed him to death.'

'What?'

'With a pretty sharp spade, made a real mess of him—nearly chopped his head off.'

'Jesus, when was this?'

'Two or three months ago, out at La Perouse.'

'Hell, who did it?' Fricker shrugged.

'Who knows? The word is another cop did it. It wasn't you, was it?'

'Jesus, no!'

'You had reason enough, mate.'

'Bloody hell, why?'

Another shrug. 'Maybe someone else who couldn't take it any longer.' Becker was amazed. Tricky Dickie Whitford was dead? Killed by another cop? There had been times when Becker himself had thought of killing the bastard, when the pressure had got so bad there seemed to be no other way out. He'd never had the chance and if he'd had the chance, he would not have been able to do it. Whitford was indestructible, or so everyone had thought. Now the ugly brute was dead. Good riddance. The world was a better place without him.

'Give me the details, Harry.'

'What?'

'The woman and the child.'

'Ah, yeah, yeah.'

So he told Fricker all he knew and gave him his mobile number. Later that day, just after sunset, the old sergeant rang him. Becker was back in Garema Place, eating a chicken burger. He had a room in a house in Ainslie, occupied by some Indians. Sometimes they treated him to a curry dish. He tried to avoid the curry, it was always too hot. He couldn't afford a restaurant and he didn't do his own cooking, so he lived on takeaways and fast-food joints. He was overdoing it, he knew. Eating bad food and putting on too much weight. His feet were beginning to hurt. Some days his ankles were swollen. He wouldn't be surprised if he were heading for diabetes. In a way he was sorry, especially now he'd met a beautiful woman. One who'd talked to him, asked him about himself, and had listened as if what he had to say mattered—at least to her, if not to anyone else. He was ashamed of himself. She must have thought him a slob, sitting on her faux-antique sofa and drinking her coffee and trying to chat like a man of the world, who might or might not be able to do her a little favour.

Fricker did not have much. The baby was adopted by Raymond and Elizabeth Billings of Murrumbeena, Melbourne.

'Billings? And where are they now?'

'Nowhere in Melbourne, I checked. Not even in Victoria.'

'That all, Bob?'

'That's all. I shouldn't be doing this.'

'Thanks, mate, I owe you one.'

'Ah, you don't owe me anything.'

Becker went to a phone box and found a directory. It was torn, they always were. This time he was lucky. He found the Crowley number, called it on his mobile. A woman answered. 'Oh, hello?'

'Mrs Crowley?'

'Yes.'

'Harry Becker.'

'Oh, Mr Becker, yes?' She sounded surprised.

'Is it safe for you to talk?'

'Yes.'

'What about your husband?'

'Oh, he's in Tokyo at present, I think.' She spoke as if he could be anywhere, such as Tokyo or New York or London or Rome. Any place except at home.

'I have a lead on your daughter.'

'You have? What is it? Where is she?'

'I don't know. She was adopted by a couple named Billings in Murrumbeena, Melbourne—Raymond and Elizabeth Billings. They don't live there now. In fact, they don't live anywhere in Victoria.'

'Billings?'

'Yes, her name is Christine Billings. If she's still in Australia, she shouldn't be hard to find with a name like that.'

She was really excited. 'My daughter is Christine Billings!'

'You'd better get someone to search the records for her parents. Try the phone books and electoral rolls.'

'Yes, of course.'

'Have you contacted the police?'

'The police?'

'About the theft.'

'Oh, no, I—'

'You don't want to?'

'No, it does not matter.'

'What are you frightened of, Mrs Crowley?'

'Frightened? Oh, I'm not—'

'You sure sound like it.'

'Do I? Oh God, is it so obvious?'

'It's the letter, isn't it?'

'Oh—'

'Are you all right?'

Suddenly, she was panting. It was a sharp, clear, loud line. Her lips must have been close to touching the phone. Now she was gasping. 'You don't want the police to see it, do you?'

'Oh, God!' He waited while she calmed down. At last she said, 'Could you come over?'

'When?'

'Oh, whenever you can.'

'Well—' He was not sure he should get involved. He might have to listen to a sob story, which might or might not be true. Still, he couldn't resist. It was hard to resist Evelyn Crowley. She was not a damsel in distress, as his wife had been when she'd told him she was in a mess because she was pregnant and her boyfriend wouldn't marry her and she didn't know what to do, because her father would kill her when he found out. So, he, Harry Becker, stupid chump that he was, had said, 'Ah, don't worry, love, I'll marry you. How's that?'

'All right, how about now?'

'Yes, yes, please.'

So he drove to the house again. The porch light was switched on. So were several other lights indoors. She must have seen him arrive, because he was about to put a finger on the bell button, when the inner door opened. Then the screen door immediately. 'Oh, thank you' she said. 'Come in. Yes, please come in.' He did so. She seemed flustered, more than early in the afternoon. Turning this way and that, as though unsure how to handle him, the situation, or herself. 'Would you sit in here? I'm a bit upset, I—' She put a hand to her breast, again not touching it. 'Can I get you a drink?' There was a half-empty glass on a glass-topped cabinet.

'What are you having?' he ventured.

'Oh, whiskey,' she said. 'I've had one already. I'm not a drinker, but this afternoon—'

'That's all right,' he said. He didn't know why he was telling her it was all right. It was her house. She could do what she liked. Already she'd gone to the cabinet, was pouring a glass. 'Ice? Soda? Water?'

'Ice,' he said.

She topped up her own glass, brought both back and sat, not facing him this time but on the other end of the sofa. It was a three-seater and the small table was between their legs. Hers were neatly crossed at the ankles. Looking at her side on he realised for the first time Mrs Crowley had a dominant nose, hooked but not too big, suggesting she was not the kind of woman to argue with. Conversely, she had a lovely mouth, the lower lip full but not protruding—the kind anyone would want to kiss. And when she smiled, it was almost a shy smile, the kind you might get from a pretty schoolgirl. He was going to say 'Cheers!' or something he hoped might be appropriate, but did not get the chance. Immediately she reached for her handbag on the table, opened it and pulled out the letter quickly, as if anxious to get rid of it. 'Please look at this.'

He swallowed a mouthful as he reached for it, unfolded it. It was a brief letter, typed and to the point. 'We know all about what you've done. Five thousand by ten o'clock Friday night or else we go to the police. You know where to drop it. We ain't kidding. Five thousand or you're in deep trouble sweetheart.' Apart from the missing apostrophes, it was well typed. A professional job, you might say. Of course, it was not signed.

'Friday night? That's tonight.'

'Yes, they don't give me much warning, do they?'

'You've had a previous letter?'

'Yes, two. They keep at me. I don't know what to do.'

'Can I see the other two?'

'What? Oh, no, I burned them. I—I was afraid my husband might see them.'

He knew that was a lie. He didn't understand why she wouldn't want him to see them, but he let it pass.

'Where do you have to drop it?'

'At an empty house in O'Connor. I mean in the letter box.'

'And you have the money?'

'Yes, no, I don't. It was in my bag. You see, when I received that letter this morning, I went to the bank in town and withdrew it, all in hundreds. It was in an envelope, a bank envelope, the logo on it. Is that the right word, logo? And I was walking back to my car—'

'And now some mugger can't believe his luck?'

'Yes.'

'Can you get another five thousand?'

'Well, no, I don't have that much in my account.'

'And you can't ask your husband for the money?'

'Good lord, no!'

'You don't want him to know anything about it?'

'No, no, no—'

'Well, no need to worry.'

'What do you mean?'

'Go to the police, tell them what's happened. Show them the letter.'

'What?' She looked terrified.

'You don't have to tell them why you are being blackmailed.'

'Don't I?'

'It doesn't matter if you've robbed the Bank of England, blackmail is a crime in itself. The cops will know what to do. They'll set a trap. You keep the appointment, drop the stuff in the box and beat it. When the villain or villains turn up, the cops will pounce.'

'But I don't have the money!'

'Look, Mrs Crowley, if the police will be there, you don't need money. Just drop anything in the box, an envelope containing a wad of paper. That'd do.'

'Oh—' She drank some whiskey. Or she tried too. Clearly, she was flustered. 'I don't want the police involved.' She was quite jumpy now. He couldn't help smiling, this woman was so obvious. 'It's not about the girl, is it?' She did not answer. 'You did something else all those years ago, didn't you?' Still no answer. 'It's none of my business, Mrs Crowley.' She slumped, almost slouching, glass in one hand, her head up, eyes closed. Slowly, she crossed her legs. Sitting that way, she looked perfect. More than perfect.

'Have you told your husband?'

'No.'

'Why?'

'I just couldn't.'

'It's something bad?'

'Yes.' He finished his drink and began to rise.

'Well, I don't think I can help you.'

'Please!' Her voice broke. 'Don't abandon me!'

When he was working at the Cross, he'd often come across women who'd beg for help. Usually because they'd been found drunk at the wheel of a car or had done a spot of shop lifting, nothing serious. But they'd immediately appeal for leniency, some of them offering themselves if he'd forget about it—even married women from good homes. Once or twice he'd weakened and enjoyed their gratitude. But as soon as they were out of danger, they'd not wanted to know him. Mrs Crowley, he guessed, was not like that. She didn't have to beg and didn't have to open her legs for any man. She was too good for that.

He thought she was going to cry, but she did not. He gave in. He was always giving in. It was his great weakness. 'What's the address?' She gave it in one big whisper, without moving. 'Is it still ten o'clock?'

'Yes!'

'When does your husband return?'

'Tomorrow, late.'

He pulled out a pen and notepad, wrote a number. 'There's an electricity sub-station across the street from your house, that large green metal box. If you see a white chalk mark on it, a circle with a stroke through it, call me.' She sat up, perhaps surprised. Perhaps not. 'What are you going to do?'

'Have a friendly little chat with this geezer.'

'What if he becomes nasty?'

'When I was at King's Cross, Mrs Crowley, we had strict rules covering our behaviour in public. Never argue with the bastards, just hit 'em.'

She stood up. 'Oh, be careful.'

'I'm never careful.'

'Thank you, Mr Becker.'

'I'll let myself out.'

She smiled. It was definitely a shy smile as if she were embarrassed, a married woman smiling gratefully at a stranger, and on her own doorstep too. 'Thank you again.'

Driving away, he didn't know why he had suggested that particular symbol.

On reflection, he realised it meant zero. This whole affair, if it were an affair at all, might amount to nothing. On the other hand, if it were something, it might still end up as nothing at all. When the woman in the play had put down the phone it was curtains, not only for someone in the play but for the audience too. In this case, Mrs Crowley was the woman on stage and he, Harry Becker, was the audience. He was in some sort of story he did not understand and yet could not put down. Once you're in, you can't get out.

CHAPTER 5

It didn't take him long to find the house. He didn't have the street number, but he didn't need a number. It was the only house in the street for sale. Also, it didn't have curtains, so that clinched it. The letter box contained a few bits of junk mail. Other bits were on the ground around it. Perhaps someone had cleared the box to make room, hadn't bothered to get rid of all the rubbish. No one, it seemed, had lived in the house for some time. It was now about twenty to ten. Becker checked the neighbourhood. Apart from a party down the road and three parked cars outside, the street was quiet. Occasionally, a car went by fairly fast, too fast for someone checking for a police stake-out before making a pick-up. Becker had parked his own car at the end of the street and walked past the empty house and to the other end. No one was watching, he was sure. He went around the house and opened the back door.

It was only an old Yale lock anyone in his profession would know how to deal with. He found his way through the house to the living room, guided by bold shafts of light from the street coming through the uncovered windows. He sat on an empty packing box in the shadows, watching the street. A man leading a dog went by, whistling. Ten minutes later, two girls went past, laughing, almost running. Next a jogger pounded down the street—right down the middle like he was the king of the road. Ten o'clock came and went. Nothing happened. Perhaps the blackmailer was waiting until the wee small hours, when absolutely no one would be about. On the other hand, he shouldn't wait too long. Some vandal might attack the box, even make off with it. Or perhaps blow it up. At that time in Canberra, sticking gelignite in letter boxes was the fun thing to do.

Becker got up several times and mooched about the house in the semi-darkness. It was an old house, one of the originals, probably built as a worker's cottage. It had cast-iron fireplaces in the sitting room and the main bedroom, even a slow-combustion stove in the kitchen. Although someone had obviously renovated the place at some point, it was still quaint. On such a block of land, close to the heart of the city, it was probably worth over half a million to someone who wanted to put up a block of flats.

He dozed, waking each time a vehicle went past.

Just before eleven o'clock, Becker snapped awake. He hadn't heard anything, yet he knew something had happened. He peeped out of a window. A big car had stopped out front, the engine still running and lights off. Becker couldn't hear the engine running. He knew it was because he could just make out steam rising from the tailpipe. It was a big Mercedes, he thought. He could almost make out the Tri-Star badge on the bonnet. A tall, thin man was getting out, just a silhouette. As he walked around the car, streetlight caught his face, but not enough. The man was wearing some kind of hat, a peaked hat, the kind that went with a uniform. A uniformed driver? A chauffeur?

A flash of light. The man had a torch. Becker jumped to one side. He peeped out again, just one eye this time. The man in the hat was at the mailbox, raising the lid. He felt around inside, even crouched down, pulled out junk mail, looked in. Next thing he straightened up, kicked the box. Becker went to the front door to get a closer view. The man was returning to the car. Becker opened the door wider, ready to dash out. The man swore as he got in, slammed the door. Becker walked out, trying to make out the registration number, but the lights were off. The car moved away, as easily and as noiselessly as it had come. Becker dashed into the street, straining to read the plate. Just before the next cross street, the lights came on. He saw nothing except the first two letters: 'C' and 'D.' Becker gave up, thinking: Corps Diplomatique.

Why the hell would anyone in the diplomatic corps be interested in Mrs Evelyn Crowley? It did not make sense. He didn't know what he was going to tell her. All he could say was the man was a chauffeur driving a Mercedes with a CD number. Nearly every diplomat in Canberra used a Mercedes. It would be impossible to trace. In the night light, he was not even sure of the colour—he wasn't sure of anything. So he walked back to his car at the end of the street and set about doing his round for the night. He hated the job, and the cold, and the loneliness. He did it only to pay for his wife's alimony and to keep the kids at school. To hell with his wife and kids, let them starve. They didn't want anything to do with him except each Christmas, when they still expected presents. They never invited him to dinner. He might quit Canberra and go somewhere, he didn't know where. Perhaps he'd head up north, lie on a beach, be a middle-aged hippie. Live off the dole. Life could be a lot worse.

The next day he drove to Forrest and stopped outside her house, hoping she'd see him although he didn't glance at the house. Instead, he made his mark on the green sub-station and left. He hadn't gone more than two blocks when his mobile phone rang.

'Hello?'

'Mr Becker?'

'Mrs Crowley?'

'Yes, I saw you stop.' She sounded exhausted. She must have waited by a window all day. 'Did anything happen?'

'Can you meet me at the gardens?'

'The Botanic Gardens?'

'Yes, in half an hour.'

'You have something?'

'Not much, I'm afraid.'

He was sitting outside the kiosk, nibbling a Melting Moment and sipping a long black coffee when she arrived, appearing out of the fine mist of the Tasmanian forest gully—and wearing a long grey raincoat and a broad, grey hat, floppy. She was a grey woman on a grey day. Obviously, she did not wish to be noticed—except she was so well dressed you couldn't help noticing her. It was not raining, although the sky was heavily clouded. She was wearing dark glasses, which she did not need on such a day. 'Can I get you something?'

'I'm not hungry.' She sat heavily, though not a heavy woman, just tall.

'Do you know a chauffeur?'

She was surprised. 'A chauffeur? No, not at all.'

'Any kind of chauffeur?'

'Well, my husband has a chauffeur sometimes—I mean when he needs a car. It belongs to the managing director. Everyone uses it—the big shots, as he calls them.'

'What does he do?'

'Donald? Why, he's with the Royal Bank of Australia. He's—he's quite important, actually.' She sounded a little flustered. 'Do you think that chauffeur is blackmailing me?'

'The man who tried to pick up the money was driving a Mercedes with a diplomatic number plate.'

'Diplomatic? Did you get the number?'

'Too clever for me. He'd turned off his lights.'

'A chauffeur?' She peered at Becker through the dark glasses. Obviously, she was not going to remove them, even on such a dismal day. Someone might spot her chatting to a mere nightwatchman—and tell her husband.

'You haven't been indiscreet, have you? Saying something you shouldn't have behind a chauffeur?'

'About what? My daughter? No, I have never mentioned her to anyone.'

'About anything else?'

'God, no!'

'What about your parents?'

'Back in Melbourne, you mean? My mother died when I was young. I told my father, a dear man. I just said that my boss had killed himself and I was pregnant by him, and I did not know what to do. He would not have told anyone. He was a proud man, who hated gossip.'

'Well, someone knows something you don't want the police to know.'

'Yes, I suppose.'

'Someone from Melbourne?'

She sighed. 'Oh, I don't know.'

He watched as she shuddered. It was not cold. At last she took off her glasses, rubbed her eyes. They looked tired. Probably she'd had very little sleep last night. She began to moan to herself, not so much audible moans as unspoken speech. Her throat pulsed, her hands fidgeted. She was a mess. 'How did you meet your husband, Mrs Crowley?'

She tensed for a moment, then shrugged. 'Oh, I never did meet him in the normal way. I was living with Papà above his greengrocery in Sydney Road, Brunswick. I used to take the money to the bank every day. Donald was the manager. Pretty soon he'd come out and smile at me and tried to talk to me, ask if he could help me in any way. I did not encourage him.' She grimaced. Becker studied her.

'Did you take the money to the bank before the child was born?'

'What? No, never. I was too embarrassed to be seen in public, especially in a bank. It would have been so obvious.'

'That you were pregnant?'

'Yes.'

'I see.' He waited. She did not wish to tell him her life's story, that was obvious. But he was entitled to a little background if he were going to help her.

'One day after my girl was born, Uncle Ennio asked me to go with him and his elder son, Alfredo, to the bank with them.'

'Who was Uncle Ennio?'

'My father's brother.'

'And?'

'They had an appointment with the manager and wanted me to interpret for them. Their English was awful. I did not care what they did. I just went along. They were seeking a loan on some real estate they had. They got the loan.'

'And?'

She sighed. 'They lied, the land was encumbered already.'

'With another loan?'

'A deed arranged with some friends.'

'Did you know this?'

'Yes, I did.'

'When did you know?'

'Afterwards, when we went home. They were laughing about it, how they had tricked that stupid man, the manager. But I had sensed that they were up to something in the bank.'

'How did you feel about it?'

'I did not care. I was so miserable at the time.'

Becker stared at her, disappointed and yet sorry for her. They were two of a kind. Someone asks you do something not too honest and you just go along with it. In his case, to keep onside with his mates. In her case, to keep onside with her family.

'After my baby was born, I'd go to the bank with the daily takings. One day, the manager asked me to have a drink with him. He was a simple little man, quite young for a manager. I was not interested in him, not interested in any man or anyone in fact. I felt pretty bad in those days. But, when I told my father, he and Ennio told me to do it, marry him. They thought being married to a bank manager was a good idea. So I married him. That's all there was to it. Security, I suppose. Isn't that what all women want?'

Becker studied her. 'And that's what the blackmail letters were all about? Someone knew he'd lent money without proper security? And that you had helped your family to deceive him?'

'I suppose so.'

'Who would know all that?'

She shrugged. 'Someone in the bank, I suppose.'

'Why would they wait seventeen years to blackmail you?'

'I don't know... I don't know.'

'Maybe it's someone much closer?'

'What do you mean?'

'In your own family.'

She bristled. 'Why would they do that? They were involved. They got away with fifteen thousand dollars.'

Becker had no answer. As he'd told himself at their first meeting, things in her story did not add up. But he let it slide. They were both guilty but for different reasons, different crimes.

'Did you have any other children?'

'By Donald? No.'

'Did you ever love him?'

'Never! It was just an arrangement.'

He finished his coffee, brushed his clothes. Melting Moments always made a mess. He must give them up, if only to save his figure. He was becoming portly, not a pretty sight after a shower. 'Mrs Crowley, why don't you tell the truth?'

She jumped as though she'd been shot.

'It's got nothing to do with your daughter, has it?'

'Yes, it has!'

He tapped the table. 'Look, no one would care a damn if you had a child out of wedlock.'

'There must be no publicity!'

He stared at her. He didn't understand her, except that she was half scared to death. And she was not telling the truth. Or, she was telling the truth, but not all of it. He stood up. 'I'm sorry, I can't help you anymore.'

'What? No, no! Please, I'll pay you anything. Please sit down. I just don't know what to do!'

He sat again, waited. She cried to herself, voicelessly for a while. Then she reached for a handkerchief in her bag—a linen one. Of course, it was a linen one. A woman like her would not use tissues, at least not when not at home. She took her time to speak again. At one point, she even moved a hand towards his, as if to hold it. But it did not quite touch.

She shrugged and sat up straight. 'Is it so obvious? I mean, that I'm in a mess?'

He said nothing.

'I must look awful.'

Again he said nothing. She pursed her lips. They were full lips without being too full, so even pursed they looked good enough to kiss.

'All right,' she said. 'I'll tell you.'

She waited until a couple had passed, hands out, feeling for rain. One or two drops had fallen. 'I became pregnant by one of the partners in the law firm for which I worked. I was his secretary. He was quite charming. I knew he was married, but he said he was separated, getting a divorce. He pursued me, I suppose. I was flattered. I went to bed with him, more than once. I was both marvellously happy and worried sick. All along I expected something would go wrong. This went on and on for months. He talked about how he loved me. His wife lived in Hamilton, a grazier's daughter, one of the landed gentry, so he said. He'd known her since they were kids. She was very snobbish, very rude, even to him. He couldn't stand her any longer.' She dabbed at her eyes again. Becker waited.

'Then I thought I was pregnant. I went to a doctor. Yes, she said, you are. Suddenly I was very happy. This confirmed it, I thought. He certainly will marry me now. Well, I was so happy next day I went to his flat to tell him. It was high in a building in Collins Street, the heart of town, trams clanging by. But outside people were gathered, shocked. An ambulance was there. I went over, I crept. My legs would hardly move. A terrible fear seized me. Somehow I knew what I would see. He was lying on the pavement, dead, crushed by the impact. Blood had dribbled out of his mouth, even filled his eyes. He must have fallen from the balcony above, six floors up. I was horrified. I was pregnant and the father of my child was dead. Why he had fallen, I did not know. People were talking around me, speculating. A policeman kept asking does anyone know this man? I began to say that I did, but no words came out. I felt so sick. I walked away, sick in my head and face and heart and belly and even my toes. It was a Saturday morning. On Monday I went to work, sure that everybody was looking at me, as if they knew I was pregnant and that somehow they blamed me. I hung on for a week or so, then I resigned, but not before I'd heard the whispers. People said he had jumped because he'd misappropriated money in his trust account. The partners had suspected, and they'd already called in the auditors. He'd had such great prospects, or so it seemed. That flat was owned by the firm. They let him have it. It was a perk. He was a very likeable man. Everyone in the office liked him. He had red hair,' she added inconsequently. Perhaps she was thinking of the blood.

Becker said nothing. All he could do was listen.

'I couldn't, I just couldn't confess. I went to pieces. I couldn't work, couldn't sleep. I kept living with Papà, hiding from the world, although I did help him in the shop. Eventually, after the child was born, I would take the money to the local bank. Donald was the manager, only twenty-eight, very bright—'

Becker pulled her up short. 'Just a minute.' She had said she could not 'confess.' Confess to what? She had said she wasn't responsible. But he let this slide too.

'Did you tell your husband you'd had a child?'

'Yes, I did.'

'When did you tell him?'

'When he asked me to marry him. Of course he would find out.'

'Did you tell him about the lawyer?'

'I just said I'd had a fling with a man and we had broken up.'

'And did you tell him what happened to him?'

'No, no, I just could not.'

They didn't speak for a while. Becker thought he'd asked enough. It was her business, not his. She'd asked him to find the child, a girl. That was all there was to his part of the deal. If someone were trying to blackmail her, she should go to the police. On the other hand, he felt sorry for her. She was a charming woman—possibly a charming liar, the kind who could string a man along.

'Why did you tell me your husband must not know about the child?'

'I don't know. I'm sorry, I should not have said that.'

'It's not about the girl at all, is it?'

She would not look at him. 'No.'

'It's about what happened at the bank, isn't it?'

'Yes.'

'The swindle?'

'Yes.'

'He made a mistake. He could have been sacked?'

'Yes.'

'So, why is someone trying to blackmail you and not him?'

'I don't know; I just don't know!'

'Did something else happen in Melbourne?'

'What? No, of course not.'

He did not believe her. She was not telling the whole story. No one would try to screw money out of a woman just because her lover had killed himself and left her with a fatherless child. The gossips around town might make a meal of it, but most people wouldn't care what she'd done.

She drew in her breath sharply. 'If only I hadn't lost that five thousand—'

'You could have shut him up? Come off it, he'd be back pretty soon, asking for more. Blackmailers don't give up. You are stuck with them as long as you've got money.'

'He didn't get the money, did he? He might kill me.'

Becker laughed. 'Why would he kill you? No, he doesn't want you dead. You are too valuable.'

'He'll be back?'

'Unless you go to the police.'

'No, no, I couldn't do that. Donald would be furious. Oh, God, he is in line for a very big job—with the World Bank in Washington. No, no, never.'

'Look, Mrs Crowley, I've told you, the police are not interested in what—'

He gave up. What was the point in trying to argue with her? She had painted herself into a corner with her fears.

'What if he talks?'

'Let me see the letter again.' She opened her bag, took it out, still in its envelope, handed it to him. 'This doesn't say what happened in Melbourne.'

'No, but that must be it, mustn't it? He must know.'

'This guy?' He tapped the letter. 'Know what? At a guess, I'd say he doesn't know. Maybe he's heard somewhere along the line you did something you wouldn't want the world to know about. He's just testing the water, to see how you react.'

'You think so? He doesn't know about my lover?'

'You didn't pay up last night, so he's probably worried you've gone to the police already. I'd better keep this letter. Maybe he was careless, left some prints.'

She sat back and tried to relax. She blinked, realising she'd told a stranger what she'd been holding back for seventeen years, that she'd unwittingly participated in a bank fraud. Her reputation was now in his hands.

'It was just an idea, Mr Becker. I suppose I hoped you might be able to find the writer.'

'What could I do?'

'If you could just warn him off—'

'Some people don't frighten too easily.'

She put her head in her hands, resumed deep breathing. 'I can't go on this way. I'm going to pieces. I don't know what to do. If I don't pay up, he might go to Donald. And I don't want him to know.'

'But he knows already about the caper at the bank, doesn't he?'

She did not answer.

Becker stood up, more to stretch his legs than to depart. It was raining now, a fine drizzle. What his mother would have called a Scotch mist, tiny drops that touched his face like occasional kisses.

'Mrs Crowley, there's very little to go on. The only clues right now are in this letter and the glimpse I got of that driver.'

She rose too, putting on the dark glasses again, even turning up the collar of her coat. 'I am sorry I've put you to all this trouble, Mr Becker. I must go. I hope no one has seen us. I don't know what I would do if Donald hears. I'm not a good liar.'

He had to agree, she was a bad liar. This yarn about the blackmailer did not add up. Why not tell her husband about a letter from someone who seemed to know what they had both done in that bank down in Melbourne seventeen years ago? He had an idea that she was not worried about that at all. It was something else. But he said nothing as they walked along the footbridge through the rain forest to the car park in the rain and mist.

'Please do not show that letter to the police, Mr Becker.'

'I don't have any love for them, Mrs Crowley. One of them shot me, remember?'

'Yes, so you said. I had no idea Sydney was so bad.'

'I thought it'd be fun to catch some crummy little villains. The villains soon caught me. They wove a net about me, trapped me. I was in it before I knew what was happening, taking their graft, little presents now and then. When I woke up to what was going on, I was hooked. I didn't know how to get out of it. Finally, I talked to my wife. She was disgusted. A bent copper, she said. To think I've shared the same bed with you, had three kids by you. After I was shot, she kicked me out. Six months later she sued for divorce. Actually, it was two kids. The first was not mine.'

'What happened about the man who shot you?'

'Nothing.'

'He got away with it?'

'They always do.'

They had reached her car. 'I sleep badly, Mr Becker. I toss and turn some nights, I have bad dreams.'

'Don't we all?'

'I never see a leaf fall from a tree without seeing that man tumbling down. I see it in my dreams—and sometimes when I'm wide awake.'

He took a punt on the next question. 'Have you thought of killing yourself, Mrs Crowley?' He expected she would deny it. She was startled at first, but relented.

'I've thought about it.'

'Maybe that's the point.'

'The point of what?'

'The whole exercise, to get you to kill yourself.'

She shuddered. 'Who'd want that?'

'Yes, who?'

She unlocked the car, got in, started the engine and lowered a window. Her lips moved as if to speak, though she said no more. She just looked at him in the way that women can do when they don't have to use words. He thought she said 'goodbye' or perhaps 'thank you for talking to me.' It was nice of her to say it, whatever it was.

He stood in the rain, watching the dark-blue sedan back out and unhurriedly depart. He didn't know why he'd said such a thing to her. Have you ever thought of killing yourself? It had shocked her, he knew. Immediately he'd regretted the question. He'd hurt her. He was a fool. Who'd want to drive her to end her life?

Walking to his own cheap vehicle, he had to admit he was half in love with Mrs Crowley, although he didn't know why. It was not because she was beautiful—which she was in a solid, tightly packed way—but because she seemed to be a kindred spirit. Maybe she had opened up to him so easily because he was a criminal, someone who knew what it was to be afraid. But there was a difference—she was miserable with fear, whereas he was just miserable with life itself.

But what had she said? I never see a leaf fall from a tree without seeing that man tumbling down. She'd said it as though she had actually seen him tumbling down. Maybe she meant that in her imagination she saw him fall. But maybe not.

And again that word, 'confess.' Why had she said confess? Just an innocent slip of the tongue or an inadvertent admission of what?

He didn't like to think about it.

CHAPTER 6

He drove home in the drizzling rain, thinking about her. She had said she'd never told a soul how her lover had died, and yet she'd told him without even prompting. Maybe because he'd needed some details to work on. Or perhaps she'd wanted to talk to someone, a perfect stranger, to get it off her chest after all these years. Once she'd begun answering his questions, it had all come out. Perhaps too easily. The lawyer had jumped because he was caught stealing his clients' money. No fault of hers. She'd committed no crime, and yet she behaved as though she had. There was more to Mrs Crowley's story than shame. Whatever it was, someone knew about it.

The house was in a street at the back of Olim's Hotel in Ainslie. It was owned by an Indian from Fiji. There was always washing on the line and about the place a smell of spices and another smell, new fabric. He used to hear the sewing machines going in the double garage at all hours, even late at night. The Indian was running a sweatshop; he knew. Half a dozen dark-skinned people seemed to live in the rest of the house at any time, sometimes four to a room. Their faces often changed. Becker suspected it was a half-way house for illegals. He'd thought about reporting them but had decided it was no business of his. Let Immigration worry about them. He'd wondered why the Indians hadn't kicked him out to fill his room with more dark faces. Perhaps they wanted to have Becker there. At a distance, he looked like a cop—dark-blue jacket, dark-blue pants. On each shoulder was an insignia which looked like a police badge, but close up said 'Stanton Security.' They might have thought it would protect them.

When he arrived, three small children were watching from the porch.

'Hello,' they said.

'Hello, kids.'

'You caught any baddies today, Mr Harry?'

'I don't chase baddies, they chase me.'

'Why do you let them chase you?'

'Well, if they're busy chasing me, they don't have time to hold up banks, do they?'

One of them, a girl of about ten, laughed. 'You gonna show us your gun, Mr Harry?'

'I don't carry a gun when I'm not on duty.'

'Mum said she'll make you some curry.'

'I hate curry, it burns my guts.'

She walked with him into the house. 'Mr Harry, a man was here.'

He stopped. 'What man?'

'A man in a car.'

'What kind of car?'

'A big, grey car.'

'What kind?'

'I don't know.'

'Who was he?'

'I don't know.'

'Police, you think?'

'No.'

'What did he say?'

'Is there a man here?'

'What man?'

'A man with ginger hair and a moustache and a bad shoulder.'

'He meant me?'

The girl nodded. Her name was Leticia, which Becker had always thought odd for an Indian girl. Maybe she was only half-Indian.

'He said you had an old Holden, a—' She screwed up her nose, thinking.

'Kingswood?'

'Yes.'

'What did you say?'

'I said you had a room.'

'Did you tell him which room?'

'Yes, the one down the side at the back.'

Becker tensed. This was serious. 'Did you give him my name?'

'I just said you were Harry.'

'Nothing else?'

'He said he'd be back.'

'When?'

'He didn't say.'

'Anything else about him, Leticia?'

'What do you mean?'

'What was he wearing?'

'A grey suit and black gloves.'

'And a hat like a policeman's? But grey?'

Leticia nodded.

'Was there a three-pointed star on the front of the car?'

She nodded again. Becker looked up and down the street, seeing no Mercedes or anything else suspicious. 'Thank you.'

'What if he comes back, Mr Harry?'

'What do you mean?'

'Are you gonna shoot him?'

'I don't know. I don't waste bullets on just anybody.'

She laughed. She was a nice kid, even if she talked too much.

He went to his room, thinking the man in black gloves was bad news. Perhaps he was death. He locked the door behind himself, knowing he couldn't keep out that kind of man. He knew which room was his. If he was going to kill you, he was going to kill you. Nothing much you could do about it. He lay on his bed, tried to get some sleep. This would be his last shift for the week, sixty hours a week doing nothing, just filling in time, waiting for something to happen. He managed to get thirty minutes' sleep, when his mobile rang.

'Yeah?'

'Harry Becker?'

'Who wants to know?'

'Keep your nose out of it, mate.'

'Out of what?'

'You know what. That caper last night was not too smart.'

'Who is this?'

'Just a friend. You're too old to take risks, Harry.' The voice sounded familiar, a voice from the past, yet he couldn't quite place it. 'Anything could happen on those lonely rounds of yours.'

'You're a cop, aren't you?' No answer. 'Or you were a cop?' The caller chuckled, a short chuckle, humourless. Becker took a punt.

'It's not blackmail, is it?'

'What?'

'You don't want money. That's just a cover, isn't it? You're out to frighten her.'

'And why would I do that?'

'To make her jump.'

'Eh?' The stranger chuckled again, this time surprised. It sounded like genuine surprise. Becker sat up on the bed, trying to get tough with a tinny voice coming from a little black instrument in his hand. 'You leave her alone, mate.'

'Yeah?'

'You can be found, any time.'

'So can you, sport.'

'The police are studying that letter.' This was not true, Becker still had it. The bluff seemed worth a try. 'If you touch her—'

'What's up, mate? Got you hooked already, has she?'

The line went dead. Becker sat there, trying to work out how he was going to find this man, when someone knocked on the door, a light knock. The girl was standing there when he opened it.

'That man came back, Mr Harry.'

'The man with the gloves?'

'He was in the street, watching.'

'He had a phone in one hand?'

She nodded. 'And he was looking at your car.'

'At the number plate?'

'Mm-hmm.'

So, that was how he'd been tracked down? The caller had been so careful last night he'd noted the numbers on each car parked nearby before he'd checked the

letterbox, just in case there was a stake-out. Only a cop could get such information—
or an ex-cop with influence.

'You tell me if you see him again.'

'Mm-hmm.'

'You're a good girl, Leticia.'

She smiled, showing big white teeth in her small dark face. She had pigtails and
a string of cheap beads about her long neck. She was painfully thin and as friendly as
a baby's smile. He'd only just closed the door when the phone rang again.

'Mr Becker?'

'Mrs Crowley?'

'I didn't tell you the truth.'

'I know.'

'I did tell my father long ago.'

'About the lawyer, killing himself? And he told someone else?'

'Yes, my husband.'

'Why did he do that?'

'He was dying. And another thing, I saw that man fall.'

'You did?' He was amused. Driving home she'd realised that she'd made a serious
slip when she'd referred to falling leaves. So now she was trying to square things off
with him.

'Yes, I was approaching the building in Collins Street, when I saw something
come down. Then I walked over and—'

'You don't have to tell me.'

She faltered. He thought she was going to gasp, but she pushed on. 'Papà believed
the shock had disturbed me, made me morose. He asked Donald to look after me. It
seems he was afraid I'd do something serious.'

'Such as kill yourself?'

'Yes.'

'How long ago was this?'

'Four or five years after I had the baby. He was so pleased I had married Donald.
He really trusted him.'

'And other members of your family? Did he tell them?'

'Not as far as I know. They've never mentioned it.' She moaned. 'Oh, I wish this thing would go away. Sometimes I feel so bad—'

'Forget it, Mrs Crowley. I'm going to find that driver.'

She didn't appear to have heard him. 'So bad I'll go to the top of a tall building and—'

'Maybe that's just what they want you to do.'

'To jump?'

'I think so.'

'How do you know?'

'The driver called me. I asked him straight out. They're not after your money, Mrs Crowley. Five thousand dollars, that's peanuts. The whole blackmail scam is just to frighten you. They'll work on you until you give in.'

'They want me to kill myself?'

'I shouldn't have said that.'

'My God—'

'Look, Mrs Crowley, just hold on. I'll think of something.'

'I am holding on—by my fingernails. I've been doing that for years. I can't hang on much longer.'

She moaned again. He could visualise her. She'd have the phone in one hand while she ran the other through her dark brown hair, even pulling at it. She was on the edge, and someone knew it. She began to cry, almost soundlessly.

He got fed up. 'Stop complaining. You're not dead yet.'

'I'm sorry, I'm sorry.'

'And stop saying you're sorry.'

'I'm sorry.'

'You're doing it again.'

She seemed about to speak. Instead, she began gasping. Probably she was patting her chest. Maybe she was having palpitations. He waited until she calmed down. 'Okay?'

'Yes, yes.'

'I'll call you soon.'

'Thank you, Harry.'

It was a long lingering word, Harry. Like a soft breeze on a summer night. Except it was not summer now in Canberra, it had turned cold. The rain had set in and so had autumn. The leaves had begun to fall.

CHAPTER 7

He spent several days checking the few clues he had. No one at work knew anyone who fitted the chauffeur's description. He asked around the hire-car firms and the guards he knew at the airport. A diplomatic driver would have to turn up there often, perhaps every day, dropping people off, picking them up. He asked one or two taxi-drivers he knew. None could help. It was possible the man was from out of town.

A few days later, Becker was sitting in Garema Place, eating lunch under a plane tree. It was one of those places that could have been something, but wasn't. To one side, a man was blowing fallen leaves into a pile. Beyond him at a table a group of loafers were sprawled, eating, chatting, smoking, yawning, laughing, scratching their heads—young women in black skirts showing their ugly legs to young men in black pants showing their ugly teeth. The clouds had cleared, and the sun was shining. It was warm but not hot, late April in Canberra. There was a burger joint on one side and Mamma's Trattoria on the other. There was also a bar where you could get a good steak if you could stand the grease and the pile of chips. Each time he went in there, he told himself he wouldn't eat more than a dozen chips. But he always did. He tended to alternate between these cheap joints. He hated the food, but it kept him alive. Perhaps that was why he hated it, it kept him alive.

He was thinking of going for a walk, when a deadbeat sat beside him.

'Mate, y'couldn't let's 'ave a coupla dollars, could yer?'

'So you could spend it on booze?'

'Eh?'

The man was wasted and unshaven. His tiny eyes had almost disappeared into his head. He wore a cast-off overcoat and a cap. And he wore boots like Charlie Chaplin's in The Gold Rush. They looked good enough to eat, except for the dirt.

'I gave you two dollars yesterday.'

'Eh?'

'I was sitting over there.' He pointed at another seat.

'Eh?'

'Here—' Becker found a two-dollar coin. He was not on duty. The firm didn't allow staff to wear its uniforms off duty and certainly never to carry a weapon, not even on duty. Becker was an exception, he had a licence. The Federal Police were decent that way. They didn't want to find a bent ex-cop floating face down in Lake Burley Griffin one day, a hole in his head. That could upset the tourists. Today he was wearing a nondescript car coat, something made in China, nice and cheap. He knew he didn't look much better dressed than the bludger, just a bit cleaner.

'Ah, thanks, mate.'

'Make sure you buy a pie.'

'I will, mate. You're a gentleman.'

'Not all that gentle.'

'Eh?'

'Never mind. Don't ask me again for a week.'

'I won't, mate, God bless yer.'

The deadbeat was about to depart when Becker called. 'Hey, where d'you get that hat?' He stood up, studied the peaked hat. It was relatively new, although superficially dirty, as if the tramp had spent the night in the open, perhaps on the grass or under a tree. There was a smear of chlorophyll on one side and perhaps bird shit or just a squashed insect on the back. It resembled a chauffeur's hat without a badge.

'This cap?'

'Yeah, that cap.'

'I never nicked it.'

'I didn't say you did. Where'd you get it?'

'Ah, I dunno.'

'You must have some idea.'

'Ah, shit, mate, I never remember things from one day to the next.'

Becker pulled out his wallet. 'I'm sure you'd remember if—'

'Ah, well, a feller give it to us.'

'Gave it to you?'

'Yeah, well, sort of.'

'Make up your mind.'

The tramp eyed the wallet. 'Well, he threw it away.'

'Where?'

'Down a lane.'

'What were you doing in the lane?'

'Tryin' to have a kip.'

'In a box?'

'Yeah, one of them big crates, packin' crates.'

'Which buildings?'

'Y'know the ones with all the col—col—'

'Columns?'

'Yeah, that's it.'

'The Melbourne Building or the Sydney?'

'Don't ask me. Never know one buildin' from the next.'

'He threw it away?'

'Ah, well, 'e was running, wasn't he?'

'Was he? Along the lane?'

'Yeah.'

'And he dropped it?'

'Yeah.'

'It fell off as he was running?'

'Yeah.'

'Why was he running?'

'Ah, dunno. Two blokes come to the end an' looked down.'

'They were looking for him?'

'Yeah, I reckon. One of 'em come down an' seen me.'

'In the box?'

'Yeah.'

'And?'

'Just said shit an' walked off.'

'Did the man come back? For the hat?'

'Nah, didn't see him again.'

'You want to sell that hat?'

'Sell it?'

'Yes, how much?'

'Ah, I dunno.'

'How about five dollars?'

'F'this cap? Ah, strewth, I dunno, a good cap like this—'

Becker wasn't going to haggle. 'I could get one at the Salvo's for a fiver and you could get a woollen beanie for a dollar.'

'Eh?' The tramp thought about it, or tried to think about. He didn't seem to have much brain left. 'Okay, a fiver.'

Half an hour later Becker was in an office in Fyshwick, a place that, when he'd first arrived in Canberra, was a tawdry joint full of crash repairers, discount electrical warehouses and men selling carpets that might have fallen off the back of a truck. Recently, it had been tarted up. There were more trees in the streets, and someone had provided off-street parking. One or two buildings looked smart, professional. Some were so new they looked as though they'd been knocked up overnight and painted just that morning. They seemed to glitter in the early afternoon sunlight with a happy sort of freshness. This particular office had a fancy name, Stern House. It glowed in its bright cantaloupe paint. The kid on the other side of the desk looked like a Harvard professor, although he was no more than twenty-one. Already he was big in genetic engineering.

One night more than a year ago, while on his rounds in the city, Becker had come across three thugs beating up the kid down a lane behind a so-called night club. It was one of those joints where singles picked up singles and creeps hung around outside waiting to set upon drunks. Becker had gone to his rescue, hitting two of the assailants, but the third, a thug with a shaven head, had knocked him flying. He was about to put in the boots, when he realised Becker had drawn a pistol, a snub-nosed Smith and Wesson, ex-police issue. He needed it. Someone from Sydney could hit him at any moment, especially on those lonely rounds.

Slowly, Becker had got to his feet. He hadn't known what to do. He'd never shot a man in his life. The bruiser had glowered at him for a moment, uncertain whether to strike or back off. Then, one of his mates passed him a bottle. The bruiser smashed the bottom against a wall. Shards fell, tinkle tinkle. All Becker could say was, 'Come on, punk, make my day!' He was not a fan of Clint Eastwood. Actors were overpaid phonies who let stuntmen take all the risks while real cops took real bullets and got no thanks, not even from the Commissioner. Apparently, this moron was impressed. Someone might have kneecapped him in the past. The three thugs beat it, so Becker got to his feet and picked up the kid, who'd been lying against a wall moaning.

It turned out he'd just left the bar and was suddenly taken ill. He'd stumbled into the lane and vomited, then had been hit from behind. His name was Ephraim Lowenstern, and he was a whiz-kid, who was going to make a billion dollars out of devising a new kind of potato, one without skin. Every housewife hated peeling potatoes. That's what he'd said, anyway. In those days, he hadn't had an office and not much future, just a thousand dollars he'd borrowed from an uncle named Joshua in the rag trade down in Melbourne. Now, he had eight kids working for him, some still at school. They all wore thick glasses and had quick, friendly smiles.

'Harry, how are you?'

'Could be better.'

'It's great to see you.'

'I need help, Effie.'

'What kind of help?'

Becker pulled out the letter. 'I want you to look for prints on this.'

Lowenstern read it. 'Hell, this is nasty.'

'So is the punk who wrote it.' He extracted the cap from a plastic Katie's bag he found in the street. 'And a profile on this.'

'Genetic profile?'

'Yeah.'

Effie stared at it. 'Isn't this a chauffeur's cap?'

'At one time it was. I got it from a deadbeat, cost me five dollars.'

'You paid good money for this?'

'You'll find at least two types of material, one from the deadbeat and the other from the chauffeur.'

'How are you gonna know which is which?'

'I'll sort it out.'

'No worries, Harry. If it's skin tissue or hair or anything else, we can get a profile.'

'How about the letter? I'm sure he would have been wearing gloves. Can you get genetic material off the letter?'

'Let's hope he sneezed on it.'

'How soon?'

The whiz-kid screwed up his mouth. He had a childish face, a mop of curly brown hair, and happened to look like Barbra Streisand. It was hard to believe he was more than twelve years old. Possibly he'd read Einstein when he was ten.

'Two or three hours. Where can I catch you?'

Becker handed him a card. 'Call me on my mobile. Don't call my office, right?'

'Got you.'

'Thanks, Effie.'

'For you, Harry, anything.'

CHAPTER 8

From Fyshwick he drove to Queanbeyan. Fricker was not pleased to see him again. He didn't want to get mixed up in anything, especially so close to retirement. All he wanted was a quiet life. 'What is it this time, Harry?'

'I want to nail an ex-cop.'

'Who?'

'I don't know.'

'If you don't know, how would I?'

'I think he was recently discharged. He's now working in Canberra.'

'Doing what?'

'A chauffeur, drives a big grey Mercedes, diplomatic—and wears black gloves, even during the day.'

'He might feel the cold.'

'It's not so cold yet. Can you think of anyone?'

'A New South Wales cop?'

Becker nodded. 'Probably from Sydney.'

Fricker rubbed his chin. 'There's a bloke who was working with Whitford.'

'Yeah? What's he look like?'

'Never met him myself, but I heard he's been seen around.'

'In Queanbeyan?'

'Someone saw him at the Leagues Club one night.'

'He was never nailed?'

Fricker shook his head. 'Named before the Wood Commission. They couldn't prove anything against him. He quit all the same.'

'Description?'

'Trim, slim, very dark hair, a natty dresser, fancies himself apparently. A bit too fast to react, if you know what I mean.'

'Hot tempered?'

'Something like that.' The old sergeant leaned back, studied a wall calendar. 'Once, so I heard, he grabbed a boiling kettle to throw it at a fellow officer.'

'Yeah?'

'The lid flew off, the water poured down his arm.'

'Don't tell me, his hand was scarred?'

'Great red-raw weals, I believe. He had to have skin grafts.'

'So that's why he wears gloves by day? What's his name?'

'That fellow? Torrence? Yeah, Vincent Torrence. Did you know him?'

'Yeah, I knew him. He was one of Whitford's men.'

'Of course, it mightn't be the same man.'

'You know where he lives?'

'No idea, mate.'

'Thanks, Bob.'

On the way back, he called again at Fyshwick. Effie Lowenstern had a result for him already. There were several sets of genetic material on the cap, and three sets on the letter. One was the same as from the cap. This clinched it. The chauffeur had at least handled the letter, even if he'd been wearing gloves. His cells were on the gloves along with some saliva. It seemed the man habitually wiped his mouth with his hand, even when wearing gloves. Becker didn't know what to do with this evidence. At least he had part of the man, his genetic code. The guy had been careful not to leave his fingerprints, yet he was leaving his genetic calling card everywhere.

Late in the day, just before the store closed, he went into David Jones and asked a friend in the credit department to check out Torrence. He'd met her in a pub soon after he'd arrived in Canberra and she'd asked him home to dinner. She was a motherly type, a widow with two grown kids. Nothing had come of the relationship, except both knew they were lonely and there was no future in it. No number of hot dinners would ever make any difference.

'I want you to check him, Rita. I need his address.'

'He mightn't be on our list.'

'He'd be on a credit agency somewhere, even if he didn't have a store account. Tell them you have to do a check on a new customer.'

'Oh, Harry, I can't do that. I'd get fired.' They were sitting opposite each other in a confidential cubicle and he was acting like a potential client.

'We used to be friends, Rita.'

'Yes, but—'

'I need to help someone. She's in danger.'

'A lady, eh?'

'I think someone's trying to kill her.'

She whistled under her breath.

'What's his name?'

'Vincent Torrence.'

'Torrence? Vincent Torrence?'

She patted his hand on the desk. 'I'll see what I can do for you, love.'

Next morning, she called Becker at about ten-thirty. He'd been dead to the world, just having come off the night shift.

In his early days in Canberra, he'd done some bank work, standing around, hands folded, his back to the window, so anyone thinking of hitting the place could see him. Young men had those jobs now, trying to look like cowboys, ready to tackle any punk who walked into the place with a shotgun in a carryall. One colleague he'd known only a few days had challenged a robber outside a bank and had been blasted for his trouble. They never found the assailant. The dead man had only just married. Someone said his wife was already pregnant when they cut the cake. It was a dead-boring job, but at least it was day work. When his wife divorced him and was awarded five hundred dollars a week in alimony, he'd had to switch to the night job. A lot more money and a lot less thanks.

'Harry?'

'Yeah.'

'Vincent Francis Torrence, he lives in a townhouse in Kingston.' She gave him the address.

'He's a client of yours?'

'No, but he's a member of a gymnasium.'

Becker wasn't surprised. Torrence would want to keep fit.

'How did you find him?'

'It's best you don't know.'

'You're a pal, Rita.'

'Mind how you go, Harry.'

He slept through lunchtime, emerging about four o'clock. Leticia was swinging on the verandah rail.

'You're going, Mr Harry?'

'Yes, off to work.'

'You always work at night.'

'Yeah, five nights a week.'

'It's a bad job, Mr Harry.'

'Many people have to work at night, Leticia. Have you seen that fellow again?'

'No, but a man rang dad.'

'What man?'

'I don't know.'

'What'd he say?'

'Get out.'

'Get out of where?'

'Out of the house. He said all Asians out.'

'Out of the country?'

'Mm-hmm.'

'He said that to your dad?'

She nodded. 'Dad was very upset. Mum burst into tears. Auntie Minnie started to have a fit.'

'Do they know who it was?'

She shook her head.

'He's just a crank. Don't worry about him.'

'You won't let him, will you, Mr Harry?'

'Let him what?'

'Burn down the house.'

'He said that?'

'Mm-hmm.'

'Forget about it, Leticia. They're just cranks.'

She followed him to his car. 'What are cranks, Mr Harry?'

'Cranks?' He'd never really thought about it. 'Cranks are people who hate people.'

Just before eight o'clock he drove to the depot out in Fyshwick and went to his locker, took out a pistol and holster as well as a torch heavy enough to use as a baton, a back-to-base radio and a bunch of keys to clients' premises, all of which he hung on his belt. Finally, he pocketed a penknife, notebook and pen. When he finished, he was surprised to see the boss still in his office, using a calculator and checking timesheets.

'Harry?'

'Yeah?'

'What happened on Friday night?'

'Friday?'

'You didn't leave cards at eight places.'

'Didn't I?'

'Not good, Harry.'

'I guess I forgot.'

'We don't pay you to forget. Those cards are important. They show we're on the job. Two clients have mentioned it.'

'Cards don't keep the villains out. They just show we've been there already and won't be back for hours. Anyway, why do you say eight?'

'Because I checked 'round next day. Six others hadn't seen any cards when they came in to work.'

'On a Saturday?'

'Some of 'em work Saturdays, you know.'

'I'm sorry.'

The boss stopped calculating and watched him. 'Something going on?'

'What do you mean?'

'Some guy was on the phone yesterday, asking about you. Said he was your cousin from out of town and wanted to meet up with you.'

'You gave him my number?'

'Yeah.'

Becker didn't know what to say. Obviously it was Torrence. The boss was watching him. He had a big black moustache and small black eyes and thick black brows and a crumpled sort of square jaw. Also, he had highly polished boots. He was a spit and polish man, who couldn't break the habit. He'd once been a warrant officer in the British Army—a man who worked strictly by the rules, so he said time and time again.

'A problem?'

'Yeah, a mate from the past. I can handle him.'

'And someone saw you with a lady at the gardens.'

Becker was surprised. 'That was in my own time. She's a friend.'

'A friend who drives a shiny blue BMW?'

'She's well off.'

'You're not moonlightin', are you?'

'A private job? No, I'm not.'

'If you can't keep focused, Harry—'

'It's okay.'

'We don't want armed men wandering 'round the streets with personal agendas.'

'I've got a licence, you know that.'

'You're the only one who has.'

'It's for my own protection. Once hit, twice shy, you know.'

The boss went back to his time sheets. 'Mind how you go, Harry.'

'It's okay, I said.'

After doing a few rounds, he went to Torrence's place in Kingston. It was a trim townhouse in a trim row. All the trendies lived there now, people who spent much of their lives at Parliament House lobbying for some big client or running a smart boutique in Manuka or playing the stock market. You couldn't get into a place like that unless you had money. Probably Torrence didn't own it, not if he were working as a driver. Someone must be paying the rent. No big Mercedes was parked in the street. No light was showing in a window.

He went back about midnight. Still nothing.

CHAPTER 9

Often, he didn't know what to do with his time. He did have two days off work each weekend and sometimes he'd see a football match at Bruce Stadium or go for a drive, sometimes down to the coast, and do a spot of fishing. Or drive to Wagga Wagga, his hometown, call on some old mates, have a few beers and then drive all the way back again. But it was those normal days, when he rose at about lunchtime and did not start until it was eight o'clock, that were hard to fill. Sometimes he simply sat in a park and tried to read a book or a newspaper or do a crossword or just sat and watched the passing parade. About four o'clock he would find a small place where he could have coffee. He'd told Mrs Crowley he did not drink much coffee, but he did late in the day, just before he went on duty, to keep him awake at night. Some mornings he did not bother to get out of bed. Just lay there until late in the afternoon, trying to catch up on sleep. Sometimes he did catch some, sometimes not. He was always tired; his eyes were itchy, and his brain was never sharp. He did a job; it brought in good money. But it was the pits, he knew. Only a dog would work such hours.

One day, towards the end of April, he wandered into the National Library just to have a look. He'd been there before, but he'd not read anything. He'd just looked around and wandered out again. This time there was some sort of exhibition—the works of a local painter. Why an exhibition of paintings was being held in a library he did not know, nor did he care. So he parked the old Holden and forced his way up the front steps. Sometimes it was a struggle. His bad knee often gave way with a stabbing pain. He'd have to hang on to a railing, embarrassed. A man like him, not yet forty, crippled like an old-timer. Needing a rail for support. The steps seemed to go up and up forever and so did the building itself, the classical style rising above him. Some people had said it was phoney and others had said it was classically simple, like the Acropolis in Athens. Others still said it was simply phoney. He went in the big brass doors and looked around. There was a bookshop to one side and a restaurant to the other. A man in a brown uniform was watching him.

'You look lost, mate.'

If you were called 'mate' by an attendant in one of the great buildings in Canberra, you knew they knew you were one of them—working class and you looked it. It was more by the way you walked than your clothes or your speech. It was the way you mooched and rambled, looking around and looking lost. This was not your world, not the world of books or pictures or maps or newspapers or even knowledge. No one called you 'sir' in this kind of place. Not a man like him, anyway.

'There's an exhibition,' he said.

'Paintings? This way, mate, through the next doors and on the left.'

He did as directed. At first, it was dark in there. It was not a large room, nor small. As his eyes got used to it, he saw spot-lit pictures on a wall, then on another wall, all done by a painter called Jennifer Jeffers, who'd died recently. There were no overhead lights, just these spotlights. Human figures occasionally moved, mostly sideways, in a slow dance of measured contemplation. He looked at the first on his left. It was of a bunch of flowers in a vase. It didn't seem to be much of a picture to him, too photographic. Below the flowers on a small silver tray were two apples. They were so realistic he could have reached out and picked them up.

He moved on. Pretty soon he too was walking sideways, one picture after another, his sight improving, his mind dimming down. He was in a dark room, where things hung in space, other humans walking along with him or standing behind him, so he had to say 'sorry' and duck out of their way. He went on strolling like a man in a dark world where nothing made any sense except that the whole senselessness was in itself a sort of sense—first one wall, then another. He was staring at a tangle of circles and dots and lines, leaning forward like the man next to him, arms folded and frowning, as if a frown could bring enlightenment. But, as he gave his mind to it, something began to appear. It was, and it was not exactly a face. Whether it was a woman or a man was not clear. He looked at the tag beside it on the wall: Diana at her toilette, it said. He didn't think it looked anything like Diana, whoever she was, and he couldn't see any toilet. He stood back, trying to get a better perspective. Diana disappeared altogether. He shook his head, defeated. If that was art, he'd eat his hat. He didn't have a hat, but that was beside the point.

'Strange, isn't it?' a voice said.

'Yeah—' He stepped back again and bumped into a woman.

'You can't see her?'

'Eh?'

He looked around. She came out of the semi-darkness. It was Evelyn Crowley. At least it was her face. The rest of her was still somewhere in that lightless space. She kept her voice down, almost reverential. It was a reverential sort of place.

'They lived together, Jenny and Diana.'

'I see.' He did not see at all. 'Why are paintings being shown in a library?'

'Oh, Jenny was on the staff here. She painted in her spare time. This is a sort of tribute to her, a retrospective.'

'I see.'

'Are you interested in art, Mr Becker?'

'No, not at all, Mrs Crowley.'

'Just filling in time?'

'Yes, I suppose.'

'Aren't we all? This one here—' She moved to it. 'I like this. Some people say it's a bit too Chagall. I, however, am impressed. It has movement, which Chagall does not.'

The card on the wall beside it called it Threnody for Dancers. There were four or five figures in long, flowing gowns, entwined. One or two were floating, one almost upside down.

'They don't seem to be dancing to me.'

'It's a different kind of dance. They're asleep.'

'How can they dance in their sleep?'

'I often dance in my sleep.'

'Really?'

'I used to kick my husband, which would wake him up and he'd snap at me, 'Evelyn! Can't you keep your feet still?' She pointed. 'They're dreaming that they are dancing. See the gestures? The long arms outstretched, the feet turned in the fourth position? The heads raised to the unseen stars, and the eyes cast down in endless sleep? They know they are asleep. The way we all are, don't you think?'

'Are we?'

'Do you think you are fully awake, Mr Becker?'

'Yeah, well, I have to be.'

'Because of your job? All night long?'

'I suppose.'

'A man who is fully awake has no imagination. He is no more than an insect, don't you think?'

'Got anyone in mind?'

'Men who stare at screens all night and day, afraid they'll miss a dollar. Such men have numbers in their brains and advantage in their hearts.'

'Like your husband?'

'He doesn't do much of that now.' She moved to another. 'This one is not so good. A bit of a mess, isn't it? Jenny was in a bad mood when she did it, so she told me. The brushwork is too thick, Van Gogh gone mad. If you stand back a bit, you get a better perspective. That, however, doesn't improve it. Now, here—'

She pointed at another.

'This is more to my taste, very simple. Any student could do it, they usually do. Jenny's got a good line on her, hasn't she? Not exactly Picasso but good enough, don't you think?'

Becker tried not to look. It was a nude of a young woman lying back with her hands behind her head, her legs both open and not open, depending on how your eyes followed the lines.

'That's one of a set of the same girl,' she said. 'I have two already. I'll buy it, if they'll let me have it.'

They moved on again. Mrs Crowley continued chatting, keeping close, leaning in, her voice soft, very breathy.

'You know, Mr Becker, sometimes I believe I am asleep all day long, and that I'll never wake. I walk in my sleep and I talk in my sleep. I'm talking to you now in my sleep. I am dreaming I'm in a dark, cosy place where it is never too cold and never too hot. And I am asleep, although I am conscious enough to know I am asleep.'

This was beyond him.

'It's where we all are, aren't we?'

'I don't know.'

She moved on to yet another. 'Well, I do know. I am in a dream and you are in a dream and it's nice to be in a dream together, don't you think? Strolling around, looking at pictures?'

He had no idea. She was a little frightening. That was his big problem—as much as he tried to stay awake in the real world, whatever it was, he could never be awake enough. He could never be fully ready when they came. There was always someone out there beyond the dream who knew what was going on. That's why he could never fully waken. And he could never fully sleep, which had been his father's problem. He'd died in Vietnam. In his last letter, he'd said that when they were out on patrol, they could never properly sleep and for that reason they were never properly awake. You could be asleep, but you were not really asleep, because you were always listening. You fought and walked and ate and pissed and shat in a dream.

Mrs Crowley moved on from picture to picture. She did not offer much more advice. For some reason, she'd reverted to her style at first meeting, sometimes vague, sometimes offhand, sometimes mysterious. But definitely not the woman who'd talked to him in the garden, in the rain and in confidence. Then she had opened up, revealing a very apprehensive woman. Last time they had spoken was on the phone, when she'd been distressed, almost crying into the instrument. Now she was offhand, indifferent. It was as though, having told her story that day, she had somehow got rid of it. Problem solved. Or perhaps it was part of some deception, a little game she was now playing to her own satisfaction. He did not know. All he knew was that she was strolling around a gallery with him in the gloom, chatting to him, teaching him something. He did not understand, but it was good to be told.

They walked out of the gallery and into the vast foyer.

'Would you like coffee?' she said.

It was just after four o'clock. He wasn't too sure. Mrs Crowley was a bit too intellectual for him. She might want to talk about art. Ask him what he'd learned. Also, she had not called him Harry once so far that day. Indifference seemed to have come between them.

'Or a glass of something?'

He did not know what to do in the circumstances. A beautiful woman was asking him to have a drink with her. Should he pay? Should he lead the way, guide her to a table? How would he order? Did you breeze up to a counter or sit and wait for a waiter?

It would not be like taking some girl you knew into a pub, perching her on a stool and saying to the barman, 'Fill her up!'

She seemed to read his mind. 'Or would you prefer to walk?'

'Walk,' he said.

They walked out. At least, he walked. Mrs Crowley, however, simply strolled in her own casual way. Going down the steps, she took one at a time, distinctly pausing between each, her hands in front, holding her bag. Now in the clear afternoon light, he could see she was casually dressed—a blue topcoat, probably a very expensive car coat, short and sharp and perfectly cut, no doubt in Milan. Also what appeared to be a patterned skirt which flipped and flapped with every step she took. On her feet were matching blue shoes and about her throat was a fine silk scarf, scarlet red. She might have been wearing a fine cotton shirt under the coat. They reached the forecourt among the golden poplars.

'Which way?' she asked.

A woman like Mrs Crowley did not really ask. Every question was some sort of subtle order, like speaking to a maid or a uniformed attendant. Or to a chauffeur? Whatever ma'am seemed to want, you seemed to do.

'Along the lake?' she suggested.

He agreed without answering. They went down to the water's edge, before turning eastward, strolling towards the land of the rising sun, which was not rising. It was moving around behind them now, heading for the Brindabella Ranges and the night.

'Do you have any more information for me?' she asked.

He shook his head. He had a few ideas, but at this stage he did not want to speculate.

'Have you heard anything more?' he asked.

'No.'

'No more letters?'

'No.'

'They may have given up.'

She did not reply.

'Maybe they fear they'd fall into a police trap.'

'Sometimes I don't care what happens.'

'Don't be that way.'

She smiled, as if surprised by his concern.

'Just an observation, Mrs Crowley.'

It was a fine day, not hot and not cool, cloudless except for a few high nimbus patterns to the east. There was no sound except the cry of a seagull and the clicking of her heels on the pavement. Way ahead were the High Court and the National Gallery, toweringly bland and functional in their concrete. He did not know what to say, so he said the obvious.

'What do you do, Mrs Crowley?'

'What do I do?'

'How do you fill in your days? Do you work?'

She laughed, short and sharp. 'Work? What would I do? I was a secretary years ago, I think I told you. In a law firm in Melbourne. I've forgotten all I knew. I'd be out of date. Everything has been upgraded. Secretaries don't take shorthand anymore. They use tape recorders and computers. No, I do not work.'

His question still hung in the air.

'Well,' she said after a few more steps, 'I don't do anything, really. I just exist. I mean, I get up in the morning, I have a shower—my hair is oily so I must wash it every day. Of course, I have to wait for it to dry. I hate electric dryers, they blow hot air in my eyes. I have sensitive eyes. I'm always putting drops in them. So, I have breakfast and read the paper and go through it, looking to see what's on. That's why I'm here today. I saw that Jenny Jeffers was showing. I love her work. I've bought several pieces. What else do I do? I check the ads to see if there's something I might buy. Usually there isn't. All of that usually takes about an hour. So I get dressed and do my nails and brush my hair. I fiddle with it. I don't care for my hair, not all those frizzy bits. Strangely, they're frizzy only on the ends. Sometimes I have my hair cut short, so that I resemble nothing on earth. Of course, it always grows back. I've tried every possible style and every possible cutter in Canberra, and I've given up. So I let it hang. It's always a mess, which gives me the opportunity to push it back, as you've probably noticed. I'm always pushing it back.'

She sighed, a short, sharp but resigned sigh, as if she were contemplating the end of the world and there was nothing she could do about it.

'Finally, I do my face, which takes at least ten minutes, because I don't like my own face. It reminds me of someone I'd rather not know. If the maid is there, I talk to her. I watch her cleaning and polishing or I read a book. Throughout all this, I have the radio on, playing the classics. It's on all day, except when I'm out. The maid comes twice a week. By the time she's finished, it's nearly lunchtime. If she's not there, I might go to a gym, have a workout, try to burn off some of the fat. It's pretty hopeless, I know. I can't beat my Italian body. It must be all the pasta and cheese and olives we eat, and the salt. Soon I shall be a big, fat Italian mamma without children.'

He felt tempted to ask why she had no children, but did not. Perhaps she didn't want them. Or perhaps Mr Crowley did not want them. He didn't sound like the kind of man who would have time to be a father.

'And what else? Oh, I might ring a friend, talk about lunch. Sometimes one will come to me for lunch, but usually I go out. I'm not much of a cook, I'm afraid. Now and then I go shopping, usually at Manuka. There's nothing worth looking at in Civic. On Fridays, I go to the National Gallery, where I serve as a guide, a volunteer guide. I don't know much about art, nor do the visitors. My husband collects art. He too doesn't know anything about it—he just buys what the dealers push at him, saying this or that will be worth a lot more in a few years. He can't resist a bargain, the poor man. That's why our walls at home are covered with this and that and no sense at all. Whenever he is at home, we drink expensive wines. Quite often we start with a Dom Perignon or a Moët. He raises his glass and says, 'Cheers.' So I raise mine and say, 'Cheers!' What we are celebrating, I do not know. Unless it is seventeen years of cheerful misery.'

Her heels went click, click, click, click, like a clock with infinite patience. They had plenty of time, at least until the end of their lives. Whenever that was.

'What else? Oh, yes, on Wednesdays I help out at Red Cross, checking in volunteers and giving them a cup of tea or coffee after they've given blood. I hate the sight of blood, but one must do something, mustn't one? At night, we might go out to dine or to a concert. Sometimes I go alone and if I meet someone I know I have to say Donald's in Paris or Frankfurt or New York once again or that he's working back. Telling little lies is refreshing, don't you think? Otherwise people might think that I am meeting someone I shouldn't or that we have had a blazing row and I have walked out on him. Donald is very strict about appearances. No doubt he will know that we have been strolling here. Someone will notice. Someone always does.'

Her voice drifted off as she looked away across the lake and up into the cold air and the thinness of the clouds behind Mount Ainslie.

'Last week we had the Sydney Symphony. They played Sibelius, the Fifth. Do you know it? I love it, especially the last movement, the glorious melodies and that great joyous bell, which is the whole orchestra at the end. He said at the time he'd been inspired by seeing sixteen white swans fly away across a lake. We have a lake here, but we have no white swans, only black ones and pelicans and seagulls. It's not the same, is it? As I sat there listening, I began to cry. I couldn't help myself. It was so lovely, I choked, a real gasp. People sitting near me turned around. An old man sitting beside me patted my hand: "Don't cry, my dear," he whispered, "Sibelius would not have wanted you to cry." Some days I wish I could fly away with those swans—up and up into limitless nothingness—and never come back.'

He was surprised by her last words. She sounded offhand but looked at him foolishly, as if she'd realised she'd given too much away.

'And so, you see, I have a rather busy life.'

You couldn't ask a woman like Mrs Crowley what was wrong, if anything was wrong at all. It was none of his business. As for the Sibelius, he did not know what she'd been talking about. He'd never been to a symphony concert in his life, but he wished he could one day. And go with her. To sit with her, listen to her, to hear what she had to say and to be educated by her. It would be like starting all over again in a different life. Or in a life that was the same but was getting somewhere. If you were getting somewhere, you were starting to be someone. And walking into a theatre or a lonely street at night or even a park like Collins Park in autumn with Mrs Crowley would be like being there, close to the centre of the universe.

And so they walked on. It was a long way. On the lake, a tourist boat headed for home. Overhead, three or four gulls floated on the light breeze. On the other side, beyond Commonwealth Park, the peak hour traffic had started to gather. Up high they could see the War Memorial, blazing in the afternoon sun. It looked final in its gravitas. Everyone who had ever died in war was buried there—if not in body, then in the vaults where their records lay.

'And what do you do? she asked.

'More or less the same—without the library and the gallery and the haircuts.'

He was going to add the sitting in Garema Place, eating a late lunch and feeding the pigeons, or going to a movie and sitting in the dark and watching big faces on a big screen. That filled in an afternoon, but it did not fill in a life. So, he did not mention them.

As they walked, he pictured himself walking beside a tall woman, who was strolling rather than walking and both looking at him and not at him in a quizzical way. He was not sure what a quizzical look was, but Mrs Crowley was doing something like it. She was watching, he knew. Testing, because she had talked too much in the gardens, in the mist and rain and the greyness of non-identity. She had given herself away, helping a bunch of Italian crooks in Melbourne take a poor sucker of a young bank manager for a ride. Not that fifteen thousand dollars was all that much to worry about, but what had followed certainly was. They'd caught him, incorporated him. He was theirs; they owned him. He could do nothing about it except play along.

She was assessing him, he knew. That's why she was so different today. Asking herself whether she had told him too much. Whether he was now a danger. If she decided that he was, what would she do about it?

They walked on a few more yards.

'Where do you come from?' she asked.

'Me? From Wagga.'

'Wagga Wagga?'

'The place with all the crows.'

At that moment one lone crow did fly over their heads and headed across the lake, cawing. Its wretchedness seemed to presage the end of a sad film, the kind with a heartbreaking close up, the kind in which the guy does not get the girl, or the girl does not get the guy, or no one gets anything except a bullet in the back and a big fade to black.

'And what did you do there?'

'Went to school, played some football, worked for a hardware store for a year or two, then got a job with a stock and station agent. I was with him for two or three years.'

'What is a stock and station agent?'

'A bloke who sells sheep and cattle and horses and anything else on four legs, as well as rural properties big and small, and does a bit of auctioneering.'

'Farms and grand old homesteads?'

'Some of them are not so grand. Some are run down and scratching.'

'Scratching?'

'For a living.'

'Really?'

'It's tough on the land. Most times, even in the good times, you never know when they are going to end and whether you are going to get through the bad ones, which always come. Some go broke, some go mad, some go for the big drop.'

'Hanging, you mean?'

'Yeah, I went out to a place not far past Uranquinty on the road going south soon after I started, only twenty at the time. I had to see a man who hadn't paid up. I couldn't find him at first. I couldn't find anyone—not a wife or a child or a dog, which was pretty strange for a place like that. Normally there's at least a dog.'

'Did you find him?'

'Well, I found his wife. She was in the kitchen, hiding behind the door. I pushed it open and saw her squatting against a wall—hands clutched, her face a horrible grey as though she had died but her heart was still beating. Her cheeks were sunken, her teeth had gone. She was a wreck. I was going to speak, but she just looked at me and said, 'There's something for you.' I didn't know what she meant. 'Where's Mr Higgs?' I said. 'Down by the creek like the swaggie,' she said.'

'What swaggie?'

'I didn't know for a minute. Banjo Paterson's swaggie, I suppose. So I went down to the creek and followed it to a big coolabah. He was hanging from a branch. He'd been there several days by the look of him, all puffed up and fly-blown. His dog was sitting on the grass looking up at him, eyes wide open, ears standing up, staring at him, as if waiting for him to speak.'

'How awful.'

'So, I went back to the house and asked the old lady what had happened. She said nothing—nothing I could understand, anyway. So I went back to town and told my boss. He rang the police. They went out, so did the funeral director. The policeman came into the office next day and said, 'This is for you,' to the boss. It was an envelope.

In it was a brief note and forty-eight dollars and seven cents. That was the fee I'd gone out for. Apparently, he'd given it to his wife to make sure all his debts were paid. He was an honourable man. She'd just sat there behind the kitchen door for days, not knowing what to do. They took her away and put her in a home. She was quite mad by this time.'

Mrs Crowley was perturbed. 'Oh, oh—'

'That's life in the bush.'

'How awful. The poor people.'

They walked on a while, coming to the landing stage and its tight little patch of nondescript gums. The High Court and the gallery were bigger now, bold in their concrete banality.

'It's not always so bad,' he said at last.

They had fallen into step. Normally he would have been a mile ahead of her by now. He'd adjusted to her swinging sort of gait, the bag still held before her body. Swinging like the dead man in the hanging tree.

'Now tell me a funny story.'

'A funny story?'

'Please!'

He was surprised. It sounded urgent, her tone. Normally Mrs Crowley would not beg. He couldn't think of a funny story. So he told her about Nil Desperandum.

'A town called Nil Desperandum?'

'No, a property west of Wagga on the Sturt Highway, beautiful red loam country. I went out there to see a bloke about a sale. The property was not big, only one square mile. That's 640 acres, big enough for wheat but not much else. If the wheat failed, you could run a few sheep. If both failed, you could always rely on bankruptcy. I drove up to the gate, opened it. On the gate was a small notice: *'Please shut the gate.'* In small print under it someone had written: *'That means you.'* A brown kelpie was watching me do all this. As I drove in, it turned 'round and led me to the house which was about fifty yards from the gate. It kept looking back now and then to see if I'd got lost. There was a huge pepper tree laden with berries to one side, so I pulled up under its shade and got out. It was not much of a house, six rooms I'd say, with a verandah 'round the front and both sides. There were the usual outbuildings such as a small shearing shed, a machinery shed, a feed store for the sheep in dry times and just about everything you'd expect, including a windmill that looked like it would fall down if you sneezed near it. All in all, it was a pretty sound sort of property. It was for sale and my boss had found a buyer.

'I stopped the car out front and a woman came out, a real bushie you could tell even before she opened her mouth.

"Ah, g'day," she said.

"G'day," I said.

"G'day," she said again.

"Nice day," I said.

"Yeah," she said.

'This could have gone on all day, so I said, "I'm Harry Becker from Thos. Thomkins & Son in Wagga."

"Old Thos?" she said. She pronounced it Thos and not Thomas, but she was not the first to do that. People had been calling him Thos since he was a kid at school, because the firm was established back before the Great War by his father, who was also Thos Thomkins. All of which is by the way, I know.'

Mrs Crowley was walking along, now in lock step with Becker, smiling as if she couldn't make up her mind whether her leg was being pulled or this story was coming from a part of Australia of which she knew nothing, a primeval place where stories sprang from the earth as if without human agency, except perhaps helped by an occasional watering with blood, sweat, tears and hopelessness.

'So, what did you say?'

'Well, I just said, "Yeah." She was looking a bit sceptical.

"Old Thos anxious for his screw, is he?" she said. I was a bit worried about the way she said *screw*. She looked the kind of sheila who could screw a man's head off the way some country women could ring the neck of a chicken. "You'd better come in," she said. "Mr Hardwick at home?" I asked.

"Ah, he's 'round somewhere," she said. So I followed her into the house. When I say '*her*' I mean a woman, although she didn't look like a woman. I didn't know what age she was, but she looked more like a boy than a woman, or at least a young man. She was wearing shorts and boots and a khaki shirt without sleeves. She had strong brown arms, the kind that could wrestle a bad-tempered steer. And her straight blond hair was cut short like a boy's, but she had earrings, small and pierced. She had small ears too, very pretty, so I guessed she must be some sort of sheila after all. She walked with one hand on a hip and the other balled into a loose sort of fist that meant business.

'Anyway, we went into the house. It was quite clean inside, much better than out. Very neat, everything set out nicely, not a speck of dust, a few pictures on the walls, even knickknacks on side tables and sideboards, and a few family photos in silver frames. You could see the woman's touch as soon as you stepped in. "You've brung the papers"' she said.

"Yeah," I said. I had the documents in a briefcase, just three or four sheets. It was otherwise empty, and I knew I looked a bit of a galah carrying a briefcase, when I could have put them in my pocket. But the boss had said, "You've got to look professional." Well, she walked straight through the house.

'I started to follow her, but she said, "Hang on there, mate." She went out onto the back verandah, which was not really a verandah but a porch, and whistled. A real blast that nearly split my eardrums. The dog came running. "Where's Ted?" she asked. The dog said '*I don't know*' with its eyes and its ears. "Well, go and find him," she said. "Tell him he's got a visitor." So off the dog went. She came back inside. "I suppose you're a bit dry?" she said. "You could use a quick one?"

"Suppose I could," I said, "coming out all this way."

'So she went to the fridge. It was old, but in good working order, I could see. When she opened the door, everything you could want was there, including half a dozen bottles of Foster's. She must have seen me looking, because she said, "He likes a bottle a day. Makes him sleep well—pisses a lot, but." Well, she took one and tried to twist the cap off. It wouldn't move. She tried again, but still no luck. So she stuck the end of the bottle in her mouth, clamped her teeth on the cap and twisted the bottle. That did the trick. They were perfect white teeth, although a bit short, probably because of her aggressive attitude towards uncooperative caps. So we sat down and had a glass each. It was nice and cold. "Been in the game long?" she asked.

"Not long," I said, "two or three months."

"Got the papers, have you?"

"Yeah," I tapped the case. "All set and ready to sign."

"Ah, I dunno," she said, "it's sad, selling up, ain't it? The old bugger's selling my own home from under me feet. Nothing I can do about it, but. It's in his name."

"Yeah," I said, "it must be a bit of a wrench. What are you going to do?"

"Ah," she said, "he wants to go to Tumbarumba, he's got rellies there. I'd prefer to go to Wagga, see a few bright lights now and then, have a bit of fun." I was going to ask her what kind of fun she had in mind, but I thought I better not. She might tell me to mind my own business.

'Anyway, by this time I was getting a bit of a glow on and she was smiling a bit and starting to look more like a girl than a boy. She was short and stocky and must have been about forty. Anyway, after we'd got through all the pleasantries she said, "Want another beer?"

"No," I said, "better not while I'm here on business." She got up and went to the back porch.

"Where is he?" she asked the dog, which'd returned without Mr Hardwick. If it ever went to find him, I don't know. She whistled again and called and cooeed, but that did no good. So, she came back and said, "Got time for a quick one?"

"Ah, no," I said, "I'd better not, not if I'm driving."

"I meant one of the other kind," she said.

"Eh?" I said.

"Yeah," she said. "If we're quick, it'll be all right. He's got a gammy leg," she said. "He'll be a while yet."

"You don't mean—?" I said.

"Yeah," she said, "if you're interested, like."

"Ah, well—," I said. She just stood up and dropped the shorts. She had nothing on underneath—and got on top of me.'

'You mean while you were sitting on a chair?'

'Yes, it was a fine-looking chair made of turpentine. You could smell it, although it was a few years old. Well, she'd unzipped me and had the old fellow out in no time flat.'

'What?' Mrs Cowley was laughing. It was marvellous to hear.

'Yeah, I was amazed.'

'I should think so.'

'Anyway, this sheila was going for her life. She went on and on, bouncing up and down, all the time smiling and looking triumphant, the way some women do, when they think they've got the better of a bloke.'

Mrs Crowley did a little dance, still laughing.

'How long did this last?'

'Until I came, which was in about ten seconds, or it seemed like it. It might have been half a minute.'

'Is this a tall story?'

'No, fair dinkum, funny things happen in the bush.'

'So, what happened?'

'Oh, she got off when she'd finished and wiped herself with a wet tea towel, pulled up the shorts and said, "Well, it doesn't look like he's comin'. Must've fell asleep under a tree." "Don't you think we'd better go and have a look?" I said, doing up my strides.

"Ah, no," she said, "he'll be right."

"I can come back tomorrow," I said.

"What's he got to sign?" she said.

"Here it is," I said, taking it out of the bag. "I could leave it, but I have to witness it before him.'

"Give it here," she said. I handed it over. She read it quickly. "Hmm," she said, "his looks all right, I'll sign it."

"Ah, no," I said, "he's the owner, he has to sign."

"Ah, he could take all day," she said. "Anyway, he's got Parkinson's. Here, where's a pen?' She jumped up and rustled through a drawer in a sideboard. I was still protesting when she sat down again and signed the deed of sale.

"Hey," I said, "that's illegal."

"No, it isn't," she said, "it's his signature, spittin' image. Even the bank can't tell the difference and they've got experts."

"Well, I don't know," I said.

"I'd better go and find him," she said.

"Oh, hell," I said, "this could be bad." I was really worried. 'How old is Mr Hardwick?" I asked.

"Sixty-four," she said, "and his wick ain't too hard these days."

"How old are you?" I said.

"I'm thirty-nine," she said, "but I still love a good root when I can get it."

Too late Becker realised his mistake, using such a word in front of a lady. She, however, did not seem shocked. No doubt Mrs Crowley was a woman of the world. In fact, she'd been chuckling through most of his story with her mouth shut.

'She said that? Good lord, what happened?'

'I was really bamboozled. She pushed me out, saying, "I hope he hasn't gone and carked it."

"But—," I started to say.

"You'd better be off," she said.

"But—," I said again. She whistled and the dog came bounding in.

"See this young bloke off the premises," she said. The dog went for my ankles. I jumped out of the way, headed for the front door. The dog followed, nipping me all the way to the car. I took off, more ashamed than surprised. I'd done a wrong thing. A woman had forged a signature, and I was carrying a false document. But I couldn't stop, because if I'd got out of the car and gone back, the dog probably would have taken a bite out of my leg. So I drove back to Wagga.

'When I showed the boss the deed, he said, "By gee, that old bloke's got a steady hand for his age."

"So has his wife," I said under my breath.

"Hey," the boss said, "you haven't signed as witness!"

"Ah, gee," I said, "I forgot."

"Well, you'd better go back tomorrow," he said. So, I went back the next day. The old man was there this time, fast asleep on the verandah.

"You want another quick one?" she asked.

"Might as well," I said, "now that I'm here." We didn't bother with the beer this time.'

'On the chair again?'

'No, on a bed. It was much more comfortable, and we took a bit longer.'

Mrs Crowley had calmed down, although her eyes were sparkling with disbelief. She was still chuckling when they reached the High Court, where the trees quietly enfolded them. She was walking jauntily now, almost skipping like a schoolgirl.

'Did you ever go back?'

'Oh, yes, every now and then till they packed up and went to Tumbarumba, just for a quick one.'

She glanced at her watch. 'Oh, my God, I must go. We're going to the opera tonight. I think it's Don Giovanni, and I think we're having dinner somewhere first. I never know until we get there.'

'You don't have your car today?'

'It's being serviced and I'm supposed to pick it up at five. Where is yours?'

'Back at the library.'

'I'll get a taxi. I'll give you a lift.'

'I'm fine,' he said.

She pulled out a mobile phone and rang a number. A taxi was waiting when they reached the gallery.

It had been a fortuitous afternoon, both of bad fun and good fun, the hanging man and the farmer's wife. He opened a door for her. She looked at him. It was an odd look, a mixture of friendship, mischief and indecision. For a moment he thought she might suggest they meet for a drink sometime. She did not. Instead, she offered a hand.

'Thank you, Mr Becker.'

They shook hands. Hers lay in his for not much more than a second. It was a lovely touch, loose and gentle and personal. In some ways it was better than a kiss. Not many women offered a hand these days, not to men like him. As she'd withdrawn it, he thought she had stroked his palm with a fingertip, but he could have been mistaken.

'I enjoyed our walk,' she said.

Just four simple words, which trailed off—not into nothingness, but into the possible future. She stepped into the cab and tucked in the skirt around her long, dreamy legs. And smiled goodbye.

CHAPTER 10

That night Becker made a few house calls, then went to the townhouse in Kingston again. This time a light was showing in a front window. Becker crept up and peeped in. He could see no other light. He heard nothing. Torrence might have been out on the town. He thought of going in and poking around, although not sure he'd find anything incriminating. Torrence would have it all in his head.

An hour or so later Becker went back. The place looked exactly the same. He returned several times until just after eleven. Now two lights were on and a small red Alfa Romeo was parked outside under a streetlight. Becker went to the front door, heard music. Someone seemed to be singing and stamping her feet, a woman. He thought it sounded Spanish—harsh wailing music, full of pain, or phoney pain. Becker raised a hand to use the knocker but changed his mind. He picked the lock quietly and just walked in. No locks could keep him out. If he ever wanted to make a fortune, he could use his skills as a cat burglar. He'd probably get away with it until some over-excited cop caught him at it one night and filled him full of lead.

The apartment was well furnished with off-the-shelf stuff, which had no class, no taste. Even the big print on the wall looked as if it had come out of a factory, very splashy with red and gold. In another room, a man coughed lightly—a short, hard sound. Becker followed the sound into a kitchen. A thin man was at the sink, swallowing a tablet with water. The glass tumbler was held by a hand badly scarred, showing mottled red and yellow patches of skin. The driving gloves were on another bench by the door. He looked around as the last gulp went down.

'Who the hell are you?'

'You know me, Vince.'

Torrence noticed the bulge in Becker's jacket, which was always open in case he had to draw fast, the pistol butt just showing—and the big hands waiting for him to make a move. Torrence was not armed. There was, however, a set of knives on the wall by his head. He smiled, almost affectionately.

'Harry bloody Becker, eh? Just look at you, eh? How d'you get in, Harry?'

'Who're you working for?'

'Me? Who'm I workin' for?'

Torrence put down the glass, leaned on the bench and grinned. He had a cheeky grin, like a little boy who's been caught pinching biscuits. In his tight pants, he really did look like a bullfighter. In the background, the woman was still yelling and stamping. The radio must have been in a bedroom.

'Just answer the question.'

'Who? Me?'

'It's not blackmail, is it?'

'What?'

'Who's paying you?'

'You're tellin' me to answer questions?'

'Someone wants her dead.'

Torrence smiled again, walking up to Becker slowly, hands on hips. He had a long, thin face, probably attractive to some women. A few black curls hung down over a low brow. The sideburns ran down almost to his chin, very neatly trimmed. He could have been someone out of an old movie—a spiv or a gigolo or a street fighter. He came up close to Becker, leaned forward and peered into his eyes. Becker closed a hand around the butt of the old Smith and Wesson. He tried not to blink. If he did, Torrence might hit him fast and hard. Might even knife him.

'Who am I workin' for?'

'Leave her alone, Vince.'

'Leave who alone?'

'You know who I mean. She's been through enough.'

'Who the hell?'

'Evelyn Crowley.'

Torrence laughed, more a giggle than a laugh. A sexless sort of giggle. 'Crowley? That dame? Fancy her, do you, Harry?' He leaned closer, so his nose almost touched Becker's. 'Been screwin' her, have you?'

'If you make her do it, I'll kill you.'

'Do what?'

'You want her to jump, don't you?'

'Me? Why'd I want that? I like the money.'

'Who told you about her?'

Torrence grinned. 'Told me what?'

'The man who jumped.'

Torrence was genuinely surprised. 'What man?'

'A lawyer in Melbourne.'

'What?'

'He fell six floors. Smacked the concrete in Collins Street.'

Torrence stood back, folded his arms and leaned against the bench. 'You're kiddin'?'

'Don't tell me you didn't know?'

'She pushed him?'

'Why do you say that?'

'Just a thought. You never know with that kind of dame.'

Becker hesitated. Deep down, he'd begun to think the same way. Most times Mrs Crowley was a cool customer, but she'd done something pretty bad sometime, somewhere. Had she pushed the bloke? That day in the gardens she had acted as though she had.

'You wrote to her. You told her you knew all about it. You demanded money, five thousand.'

'Hey, now, wait on—'

'I saw you try to collect the money.'

'All right, so I did. It was just a caper. Everyone likes to make a fast buck.'

'You mean you didn't know?'

'Didn't she show you the letters?'

'She showed me one of them.'

'There was nothin' about killin' anyone in any of 'em.'

'How do you know that?'

'I wrote 'em, mate, that's how.'

Becker was surprised. 'You wrote them?'

'Well, not actually wrote 'em. I typed 'em.'

'Typed them? Who for?'

Torrence laughed. He seemed such a happy man. 'Uh uh!'

'What's going on, Vince?'

'Uh uh, not telling!'

'Stop the bullshit.'

Becker thought of shooting the stupid bastard, just a flesh wound in a leg, to make him talk. He didn't do it. Torrence might not talk even then.

'It's not blackmail, is it? You were to get the five grand for being a good dog, weren't you? The real purpose is to frighten her, isn't it? Frighten her about what? Just getting herself pregnant when she wasn't married wasn't enough to shake her down. That was years ago. But it's not money, is it? Someone wants her dead.'

Torrence just laughed. It was a fast little laugh, the kind a boxer might give you just before he lands the knockout. 'Someone is tryin' to kill her, you reckon?'

'Is it her husband?'

'Eh? That turkey?'

'You drove for him once. Did he put it to you? Frighten her to death?'

'Frighten her?'

'That turkey, as you call him, is very big in a very big bank. And he's after a big job in Washington—a seat on the board of the World Bank. Maybe he wants to get rid of an embarrassment? If it got out she'd done something bad—'

'Ah, Christ, mate, I know nothin' about this. I just do what I'm told. I'm still waiting for my money.'

'Am I right?'

'Ah, Christ, you and me, we're just a couple of creeps in all this, like those two guys. What was their name? Rozencrantz and somebody? Wanderin' in an' out of a story we don't understand. No one gives a shit about us, mate. So leave it, Harry.'

'It's big?'

'Yeah, mate, big.'

'A lot of money?'

'Yeah.'

'And you?'

'I don't know. I'm just the messenger boy.'

'You want to talk about it?'

Torrence didn't answer. He had turned and was staring out the kitchen window. Someone out there could have been watching and listening.

'I was kicked out three years ago, Vince.'

'I know.'

'I was gonna talk and someone shot me.'

'I know.'

'It was Whitford.'

'Yeah, I know.'

'He paid someone to hit me.'

'Yeah, he did.'

'How do you know?'

'Because he asked me to do it.'

Becker was surprised. 'You?'

'Yeah, me.'

'Why didn't you? Didn't he offer enough?'

Torrence shrugged. 'We were mates, remember?'

'Who did he pay?'

'I dunno. Some crackhead, who'd shoot his mother for a fix.'

'Whitford was a mongrel,' Becker said. 'I saw him belt a man half to death.'

'Yeah, I was there.'

'Who killed him, Vince?'

'I did.'

'You? Why?'

'Ah, I'd had enough by then.' Torrence was still staring out the window. Becker waited. There was no point in pushing him. He had a feeling it would come out, one rat to another rat. 'One night we took this guy out to La Perouse. I thought Dickie was just goin' to give him a beltin' but he pulled out his piece and shot him.'

'Shot him?'

'Yeah, we were standing' there lookin' across the bay at the lights at Port Botany. It was lit up like a Christmas tree. And he shot him. Through the back of the head. Dropped like a stone.' Torrence wriggled a bit, sucked on his teeth. 'Then he told me to get a spade out of the car and start diggin'. I was astonished. "You want me to dig a hole?" I said. "Why do you think you're here?" he said. "I've got a crook back." I started walking back to the car. Then I heard him say to himself, "Stupid fuckin' Dago." That got me. I've been called a Dago all my life, but this time—'

Becker did not know what to say, so he said nothing.

'I got the spade, a nice new one, as sharp as a razor, from the boot. Then I walked back and hit Dickie with it. I'd intended to whack him with the flat of the blade, just to flatten him, but I slipped in the sand. The blade hit him edge on, nearly cut his head off. I walked off, left him lyin' there with the other bloke, caught a bus and went home.'

'What did you do with the spade?'

'Left it there.'

'What about prints?'

'Never thought of that.'

'There must have been an enquiry?'

'Yeah, nothin' came of it.'

'Nothing?'

'Nah, no one missed Dickie. No one went to his funeral. He was an embarrassment, bringing the force into ill repute. Some big people up top were glad to be rid of him.'

Becker stared at Torrence, thinking about it. It was like being back in the pub by the docks. Having a beer with the boys and Dickie Whitford walking in and grinning all over his great ugly face and pulling a roll of notes out of a pocket and saying, 'What are we all drinkin'?'

'I'll let myself out, Vince.'

'You want a drink, mate?'

'I've got a job to do.'

'Yeah, ain't we all?'

At the door, Becker looked back. 'Vince? Who was chasing you?'

'Chasin' me?'

'Down a lane in Civic.'

'You heard about that?'

'Who was it?'

'Best you don't know, mate.' Torrence said. 'And Harry, keep away from that Crowley dame. She ain't what she seems.'

Becker paused. He'd already been thinking Mrs Crowley was not what she seemed. But he let it go. He was like that these days. He let a lot of opportunities go. Sometimes, he felt that life was a lot better now that he'd met her. Then, he'd think it would be better to forget her. There was no hope there. Not with a woman like that.

CHAPTER 11

He went to Forrest and got out the piece of chalk he had in the car. He made the sign again on the green box and continued on his round. Someone was talking about the Dead Sea Scrolls on Radio National, so he switched to a local station. At midnight the local news came on, the reader talking about a fire in Ainslie. In fact, it was in his own street. He went there as fast as he could, found the fire truck outside the house. The Indian and his family were on the footpath, near a police car and two officers in uniform. One was talking to them, taking notes.

Becker went up to the other.

'What happened?'

'Someone tried to torch the place.'

'What time?'

'Forty minutes ago.'

Becker nodded. It couldn't have been Torrence. He was at home then.

'Some crank?'

'Yeah, he's phoned before.'

'I know, I live here.'

'With all these Indians?'

'What's wrong with Indians?'

The officer looked at the Stanton insignia on his shoulder. 'You have any idea who it is?'

'Probably some bloke who's been sacked from his job in the garment industry.'

'We don't have any garment industry in Canberra.'

'How much damage?'

'Pretty superficial, really, a fire under the wooden verandah. The walls are solid, double brick. Hard to make a place like that burn.'

'Just a warning, eh?'

'Could be.'

'Okay to go in?'

'Yes, okay.'

He talked to the Indian and his wife and sister and skinny Leticia. Some child was crying in the background. Toothless Grandpa was peeping around a corner, afraid. None of them had expected anything like this would happen in Australia. Becker went to bed, thinking about it. Maybe he was the target. This was another warning. Someone was going to kill him and make it look like a racist attack on a bunch of Indians. The fire was only a warning. Next time it might be a bomb.

He was still asleep next morning when the phone rang. He woke up, blinking and squinting against the harsh morning light in the window. Almost every night he forgot to draw the blind. Occasionally he enjoyed forty winks in the early hours, while still on the job. If he were caught, he'd be sacked. He didn't care. To hell with the job. He was getting out, one way or another.

'Hello?'

'Harry, it's Evelyn Crowley.'

'Oh, yes.'

'I saw your sign, the second one.'

He drew a breath, trying to work out what to say to her—a woman he did not quite trust. What had Torrence said about her? "She ain't what she seems." And worse than that, he'd said quite spontaneously: "She pushed him?" Why would Torrence think Mrs Crowley would push a man to his death?

'I've found him, Mrs Crowley.'

'Who? The chauffeur?'

'Yeah, he had quite a story to tell.'

'What story?'

'We'd better meet.'

'Donald is at home at present.'

'Where, then?'

She did the thinking. 'I'm about to go to Manuka. I have to pick up a dress.'

'Manuka?'

'We could have coffee and perhaps a bite to eat.'

'Where exactly?'

'On the strip.'

'When?'

'Give me thirty minutes.'

He hesitated, not keen on Manuka. Everyone went there, but what did it matter now? His boss knew he'd been seeing her. What secrets did he have? None at all, except he'd wanted to kill Whitford. Now Torrence had beaten him to it. As a result, he didn't have much direction in his life. He may as well go and drink coffee with a rich dame who drove a smart car, who'd been stringing him along like a poodle on a leash, a lapdog. Some women were like that.

Even so, he went to some trouble, putting on his only casual outfit, denim pants and an as-new jacket over a white t-shirt. Also his new boots, hardly a scratch on them. He'd bought them some months ago, because he'd had a date with a checkout chick in Woolworths, a girl with a terrific figure and a welcoming smile. But she'd not shown up. He'd gone into the store next day and asked for her, but she was not there. She'd quit, they'd told him. Had had a fight with her boyfriend and cleared out. They'd wanted to know whether he was the boyfriend. He'd not answered and walked out while they watched him suspiciously. People were always watching him suspiciously. Or, if they were not, he always felt they were. Such was life.

He thought of putting on a golden neck chain but realised he might look foolish—a nobody trying to look macho. Mrs Crowley would probably laugh at him. Then he thought of cologne. It would not improve his appearance, but it might make him feel a little fresher, less worn out by lack of sleep. But he abandoned that idea too. He did, however, trim his moustache, which was darker than his gingery hair, almost reddish brown. Eventually, he looked at least half decent.

Driving across town, he pulled up beside a big grey Mercedes with a diplomatic plate at red lights in King's Avenue. In the back, two swarthy men were talking. One was waving an arm. He looked Italian, the other more of a Greek or a Turk. The second had a shiny brown head, bald on top, nut-brown. He was smoking a cigarette. There was no flag on the front of the limo, so Becker couldn't guess what country owned it. As he stopped, the driver looked at him. It was Torrence. The phoney toreador watched him, gesturing with his eyes. He seemed to be indicating the men in the back. Next, he half smiled, raised one hand and made a shooting sign. Becker wasn't sure what it meant. The lights changed, and the limousine shot off, too fast for the old Holden. Soon Becker lost it on Canberra Avenue.

This time he did get the CD number, the full number.

When he arrived, most of the tables were taken by loafers eating either a late breakfast or an early lunch. It was about five to eleven. As for Mrs Crowley, she was sitting by herself at a table outside a bookshop, legs crossed and looking idly absent. As he came up, he paused and studied her in the way you might study a rare bird you had come across in a mountain glade. She was some woman. She had a way of sitting, as a model would sit on a chair and be told by the artist not to move, not even an eyelash—except of course she was clothed, but in such a way she might just as well have been naked. The fine jersey dress fitted like a glove, so that she looked like a woman on whom someone had painted a dress.

Her hands were folded on a magazine on her lap, although she was not reading. Her chin was slightly elevated, as if debating with herself and perhaps losing the argument. Her full lips were slightly open, as though about to speak, but not too open, just relaxed. She'd have a perfect head, a perfect face, if it weren't for that hooked nose. A Roman nose, he thought was the right name for it. She was holding her sunglasses open as if she'd just slipped them off, the better to see something across the way. The glasses were similar to others he'd seen her wear, and yet subtly different. Quite possibly, as with her handbags, she had a pair to go with every outfit. By her feet was a large Carla Zampatti bag.

Becker came up to speak to her. Hello seemed too banal for Evelyn Crowley— she'd probably think it unworthy of a reply. So he launched into chatty conversation, a bit more casual but also a bit more abruptly than he'd intended.

'What's the big occasion, Mrs Crowley?'

She glanced up at him. 'Pardon?'

'The new outfit?'

'Oh, this?' She nodded at the shopping bag. 'Just something for Friday night.'

'Your husband?'

She watched as he pulled up a chair. For a moment, it seemed she was not going to reply. Thoughts hung heavily in her eyes. She might have been staring at St Christopher's cathedral, perhaps wondering whether she should be inside, praying. Praying for what, he did not know. A clear conscience? Absolution? An Italian girl, a good Catholic girl, convent educated, would know all about it. All she had to do was go in there and wait for the panel to slide open and say, I have sinned, Father. If she did, would it have made any difference?

As for Becker himself, he wasn't a Catholic. He wasn't anything in particular. One of his grandfathers had been Lutheran, the other Anglican. The rest of his family had been no-account Welsh and Irish with no particular affiliations. Becker hadn't been in a church for many years, mainly because he felt God was not interested in him, had given him up as a bad job. Anyway, he had nothing to confess—at least nothing God would be interested in. If he had, he should go to Sydney and talk to Mr Justice Wood, tell him the whole story about Whitford, even if it meant next day he'd be dead. People up the line would not want him to open his mouth. No, he did not admire the Catholics; they could confess their sins and get off scot free. That took no guts at all. But to stand up before a royal commission and say you had witnessed Whitford flog a man, his eyes hanging out of their sockets, his teeth flying like broken crockery—that took guts.

He sat beside her, so both were now looking at nothing in particular.

'Yes,' she said at last, 'the big announcement.'

'The World Bank job? Is he going to get it?'

'Donald has his fingers crossed.'

'What exactly does he do?'

'At the Royal Bank? He's in charge of international operations.'

'What does that mean?'

'I really don't know.'

'You must have some idea?'

'I think he just moves money around the world, paying people's debts.'

She was looking at a waitress and raising a hand. It was the hand that she'd offered at the gallery, thanking him for his stories. He'd thought he would tell her another today, just to cheer her up. He did not get the chance. Mrs Crowley was not in a good mood today. She put back the glasses, so that he could no longer see her eyes, an action he thought discourteous. Even a lady should take off her glasses when she is talking to a gentleman. Perhaps she hoped no one would recognise her talking to a man like him.

'Millions, you mean?'

'Billions, more like it.'

The waitress came over. 'Yes, ma'am?'

'What'll you have?' Mrs Crowley said to Becker.

'Apple pie and cream and a long black.'

'And you, ma'am?'

'Just a latte.'

'Thank you, ma'am.'

Both waited until the girl had retreated. 'Why do you ask?' she said.

'Why do I ask what?'

'About what he does?'

He leaned forward, dropping his voice.

'Some people would say a man in his position would be a good friend to have.'

She flinched. 'Are you implying that he is involved in something?'

'I'm not implying anything. I don't know.' Becker leaned even closer. 'But I know one thing, Mrs Crowley—you are a liar.'

'What?'

The magazine slipped from her lap. He retrieved it for her.

'As I told you, I found the chauffeur. He's an ex-cop like me. We had a heart to heart. He says he sent you that letter. Not only that, he sent three letters.'

'I told you that. There were three, but I burned the first two.'

'So you did, and he also says there was nothing in them about anyone jumping to their death in Melbourne.'

She was astonished. 'But there was.'

'Not in the one I read.'

She began to tremble, not quite knowing what to do with her hands. Things were not going too well. She was annoyed, he could see. He'd been too firm with her, trying to be smart, business-like. You couldn't push such a woman, she had powerful friends. The waitress came with the two coffees and the pie. Again, they waited until she had gone.

'Rather convenient, isn't it? That you burned them.'

'How dare you!'

She took off the glasses and glared at him. Anger lit up her eyes. 'What are you saying? The first one said we know what you did to that man in Melbourne.'

'Which man?'

'Why, the lawyer, of course.'

'What did you do to him?'

'Nothing, I swear it. I was in love with him. Perhaps someone thinks I was responsible for his death.'

'And who would think that?'

'I've no idea.' She was shaking a little. 'Perhaps his wife?'

'After all these years? Why should she care now?'

He waited, watching her uncertain lips, her nervous hands. She cleared her throat, dropped her voice as she inclined her head. Her lips were so close he could feel her breath on a cheek. She was going to say something but did not seem to be able to find the right words. So he said it for her.

'And the second letter?'

'Oh, it said—What was it? "Got the money? Good girl. If you don't pay, your man can kiss Washington goodbye. We'll be in touch with the time and place." Or something similar.'

'Just that?'

'Yes.'

'The first one didn't mention the lawyer. In fact, the chauffeur did not know about the lawyer. The letters are about you and another man, aren't they? What exactly did you do to him?'

'What man?'

'Washington sounds like your husband.'

She was puzzled. 'Donald?'

'Is he in some sort of trouble?'

'Of course not!'

She was still angry, yet she did not get up and leave.

He put sugar in his coffee, just one spoonful, stirred slowly. At the other tables on each side, chatterboxes were shouting on mobile phones. All along the strip, smart young things, such as used-car dealers and land-sharks, were stitching up deals. One or two prostitutes, who'd just got out of bed, were recharging their batteries. Everyone, it seemed, was wired for sound these days. All were interconnected, and every conversation could be intercepted. Across the way, the cinema was showing a movie, Run for your Life. Below the sign, a young man was taking snaps of a young woman standing on the kerb, posing. She was standing with her back to Becker and Mrs Crowley. Becker was sure the camera was pointed not so much at the girl as over her shoulder. Someone was watching them through the telephoto lens. And snapping them.

'How did your husband get his present job, Mrs Crowley?'

'Oh, well—' She shrugged, more with her lips than her shoulders. 'He was very ambitious. He applied for a good job here in Canberra, and ever since—'

'He's had a fast rise to the top?'

'What's wrong with that?'

'Is he in trouble? At the bank? Has he been dipping into the till?'

She was annoyed. 'Stealing money? Absolutely not!'

'How do you know?'

'If anything like that had happened, he would have told me.'

'Why?'

'I am sure he would.'

'You don't know, do you? Or do you?'

She did not answer. Instead, she looked around without really seeing anything. She was frightened, he could see. She was squeezing one hand with the other.

He persisted. 'Why don't you tell him?'

'Tell him?'

'About the letters.'

'I couldn't do such a thing.'

'Just show him the last one and ask what it means? What are you supposed to have done in Melbourne? What about the swindle your relatives put over him?'

'How would anyone know about that?'

'Your Uncle Ennio knew about it.'

'Why would my family threaten him with that? They were part of it.'

'Then it must be someone else.'

'If it's really Donald they're aiming at, why not send it to him instead of to me?'

'If they did, he might not show it to you. They want you to know all about it—to ask him about it, to really frighten him. No secrets from his wife, who might blab to someone, perhaps a close friend, perhaps the police.'

'Oh, no, no—'

'It's a natty way of applying pressure to a man. It sounds like they're squeezing you to get at him.'

'No, no!' Several times she'd tried to sip coffee but had failed. 'What is happening? Who are these people?'

'I don't know, but it could be someone else—like the police.'

'Why would the police do that?'

'Trying to make him talk. On the other hand, it might be someone warning him not to talk.'

'Who?'

'I don't know.'

'My husband? You're saying he is mixed up in something crooked?'

He did not answer. She was still annoyed, but she did not snap at him. Mrs Crowley was a very constrained woman. She put a hand to her head.

'Oh, dear God, why is everything so awful?'

'I'm sorry. I shouldn't have called you a liar.'

'What am I going to do?'

'Show him the last letter. Tell him about the other two.'

'If he is involved in anything—'

'He might be arrested.'

'Arrested?'

Becker shrugged. He didn't care if someone did nail her husband, but he did care about her. He waited while she tried the coffee once more, managed a sip or two then gave up altogether. She sighed, then dropped her voice very low.

'I think it's something to do with Washington.'

'Someone doesn't want him to go? Why?'

'I don't know! I don't know!'

She was suddenly quite rattled. She gulped air, then opened her bag, took out a purse. 'I'm sorry, I—' She shuddered.

'It's my treat, Mrs Crowley.'

'No, no—'

She put down money, then rose awkwardly. Becker picked up the shopping bag.

'Thank you.' Her face was tight, the colour suddenly gone.

'Are you all right?'

'Yes, I think.'

'Where's your car?'

'I walked, it's not far.'

'You want me to drive you home?'

'No, thank you. Goodbye, Mr Becker.'

He watched her go, smiling to himself. She had not asked the obvious question: What was the name of the chauffeur who had been trying to blackmail her? He guessed she knew it already. Mrs Crowley was a strange woman, a bundle of contradictions and evasions and half-truths, not a woman to be trusted. Still, he was sorry to see her go. He enjoyed being with her. Every time he saw her, she made his day.

'Goodbye, Mrs Crowley.'

CHAPTER 12

He waited until she disappeared from view before he resumed his seat. As he did, he noticed a man had been sitting at an adjacent table. On it was a brown paper package, big enough to hold a large book—or a small recorder. The end facing him was open, but he could not quite see what was in the bag. It could have been a book after all, but it did not look like a book. The man was short and round and bald, sporting a thick grey moustache and wearing a light-brown three-piece suit, possibly alpaca. He was leaning back, smoking a long, fat cigarette and apparently squinting into space. The cigarette smelled like aromatic camel dung.

In those days in Canberra you were not allowed to smoke where food was served, even outdoors. The stranger seemed unaware of this, or he was aware but totally indifferent. If you'd asked him not to smoke, he looked the type who'd rise quickly and apologise profusely in some foreign language, before sitting again and squinting thoughtfully at nothing at all. On his table was a very short cup of coffee, no more than two mouthfuls. No doubt it was that strong stuff called Turkish. Becker couldn't drink it, it burned his guts.

In a way, the man in brown reminded him of one of the two men in the embassy car he'd seen Torrence driving, probably the bald one who'd been smoking and waving his hands around. He couldn't be sure. The man certainly could be a Turk or a Greek. He was about to challenge the man, even seize his package, when a young woman spoke beside him.

'Excuse me, sir.'

At first, he thought it was the waitress. When he turned, he saw a greenish-blue uniform. It was a girl from Canberra Church of England Girls' Grammar. She had reddish brown hair, white skin with a few freckles, and green eyes. Even without makeup, she was quite pretty. She looked about seventeen. Another girl in the same uniform was standing back and watching, half-smiling.

'Yes?'

'Would you please tell me—' She cleared her throat and tried again. 'Who is that lady?'

'What lady?'

'The lady to whom you were speaking.'

Becker was surprised. The girl spoke with the effortless precision of Mrs Crowley.

'You know her?'

'No, not exactly.'

'Why do you ask?'

'I came out of the bookshop and I saw her.' The girl was holding a paperback.

'Is that all?'

'Well, you see, I saw her two days ago, sitting in a car outside our house, looking at me. She smiled as though she knew me. Even raised a hand as if to wave, but changed her mind.'

'Changed her mind?'

'Yes.'

'Perhaps she thought you were someone else, then realised her mistake.'

'Oh, she was outside the gates at school this morning.'

'Was she? What, may I ask, is your name?'

'Oh, it's—' She hesitated, but she'd ask for the name of a strange woman, so she felt obliged. 'Christine Billings.'

Becker was annoyed. Mrs Crowley had found the girl. As he'd remarked, with a name like that she wouldn't be hard to find. As it had turned out, the girl was living in Canberra—and Mrs Crowley had not been able to resist the temptation to get a glimpse of her long-lost daughter. More than one glimpse, in fact.

'That lady?' He was inclined not to help, yet what did it matter now? 'Her name is Crowley.'

'Crowley?'

'Yes, Mrs Crowley.'

The girl was puzzled. 'Why is she interested in me?'

'Is she? I have no idea.'

'Please, where does she live?'

'I don't think I should tell you.'

'Oh, please—' She looked back at her friend, dropped her voice. 'You see, I was adopted and—'

'Is that so?' He pointed to a chair. 'Why don't you sit down and tell me all about it, Christine?'

She sat quickly and correctly, straight-backed and respectful, cleared her throat again. 'You see, Mother—that is, my adoptive mother—was told that my biological mother lived in Brunswick.'

'In Melbourne?'

'Yes, I've been trying to find out who she was, but I can't. The adoption agency will not tell us anything. Mother says it's not allowed by law. You are not supposed to know and not allowed to go near your real mother and father. Then, when I saw her— I mean that lady—'

'Mrs Crowley?'

'Yes, I thought she knew me. And the funny thing was I thought I knew her, although I couldn't remember ever meeting her.'

'How long have you known you were adopted, Christine?'

'Since my last birthday.'

'A bit of a shock, eh?'

'Yes, although I'd thought that might be the case. I don't look anything like Mum and Dad. You see, they are both blondes and I'm a—' She pointed to her hair.

'Coppertop?'

She grinned. 'Yes, everyone used to remark on it. So, they decided to tell me. Do you think I resemble Mrs Crowley?'

Becker did not answer, but he had to agree. Except for the coppery-brown hair, the reddish freckles and the green eyes, she did resemble a young Evelyn Crowley. Her nose, however, was not so dominant.

'You want to meet her?'

'Yes, but I don't know whether she'd want to see me.'

'Why don't you just knock on her door? She lives in Forrest.'

'Forrest? Really? I live quite near, in Red Hill. Oh, that's not allowed, is it?'

'I don't think anyone would know.'

The girl shook a little. 'Oh, no, I would be too scared.'

'Be brave, Christine.'

'What if she didn't wish to see me?'

'I see your point.' He had finished the pie, not the coffee, which was almost cold now. 'Can I get you something?'

'Oh, no, thank you.'

'What are you doing out of school so early in the day?'

'Oh, we senior girls are allowed to come and go as we wish, as long as we attend compulsory classes.'

'Like being at university?'

'Yes, it is. We're trusted to be responsible.'

'I'm sure you are.'

She seemed to be a model student. No doubt she won prizes and was a credit to her family.

'Are there any others at home?' he asked.

'Siblings, you mean? Yes, I have a brother and a sister.'

'Adopted?'

'No, Mother had them. Apparently, that sometimes happens after you adopt a baby.'

'Does it really?' He could see how she might feel, illegitimate among legitimate children. She was waiting for an answer. 'Well, Christine, I think she'd want to see you.'

She was delighted. 'She would?'

'But it might be difficult right now.'

'Oh?'

'She could be upset. After all—'

'Would she?'

'I tell you what, do you have a dog?'

'Yes, we do.'

'She lives in Empire Circuit, quite near Collins Park. Do you know it?'

'Yes!'

'There's a clump of trees, bright red leaves beginning to fall.'

'You mean oaks?'

'I believe they are. Do you know the spot?'

'Yes, I do.'

'There's an old seat among the trees—'

'I know it. I often sit there.'

'She can see that seat from her house.'

'Can she really?'

'I suggest you walk your dog among those trees—quite casually, you understand? Don't go near her house. In fact, I won't tell you the number in Empire Circuit. If you meet, it'd have to be quite accidentally.'

'Of course!'

'As if you just happened to run into each other and got talking. Is that clear?'

'I understand.'

'You might have to do this several times, but she's sure to see you eventually.'

'Oh, I will!'

'If she feels she's up to it, she'll approach you. In fact, she might not mention who she is. I think she'd be embarrassed to meet you, because she had to give you up for adoption.'

'Yes, I understand.'

'You could just get chatting about any old thing and, you never know, it might all come tumbling out. That way neither of you would be breaking the law.'

'How marvellous!' She was so excited she couldn't keep still.

'Don't rush it, Christine. You might frighten her off.'

'Yes, of course. Oh!' She jumped up, sending the chair flying. Her friend picked it up. 'Oh, thank you, sir. Oh, thank you, Mr—?'

'Becker, Harry Becker.'

'Oh, thank you, Mr Becker.' She ran to her friend, but immediately ran back. 'Oh, could you also tell me, please? Who was my father?'

'Your father?' Becker stroked his moustache. He was enjoying this, bringing joy to the world. 'I never met him. That was well before my time. Apparently, he fell off a balcony in Melbourne, broke his neck. Just mucking around at a party, you know. One drink too many. One of those stupid things people do when they're happy.'

'Oh, how awful!'

'Mrs Crowley does not like to talk about that, so don't mention—'

'Oh, no, I wouldn't! Oh, oh—' She was about to leave, but had another thought. 'Were they—?'

'Married? Apparently not.'

'Oh, and was she—'

'Pregnant at the time? Yes, she was.'

'Oh, how tragic!'

She clapped her hands. The book fell. The friend picked it up.

'Thank you, Mr Becker!'

'Harry.'

'Thank you, Mr Harry!'

She stood up straight, panting and delighted. For a moment, he thought she was going to throw her arms about his neck and kiss him.

'Goodbye!'

She waved, but had gone only a few steps when she ran back. 'Oh, please, what is her name?'

'I told you, Mrs Crowley.'

'But her first name?'

'Oh, Evelyn.'

She raised her eyes to heaven. 'My mother is Evelyn Crowley!'

CHAPTER 13

Becker didn't know where to go from there. As far as he was concerned, the job was finished. He'd located Torrence and had reported to Mrs Crowley and set up a meeting with her lost daughter. Most likely she was now lying on her bed, an arm over her eyes, sighing to herself and wondering why on earth she'd ever confided in that wretched ex-policeman. Would he turn nasty? Would he use the information? Threaten her? Blackmail her? Give her away to the police? Or expect payment in kind? He would never do any of those things, but she was not to know that. Looking at it from her point of view, he could be a problem. He wasn't sure how he'd got involved in this business in the first place. Picking up a handbag in a litter bin didn't seem to be an adequate reason. It was queer how a simple act of kindness could get you mixed up in something bad.

He did see her, however, only at a distance.

One day he was standing in front of a record shop in the Petrie Plaza, idly looking at albums through a window. He didn't have a player, so there was no point in buying anything. In the old days, when he still had a home and a wife, he'd collected a few classics, such as Neil Diamond, Johnny Cash, Glen Campbell, Dionne Warwick, mostly country stuff. He was a country boy at heart. He should never have left. If he hadn't, perhaps he wouldn't be in this mess now. He began to sing to himself, 'Do you know the way to San Jose, I've been away so long...' when he noticed a familiar shape in the window. It was a woman—not a real woman, but a reflection in the glass. Behind him the sun was full on David Jones and the woman was standing with her back to him and studying something in a corner window over there, possibly a dress or a display of hats and bags and gloves or whatever rich women bought. He could not see her face, not in the glass. She was just a shape, an elegant shape dressed in dark blue. He thought he recognised the car coat, the one she'd worn when they had strolled by the lake on that bright day of stories and youth and exuberance and good fellowship.

He thought of going over and saying hello, even apologising for upsetting her at Manuka where she'd walked out on him, annoyed. He'd as much as called her husband a crook, which undoubtedly, he was. But he'd blown it then. Blown what could have become something worth having—perhaps nothing more than a casual acquaintance. It could have been something, maybe a cup of coffee now and then and some funny stories and perhaps the touch of her hand.

Then, as he stared, he realised she had turned and was gazing at him, or at least his back. He thought of turning and going over, now that he'd been spotted. But he did not, because he did not know what to say to her. How do you win a woman's smile without crawling to her? He was finished with her, he knew. And, no doubt, she with him. He turned and walked away.

Then, one evening a few days later, he saw her much closer. Almost too close for comfort.

He'd been wandering along London Circuit and had found himself in Ethos Square. Up ahead, people were walking towards the Theatre Centre. On one side was the big auditorium with 1,200 seats, and on the other side was the Playhouse with little more than a quarter of that capacity. Between them was the Link. It was all glass on each side. He thought he'd mosey up and have a look—at what, he was not sure. At the people perhaps, well dressed and not so well dressed in some cases, making for the doors on one side or the other or the Booking Office in the Link. He did not know what he'd do if he put a foot in the place. He wasn't dressed for a night out. He looked a lost dog. But a young couple went by. She was in patchwork pants so tight they must have been painted on and he was hopping on one foot, supported on one side by a single crutch and on the other by the giggling girl. So he followed them.

They went up and up, laughing and struggling, past the statue of Ethos and into the Link. It was brightly lit in a mellow gold. There was a small crowd at the counter, collecting tickets. Behind the counter were big posters, buoyant colours, buoyant bodies. In one he saw a ballerina on points, head back, flinging herself at the stars. Another poster was saying: Waiting for Godot and showed two tramps grinning at him hopefully. They could have been clowns without makeup. Oddly, he had heard of the play. He'd never seen it, but someone in a newspaper review had said it was a great classic all about nothing, but was hilariously funny. He mooched up to the counter, following the young couple. He had his wallet out and was about to speak, still not sure whether he should be here at all. But the two tramps in the poster seemed to be appealing to him. Appealing for what? Sympathy, help, a way out? A way out of what?

'Yes?' a young woman said. She was behind the counter. She did not address him as '*Sir*.' He could have been anyone who'd wandered in off the street, looking for the nearest bar. Or a toilet. He certainly didn't look like anyone you'd address as '*Sir*.'

'One,' he said.

'One what?'

'One to—' Stupidly he looked around. He couldn't think straight. The tramps were begging him now. Begging for what?

'The ballet or the play?'

'The play, yes.'

'Thirty-three dollars.'

'Thirty-three?'

'Thirty plus GST.'

He was surprised. He'd had no idea the theatre could cost so much.

Desperately he searched his wallet, found enough.

'The performance begins in five minutes,' she said.

'Yeah, thanks.'

It was oddly exciting. He'd been to only one play in his life. He hoped this one, with the wretched clowns waiting for some bloke who never arrives, would be a lot better than the one with the woman on the telephone saying 'Yes' three times as the curtain came slowly down, inch by inch.

He turned left, dodged a few people, all talking loudly, excitedly. He wandered, dazed by the sumptuous light. He was going the wrong way. The Playhouse was on the right, but that did not matter for the moment. He'd have a quick look at the main theatre, at least at the foyer. It was wide and long, filled with people. Some were buying programs from women in long gowns standing behind stalls, others sipping champagne. The buzz, the breaths and the bodies closed around him. He edged through the crowd, dodging elbows and feet. It was a happy sort of crush, sixty dollars a ticket to the ballet, a hundred in the best seats. It was about to overwhelm him, like an embrace by a strange woman you had never seen before and who you suspect is blind drunk with goodwill. Becker looked around. He'd had enough. He turned, headed back towards the huge glass doors in their huge brass frames, but as he did a bell began to ring, insistently, even rudely. The crowd began to move towards the stairs.

A gap opened up, and he saw her, not far away at all, no more than twenty feet.

She was with three others, two men and a woman.

Evelyn Crowley was holding a glass and laughing, throwing back her head in a politely ebullient way. She was splendid. Her hair was piled high and from her ears hung twinkling points of light. From her throat hung a blue diamond. Her dress was greenish blue, shimmery. It seemed to be sown with a thousand glittering eyes, none of them focused on Becker. Her shoulders were bare, and he wondered why on a cold night, but he realised. A woman like that would have arrived in a mink and checked it in at the cloakroom. Or her husband had checked it for her.

One of the men was obviously her husband, the man in the press photo he'd noticed that first day at her house: 'Canberra man tipped for World—' World what? Now everyone knew. The big job at the World Bank. He tried to get a good look at Crowley, but saw only a bald head on a small man with a small mouth. His was a stern face, thin lips, deeply concentrated eyes, probably black or dark brown. His expression was neither irritated nor bored nor enthusiastic. No doubt Crowley was a good listener, he absorbed everything. He said almost nothing, or nothing that later could be pinned on him. He was holding a glass and listening to the other man, who was large and overbearing and over-talkative. Evelyn towered over her husband. In high heels, she was at least three inches taller. She made him look to be the insignificant insect he no doubt was.

'Please take your seats, ladies and gentlemen,' someone announced on a PA. 'The curtain is about to rise.'

People tossed down the last of their drinks.

The Crowley party turned. For a moment Becker thought she'd see him, but she happened to be passing a glass to her husband, who took it, placed it on a table, then offered an arm as they walked towards one of the two inner doors. He handed their tickets to a man in a dinner jacket. Becker had been to this theatre more than once— mainly to see country and western stuff. The stairs ascended to the gods. From there they would walk down and down and down, slowly one step after the other on the red plush, following their friends. Until they reached the best seats in the house, five or six rows up from the stage.

But first they had to go up the steps.

As if in a dream, Becker watched that female body. The dress hung loosely from the shoulders, barely touching her breasts and bottom, and ended below her calves. She moved with grace, one careful step after another, as was her custom. Nothing hurried, every move well thought out. And that body, something must have happened. No longer was she incipiently plump. Instead, she was long and lithe. She must, he guessed, have done something about it. Perhaps one of those things women struggled into, as tight as a drum which pulled in tummies and lifted the breasts. He watched as her hips slid this way and that beneath the gown, almost impertinently. And her shoulders and back muscles rippled as if saying: Are you coming up or are you just going to stand there, gawking? He waited until all the latecomers had passed him. The lights inside had sunk like the world going to sleep and the first bars of Scheherazade had blared out and filled the world with brass.

Then the man with the tickets closed the doors.

Becker did not go to the Playhouse. He never saw *Waiting for Godot*, although for the rest of his life he wished he had. It might have explained something.

He went home and sat on the edge of his bed for a while. It was his day off and his night off. He was not doing anything tomorrow either. He could not think what he would do for the rest of his life, now he had seen Mrs Crowley at her best. She was made to be looked at. If others did not look at her, she would not exist. And, in some perverse sense, nor would they.

CHAPTER 14

He did not see her again until well into May. He did, however, see Torrence, usually driving the diplomatic limousine. Once he thought he saw an Alfa Romeo parked in the street where he lived with the Indians, but it was not red. It was a big one, black and brutal in its own urgent way. On another occasion, he'd just left a card after checking a warehouse when he noticed headlights switch on in his rear-view mirror. He called on a few other places and finished his shift, certain he was being followed. One morning, just before dawn, a small, red Alfa pulled up beside his van on Northbourne Avenue. Torrence signalled to him to wind down his window. Becker did so, wondering whether he was about to be executed in the street. No one was about. You could have fired a canon down the main street of Canberra at that time of day without hitting a soul. Not even the taxis were out yet, starting the early morning run to the airport.

'Get out of town, Harry.'

'What?'

'I said get out of town, if you don't want to be popped.'

'What the hell?'

'You and that Crowley dame, people are watchin'.'

'I know that. Who?'

'You wouldn't want to know.'

'Why?'

'Figure it out for yourself. Big bank, big money.'

Torrence took off. Becker didn't try to follow. There was no point. Torrence could lose anyone. He went home, feeling cold in his guts. He'd advised Mrs Crowley to try to get her husband to talk. That had been a bad move, he now realised. If she succeeded, if Crowley confessed, he might soon be dead. So might she. And so might he, Harry Becker, just because he knew too much—which was next to nothing. But the killers weren't to know that.

He lay on his bed thinking he should phone her, but her husband might be at home. He might answer the phone, want to know who was calling so early. Becker waited and waited, trying to sleep. At best, he dozed for half an hour. He got up about eight, had a shave and shower, had some breakfast. The house was stirring. Already Leticia was dressed for school and in the kitchen.

'You not in bed, Mr Harry?'

'Couldn't get off to sleep.'

'You got your gun, Mr Harry?'

'I have to check it in after each shift, Leticia.'

'They don't let you bring it home?'

He shook his head.

'Dad says you must stop them.'

'Stop who?'

'The bad man, he rang again.'

'The nut? The one who said Asians out?'

'He said this time last warning.'

'Or what?'

'Boom!'

'Boom?'

She nodded. She was spreading sultanas on top of a slice of bread thick with peanut butter. She always got her own lunch. Grandmother walked through the kitchen, swishing her silk robes and scraping her flapping sandals. They always wore sandals, even in mid-winter, which it was not yet. It was still May. The old lady never spoke to him, possibly because she didn't know a word of English even though she came from Fiji. Or did she? Maybe she'd been slipped into the country without a visa. There were also two brothers, cutters at the big table in the garage. They too didn't speak, but they did watch him carefully, smiling in their yellow teeth each time he appeared. He didn't care how many illegals were in the place. They were welcome to the country. He was getting out, one way or another.

'You mean a bomb?'

'Dad is much frightened.'

'Did he call the police?'

'No, he crawled under the house last night with a torch.'

'Looking for a bomb?'

'I think so.'

'Did he find anything?'

She shook her head, munching.

'He must go to the police.' It was a pointless suggestion, he knew. A man running an illegal workshop in the back garage and housing illegal immigrants was not going to call in the police. Besides, the warnings were not being made against the Indians but against himself. Torrence had made that clear.

A few minutes later, he called the Forrest number and waited.

At last a woman answered. 'Hello please?'

'Mrs Crowley?'

'Mrs Crowley, she not home.'

'Where is she?'

'She gone gym. Who this, please?'

'This is Harry Becker, a friend of hers.'

'How you spell please?'

He told her slowly, visualising her writing it on a pad by the phone, slowly, carefully. One letter at a time, printing. She sounded like a Filipina.

'Tell her I must speak to her urgently.'

'Okay, I tell her, urgent.'

'Do you have her mobile number?'

'Mobile?'

'Another phone, in her bag?'

'Yes, I think. I not know number—Excuse, please, man at door.'

'Which man?'

She paused, possibly going to a window.

'Security man.'

'What security man?'

'I think he Stan—Stan—'

'Stanton?'

'Yes, Stanton. I go now, Mr Harry.'

He was about to ask her to let him speak to the visitor, but she hung up. On second thought, he went to the depot, called on the boss. 'Who's doing the job in Forrest?'

'What job in Forrest?'

'The Crowley house in Empire Circuit.'

'Crowley? Empire Circuit?'

The boss punched a few keys on a computer. 'We don't have anyone there today.'

'Yes, we do.'

The boss evaded the question. 'What's going on, Harry?'

'What do you mean?'

'The Crowley woman. You've been seen again, Manuka this time, drinking coffee.'

'Who told you?'

'Word gets around.'

He explained as briefly as he could. The boss was a bit thick at times, or deliberately thick. His name was Pickles, and he had no sense of humour. Everyone called him Wilfred, which was not his first name. He had a nervous cough and a runny nose. Becker was sure he was on coke. He told him about the handbag and the letter, although not the contents. Mrs Crowley had been friendly, grateful for his consideration, and bought him a coffee once in the gardens and again in Manuka. That was all.

Pickles thought about it. 'You'd better get out there, Harry.'

CHAPTER 15

Becker parked across the street near the trees. There was no Stanton vehicle to be seen or anything else of note. A few leaves came down from the small group of trees, all blood red. It was that time of year. It made him think of King's Cross blood. All the blood he'd seen on the job, the car smashes and the drunken brawls and the gunshot wounds. Once he'd been on the beat with a young cop named Branson. Branson was new, enthusiastic as a puppy in a playground. The Cross had not been a playground, except for the young and drunk and stupid and the crims and the shady operators, pushing booze and titillation and dope. Branson was happy, his first week in the Cross. They were strolling along Darlinghurst Road one Friday night, except Branson was tending to stride off. He was so keen, a hand on his sidearm, his tongue hanging out and grinning like a kid at a funfair. He was from Tenterfield or someplace up north where the Traveller came from. They'd just passed the Lucky Streak strip joint when something happened. It was a shot, or not a shot. More like a soft whop! Or a pop! Hard to describe exactly. A bloke behind them fell, howling. Clutching his guts. At the same time, a car sped off. The poor bastard had been popped, right there on Darlinghurst Road, the neon blazing and the young sheilas screaming. One of them was leaning against a wall, vomiting. Which had nothing to do with the shot. She was full of speed at the time.

'Ah, shit,' Branson had said, pulling out his Smith and Wesson.

It was too late. The car had gone, tyres screeching.

'Ah, shit,' he said again, looking at the little creep rolling on the sidewalk, holding his guts. His mouth was open and he was screaming voicelessly.

Blood was gushing out between his fingers. It was pretty obvious what had happened—the bullet had hit the aorta just above the navel. Already Becker was on the blower, calling in the first letters of the rego, but not the numbers. He'd missed them. It was an old souped-up Chrysler Charger.

'Don't just stand there gaping,' he'd said. 'Get down there and stop the flow.'

'What with?'

'Use your hand.'

'Ah, shit,' Branson had said again.

'No, mate, that's just blood. An ambulance is coming.'

They'd waited, the blood still oozing out, the man on the ground writhing. Branson was covered in blood.

He'd even taken off his cloth cap and was trying to stop it with that. He looked up, close to crying. He was more shocked than the poor bastard who'd copped it.

'Jesus, Harry, I didn't know it was going to be like this.'

'Welcome to the Cross,' he said...

The small BMW came down the road and pulled in. Becker went to it. She wound down the window slowly, as though not sure she should. They had not parted on good terms at Manuka.

'Don't go in, please.'

'Why not?'

'I think we'd better take a little walk.'

'Really?'

At first, he thought she was going to refuse, but she left her car standing in the driveway and said nothing as he led her into Collins Park. It was cold now, and she was wearing a short coat without a hat.

'What is it now, Mr Becker?'

'I think your house is bugged.'

'You mean someone is listening?'

'Yeah.'

'Who?'

'The police.'

She was startled. 'The police? They can do that?'

'Probably have a court order. Probably someone else too.'

'Who?'

'Someone working for Stanton Security. When did you have that system put in?'

'Oh, when Donald bought the house, I think. Yes, seven or eight years ago.'

'Have they been back recently?'

'Once or twice, to make adjustments, so they said.'

'To the equipment? Did they install anything else?'

'I don't think so. I didn't watch them at work.'

'When were they last here?'

'Several weeks ago, I think.'

'Just before you received the first letter?'

'I suppose so. What is this all about? Why are we walking through here?'

'So no one can hear us.'

'What is it now?'

'Have you spoken to your husband?'

'About the letters? Yes, I have. That night after our meeting at Manuka. When I came out of my bathroom, I found him lying on my bed. So I told him. I said it seemed someone knew something about him. Something to do with the bank back in Melbourne. I thought that would get him off my bed.'

'You don't sleep together?'

'We haven't for years.'

They walked among the trees, occasionally kicking at leaves that quickly settled again, like giant dead butterflies or birds too dispirited to fly away. There was little breeze, although the sky was heavy and grey. It might rain again soon.

'How did he react?'

'He didn't react at all. He just lay there, listening or not listening, I don't know. Then he said not to worry, everything would be all right.'

'He had something else on his mind?'

'I think so. He looked very worried. He said two policemen came to see him. A big bald man, who was a chief inspector, and another man, who seemed to be an expert in computers. They said someone was laundering the proceeds of crime through the bank without it showing in the records. They asked did he know how this could be done.'

'Jesus, they did that?'

'I think that was on his mind.'

'When the police ask you a question like that, they mean they know you did it, but they can't prove it.'

'Why would they say it if they can't prove it?'

'To make him break down and confess.'

They walked on a few yards. 'Mrs Crowley, I hope he doesn't tell you what it is or tell anyone else.'

'Why?'

'They may kill him.'

'Who?'

'The people with the money.'

'Oh, God, who are they?'

Becker strolled on, shoulders slumped, hands behind his back. He felt defeated. When you were up against people like that, you didn't have a chance. If Crowley were a crook and he, Harry Becker, went to the cops, the banker would be arrested. His wife would be devastated. On the other hand, she might be in on the scam. Indeed, she might be the brains behind it. Maybe her husband was just the fall guy. After all, the first note, according to her, had said, '*We know all about you.*' It might have meant 'you' plural, not 'you' singular as she'd said.

'I don't know,' he said, 'but I've been warned.'

'By whom?'

'The chauffeur. He had no reason to lie, not to me anyway.'

'What did he tell you?'

'To keep my nose out of it.'

'He knows who's behind it?'

'It looks like it.'

They had crossed the park and begun to turn back. She sighed, pulling her jacket tighter around her body. 'Oh, God, my house bugged?'

'I think you'd better tell your husband, but not at home. Can you meet him during his lunch break?'

'Yes, I suppose.'

'Do not eat at a restaurant, go to some lonely place by the lake with wide-open space all around.'

'Oh, oh—' She began to moan, her feet dragging, her eyes screwed up.

'I'm sorry.'

'What's gone wrong? What've they done to Donald?'

'What has he done to himself?'

'You really think he's a crook?'

'Someone does.'

He studied her, sorry for her. Her distress seemed to be genuine. Conversely, she might have been a good actress. She put her hands to her face, her teeth gritted.

'I can't bear this. It just goes on and on. Can there be no peace?'

She began to moan, her knees bending. For a moment, Becker thought she'd collapse. He took her by an arm.

'Mrs Crowley—'

'Oh, no, no—'

'You want to go somewhere? Have a drink?'

It was a stupid suggestion, he knew. Wherever they went, the others would follow, watching and listening and even catching them on camera, hoping to learn whether she knew what her husband was going to do. Talk or shut up? She didn't answer his question. Her face was wretched, her eyes still closed. She did manage to take a few more steps, generally heading homeward, while he steadied her with a hand.

'I saw your daughter that day.'

She stopped dead, her eyes flying open.

'What did you say?'

'She saw me with you at Manuka. She wanted to know who you were.'

'And you told her?'

'Yes.'

'Did you say where I live?'

'I said in Empire Circuit. It's a long street.'

'Christine? My daughter wants to see me? Does she really?' She stumbled but checked herself. Becker feared she'd collapse before they reached the house. 'No, no, I couldn't. I mean, I'd love to, my own dear daughter, but—' She was struggling now. 'She'd want to know about her father.'

'I told her he had an accident, fell off a balcony one day, too many drinks at a party.'

'You told her that?'

'He was skylarking.'

'You didn't say I was there?'

'Not at all.' They had reached the old seat among the oaks. For a moment, he thought she was about to sit on it, but she did not. Instead she turned slowly, her eyes searching the street and the park, as if hoping to see the girl. 'Did I do the right thing?'

'I suppose you did.'

'You want me to come in for a minute?'

She shook her head. 'Not with the maid there.'

'Don't do anything about the bugs. Do not try to find them.'

'Where are they?'

'In the ceiling, in your phone, probably in your bedroom.'

'They listen to a people in bed?'

'That's when the secrets come out.'

'How disgusting.'

'If you interfere with them, they'll know you know. Even if you just look for them without touching them, they'll hear you breathing close at hand.'

'Such an awful thing.'

'I'll try to find out who's behind it.'

'The chauffeur?'

'I don't think he'd say any more.'

'Can't you make him tell? If he wants more than five thousand—'

'I don't think he'd risk it.'

'Couldn't you make him? I mean, if you're an armed guard you must have a gun?'

'I have a gun, but I'm not officially armed. Anyway, I wouldn't trust my chances with him. He's still young and fast and I'm slow on the draw.'

He watched her. Something told him that Mrs Crowley wanted Torrence out of the way. He recalled again his words at that flat in Manuka: That dame ain't what she seems.

She put a hand to his shoulder. 'You have gone to a lot of trouble for me.'

'You're worth it.'

She almost smiled. 'I haven't paid you for all you have done.'

'Forget it.'

'I'll never forget it.'

He thought she was going to kiss him, which would have been unwise in public. Anyone could be watching. The maid might be at a window, someone next door. He looked around, particularly at cars parked along the street. None looked suspicious. Which didn't mean the people behind all this trouble weren't listening. And watching.

'I'm sorry,' she said. 'I was rude to you at Manuka, wasn't I?'

'I got a bit too cheeky.'

He reached up, turned up the collar on the soft woollen coat.

'What are you doing?'

'Looking for bugs.' He felt the lapels, then the collar. 'Nothing there.'

She smiled. 'Thank you.'

'You feel well enough to drive?'

'Yes, yes.'

'Go to a payphone and call your husband.'

She nodded, then looked at him uncertainly, as if embarrassed to ask the question.

'Did you enjoy the ballet?'

'What?' He was surprised.

'I saw you come in.'

'Oh, I didn't go. I had a ticket to the other—' Again, he couldn't remember the name of the play. His heart was jumping.

'The Beckett?'

'Yeah.'

'And what did you think of it?'

'I—' The words would not come out. He couldn't admit he'd been a coward, not gone to the play. Could not face something he did not understand after he'd seen her walk up those stairs, holding the arm of her measly little crook of a husband.

She was smiling. 'You did not see it? Oh, you should have. It's very simple, and very funny.'

Was she saying anyone could understand it, even a simpleton like him? Or saying it's the kind of play only a truly simple person could truly understand?

'Well, I wasn't feeling too good.'

'It's on for a week or so. You should see it. In fact, we could go together.' She shrugged, hands still in her pockets, looking away and looking back at him, perhaps shyly. Perhaps not. 'Come on, Harry, my treat. I owe you a lot.'

His heart jumped again. It was like that time he'd lain on the pavement outside that nightclub in Civic and the slob had the broken bottle and was going to cut him pretty bad. He'd go for the throat. And he'd said the corniest line ever written: Come on, punk, make my day. And his finger was closing on the trigger. The trigger was moving. Another two or three millimetres and the hammer would hit and someone would have a big hole in his guts. He'd never shot anyone in his life. But the slob had backed off and slunk away with his mates, laughing. And Ephie Lowenstern had been saved.

That had been the fear of pain and death. This had been the fear of pain and beauty.

She was waiting, smiling.

'What about your husband?'

'Donald and I lead separate lives.'

'You didn't look too separate when I saw you.'

'That's only for show,' she said.

He shrugged. He did not know how to say anything, which would not be a monumental failure. She seemed to understand.

'Think about it.'

She turned on her heel and made the peculiar clicking sound she'd given in that small, darkened galley a week or so ago. Which he now realised was not a click of the tongue at all, like the click his mother habitually gave to a world she could not understand, but a sort of kissing sound without pursed lips.

'I'll do it now,' she said.

She meant the phone call to her husband.

'Goodbye, Harry.'

He stood with hands in his jacket pockets, watching as she went to her car. He thought of following her as she drove off, heading for Manuka post office, to keep an eye on her. But he did not. A fairly strong breeze rattled through the trees, sending down more red leaves, the cold air cutting his ears and eyes. One or two stuck to his jacket and even to his hair. He blinked, turning up his collar. Rain began to fall, at first thin and cold like frozen breath. As he stood there thinking, it began to pour. Big drops hit him like bullets of ice.

CHAPTER 16

Becker went home and got three or four hours of sleep, expecting the house would be blown to bits at any minute. They'd place the bomb beneath the floorboards under his bed. That way they'd be sure to get him. They couldn't have done it during the day, because of all the Indians around the place. They'd do it at night, while everyone was asleep. Of course, he wouldn't be there, he'd be out on his rounds, although they'd know that. Already they knew he came home soon after six or sometimes seven. All they had to do was wait until he switched on the light in his room and then push a button, remote control. As Leticia had said, Boom!

How many would go with him? He hoped the little girl would survive. He liked her, a gentle girl, intelligent and friendly. Sometimes he felt she was a kind of daughter. He had two daughters of his own and a son who'd abandoned him long ago. Their mother had told them why he'd been shot in the shoulder and why he'd been kicked out of the police force. He'd been invited to his daughter's confirmation years ago and had worn a new suit with a white buttonhole. He'd not enjoyed himself, although he'd shaken a few hands. He seemed to stick out like a sore thumb, as if everyone knew about him. He could sense his daughter's embarrassment. He still had the suit, although it was tight around the waist and shoulders now. These days, he wore it only to funerals. He wondered whether the undertaker's staff would find enough bits of him to stuff in the suit. Or would they just stick them into a bag, a plastic bag, a garbage bag? He deserved no better.

At eight o'clock he checked in at the office.

The boss was not there, so he wandered into the operations room, a misnomer. There was a bank of lights and numbers, but nothing was happening. One of the men was dozing before a television set, on which the ABC was showing Mother and Son for the umpteenth time. A glass coffee pot was steaming in a corner.

'G'day, Tony.'

The operator sat up.

'G'day, mate.'

'Anything happening?'

'Nah, bit of a fracas out at Phillip. Someone tried to break into a Chinese.'

'Restaurant?'

'Nah, food store.'

'Why'd anyone want to do that?'

'Maybe they like rice.'

Becker watched Mother and Son for a few seconds.

'The boss say anything?'

'About what?'

'About me.'

'Such as?'

'Mrs Crowley.'

'Who?'

'Someone's been posing as one of us, bugging her place.'

'Not me, mate.'

'It's probably the Feds or someone from out of town.'

'What's goin' on?'

'Haven't a clue, mate. Are you the only one on tonight?'

'Yeah, till midnight.'

'Who's next?'

'Russo.'

'Russo, eh?'

'What d'y'mean?'

'Didn't he do time for burglary?'

'No idea, mate. Why?'

'Nothing. See you around.'

He went to his locker and drew his pistol. The company had a rule saying he had to sign it in and out, even the serial number. It was his own pistol, not the company's, it was registered, and he had a licence. But he hadn't cleaned it in months, simply because he'd not fired it. One day he was going to pull the trigger and the damned thing would explode in his hand. He'd be like Torrence, a man with a maimed mitt. He might have to wear a glove too.

Nothing much happened that night. He did his rounds, thinking about Mrs Crowley. Had she met her husband at lunchtime? Had they managed to meet without being seen? Had she told him she knew something was going on at the bank? What'd been his reaction? This time, had he just listened without comment or had he broken down and confessed? Becker didn't know. Most likely he'd not be told. No one would think of him. He was just a bit player in this comedy. He walked on stage and said a few lines, then walked off to watch again from the wings. To be heard no more.

More than once, he thought he was being followed. Each time he slowed the company van and waited, the following car went past at normal speed, the driver apparently not looking at him. It was a woman, he was sure, but he did not get a good look at her. Just a big blonde. Later he came out of a car yard and saw a car parked in a side street. At the wheel was a woman, not the same one, not so big. Of course, if they'd used enough cars they could watch him all night, one in front, one behind, sometimes passing, sometimes dropping off, keeping in touch by mobile. When he finished his rounds, he was sure no one had been interested in him for at least two hours. He went back to base, checked in his gear including the Smith and Wesson, and got into his Holden. Russo had come out, leaning on the door of the squad room. He was a sloppy sort of fellow with a sloppy walk and a sloppy grin. His face was screwed up on one side and his mouth hung down below it and tended to dribble. He had a dribbly way of speaking.

'Everythin' all right, Harry?'

'Yeah, mate.'

'Nothin' happen?'

'No, nothing.'

'How's Mrs Crowley?'

'Pickles told you?'

'Yeah, I hear she's quite a dish.'

'How do you know?'

'Saw you at the gardens with her one day. Take her out to dinner tonight, did you?'

'Get lost, Russo.'

Back at Ainslie, he sat in his car outside the old double-brick house, undecided what to do. Get out of the car and go to bed, or sleep somewhere else for a few hours. If they were going to bomb the house, they'd be sure he was in bed before they blew it. The sun was about to rise and yet he was getting cold, not in his feet but in his belly. Finally, he turned the car around and went into Civic, checked in at a motel. He had to bribe the night manager to let him have a room that some early risers had vacated. It was overpriced and not yet made up. The manager claimed nothing else was available. The room was upstairs, a cold, stale, inhuman room, which smelled of cigarette smoke, air-freshener and the last inhabitants. He lay awake, waiting until the sun was up and shining. When it was, he got up and pulled the curtains, put a Do Not Disturb on the outer door handle, tried to get some sleep. If they were watching the house in Ainslie, they'd have assumed he had not come home. The Indians would be safe for at least another day.

He slept through breakfast, being wakened just after eleven by a knock on the door. He opened it, expecting to see a maid. He was going to snap at her about the sign, but it was not a maid. Two men stood there. They looked like cops, but you never could tell. Then he realised they were cops. They had the tired expressionless faces of men who'd had a bad night and the day was not going to be much better. And their calm politeness was scary. It meant they could wait as long as it took, because the fact they were there at your door meant you had a problem. And the sooner the matter was cleared up, the better for everybody.

'Mr Becker?'

'Yeah.'

'Harry Becker?'

'Who wants to know?'

One of them pulled out a warrant card. 'Senior Detective Adams and this is Detective Paesch, both from Criminal Branch.'

'What's the problem?'

The senior man put a hand on the door. 'You know a man named Vincenzo Franco Torrenza? Known as Vincent Torrence?'

'I've met him.'

'Where were you last night?'

'On my rounds, why?'

'Were you with him?'

'Torrence? Last night? No, not me.'

'You'd better come down to the station.'

'Why?'

'He's been found dead.'

'Torrence? Dead?'

'Yeah, shot dead.'

'Hell, no!'

'No doubt about it.'

'What's this got to do with me?'

'It was done with your gun.'

'What?'

'No doubt about it.'

'When?'

'Sometime late last night.'

'I had my gun all night.'

'Got any gear, mate?'

'No, nothing.'

'Travelling light, eh? About to flit, eh? Better get your pants on.'

'Look, I didn't kill him.'

It was pointless protesting. He went with them, astonished. Torrence had warned him to be careful, now Torrence himself was dead. He couldn't believe this, he must still be asleep, having a bad dream. He wasn't. After half an hour at police headquarters, Becker was convinced Torrence really had been shot with his gun. The police had the number registered to him and they had the ballistic results already, irrefutable evidence. The body had been fished out of the lake about six thirty after a jogger had spotted it. There was one hole in his head and another in the lower back. A bullet had been extracted and sent to ballistics already. The police had gone to Stanton and commandeered his pistol. They'd been watching him for some time. They even knew about Mrs Crowley and her problem, even suggesting she'd got him to kill Torrence. They knew the chauffeur had been blackmailing her. It was a neat explanation, perhaps too neat. Becker could see it might stick if it went to court. On the other hand, why had they been watching him and her in the first place?

'I can't tell you.'

The man in charge was a young sergeant named Palfreyman, younger than Becker, amiable, self-confident, sure to be on his way up the ladder. Inspector next stop. The kind who was confident he couldn't fail. Becker had met him once or twice on his rounds, usually because of break-ins he'd reported. He thought he'd seen Adams somewhere too, a slouching sort of man who tended to lean against walls with his hands in his pockets and his balding head slightly down, so he looked up with wide-open eyes, tired eyes, indifferent eyes. It might have been on his rounds too, the kind of face that always seems to belong to another world, a world where things never quite add up.

Palfreyman was leaning back and smiling as though he hadn't a care in the world—and tapping a pen on the ballistic prints on his desk. Beside them lay a Smith and Wesson in an evidence bag.

'This your gun, Harry?'

'Looks like it.'

'This,' he said, tapping the prints again, 'says it is. Serial number so and so, registered to Henry Brinsley Becker of such-and-such address in Maroubra, New South Wales.'

'So what? I carry a licence.'

'Let's see the licence.'

Becker fished it out, handed it over.

'New South Wales, no good here, Harry.'

'I'll get another.'

'Yeah? Maybe you will, maybe you won't. This is evidence now.'

'I didn't shoot anyone.'

'Yeah? We hear someone tried to kill you in Sydney?'

'That's why I need a gun.'

Palfreyman was flicking a finger at the licence. 'This was signed by Bob Fricker in Sydney three years ago, I see. Bob's now at Queanbeyan. Old mate of yours, is he?'

'I've got a few left.'

Palfreyman looked at the other two men, both leaning against a wall, both grinning. The young one looked an idiot, just out of school. Adams looked as though he knew exactly where you'd been in the last twenty-four hours and knew you were innocent, but was going to let you fry, just for the fun of it.

'He'd be the only one, from what I hear.'

'Get stuffed.'

'Don't tell me to get stuffed, Harry. I'm a cop and you're not.'

'You've been taking pics of me, haven't you? And Mrs Crowley.'

'Have we?'

'And eavesdropping?'

'Yeah?'

'I'm not blind. I was a cop once.'

The sergeant laughed. 'Yeah, drummed out of the force, I believe?'

'Because I had a conscience.'

'Didn't do you much good, did it? Copped a bullet, I hear?'

Becker felt like getting up and hitting the bastard. Palfreyman was a strapping fellow with a clean shave who'd probably hit him back, then pat him on the back. He looked casual, even amiable. He had bright-brown eyes and a ready smile. He didn't look like a cop at all. These days you didn't know who you were dealing with in a cop shop—a professional thug like Whitford or some geek with a PhD in marine biology. In the old days at Darlinghurst, there was no point in throwing a punch at anyone. If you did, they'd take you into the Gents and break an arm. Becker didn't know how straight the Feds were, probably a lot straighter than the cops in Sydney, so he tried to appeal to reason.

'You know about her husband?'

'Donald Crowley? What about him?'

'Why are you so interested in his wife? It's him you want.'

'Yeah? Why would we be interested in him?'

'He controls a lot of money.'

'So what? He's a banker.'

'Torrence told me someone is shifting millions.'

'Did he?'

'Now he's dead.'

'And you killed him?'

'Why would I kill him?'

The sergeant pulled a face. 'Why not? Mrs Crowley is a delicious drop, isn't she? Pretty good in bed too, so we hear.'

Becker was furious. 'You listen, don't you? You've got the house bugged.'

Palfreyman laughed. 'Calm down, Harry.'

'You bastards.'

'Look, mate, I don't care if you're poking Mrs Crowley, good luck to you. The fact remains, Torrence was killed with your gun. How do you explain that?'

Becker just sat there and took it. That was how the world saw him, a no-hoper who couldn't help himself. He was no better than the tramp who'd touched him for two dollars in Garema Place.

'I didn't kill him.'

'Did I say you did?'

'It was a set-up, wasn't it?'

'Yeah?'

'Look, someone switched my piece before I came on duty. I didn't check the serial number, why should I? I carry the same one every night. Someone substituted a ring-in, didn't they? Same make, same model, same weight, same in every detail except the number. Later, after I'd finished my shift, but before you arrived, they put back my weapon and took out the ring-in.'

Palfreyman screwed up his face in a sort of wink.

'That how you see it, Harry?'

'Yeah.'

'Who'd want to do that?'

'Someone with a problem, such as cocaine.'

'And who'd that be?'

'My boss, Wilfred Pickles. He's always sniffing it.'

'And someone put the hard word on him?'

'Someone with a lot of money.'

'Who'd that be?'

'Someone who has Crowley under his thumb.'

'You should be careful, mate. Mr Crowley is big in the world of finance.'

'So what?'

'Just be careful.'

Becker looked from Palfreyman to his two offsiders. They were smiling with unfriendly eyes. No sympathy there. He was tired and afraid. In a way, he was sorry for Torrence. The man had been a mongrel, a corrupt cop who'd taken money from crooks. He'd probably started as himself years ago—a starter with fine ideals, an innocent who'd thought there really was a Father Christmas when he'd found money turning up in his bank account for overtime he'd not worked. He might have said he should return the money, but had been told to forget it. Just keep it, mate, and don't tell anyone. In time, he'd have realised he was being paid for services not yet rendered. He might have thought of going to a senior officer and reporting it, but he'd have been warned if he did he'd be charged with receiving secret commissions. Other officers would be prepared to swear on a stack of Bibles he'd been seen chatting to disreputable characters. Obviously, he was on the take, a young constable who could be bought. After that, he'd have been sucked in, soon so deep he couldn't get out. That's how they did it. That's how Becker himself had been trapped. Having a conscience was not a good idea, not if you wanted to live.

'You know I didn't do it. Your boys were following me all night.'

'Is that so?'

'You going to arrest me?'

Palfreyman clicked his tongue, then flicked the licence at Becker. 'Go home and get some sleep, Harry. You look knackered.'

Surprised, he picked up the licence and stood up.

'What about my gun?'

'Evidence, mate.'

He started for the door, but looked back.

'Who was the man in brown?'

'What man in brown?'

'Sitting near me and her outside a cafe in Manuka. You got him on camera. The two rookies across the way were pretty obvious.' The police looked at each other blankly, so Becker nudged them. 'He's diplomatic. Who was Torrence driving for?'

They did not answer.

'I've got the number.' He gave it to them, the number on the diplomatic plate. 'You could easily check it.'

'Yeah?'

'What's going on? Why are you tailing me?'

Palfreyman threw down his pen, sat up straight.

'Keep your nose out of this, Harry.' Torrence had said the same thing, keep your nose out of it. 'And keep away from Mrs Crowley. That woman has dangerous friends.'

'What kind of friends?'

'Best you don't know, mate.'

'Yeah?'

'Stay in town, Harry. Don't think of doing a runner.'

Becker paused at the door. He was going to ask, Why not? He didn't, possibly because they knew he had nowhere to run. He was a comic turn wherever he went. So, he went home and tried to sleep. It was impossible. Whoever was watching him knew he was at home. All they had to do was press a button or even dial a number on a mobile phone. He lay there for some time, expecting the house would blow up, and thinking about what had gone wrong with his life. Once upon a time he'd been a country boy. He'd been happy then. He should have stayed there. It was too late now.

CHAPTER 17

Early in the afternoon he went to the office, found Pickles sitting at his desk, reading
The Canberra Times. He looked nervous and tended to cough with his mouth closed,
making his belly jump. He'd been a dapper man in the old days when he was in the
British Army. He had pockmarked cheeks and a trim little black moustache, which
might have been tinted, like his black hair. He had one brown eye and one black. The
latter was deformed, so it seemed to have one large pupil, no iris. He glanced up as
Becker entered.

'Looking for a job, Wilf?'

'What?'

'You may be out on your ear soon.'

'What?'

'Not just for sniffing happy dust—'

'What're you talking about?'

'But for trying to frame an innocent man.'

'What is this?'

'You switched my piece, didn't you?'

Pickles lowered the paper. 'What're you talking about?'

'Torrence was fished out of the lake this morning. I think you know who shot
him.'

'Torrence? Torrence?'

'Don't try to kid me. The police came and got my weapon, didn't they? They did
a ballistic check on it and it matches a bullet taken from Torrence.'

Pickles tried to huff and puff. 'They did come, making enquiries.'

'They let me go. Why would they do that?'

'How should I know?'

'Because they were following me last night and know I wasn't with Torrence at any time.'

'Why should they be following you?'

'They just want to know what I know.'

'About what?'

'I've no idea.' He sat on the edge of the boss's desk. 'They've kept my gun, naturally. So, when do I get another?'

'I don't know what you're talking about, mate.'

'I'm not going out tonight without one.'

'That's your problem.'

'No, mate, it's your problem. How'd you like me to phone head office? Have a little chat to someone about your habit?'

Pickles went to his own locker and took out an old Webley .45, a long-barrelled British Army pistol, complete with a ring at the base of the handle to take a lanyard. Becker was not impressed.

'This thing came out of the Ark. It weighs a tonne.'

'It's all I have. I was issued with it thirty years ago, one of the last Webley's ever made. I took it to the Falklands.'

'Is it registered?'

'Yes, but—'

'Where's the holster?'

'It fell apart years ago.'

'It's too big to fit in mine. What about ammo?'

Pickles produced a box that rattled loosely.

'How old is this stuff?'

'Hasn't been fired in years.'

Becker opened the box and started to load the Webley.

'Who's behind it, Wilf?'

'Behind what?'

'Who made you do it?'

'Do what?'

'Don't come the pompous Pom with me. What've they got on you, apart from a filthy habit?'

'Look here, Harry, I don't know what—'

'Only you have a set of keys to all the lockers.'

'Someone must have taken them.'

'Who? Tony? Russo? Boxall? Wendt? Who's the insider here? Or did someone creep in before eight last night and pick a lock?'

'Well, I suppose they could have.'

'How would they know which was my locker?'

'I don't know.'

'Maybe you told 'em?'

'Look here, if you attract the attention of the police—'

Becker snapped the cylinder shut and pointed the Webley between Pickles' eyes. 'Some days I feel like killing someone, Wilf. I don't know who, and I don't care. It might as well be you.'

Pickles gulped as Becker stood up, stuck the pistol in a pocket of his jacket. It was not the regular Stanton jacket that was only hip length, but his own car coat, big and floppy and padded and faded. Cheap stuff made in some Chinese sweat shop for a couple of dollars. He'd paid a hundred for it when he'd hit Canberra in winter three years ago. It was a cold place, you needed something padded then. It had big pockets in which you could conceal almost anything, even an antique piece such as the Webley.

'Don't make me any madder, mate.'

'Where're you going with that thing?'

'That's my business.'

'You can't take it now. You're not on duty.'

'Duty? Yeah, you'd know all about duty, wouldn't you? God, Queen and Country and all that stuff. Did you ever take a bullet for your country?'

The boss shivered. Maybe he'd felt one whiz by in the Falklands or perhaps Northern Ireland or wherever the British Army got to these days. Becker turned and made a shooting gesture, same as the one Torrence had made from his limousine.

'Maybe you'll know all about it pretty soon.'

He went home and got four or five hours sleep.

Next day he was back in Civic having a late lunch. He'd bought a shish kebab at Ali Baba and a bottle of orange juice and sat in the sun in City Walk, near the carousel. It was a famous carousel, the one that had been at Luna Park in Melbourne for many years. Some kids were on it, going around and around to pipe-organ music. And laughing, their mothers watching, hearts in their mouths. He leaned forward and began eating in huge bites until he realised he was eating like a dog, quickly before some other dog snatched it—or killed him for it. So he slowed down, drank some juice. He still felt like a dog, a lost dog, perhaps a mangy dog. No one cared if he lived or died, except someone who'd prefer him dead. On the other hand, Mrs Crowley had called him 'Harry' as if she cared for him. And smiled at him and suggested they see a play together. If she really did care, she'd be the only one in the world.

He thought again about the moment when he'd lifted the collar of her coat and felt behind it for a bug and even behind the lapels and had, for a split second of happiness, rested his hands on her chest, almost touching her breasts with his knuckles. Something had shown in her eyes. It was not delight, although it could have been hope. She might have moved in, pressed against him, raised her hands and held him—for a second or a lifetime? It was not important how long, because it would have been forever, whichever way it turned out.

Again he wondered what it would be like to go to bed with her, to see her lying naked on a bed of infinite possibility. Would she be delightful or a dismal disappointment, a woman past her prime? Would her breasts be too big and her belly too loose? And her legs, even wide open, would they be the end of all temptation? Would entering her be the end of the pain and disappointments, or the end of all hope? He did not know. What is more, he would never know. Evelyn Crowley, she was beyond imagination.

'Excuse me, mate.'

'What?'

'Excuse me—' A man sat beside him, uninvited. 'Y'couldn't let's have a coupla dollars to get a pie, could yer?'

'It's you again?'

'Eh?'

'I gave you two dollars week before last. In fact, I gave you five dollars for your titfer.'

'What?'

'Tit for tat, hat.'

'Eh?'

'You don't remember?' It was a futile question, he knew. A man like this, a booze-artist, was probably brain-dead or well on the way. He was all skin and bones and there was a week of white bristle on his face. His cheeks were hollow, half-starved. His hands were pressed into a shabby coat that seemed to be part of a suit, which had seen better days. The cuffs were threadbare. His accent, however, was educated. Or had been educated years ago. He could have been an actor or a teacher or a salesman in David Jones, back when the world was wide and he could have been someone.

'How much do you make botting off people each day?'

'Ah, I dunno, maybe ten.'

'Ten dollars?'

'On a good day.'

'What's your name?'

'Buster.'

'Buster who?'

'Keaton.'

'Same as the actor?'

'Yeah, what they called's at school.'

'Must have been a long time ago?'

'Yeah, was.'

'Any family?'

'Nah, not now.'

'What did you do?'

'What do yer mean?'

'For a living, when you had a living?'

'Ah, I was a schoolie.'

'A teacher?'

'Yeah, out west.'

'What happened?'

'Ah, they kicked me out.'

'Misbehaving?'

'Yeah.'

'Interfering with the girls? That sort of thing?'

'Something like that.'

Becker almost smiled, he knew the feeling. No family, no friends, no one cared a stuff. And the disgrace. People were more interested in him dead than alive. Except perhaps Mrs Crowley. They sat there together, both looking and not looking at nothing in particular.

Across the way, under a tree, two young women were seating themselves at a table, a brunette and a blonde. The blonde was taller and quieter. The brunette was facing away from Becker so he could not see her face, but the blonde was watching him as she sat, an ice cream in hand, overflowing the cone, dripping already. There was a parlour behind the carousel. It had thirty-six varieties. Sometimes he'd go in there and have a pistachio. He didn't know why, but he always had a pistachio. He was a creature of habit now. He always did the same things, said the same things, thought the same. He couldn't see what the brunette was eating. It must have been good, because she was tucking into it fast and talking fast and waving a hand around. The blonde was taking her time, apparently more interested in Becker. She said something to the brunette, more in body language than actual words. But she was looking at him when she said it.

The derelict was sniffling. 'Y'remember—y'remember that bloke?'

'What bloke?'

'One that lost the cap.'

'What about him?'

'Seen him last night.'

'Where'd you see him?'

'Down b'the—'

'The lake?'

'Eh? Yeah.'

'How could you see him in the dark?'

'Was standin' under a light.'

'Was he? All right, what was he doing?'

'Talkin' to coupla blokes.'

'What blokes?'

'Just two blokes, one had him by the arm. Real friendly they looked.'

'Then what?'

'One of 'em shot him.'

'Shot him?'

'Yeah, one in the back an' one in the 'ead.'

Becker shook his own head. 'And dumped him in the lake?'

'Yeah, how'd y'know?'

'Heard about it this morning. Where were you?'

'Havin' a quiet kip under a—under a—'

'Tree? You saw their faces?'

'Nah, only his, too dark.'

'What were they saying?'

'Dunno. The skinny bloke, the one who'd had the cap, was sayin', "When do I get my dough?"'

'Well, did he?'

'Ah, I dunno. He took out somethin' from his pocket—'

'The fat man? What was it?'

'I dunno. Could've been a wallet, y'know.'

'And did he pay him?'

'Yeah, but not much.'

'How do you know?'

'The skinny bloke said, "Five dollars? We had a deal, five thousand!"'

'What happened then?'

'They went on arguin'. The skinny feller was swearin' all the time. The fat bloke just kept pattin' him real friendly like, trying to calm him down, I reckon. He said, "You want five thousand? It was your job to get information. You've been pokin' that bitch for weeks and you've got nothin' out of 'er. Is he gonna talk, or isn't he?"'

'He said that? He called Mrs Crowley a bitch?'

'Who?'

'Never mind. What then?'

'The skinny bloke said, "I told you she doesn't know nothin'."'

'The chauffeur said that?'

'Eh?'

'The skinny bloke, the one who had the hat?'

'I reckon.'

'So what happened then?'

'Ah, the fat bloke said, "She's talkin' to a cop and you're tellin' me she don't know nothin'?"'

Across the way, under a tree, the blonde had finished her ice cream. She was leaning forward, arms crossed on the small table and listening to the brunette still talking fast. Both were dressed in much the same way, not uniforms of any kind but the same sort of rig—tight pants, working boots and leather jackets, one blue and the other brown, not exactly police issue but near enough.

'Yeah? So what'd the skinny guy say?'

'Ah, somethin' about him bein' kicked out.'

'Who was kicked out?'

'The cop, I think. "He's all right," he said, "he won't talk. He's been shot once for talkin'".'

'And what did the fat man say?'

'"You're right, he won't talk."'

'He said that?'

'Yeah.'

'Then what?'

'Nothin' for a while. Just starin' at the skinny bloke. Then he said somethin' to the other bloke.'

'The third man? What'd he say?'

'I dunno. Some foreign language by the sound of it.'

'Italian?'

'Ah, I dunno. The fat man was holdin' the skinny bloke by one hand and pattin' him with the other, like a father.'

'And?'

'He said, "You want five thousand? All right, I'll give you five thousand."'

'And did he?'

'Nah, he just went on talkin', saying somethin' like, "How d'you want it? How d'you want it?"'

'What was the skinny one saying?'

'Couldn't tell, really. This big truck was comin' along the road behind us and makin' all this noise with those air brakes, goin' Tschiooh! Tschiooh!'

'Yeah?'

'Then the other bloke—'

'The third man?'

'Yeah, he just put somethin' to the skinny bloke's head and there was a sort of pop or crack or somethin'. Then another one.'

'He shot him twice?'

'Yeah, twice by the look of it.'

'They used the truck as a cover?'

'Eh?'

'For the sound. Go on.'

'So they just pushed him over.'

'Into the lake?'

'Yeah, and walked off.'

'Jesus!'

'Yeah, didn't muck around, did they?'

Becker was afraid. That's how they did it in this brave new world. Just take a bloke for a walk in the middle of the night and all you get is bang, bang. Now things were beginning to make sense. Some punks from out of town were worried about Mrs Crowley's husband, worried he'd talk. About what? Something happening at the bank? And Torrence had made a mess of it. He'd paid the price. And now the killers knew about himself, Harry Becker. He didn't know as much as Torrence, but that would not matter to those guys.

'What'd you do next?'

'Went down an' had a look.'

'At the bloke who'd been shot?'

'Yeah.'

'Floating in the water?'

'Yeah.'

'Then what?'

'Picked it up.'

'Picked what up?'

'This here—'

The tramp pulled out a card. It was a credit card and on it was a foreign name. The name was not Scarafini or anything resembling it. Across the way, the blonde nudged the brunette who pulled out a small compact and touched up her lips. Or pretended to touch them up. Becker was sure he could see an eye in the mirror.

'So what did you do?'

'Got out of there fast. Thought they might come back.'

'For the card?'

'Yeah.'

'Mind if I keep this?'

'Ah, I dunno. Might be worth somethin'.'

'Not to you. You don't have the PIN.'

'The what?'

'A secret number. How about ten?'

'Dollars? Ah, I dunno—'

Becker took out his wallet. 'Twenty?'

'Ah, all right.'

Becker finished the kebab and the orange juice, thinking about it. Evelyn Crowley was right. The man in the brown suit at Manuka was not her cousin. And Torrence was right. He was getting in too deep. Becker should get out while he could. Talking to the tramp had done him some good. He'd eaten slowly and didn't belch when he threw the bag in a bin. For some reason, he never missed. It did not matter which bin or from what distance. That was about his only talent these days.

He got up and so did the two women, scraping their chairs and looking away from him. Making a deliberate show of disinterest. Casually they walked past, talking about shift work and lack of sleep and men.

'Oh, Jesus,' the brunette was saying. She'd covered her mouth with a hand and was yawning. 'I'm rooted, really rooted.'

'No wonder, the way you behave, shagging blokes all night.'

'It was only one bloke.'

'You're stupid, Polly.'

'Ah, no harm done.'

'You're stupid.'

He watched them saunter off, casually chatting. They seemed to be in no hurry. They were tall and tough women, no more than thirty. The blonde looked like she could flatten you with one hit. She was putting small change in a pocket. As she did, her arm brushed her jacket and for a flash he saw the weapon on her right hip. It was a Smith and Wesson .38 revolver, just like the one he had. Or, like the one he did not have, because the police held it. These, he was sure, were the pair who'd tailed him two nights ago. Two women in two unmarked cars. They knew he'd not been near the lake. Palfreyman had nothing on him and knew it. He felt thankful. There was still some justice in the world.

Just then his mobile went off. 'Hello?'

'Harry?'

'Yes.'

'It's Evelyn Crowley. Something terrible has happened.'

'You mean Torrence?'

'Who?'

'Never mind, what is it?'

'My husband—'

'What about him?'

'He's dead.'

'Him too?'

'What do you mean?'

'Where are you?'

'At the morgue. I feel awful, I just can't take it any longer, I—' She was gabbling.

'Be careful, don't say anything more. Can you drive?'

'I don't have my car. I was about to get a taxi—'

'I'll pick you up in ten minutes. Wait out front.'

CHAPTER 18

She was wearing the black coat and black hat again when he arrived. Quickly she got into the Holden, making Becker feel ashamed. No woman of her class had ever graced an old bomb like his. She pulled the coat tightly about her body as they drove off, sitting stiffly, elbows dug into her sides, as if she hurt badly. She was not wearing dark glasses and looked bad in the eyes. They were shut tight, screwed up in two whorls of tiny lines, showing her age. Yet she still looked lovely. Unexpectedly she sat in the middle, next to him. It was that kind of car, a six-seater, made in the old days when every Holden had a bench seat up front. An ex-taxi, it had more than three hundred thousand on the clock. It had had a rebore, but it was blowing smoke again.

'I feel so sick, what am I going to do?'

'Where's your car?'

'At home. The police brought me here. They offered to take me home but—'

'You called me instead?'

'You're the only one who seems to know what's going on.'

'I wish I did.' He had a good idea now, but wasn't going to tell her. Not yet, anyway. He could still hear those words: She's talkin' to a cop and you're tellin' me she don't know nothin'?

'I feel so bad I could just lie down and die.'

'I know what you mean. Do up the belt.'

'What?'

'The seat belt.'

'Oh, yes.'

She was sitting on the belt, so he waited until she'd wriggled enough to retrieve it. He drove her to Weston Park, stopped under a kurrajong and faced Black Mountain across the lake. It towered over them, dark and majestic and at the same time primitive in its monumental shadows. He opened a window, just a crack. Today she was wearing perfume, very subtle, something very expensive, of course. She put her hands to her face, began to cry. He thought of putting an arm about her shoulders, but that would have been impertinent.

'What'd the police say?'

'Nothing really, only that they were making enquiries. If I only knew what he meant—'

'He left a note?'

'Just a piece of paper in an envelope on his desk.'

'At home?'

'No, at work. Apparently, he got up, told his secretary he was going out for a minute and—Well, it seems he went onto the roof and—'

'Jumped?'

She nodded. 'Eight floors.'

'Oh, Jesus.'

'Yes, my lover and now my husband, the same way.'

'What was in the note?'

'It just said, 'One day long ago there was a pretty girl in Melbourne town—'

'He signed it?'

'No, but it was his handwriting. Why did he do it, Harry?'

He had no idea. 'Did he get the Washington job?'

'No.'

'Maybe that was it.'

It wasn't, he knew. Crowley had jumped because he was at the end of the line.

While speaking, she had taken off the hat. Now she reached into her bag for a handkerchief, wiped her eyes. No mascara came away. She did not wear it, did not need it. Her eyes were naturally ringed by black lashes. Cars whizzed along the road on the other side of the lake. Birds took off, cars came up behind them silently, just cruising, seeing the sights, then drove off.

'Hold me,' she said and collapsed against him, her head still in her hands, crying.

This time he did put an arm about her. They stayed that way for some time, both thinking and not thinking. She sighed, a long suspiration. Nothing more happened, as though she had given up breathing. She was both alive and dead in his arms.

'I killed him,' she said at last.

He was surprised. 'Your husband?'

'My lover.'

'The man in Melbourne, the lawyer?'

'Yes.'

'You said he jumped, because he was misappropriating—'

'Yes, he was, but I did not tell you the full story. I didn't care about you then. Now I do, I don't know why. Perhaps because you talk to me, tell me about yourself. I enjoy your stories. I think you are an honest man, Harry.'

He didn't know what to say. But he was sure she was going to tell him something he'd prefer not to hear. She lay back, relaxing in his arms like someone who has fallen from a great height, but was not broken. Just defeated.

'He didn't jump?'

'No, I pushed him.'

'Oh, Jesus.'

'Yes, that's what I thought when I realised what I'd done. Did I tell you? That I went to his flat to tell him? I didn't ring him, because I wanted to tell him to his face. I was so happy. I rang the bell, he opened it. He was in gym clothes. He'd been doing exercises. He tended to do them on Saturday mornings. We went out onto the balcony. I was smiling and dancing around as bright as a button. He asked what was wrong. What had happened? I told him, standing back. "Darling," I said, "we are going to have a baby!" He was astonished, his face fell. I said, "What is it? Aren't you pleased? You said you loved me. You said you wanted to marry me. You said you were getting a divorce.".'

She stopped, quite ashamed. It was obvious.

'What happened then?'

'He—' She gulped air. 'He said he couldn't marry me. His wife's father had just died, and she had inherited a lot of money and—well, it was impossible now. He was afraid, I could see, a frightened little bastard. He had used me. And now he was rejecting me, just because his wife was suddenly rich. I couldn't believe it. I was shocked. The shock, the shock, it was awful!'

'I bet it was.'

'The bastard, suddenly I hated him. I wanted to tear his eyes out. He was leaning back against the balcony, smiling. And saying, I'm sorry, Evelyn, but that's how it is. Of course, I'll help you. He was saying that he'd pay, pay to have my lovely baby killed. I was horrified. I am Catholic. I would never do such a thing. I rushed at him, tore at him with my nails. He jumped back, startled. I tore at his face. He tried to stop me, tried to catch my hands but—'

'But what?'

'I pushed him. I did not mean to. I didn't know what I was doing. He went over.'

'Jesus!'

'He began to fall. I came to my senses. I grabbed him, tried to pull him back as he was going over—and taking me with him. Evelyn, he shouted. He pushed me back. That just made him go out further. I lost hold of him. He went down and down and down—six storeys! I stood back out of sight, horrified. I couldn't believe I could have done such a horrible thing—pushed a man to his death. I refused to believe it. I began to cry, tried to take hold of myself. At last I crept forward, peeped over the edge. People were rushing to the spot. He was spread-eagled on the pavement below. I jumped back. Some began to look up. I didn't know what to do. At last, I gathered my bag and my wits and went down, down, down in the elevator—sneaked out onto the street, crept up to the crowd gathering around him. And just stood there, gaping. He lay on his back, his body twisted, his arms out and twisted, his neck broken. It must have been an awful impact. Blood was welling in his eyes. A taxi driver was calling for an ambulance. Someone else asked where did he fall from? They looked at me as if I might know. I just stared, horrified. I don't think anyone really associated me with his fall. They were just as shocked as I was. I stood there in a fearful stupor for a while, I don't know how long. A policeman appeared. He said, "Anyone know this man?" Looked at all of us. We shook our heads. I think I tried to say I knew him, that he had fallen from a balcony on the sixth floor, that it was an accident. Nothing came out. I fully intended to confess, I really did—to tell the police everything. Then, as I tried to think what I'd say, something strange happened. I began to walk away—at least my body did. It was quite eerie. I was still there on the edge of the crowd staring at him, but my body was not. I could see it walking away along the street. Somehow, I ran after it, got in it. I couldn't stop it, so we ran away together—got clear away.' She gulped air again. 'I never spoke up, Harry. I was a coward, a dreadful coward. I still am.'

She had turned during the telling, cringing against him, her knees pressed against his legs, her eyes now full of shame. She looked crushed. He gave her time to relax, her breath coming in spurts like an old machine, which cannot take too much pressure. So Torrence was right. She had pushed him. Maybe it was an accident, but it didn't make that much difference. Evelyn Crowley was a killer.

'Did you ever tell anyone?'

'Not a soul.'

'Not your father?'

'Yes, I did. But he would not have told anyone.'

'A friend?'

'No.'

'A priest?'

'No, no one.'

'Was there an inquest?'

'Yes, of course. The verdict was suicide. He was a money-hungry man. Unknown to me, he had been misappropriating his trust fund, living beyond his means. His partners had begun to suspect. In fact, they'd decided to call in the auditors. I think I told you that.'

Becker rubbed his hands, weather-beaten hands, prematurely old. Some men on the job wore gloves to keep out the cold. He never did. He knew he'd fumble if he had to draw quickly, not find the trigger in time.

'So, you got away with it?'

'Yes, I got away with it.'

'It was an accident, Mrs Crowley.'

'I feel that I killed him, nevertheless.'

'Well, I don't know what the coroner would've decided, if you'd confessed. He might have let you off, found it was an accidental death.'

She did not reply, but simply lay there, twisted against him, until her breathing evened out, became normal, thoughtful. He watched her black lashes flicking now and then as she stared at the water and the dark wall of the mountain and the traffic flitting along the distant shore.

'Now it has happened to my husband,' she said at last.

'Why did he do it?'

'He was under suspicion, I think.'

'For what?'

'The police would not tell me. Donald wouldn't take money, he had no need. Do you know, he was paid nearly a million a year, including bonuses.'

'Some people want more.'

'No, please understand, he was not greedy.'

'Maybe he was under pressure from someone who was.'

'Who?'

'Your relatives in Melbourne.'

'Uncle Ennio? Why would he blackmail him?'

'Maybe he's playing a game?'

'What sort of game?'

'Threatening to expose him unless he does something for them. Something big, something to do with the bank?'

She did not reply. Over the lake, a flight of pelicans came down and down. They hit the water, skidding on their webbed feet. After a few seconds, they seemed to organise themselves. One of them, which looked exactly like the others, moved off in the thoughtful manner of pelicans. They followed, swimming effortlessly, not disturbing the surface at all. The leader moved towards the bank, near where Becker had parked. A few feet out, he dived. One or two others did the same. Something was down there, something very simple, like a meal. Birds lived in a world where you ate all day—if you didn't, you died. Humans, on the other hand, lived in a world where you just died. It didn't matter whether you ate or not.

She stirred, sat up. 'Thank you, Harry.'

'What for?'

'Talking to me.'

'You feel like a drink?'

'No, no—'

'You want to walk along the lake?'

'It's too windy.'

'I'll take you home.'

He did so, watching each side. Once he thought he saw two women in an unmarked car following them, but it soon dropped out of sight. They said nothing for the first mile or so, Mrs Crowley sitting up straight, arms folded, tight-lipped and frowning as though in pain. At last she said, 'Tell me about yourself.'

He was surprised. Why would she want to know his story? But perhaps that was just her way of not thinking about her husband.

'There's nothing to tell.'

'You said you'd been married.'

'Ah, yeah.'

'What happened?'

'What do you mean?'

'To your marriage?'

'That went bust, after I was kicked out of the force.'

'She couldn't take the shame?'

'No, she couldn't.'

'What was she like? Pretty?'

'Yeah, real pretty. Only eighteen at the time.'

'So you fell for her?'

'No, not quite—'

Mrs Crowley was puzzled. 'Why did you marry her?'

'Well, it was like this. She was one of the cheerleaders for St George. You know, the girls who dance around in bikinis, wearing silly hats and waving streamers. Mad about footballers, she was. Anyway, I'd taken her out a couple of times, kissed her now and then. But I hadn't seen her for months.'

'And?'

'Well, one day I was called to a smash and grab at a jewellery store in Hurstville. She worked there, and she was crying her eyes out when I arrived. "Gee, Addie," I said—'

'Addie?'

'Yeah, Adeline Atkins was her name. Anyway, I said, "What's up?" "I'm all right," she said. "So, why are you crying?" "Because," she said, "everything's gone wrong." "You know who did this?" I asked, thinking she might have been involved in some way. "No," she said, "it was a dreadful fellow. He just walked in and started smashing cases with a hammer and stuffing things in his pockets." "Hey," I said, "don't cry. It's not your jewellery, you're not responsible." By then another patrol car had arrived, and they sorted things out and did all the interviews. They thought they knew the bloke. So off they went after him, and I was left with Adeline and the manageress who'd just walked in screaming. She'd been down the road at the bank. So we cleaned the place up a bit and closed the door and tried to restore things as far as you can with a crying girl and an irate shopkeeper who seemed to be blaming the girl for not stopping the thug with the hammer. Anyway, the manager calmed down a bit, especially when a woman who worked part-time for her came in and gave a hand. The boss told Addie to go home and not come back until she'd stopped crying. What did I do? I said I'd take her home. I was going her way.'

'That was kind of you.'

'Yeah, so off we went in the patrol car. You're not supposed to give people a lift, but she had been the victim of a smash and grab and was pretty distressed, so officially it was all right.'

'She must have been grateful.'

'Ah, yeah, well, as it turned out, she wasn't upset about the robbery. It all came out before we got to her house. She was pregnant and her boyfriend had deserted her.'

'Oh, dear.'

'It was worse than that. She was a good girl who'd sworn she'd never have sex before marriage. But he got her drunk one night, and it happened.'

'Oh, dear.'

'Yeah, she was a strict Baptist and terrified she'd go to hell.'

'Had she told her parents?'

'No, that was the problem. She could not, she was so ashamed. She was almost three months gone, and she didn't know what to do.'

'The poor girl.'

'She kept crying and saying no one'll marry me now.'

'So what did you do?'

'Ah, well, muggins me, I said I'd marry her.'

'You did?' Mrs Crowley was surprised.

'Yeah, so she took me in and introduced me to her parents, who I'd already met because I'd dated her twice and brought flowers when I'd called for her and all that. The worst thing was she told them she was pregnant, and I was the father. I wasn't prepared for that, but I suppose they had to know sometime. She was starting to swell a bit.'

'My goodness, what did the parents say?'

'Nothing much at first. They just stared at me for a minute, like I was something from outer space. The old man said, "What've you go to say for yourself, young man?" I was a bit perplexed, trying to point out I was only trying to do their daughter a favour. "A bit late, aren't you?" he said. "Well, sir," I said, "I didn't know until today she was expecting." "You knew you'd deflowered her, didn't you?" he said. I didn't want to say I'd never had sex with her, which was true. I never had. She always seemed a bit too pretty and unsophisticated for that. A really clean-living girl. She read the Bible every night. Anyway, if I'd protested my innocence, that'd give the game away for her, wouldn't it? So I said I was sorry and would they forgive me? "That'll cost you a bit," he said. His wife was present, staring at me all the time with her snake's eyes, while young Adeline was in the corner, sniffling into a handkerchief. "What?" I said. "One thousand dollars," he said, "for the hurt." "Eh?" I said. "For the hurt and the shame you have brought on this family!" he shouted. By gee, I was pretty knocked back by this. They were taking it out on me and I'd never even given her as much as a tickle!'

'Did you go ahead?'

'Yeah, well, I had to, didn't I? If I hadn't they would have skinned her. Or, she would have done away with herself. Yeah, we got hitched in a little wooden church in Stony Creek Road between a spray painter and a chicken takeaway. There was a white cross on top and paper flowers in the windows. There were only half a dozen people, and they were looking even more miserable than Addie and me. The minister said I would have to be baptised. Her parents objected, saying I was not clean enough. So, I got out of a good dunking.'

'No reception afterward, I suppose?'

'Yeah, there was, only tea and scones, back at their place.'

Mrs Crowley almost chuckled. 'You poor man.'

'We went to bed after that. She wouldn't let me do her, because she was pregnant. It was a pretty miserable time, but she'd already read a book on what to do in such circumstances.'

'I see.'

'This went on until the baby came. Then we got down to real business. She got to like it after a while, so much so she was all over me like a rash as soon as I was in the door. When I was posted to Darlinghurst, we got a place in Maroubra and had two more kids.'

'And what happened when you were shot?'

'She kicked me out—'

'Really?'

'Saying she couldn't live with man who'd sold his soul to the devil.'

'After all you'd done for her?'

'Ah, I think it was those parents of hers. They were a pair of pissants, who'd never liked me. Her old man, I heard later, had done time for cracking safes in Brisbane, where Addie was born. He might've been still at it, so he wasn't too keen on having a copper in the family. Yeah, they got at her, saying I was sure to go to hell now I'd been kicked out of the force. They were strong believers in hell. Heaven didn't seem to matter much to them, not even in bed.'

'You're a good man.'

'Ah, well—'

He was going to tell her about a girl he knew in Cootamundra years ago, just to cheer her up, but did not get the chance. They had arrived at her house.

As he helped her out of the Holden, he noticed the girl walking a dog in Collins Park. She was eyeing them without faltering in her stride. The dog was a big, red, Irish setter with a studded collar, well groomed. It looked a happy dog—happy to be walking with a pretty girl. Mrs Crowley did not seem to notice. Or, if she did, she was trying not to show it. He escorted her to the door.

She paused, inserted a key in the lock, but she did not turn it. Instead, she leaned against the wall, her hand on the key, looking at him, her eyes now and then flicking at something else over his shoulder. No doubt the girl.

'She's lovely, isn't she?'

'The girl? Yeah, she must've got that from her mother.'

She snorted modestly. 'Would you like to come in for a drink?'

He was tempted, but declined. 'Not a good idea. They're sure to be listening.'

'Still? The police?'

'Not necessarily the police. Don't talk to anyone. If you must contact me, use a payphone.'

'Thank you for your help, Harry. I owe you a lot.'

'That's all right, Mrs Crowley.'

'Evelyn, please call me Evelyn.'

For a fraction of a second, he thought she was going to kiss him, or at least stand close, let him feel the heat of her body, its shape and its womanliness. Let him have her. But she did not.

'You're a good man,' she said again. And turned the key.

As he drove away, he saw the girl again. She was now seated on the old wooden seat. The dog was snuffling among fallen leaves. Becker nodded to her, raising a hand. She smiled cautiously. He wondered whether she'd take a risk now and go to the house, knock on the door. He hoped not. In the mood she was in, Evelyn Cowley would probably break down, tell her newfound daughter everything—including what had really happened to her father. The poor girl would probably run a mile, horrified.

He thought he had it worked out now. Crowley had been in thrall to a family of creeps down in Melbourne. They'd had him by the balls, so to speak. If he'd refused to launder money, they'd threaten to reveal what he'd done years ago in Brunswick. He'd probably given in each time. He was trapped, and each year the trap bit harder. Crowley had been desperate. He was thinking of going to the police, confessing all. The Scarafini gang worked out a nice little scheme for getting rid of him. Instead of cutting his throat, they'd scare him to death. They'd send a note to his wife demanding money or else. She'd ask him what was this all about? He'd take fright, kill himself. Problem solved.

Yes, it was a smart caper. And it had worked.

Except they didn't know the wife had taken it the wrong way. She'd thought it referred to the big drop in Melbourne. And she'd appealed to a born loser called Harry Becker for help. And now they were worried, because he was a cop. It was a neat theory, but was it correct? Someone else was involved. As Buster had said, someone who didn't muck around.

So, here he was driving home on a cold May day in Canberra in two minds.

What was he going to do? Try to help a woman who didn't seem to have much future? Or should he forget her and go to Sydney, have a chat with Mr Justice Wood.

Tell him what he knew about corruption in the New South Wales Police Force? And risk another bullet?

He'd have to make up his mind soon. The commission was going to wind up hearings next month. He didn't know what to do, so he did nothing.

CHAPTER 19

He didn't see her again for nearly two weeks. He thought of phoning her or dropping by, but it was not a good idea. A new widow shouldn't be seen with a man she couldn't explain. He just hoped she didn't say too much to her friends in Melbourne. Anything could happen to her, a pre-arranged car smash or a simple electrocution when she switched on a metal toaster or a coffee pot. He'd become quite paranoid about safety. He checked his car each day, expecting to find a planted bomb. He searched it for bugs, found none. Even so, he installed a simple buzzer which he could turn on whenever he wished to have a private conversation. Anyone listening wouldn't be able to hear above the racket. It played havoc with radios in the area, but that was the price the citizens had to pay to keep him alive. As for the Indians he lived with, they received no more racist calls. Perhaps someone had got the message. Frightening him was not going to work.

He was mooching along City Walk one late afternoon towards the end of May, when a woman fell into step beside him and said, 'Penny for your thoughts.'

'Oh, hello. Where are you going?'

'To my car.' She smiled. 'What were you thinking?'

'Oh, I might get out of Canberra.'

'Really?' She laughed, but it was clear she was surprised, perhaps a little apprehensive.

'Yeah, go out west, perhaps go back to Wagga.'

'Your hometown, I think you said?'

'Yeah.'

'Fed up, are you? Fed up with me? And all my problems?'

'Fed up with everything, really.'

'The job getting you down?'

'Yeah.'

'I'm sorry, Harry.'

She must have come out of the Monaro Mall. That's what it was called before the place was expanded and became the Canberra Centre. On this day, her hair was piled up behind her neck in a sort of loop, perhaps to keep it out of her eyes. The breeze was light but occasionally gusty. Even so, a few long dark strands hung about her face. In one hand she carried a handbag, in the other a David Jones shopping bag.

'Another dress?'

'No, just food, bits and pieces of this and that.'

He walked along with her, thinking he'd see her to her car. It was almost five o'clock.

They came to Garema Place, where the plane trees were fast losing their leaves. Soon they would be bare. The concourse was decorated with two or three piles of leaves. Someone had been raking them up and had left the job unfinished. Perhaps a public servant impatient to get to the nearest pub. An occasional breeze was gently undoing all his good work.

They slowed to a dawdle. This was where it had all begun six weeks ago, when he'd spotted her handbag in a bin. He looked at the bin. It had been cleared—nothing significant about it, except suddenly it looked unbearably empty. She seemed to read his thoughts.

'Is that the one?'

'Yeah.'

She paused. 'Poor bin, it looks so lonely.'

She halted altogether, looking around, spinning on a heel. For some reason, he thought of a French film he'd seen late one night on television. A couple were walking along a Parisian street, lined with plane trees. He was very tall, and she was very short, just a slip of a girl. She was wearing a belted coat and a black beret. In French films of that time, all the women seemed to wear tightly belted coats. And berets. It might have been soon after the war. Suddenly he stopped, picked her up, said something Becker did not catch, because he couldn't read the captions fast enough, kissed her on the nose and then set her down. She'd just laughed, and they'd walked on.

On an impulse, he thought he'd do that to Evelyn Crowley, but he did not. She'd be much too heavy. She was not a slim waif like that girl.

'Now what are you thinking?' she asked.

'If I hadn't seen that bag—'

'This is the one.' She held it up. 'We never would have met, would we?'

'I'm glad we did.'

'So am I.'

Garema Place has three wind tunnels, one at the Mall end and two at the end leading to Bunda Street and the car parks. With each gust, the wind whistles through the tunnels, then dies. It seems some giant is respectfully trying to fan your cheeks. In winter, it is a place of blizzardly draughts, but it wasn't that bad yet. A few people were about, although none sitting outside Mamma's Trattoria. To one side was a bar and steak house called El Rancho, into which he sometimes went. There was nothing ranch-like about it, except for a pair of buffalo horns stuck on a wall and some pictures taken at a rodeo somewhere. It could have been in New Zealand. He'd have a whiskey, sometimes with a beer chaser. He did not like it, not so much the whiskey as the place. It was always half empty and so dark you couldn't really see who was sitting alone at a table, except for a pair of eyes staring at you as if you were in some sort of trouble you didn't want to talk about. Everyone spoke in whispers, even some drunk who'd been there all afternoon. Any conversation you struck up got nowhere. The emptiness was emptier than the emptiness of the bin outside, where it had all begun. He'd been heading that way when she'd spoken to him.

'Do you have time for coffee, Harry?'

'I drink too much coffee.'

'Yes, I remember you saying.' She paused, weighing up her words. 'I have some veal and prosciutto and things here—' She lifted the bag. 'I'm going to make saltimbocca and perhaps gnocchi—' The wind blew thin threads of hair across her face. The loop behind her head was unravelling. Thoughtfully, she pushed it back. 'Would you like to dine with me?'

'Do you think that's a good idea?'

'When I am supposed to be a grieving widow?'

She looked away, frowning. She too was wearing a belted coat, but it was not a raincoat. Rather, it was short and black and classy, like her. Except she was not short and black. She was a bit over average height and, in boots, she looked a bit mannish, though sexily mannish. From just outside the coat at her neck peeped the collar of a deep-pink blouse, tied at the throat by a neat little bow of strings, which was what gave her away as still sexily womanish. She wore a thick grey woollen skirt, on which he saw black leaves, which did not look right. He'd never seen black leaves. But they went with her black coat and black bag and her long black boots—caballero boots, he noted, without all the flash embossment.

'Despite appearances, I'm not in mourning. No, I don't grieve for Donald. I didn't love him, I didn't even like him. But I got used to him, in the way you get used to a physical defect that is unattractive, such as a hairy mole on your neck or a stye in your eye. But you can live with it, especially when everyone else, once they've seen it, can get used to it too.' She glanced around. 'But I'm sorry about him and sometimes sorry for him.'

'Because of what your family did to him?'

'Yes.'

She sounded genuine, a woman who regretted much that had gone wrong in her life. A modest convent girl, perhaps shy originally, but too pretty to be safe from men. She'd been conned by some fast-talking lawyer in Melbourne. And used by her own family, because she was pretty and easily talked into going along with them, trapping a young bank manager into a fraud and a marriage he could not get out of, even if he'd wanted.

'You should be careful, Evelyn.'

'About what people might say?'

He nodded.

'I don't care what people say, not now. I'm not married anymore. Like you, Harry, I am thinking of getting out of Canberra. I don't know where I'll go, but—' She looked at him, frowning against the wind. 'I can't just yet. There are things to be done. Donald's estate, you know. But, in a few weeks perhaps.'

He watched her. She was vacillating. She wanted him to come home with her, but did not wish to beg.

'Harry, I'm not trying to get you into bed, if that's what you're thinking. It's just that—well, I like you. I like you very much. I don't know what I'd do without you. I mean, I have no friends now, at least none who'd want to be seen with me in public and—' She shrugged. 'You've heard about me, haven't you? I used to pick up strange men and take them home, when my husband was not there. I am not trying to pick you up. We are not strangers, are we? We've seen a lot of each other over the past—how many is it? Six weeks? Also, you know more about me than anyone, now that Donald—' She pulled a bitter-sweet face. 'I just want to talk to you, as one friend to another.'

'What about?'

'Your job, those dreadful hours. You should not be doing that.'

'I need the money.'

'I know, I know. If you'd allow me, I would help you to get out of it.'

He was both tempted and shocked. Not shocked because of what she had said about men. It was none of his business who she went to bed with or how many. It was because of her offer. She was willing to help him to get out of this life to which there had seemed to be no end, except death. But he couldn't do it. He'd be obliged to her, perhaps bound to her. Which could be dangerous.

'I don't want any help.'

She smiled and shrugged.

'All right, just a glass of wine and a bite to eat? No sex, I promise.'

She waited for an answer, smiling, but prepared to be disappointed. He did not answer. She twisted and turned a little on a heel. 'Harry, what do you think of me?'

He shrugged. 'I just think of you.'

'And what do you think about me?'

'Nothing at all, I just think.'

'No one can think of someone without thinking about them.'

'I just like to look at you.'

She laughed. 'Really? Like a work of art? My God, how awful. I assure you I am not like that at all. I'm quite—how should I put it? Affectionate, when you get to know me. I'm just a little girl who loves to be kissed and cuddled, but no one sees me that way now, do they? Because of the awful way I have had to live all these years, withdrawn, careful, suspicious. Afraid someone would find me out. That someone would go to the police. That's how Donald trapped me, always threatening to expose me if I ever tried to—to—'

She shuddered.

'Run away?'

'Yes.'

She pushed the hair back again. The knot had undone now and was blowing across her face. 'Oh, I must look a mess.'

'You look beautiful.'

She gasped. 'Really? Oh, a beautiful mess, I'm sure.'

They stood there, not speaking for a while. She looked about, both happy and miserable. She shrugged again, perhaps embarrassed. He just looked at her. She glanced up, squinting. 'You don't like me, do you, Harry? You're afraid of me. I can see it. I don't blame you, after what I told you.'

He was about to say that he loved her, but something stopped him just in time. He looked away, knowing he shouldn't have said she was beautiful. She'd realise he loved her, if she hadn't worked that out already. Now she had the advantage on him. He did not answer, but that in itself was answer enough.

'What I did in Melbourne so long ago, I'll regret that for the rest of my days, Harry. What am I to do? Please tell me. Should I go to the police and tell them?'

She was pleading with him. He had an impression that whatever he advised, she would do it, even go to the police. And then what would happen to her? Prison? Or possibly a verdict of misadventure? Let off with a reprimand for not reporting an accident?

'Tell me, Harry, what am I to do?'

He did not know. 'Just go on as you are. Live with it.'

'Live with it? That's what I have been trying to do for nearly eighteen years!'

She gazed at him intensely. He looked away at passing people, not many. Some had hands in their pockets and heads down. One woman, her arms full of shopping, was trying to hold on to her hat. The wind subsided, and the leaves came back to earth. He thought Evelyn was going to add something. Her throat moved, her lips paused in mid-thought. Her eyes were wide and deep and kind and hurt. She stepped forward and kissed him on a cheek. 'Good night, Harry.' Then she turned and walked away.

'Good night, Evelyn.'

He went into the bar and had a whiskey sour. It went down in a few minutes without achieving anything. So he went home, intending to get a couple of hours sleep before starting work. He just lay on his bed with his hands behind his head, thinking about her and her invitation and all the good reasons for rejecting it. On the other hand, he now wanted to live. Some strange and possibly dangerous woman wanted to cook for him, as if she really did care about him. Also, she had a pretty daughter. One day, if the girl didn't bring them together, he'd see to it that they did meet. To hell with the law, Evelyn Crowley needed someone now, someone to live for.

Fifteen minutes later, he walked up to her front door and rang the bell. He waited, a few cars went past along Empire Circuit, even a Rolls. The man driving looked like a bricklayer who'd made a pile. There was a car parked a few yards up the street, not outside a house but on the other side, by Collins Park. Someone was in it, but he could not see clearly. The light was fading now. He was being watched, he knew. The police or someone else?

The door opened. From inside came lovely singing.

'Harry? You changed your mind?'

'I just want to talk to you.'

'About my idea? Yes, of course, come in, come in! Oh, what a surprise! This is lovely. Come in here, I've just opened something. Sit anywhere, sit by me on the sofa. No, you sit there, I'll sit over here where I can see you. I was just about to have a drink and... How are you?'

She was as excited as a schoolgirl on her first date. He sat on one of the chairs, watching her waltzing around, waving her hands. A woman was singing, a soprano, going up and down the mountain tops of a sad song. He looked around but saw no audio equipment. The sound seemed to come from the whole room, from of the walls, the furniture.

'Will you have a glass?' She went to a cabinet where a bottle stood on a silver platter. 'It's Tarrango, quite light and dry. I drink it cold in summer, but it's all right to sip at any time.' She was looking back over a shoulder. 'Can I tempt you?'

'Yeah, sure.'

He watched as she poured two glasses. She'd left her hair down and dispensed with the black coat and the boots. On her feet were high-heeled sandals that looked more like slippers. He thought the Americans called them mules. The skirt was the same. It was not all black and grey as he'd thought, but had three colours if you could call them colours at all—black and grey and a sort of off-white, like the colours of the butcher bird. It was a terrible bird. Often he'd been pecked by one or more in the nesting season in Sydney. They had lovely calls but nasty habits. They devoured the young of other birds, stole them from their nests and ate them alive. The poor little things, shrieking.

The blouse was the same, deep pink with a small bow at the neck.

'What is it?' he asked.

'The singing? Oh, sorry—' She picked up a remote control.

'It's all right,' he said. 'What is it?'

'Oh, my favourite at present. Marietta's song from The Dead City. It's too loud, isn't it?'

Before he could protest, she had clicked the volume down and down.

'How's that?'

'Good.'

'You like music?'

'Yeah.'

'Here,' she said, handing him a glass before sitting on the sofa and relaxing, immediately crossing her legs, casually flipping a slipper as she chatted, the foot half in and half out. Quite different from the Evelyn Crowley he'd met on that day six weeks ago, when she'd sat in front of him, so prim and proper, her knees and ankles pressed together, calculation in her eyes. They were friends now, almost intimate. But, for some reason, he recalled an early scene in an old movie, when Barbara Stanwyck walked downstairs wearing a gold anklet. And that poor mug, Fred MacMurray, couldn't take his eyes off that anklet and that ankle and that dame, fresh out of a shower and chatting amiably as she descended upon him. Pretty soon they were talking about insurance and the extra payout to be expected from a double indemnity, and soon after that how to kill a man and get away with a packet. Evelyn Crowley was nothing like that dame. There were none of the tricks of the screen sirens of those days. But she was just as dangerous. She had dangerous friends somewhere out there in the unknowable world. They could be quite close or far away. You did not know where they were or when they might pop up.

'Good health,' she said.

'Yeah, good health.'

They sipped. As she had said, it was a light, dry wine, similar to Chianti but not so rough. Very drinkable. It didn't seem to go with the lovely song, a sad song, full of loss and longing. But it went with Evelyn Crowley. She settled back, watching him. And almost smiling to herself.

'How is it?'

'The wine? Oh, okay.'

'Good... Oh, I'm sorry, would you like cheese with it? You are probably hungry?'

'It's okay.'

She took another sip, then sighed, almost slouched on the sofa, as if about to close her eyes for a minute's rest.

'I love music,' she said. 'If I did not have such music every day, I think I would just give up and die.'

He did not comment. He didn't want to think about dying now that he was with her.

They sat there for a while, neither speaking, just listening. He never did find out where the sound came from, he could see no loudspeakers. Music without speakers seemed magical. Like being in a cave in a forest on a warm day, although not warm in the cave, which was open to light flickering through the trees. And the tinkling chatter of bellbirds. A secret world where there was no one else but a magical woman, who was both there and not there. A shadowy woman, indistinct, one you could talk to as if in a dream. Who talked back at you, but whatever she said was indecipherable. Not the words, but the thoughts behind the words.

'So, Harry,' she said, 'what do you think?'

'It's a lovely place.'

'I meant, have you thought about my suggestion?'

He'd known what she'd meant, but hadn't wanted to beg.

'About helping me?'

'Yes, I really meant it.'

'Why do you want to help me?'

'I told you, didn't I? You didn't react when I made my little speech today. I was quite hurt, you know.'

'What sort of help?'

'Well—' She waved a hand. 'You must get out of that dreadful job. You deserve better. Don't you want to be your own boss? Don't you ever think of having your own shop or business? I know I'm sticking my nose in where it may not be wanted, but I really like you, Harry. I owe you a lot.'

'I don't want to be paid.'

'I know, but if it had not been for you—'

The song ended. A man began to speak, but she reached out and clicked the control again. No sound now. She sat back on the sofa, gazing at the opposite wall. There was a hiatus. Respectfully, he waited for her to fill it.

'Horrible, isn't it?' she said at last.

'Pardon?'

'The whole mess. Nothing goes with anything else.'

He realised she was referring to the pictures.

'This whole room is a magpie's nest or a shop full of stuff, which may or may not sell. Now and then I'd rearrange the lot, try to get some balance into this jumble, some sense of cohesion, but he'd come home with another masterpiece he'd picked up somewhere and put them back the way they were or even worse. Then, one day, I realised that there was a pattern in it after all—'

'Yeah?'

'They are all arranged according to price or fame, the same thing to Donald. If it was pricey it must be famous, or if not, it would be.'

'Really?'

'Yes, see the small drawing there?'

She pointed, but he had to squint before he made it out, a framed drawing of what looked like a man wearing a helmet, his mouth wide open in anger or horror or malicious glee. Maybe it was just a Roman centurion yelling at his troops or a soldier about to hack someone to death.

'That,' she said, 'is a Leonardo, which he picked up at Sotheby's in London—for a song, he said. He seemed to think he was clever, but in fact there are thousands of Leonardo drawings around the world. Yet he'd steer visitors to this one when he'd bring them in, his pride and joy. He owned a Leonardo! The poor, simple, little man.'

She sighed, taking another sip. She was drinking faster than Becker, as if eager to talk, eager to be friendly, eager to please him.

'I never did understand his brain, if he had one. I think that he was really a mechanical man, a walking and talking cash register. All you had to do was press the right buttons and he'd go ping! But I do like that one.' She pointed again. 'The poor man outside the factory gate. Has he been sacked? Has he come to the wrong place? Did he come to the right place but there was no job for him after all?'

It was a simple painting. A short fat man, reminding him of Alfred Hitchcock without the prominent lower lip, was standing in front of a factory wall painted in great garish stripes of colour—nothing else in the picture. Except the end of a word, '—*tries.*' Industries? Or was it the complete word: Tries? Who tries? No one. Or everyone tries but gets nowhere?

'It's a Jason Guthrie, just a sad man staring at nothing. Or is he staring down the road, hoping something will turn up? Don't you think the poor, little man looks sad?'

'Yeah, he does.'

'Sad and bewildered, that's how I feel some days. I felt it when you knocked me back today. It was as though my last resort had vanished. My intentions are honourable, Harry. I'm not trying to seduce you or get you into bed or trying to trick you into doing anything immoral or... or...' She shrugged. 'What do you want to do with the rest of your life? Starting from now?'

He was impressed. She had a way with words, simple, fluent, frank, intimate.

'I'd like to get into something, maybe something to do with the land.'

'A farm?'

'I'm not a farmer.'

'I'll buy you a farm, if you wish. How much would it cost?'

'I don't want anything.'

'Well, how about a shop? A petrol station? A supermarket?'

'I guess it'd have to be in a town.'

'What sort of town?'

'I used to live in Wagga—'

'Yes, you told me. You worked for a real estate agent?'

'Stock and station agent.'

'You'd be happy to go back to that?'

'Yeah, I would.'

'How long is it since—'

'Fifteen years.'

'It would take some catching up, wouldn't it?'

'I reckon.'

She sat up a little, turned towards him. 'But you could do it, Harry. I know you could. You want to start up such a business? Selling farms?'

'That'd be no good, I wouldn't have any clientele to start off, and I'd be out of touch.'

'Why not buy into an existing business?'

'That would be better.'

'Do you know one?'

'There might be one in Wagga.'

'Really?'

'I heard old Tommy was trying to retire.'

'Tommy?'

'Thomkins. You remember? The bloke who sent me out to get old Ted Hardwick to sign a bill of sale. I told you about this.'

'So you did. And his wife signed instead. What was her name?'

'She never did tell me.'

Mrs Crowley was laughing. 'I'll bet she was too busy with you on that chair. Do you know any other funny stories?'

'Oh, well, there was this girl in Cootamundra.'

'Where is that?'

'Out west, north of Wagga. Did my first posting there.'

'What happened?'

'Ah, well, I'd been there only a few weeks when this girl, who worked in the local cafe where I'd go in for lunch, asked me to take her to the local dance.'

'How old were you then?'

'Twenty-four. Anyway, I was a bit surprised, because she'd already told me she was getting married soon. Even had a ring on her finger.'

'Did you take her to the dance?'

'Yeah, but I was a bit mystified. Why didn't her fiancé take her? Oh, she said, he was away in Sydney at the time, attending a religious convention. He was an Adventist pastor, she said. Well, I picked her up at her place and off we went down the main street. But when we reached the local park, she stopped and said she didn't want to go to the dance at all.'

'She didn't?'

'No, she said she wanted me to have sex with her.'

'Really?'

'Yeah, well, I was a bit surprised. I asked her why? She said she was pretty nervous, because she didn't know anything about sex, and she was afraid she'd be hopeless on the wedding night.'

'This sounds like a tall story to me.'

'That's what I thought. I wasn't too keen on this idea, but she said it would be all right as she couldn't get pregnant at that time. Oh, yeah? I thought. I've heard that story before. But she was pretty determined. She took a condom out of her bag, saying she realised I might be a bit wary about doing it with a girl I hardly knew, so she'd borrowed one from her married sister.'

Evelyn Crowley laughed. 'She borrowed one? From her sister?'

'This is fair dinkum. Anyway, I thought, well, I can't get into trouble here. So we went into the park, right up the back where there wasn't much light, and got to work. At first, she was pretty nervous about it but soon got into the swing of it. When we finished, she was thanking me like mad and brushing the grass off her dress. "Now I know all about it," she said. "Oh, I'm so happy. Oh, now I know everything will be all right!".'

'And was it?'

'I reckon so. Every time I saw her after that, she'd give me a big wink.'

'I should think so.'

'But on the way home, I asked her why she hadn't practised for the big night with her boyfriend. "Oh, no," she said, "I could never ask him to do a thing like that. He's a virgin and proud of it!".'

Evelyn laughed so much that, after a while, he thought she was crying. She'd sat up, slapping a thigh with one hand and holding the glass high with the other and shaking. The wine was spilling, trickling over her hand and down her arm. She couldn't get out a handkerchief or tissue in time, so she licked it, still laughing.

'Are you all right?'

'Oh, yes, oh, yes! Oh, goodness me, did this ever happen again? With those Cootamundra girls?'

'Ah, yeah, five or six times, some of them married too. They'd come up to me in the street and ask me to take them to the dance. And wink.'

'Word had got around?'

'Yeah, and the funny thing was they always brought their own condoms.'

'How considerate of them!'

She took another sip of wine, kicked off the slippers and curled up on the end of the sofa near to him.

'Harry, you are the funniest man I've ever met. I think that's why I—'

He thought she was going to say 'love you,' but she didn't.

'Love to talk to you. You make it worthwhile.'

'Make what worthwhile?'

Her mood changed. She scratched her forehead with the little finger of the hand holding the glass. 'Life,' she said.

'You feel really bad some days, don't you?'

'Yes, terribly. Several times I've been close to—'

'You had a bad marriage?'

'Yes.'

'Sounds like you were not compatible?'

'No, we weren't.'

'Why did you marry him?'

'I told you, I was forced into it by my family.'

'Told to hook the bank manager?'

'Yes, I suppose that was it, that and the deception.'

'What deception?'

'The fifteen-thousand-dollar loan, years ago. They used me as the honey pot. Is that the right expression? I think I read that somewhere. Donald fell for it. He gave them the money. I think I told you all this. Well, an auditor picked up the discrepancy months later, that is after we were married. Donald was horrified. He persuaded the man to say nothing by paying off the loan himself. He had some money put away, but he had to borrow from his own family. Soon they put another little proposition to him, Ennio and Alfredo I mean. If he did not agree, they threatened to tell the bank. They'd say they hadn't understood, when he'd asked if it was encumbered. They'd even blame me, saying that their interpreter had got it wrong. It was an innocent mistake on their part. They were very sorry. They'd get off, they knew. But Donald would be sacked. So they tried that little scheme again and again and again, each time asking for a bigger and bigger favour. Each time, he gave way. Now it has grown to a massive scam. Is that the right word? It sounds too silly a word to describe what they are now doing?'

'What are they doing?'

She began to answer, but immediately he realised his mistake. He waved at her, indicated silence. She was puzzled but obeyed.

'They wouldn't tell you?' He was still pointing around.

She caught on. 'No, they would not tell me.'

He smiled approval. 'Now you tell me a funny story.'

'Me? I don't have any funny stories, only sad ones.'

'Tell me a sad one.'

She thought about it. 'All right—' Evelyn Crowley did a strange thing. She turned and stretched out along the sofa, her head on a cushion, her free hand inverted on her brow. And facing away from him. 'I'll tell you how I became a whore.'

'You're not a whore.'

'Yes, I am, but never a prostitute.'

He was surprised. A woman doing a thing like that, stretching out before a man she hardly knew. But it was her house, so she could do what she liked.

'When we moved to Canberra, about eight years ago, I was thoroughly fed up with Donald. I hated him, but I could not get out of the marriage. He knew what I'd done in Melbourne. I'd told only one person, my dear father and he, it seems, just before he died had told Donald, probably in the hope that Donald would understand me better and look after me. But he did nothing of the sort. He made it quite clear that if I ever revealed what he'd done in Melbourne—and has gone on doing for those ugly creatures, Uncle Ennio and his dreadful sons—he would tell the police about me.'

'About the man in Melbourne?'

'Yes.'

'You had a tough time.'

It was a banal sort of remark, but Becker could think of nothing better. He knew that she had changed her story about her father. He had told her husband. She was inconsistent, but it didn't seem to matter. Obviously, Evelyn was that kind of woman. She changed her story as it suited her, without explanation or apology.

'Tough is correct. I hated him.'

She took yet another sip and then opened up.

'I had an affair—with one of his colleagues I'd met at one of the bank's social get-togethers. He was a nice man, the complete opposite of Donald—outgoing, fun-loving, kind and flattering. I fell for him. He drove me home one evening, except we did not get this far. We parked up on top of Red Hill to look down at the city lights and did it in the car. I was pretty nervous at the time. I'd never done such a thing before, not while married. But he said he loved me and could not take his eyes off me. Well, he was not married, so I thought, after this had happened a few times, including here at home while Donald was away, it would be all right. In fact, I was getting ready to leave him. Everything was going along fine until one evening, when Donald took me to a big convention—bankers from all over Australia, some from overseas. I think the Governor of the Reserve Bank was there as guest speaker. We talked to all sorts of people, then I realised Donald was not with me. I had lost sight of him. So I wandered around, but in the great crush I had lost him. I stopped with my back to a high screen which cut off the cocktails area from the dining area. It was one of those wooden structures of vertical slats, which overlap but leave a space between each. I was standing there, hoping to spot Donald, when I realised two men on the other side were talking about me.'

She paused, raising her head and sipping wine before she continued.

'One of them said, "Do you know Don's wife?"'

'Yes, I do," said the other.

"Well?" asked the first man.

"Pretty well," said the second.

"Ah, she's beautiful, isn't she?"

"A knockout," the second one said. Then he lowered his voice and said something about me. It was horrible, disgusting.

"Yeah?" the other said.

"Yes," he said, "you can't stop her once she gets going. She's mad for it." I didn't hear any more, I was so shocked. They seemed to move away. I just stood there, shaking with humiliation. I felt sick; I often feel sick when I think of it.'

The glass was shaking in her hand. Becker feared it would snap.

'Let me take that,' he said.

'It's all right.' She reached out and placed it on the small table. Then she let that hand hang down, so that the nails just touched the carpet.

'And the second bloke? He was your lover?'

'Yes. I was so sick I could not stay for dinner. I had to make an excuse. I got a taxi and cleared off. When I reached home, I lay on my bed face down and cried with rage. I thought of killing him, then I thought of killing myself.'

'I'm glad you didn't.'

'Thank you, Harry.'

'So that's how it started?'

'Yes, I decided I hated all men. When I calmed down, I decided I'd fix Donald once and for all. I'd become a real whore just to humiliate him. This, I thought, was one sure way of getting rid of him. I'd behave so scandalously he'd have to divorce me. So, I began picking up men and bringing them home whenever he was away, mostly bankers. But after a while I did it for the mischief of it with just about any man I fancied. I did not care who knew about it. Then one day I told Donald what I was doing, but my little plan backfired. I expected him to be disgusted, to throw me out, perhaps hit me. But he did not. In fact, he said he knew about it already and didn't care. I could have as many men as I wished. I think that was his way of taking revenge against me, against my whole family, for what we had done to him. I felt awful. I had degraded myself all for nothing. Now I was caught in a trap of my own making.'

Evelyn was close to crying. Her body was shaking. The fingers of the inverted hand on her brow were opening and clenching, the long nails cutting into the flesh.

'Hold on,' he said. It seemed to be a hopelessly inadequate thing to say.

She gasped. 'Oh, I'm all right. I'm pretty well used to it now, Harry. I have no friends; no woman will speak to me. And all the men I knew don't care about me, they just want to have their fun with me. That's how they see me, something pitiful and stupid and trapped, a poor silly trophy wife. That's what they call a woman such as I, don't they? A trophy wife, good for nothing but looking good.' She winced.

Becker didn't know what to do to help her, so he just let it all come out. Perhaps that was all she expected.

She ran a finger through her hair.

'You know, Donald has been dead ten days and already I have had phone calls from six former lovers offering their sympathy and wanting to call on me, flowers and wine in hand—' She shrugged. 'I am tired of this life, Harry, so very tired. The only thing that keeps me going is that I've found my daughter, but I cannot speak to her. She's sure to ask me what happened all those years ago. I'm afraid I'd tell her the truth, that I'd killed her father.' She exhaled, took a long, deep breath, and held it. It was as though she'd decided never to breathe again, but she did at last. 'So there you have it, the sorry story of Evelyn the tart.'

'You're not a tart.'

'Thank you, Harry.' She glanced at her wristwatch, then sat up. 'My God, six thirty! I'd better put the rice on and start chopping things.' She shot to her feet, stepped into the slippers.

'Come and talk to me in the kitchen. Get yourself another glass, then come and tell me another funny story while I work. After that confession, I need cheering up.'

He stood up, but hesitated. 'I won't stay.'

She turned on him. 'You won't? I thought that's why you came?'

'Just for a drink and a chat.'

'About my offer? It still stands, Harry. When are you free for a day or two?'

'This weekend.'

'Good, let's do something together, and I don't mean in bed. Let's go to the coast, walk on a beach!' He did not answer. 'Let's go to Wagga? You'd like that, wouldn't you? See if that man will sell you a share?'

'No—'

'We could go in my car. It's quite comfortable. You could drive. It would be good for both of us. You look so unhappy sometimes. It hurts me to see you like that. I need a break too, Harry. I'm going out of my mind. That awful little man has left me all this money, lots of it, God knows why. I'm not worthy of it. I hated him, I loathed him for being the calculating little insect he was. It was hell being married to him for seventeen years. He used to tell me over and over that he adored me. He used to ask me to lie naked on my bed and let him kiss me all over.'

'All over?'

'Yes, everywhere—on my feet, my bottom, between my legs, everywhere.'

'How did you feel about that?'

'Disgusted. All that kissing. It was like being crawled over by a big, fat, slimy slug. I'd wake up some nights and realise he was sucking my nipples or sniffing my...

God, he couldn't get it up unless I—' She shuddered. 'I hated him. I don't want to be adored. I'm not a piece of art, something you can show your friends. I think he wanted me to be a whore. That way he could show me off, saying in effect: Isn't she wonderful? The greatest whore in Canberra, and she's all mine!'

He was startled, not knowing how to handle such a woman.

'You're free of him now.'

'That's not the problem! I'm not free of myself. I can never be free unless I change and I can't change, not by myself. I need help, Harry. Please understand, I need someone like you. A good man, an honest man.'

'I'm a crook, Evelyn. I was thrown out of the force for corruption.'

'You've made mistakes, but none as bad as mine. We need each other, Harry. I'm not trying to trap you. I just want to be with you and talk to you and hear your stories and try to be like you. You know the story I liked best? The one about your wife—how you came to marry her. You married a woman you hardly knew to save her from shame and possibly death. You are a most unusual man, Harry.' She squirmed. 'Please, let us be friends, good friends, good companions. I trust you. Let's go away together, somewhere far from here. Let's start anew. I'm Evalina Scarafini now. I'm going back to what I was when I was a girl, young and innocent. That's a new start, isn't it? I'll never be Evelyn Crowley again.'

'Evalina?'

'Yes, Evalina. I told you that first day, I—'

She was standing close, her arms open, hands open, palms turned upward, pleading.

'I'll give you the money, whatever you want. You won't have to pay it back. No strings attached. Please help me, Harry. I understand how you feel. You have your pride. You don't want to be a kept boy, do you? I would not keep you. In fact, I'd give you a million dollars if you like. I wish I were poor again. I was a better woman then. I was innocent, a shy woman, ashamed of what I'd done to that man. I would help Papà in the shop, polishing the apples, stacking the shelves, working the cash register, my fingers aching with pain, and smiling at the lovely customers and asking about their children and thinking about the child I had lost. But I was sort of happy then, my breasts used to tingle with happiness every time I'd see a little girl. Now I'm sick and sad, a wreck. I've done some terrible things. I want someone just to... to... look after me, a lovely man who'd give me a—'

He thought she was going to say, Give me a child! But she did not. She did not get that far. She broke down. Her head went down, her hands went up to her face, but did not touch it. He put his arms around her, loosely, both touching and not touching. In the car that day by the lake, the day Donald Crowley had died, she'd asked him to hold her and it had seemed to help. So, they stood that way for some time. Occasionally, there was some noise from outside, perhaps a car tooting, or children calling. Or even a magpie carolling. Something was happening out there in the world, but for them, at that moment, there was only one story.

She stood with head bowed, her elbows against his chest. He could smell her, the scents of her body and the dry wine of her breath. He wanted to run his hands over her back, up to her neck and down to her hips. And pull her in close. But if he did, she would kiss him. She'd go for him and he'd have to go for her. He'd not be able to stop. He'd have her in bed in no time flat or up against a wall, banging away at her, like they did it in the movies these days, knocking the pictures off the wall, the house rattling with lust, while she moaned and groaned. While he gave it to her, everything she wanted.

'I'm so sorry,' she said at last.

'Are you all right?'

'Yes.'

'I don't want any money, Evelyn.'

'I understand.'

'You are a lovely woman.'

'Oh—' She raised her head. Her lips were so close he could have kissed them. She was waiting for him to do it, but he did not. It would have been easy to give her a child, if that was what she wanted, if it were not too late. She was not all that old, just nudging forty, but he could not live with her. She was too generous, too overwhelming, too demanding. Besides, he did not trust her. He loved her but did not like her. What if they had a child? Was that all she wanted? Just a stud to service her? What would happen if he did give her a substitute for Christine? Would she get rid of him, as his bitch of a wife in Sydney had done, when she'd kicked him out—no longer wanted on the voyage. And if he proved to be a problem, would she pay someone to solve it for her?

He didn't know what to do with her, so he stepped back.

'I'll give you a call,' he said.

He didn't mean it, and she knew he didn't mean it.

'I understand,' she said.

'Are you okay?'

'Yes.'

'You're sure?' He was holding her shoulders now.

'Yes, yes, don't worry. I've been stupid, I know. I've insulted you, haven't I? No one can buy a good man. Go on, Harry. Thank you for dropping in.'

He kissed her on a cheek, the way she had kissed him that afternoon, but it seemed like kissing goodbye at a train station or an airport, perfunctory. She walked behind him to the front door. It was the same slow, thoughtful walk he'd known from the start, as if a decision had to be made. Like asking a stranger if he did private jobs.

He opened the door, stepped out.

When he reached the car, he looked back. She was standing in the doorway, arms folded, leaning against the frame. Her face showed nothing, not a flicker. He drove away thinking he'd made a serious mistake. He had rejected her, a Calabrian woman. She could be more than dangerous. Look what she'd done to that man in Melbourne.

CHAPTER 20

He did not work on the weekends. Some bloke who worked full time in Treasury did that shift. The poor bastard, some Indian or Pakistani trying to save a packet so he could buy a petrol station, get into business, make some real money for his family, for himself, for the future. Becker admired him, admired his faith in the future. He, Becker, had no future. Several times he thought of ringing Evelyn. He'd promised he would, but each time he decided to do it, he decided not to do it. He didn't want another emotional scene. He was a coward; he knew. He didn't know how to handle such a woman. He had to get out of Canberra, try to forget her. He'd go back to Wagga, see what was doing there, perhaps get a job. To hell with Adeline and the kids. Let her sing for her money. She had a bloke living with her now, so he'd heard, a live-in lover, who was getting free bed and board for which Becker was paying. That hurt him. She was a cheat. The more he thought of her, the more she looked like her mother.

On Saturday afternoon, he went out to Bruce Stadium to watch the Raiders play the Panthers. The Raiders won by a mile. He tried to be thrilled, but it was just a way of filling in time. In the old days, when he was stationed at Hurstville, he'd played for St George. He'd never made it to the big-time, although occasionally he had played in Reserve Grade. He was no great shakes as a player—only two tries in a season. But it had been fun. That's why he'd been at the Leagues Club, and that's how he'd met Adeline. She'd been sitting beside him at a large table and they'd got talking. And he'd asked her for a date. She had been a shy girl, dolled up in skin-tight red satin with a little black bow at the throat, thrilled to be chatting to a footballer, a real glamour boy who'd scored a try for Saints that very day. He'd asked her for a date and she'd agreed, uncertain because she was young and eager and a virgin. You hadn't needed to ask her if she was. You just had to look at her and you knew she was. It was the innocence and desperate friendliness in her pretty pussy-cat eyes.

That night he treated himself to whiting and salad at the Seven Seas Cafe in Bunda Street, then drifted along to the Centre Cinema and saw the director's cut of Mildred Pierce. He watched Joan Crawford working her fingers to the bone, trying to satisfy the greed of both her indolent lover and her bitchy little daughter. Finally, she realised the lover was also screwing her daughter. At least that's what was implied. In those days, there was never any actual screwing on screen, not like today. You couldn't go to the movies without seeing heaving bottoms, and that's not all. Well, Mildred got so mad she shot the bastard. That's what the police thought. But the catty little daughter had killed him in a fit of rage, because he was laughing at her. He wouldn't marry a little tramp like her. Besides, her mother had a lot more money.

Becker left the cinema thinking love was a trap. No one really loved anyone else, they loved only what they could get out of others. And yet he told himself he'd have to go to Evelyn, talk it out with her. Tell her he loved her, but he didn't want anything from her—not any favours, not any money, not even her lovely body—just her bemused smile when he told her stories and the sweet sound of her womanly voice. Or, if not her voice, then a few resonances such as the ring of her footsteps by the lake and the secrets of her smile.

'Hey, Harry!'

He stopped dead. Palfreyman came up to him, hands in pockets and grinning like an ape.

'What is it?'

'Where's the card?'

'What card?'

'The one the derro gave you.'

'Buster?'

'Is that his name?'

'I don't have any card.'

'Don't frig around, mate. You were spotted a week ago. He gave you a credit card.'

'Where is he?'

'In hospital. Someone ran over him last night.'

'Deliberately?'

'You could say that.'

'Why?'

'They went through his pockets, looking for that card.'

'How did they know he had a credit card?'

Palfreyman baulked. 'Eh? I don't know. Maybe they saw him pick it up.'

'And maybe they didn't. Maybe some cop told them.'

'Eh?'

Palfreyman was stumped, you could see. Maybe the thought had just hit him too. Behind them, Adams was watching, his little head down. It was not so much a little head as the head of a little boy. A nasty little boy with a nasty little smile.

'How is he?'

'Who? Buster? He won't walk again. Lucky one of our patrols came along a few seconds later or they'd have finished him off.'

'Who were they?'

'You know who, the guys who killed Torrence.'

'How do you know about them?'

'Buster told us, in hospital.'

The cinema crowd was dispersing. Soon he would be alone with these cops. He wondered how they knew where he was. It wouldn't surprise him if he found a tracer in the lining of his jacket, or at least in his car.

'I don't have it.'

'You'd better find it, mate. That's evidence.'

'Get stuffed.'

Palfreyman smiled. He was tall and hard, built like a second row forward in a Rugby pack. Becker wouldn't have a chance against him. He tried to walk away, but the policeman caught him.

'Listen, Harry, you're in deep shit.'

'Keep your hands off me.'

'Just be careful, mate. People are watching.'

'You keep away from Evelyn.'

Palfreyman laughed. 'Evelyn, eh?'

'She's had a hard time.'

'Yeah? Giving her a hard time, are you, Harry?'

Becker tried to ignore it. 'She can't take any more.'

'Why'd that be, Harry?'

'What do you mean?'

'She knows more than she admits.'

'Knows what?'

Palfreyman smiled, even winked. It was a matey wink. He had that kind of manner, so matey that one day, irrespective of what you'd done, you'd be telling him everything, as one mate to another over a beer at the local. He came up close, patted Becker's jacket.

'What've you got here, Harry? A shooter? Where'd you get that?'

'My boss lent it to me.'

'Is it registered?'

'He said it was.'

'He's not supposed to do that, Harry. Not without notifying us.'

'I need something.'

'Yeah? Worried, are you?'

'Nothing worries me more than a smart-arse cop.'

'Going to drop me, are you, Harry?'

Becker was about to hit the impudent bastard. Instead, he began to walk away.

'Hey, Harry! You see a lot of movies? You ever see that one, Body Heat? Remember that scene where this dumb lawyer is at this jazz concert and this dame, dressed all in white so he can't fail to see her, comes walking up this aisle, swinging her hips? And this guy is looking at her and getting hard for her? He can't help himself, can he? Pretty soon she's asking him to do a little job for her, like kill her rich husband. What does he get for his trouble? Life in the slammer while she does a bunk with the loot.'

Becker tensed, something cutting into his brain. It wasn't the pain he got when he turned his head quickly. It was cold, hard, paralysing fear. Something was coming, he knew. Bad news.

'What about it?'

'You see the resemblance?'

'She doesn't look like that.'

'We've been watching her for some time.'

'Her?' At least he got that much out.

'Her and her husband, both of 'em. Now he's dead, and where does that leave her? A filthy rich widow. Yeah, we've seen his will. She gets the house, the money, two smart cars, all those paintings, all his shares in blue-chip companies and half his big fat superannuation payout from the bank. She's rolling in it, mate.'

He felt sick. His knees went weak. His face, he knew, must be white with fear. Palfreyman was patting him on a shoulder. From the police point of view, it was open and shut. Evelyn Crowley had killed her husband for a bagful of loot.

'She wasn't there. He did it alone, he jumped.'

'Yeah? What's that prove?'

'She didn't kill him.'

'Yeah? You know the best way to kill a man, Harry?'

'No idea.'

'Get the poor bastard to do the job himself. That way there's no evidence, no prints, nothing—and best of all, no connection. You can be miles away at the time with a dozen witnesses to back you up. You hear what I'm saying?'

Becker was surprised. These were very much his own thoughts.

'How could she make him jump?'

'What do you think all those letters were about? You were the poor sucker. She needed someone to swear in court there was a genuine blackmail attempt, when there wasn't one at all, was there? It was all a set-up, Harry, and you fell for it. Hey, mate, did Torrence tell you who dictated those letters?'

He dared not think. His body was shaking.

'She did! Yeah, they cooked up the plot between 'em. She knew old Donald was teetering on the edge. All he needed was a little shove and goodbye hubby.'

'You're lying!'

'Lying? Hey, George—' He was addressing Adams. 'Harry here says we're lying. Look, mate, we've got it all on tape. You want to come around to the office and listen? Come on, come around now!'

Becker stared at him. He couldn't speak and he couldn't think. His brain had seized up. Unwittingly, he put a hand in a pocket—the one with the Webley.

Palfreyman laughed. 'Go on, Harry, pull it.'

'Why don't you arrest her?'

'Ah, mate, there are bigger things at stake.'

'What things?'

'Can't tell you, not at this stage.'

Becker glanced at Adams, whose fingers were now inside his coat, no doubt touching his Smith and Wesson, police issue. He was using his left hand. At last Becker remembered where he'd seen that cop—on the range at Majura. He was a member of the gun club. One day out there he'd watched as Adams had hit five bulls in a row at fifty metres. Just like swatting flies. He'd used a heavy, long-barrelled weapon, very little kick—someone had told him, but he couldn't remember what it was. Adams was fast, very fast. Becker would not have a chance, especially with the Webley. It was old, and the ammunition was old. It might not even fire.

'You're not worth it.'

'Nor is she, mate. Ask her, Harry, what was her maiden name?'

He'd taken a slow, deep breath. He felt better now. 'Scarafini.'

'Yeah, same as those monkeys down in Melbourne, Uncle Ennio and his two obnoxious sons. They were all in it together. The pickin's were good, eh? And now she doesn't have to share them with Torrence, does she?'

He felt sick. For a moment, he thought he'd faint. His heart had stopped, then picked up again. He was going to protest that they'd got it wrong, Evelyn would not do such a thing. But he did not. Maybe they were right.

'How do you know all this?'

'We know a lot of things, mate.'

'She didn't kill Torrence. It was someone else, much bigger.'

'How do you know?'

Becker was going to give him the credit card, but he did not. He hated this cop. He could have shot the bastard and to hell with everything. He was going to die soon, so what did it matter? Yet, while there was still Evelyn Crowley and her kind words, her friendship, her sweet chuckles when he told her stories, he couldn't.

Palfreyman persisted. 'Where's the card, Harry?'

'Get stuffed.'

'That's withholding evidence, you know.'

He did not answer, still walking. Palfreyman came after him. So did Adams sauntering, one step at a time, but a bit to one side, so Palfreyman would be out of the line of fire.

'It's the law. I can arrest you, mate.'

Becker kept on walking.

'Go on, Harry, go out there tonight and shag her! In no time, she'll be asking you to do her a little favour, like kill Uncle Ennio. That way she won't have to share the loot with anyone, except you. But that wouldn't be any problem, would it? All she'd have to do is import someone and it'd be goodbye Harry, wouldn't it? You're the fall guy, mate. See if I'm not right.'

'You're shit, Palfreyman.'

The policeman fell back, grinning. He had a happy grin, just like a great big overgrown schoolboy. Too clever by half.

'Yeah, I know, but I'm good shit. There's a difference.'

Becker was still angry when he reached Forrest. He'd gone through two stop signs, nearly collecting a bus at one. He sat in his car for a while, looking at the house, uncertain. Somehow what Palfreyman had said had made sense. Was it all a set-up? Had he been taken for a sucker from the beginning? Was she innocent? Or was she a scheming bitch? He seemed to have entered a world where the good things of day turned into the bad things of night at the flick of a switch.

On his first day at Darlinghurst, everyone had been friendly, shaking his hand and calling him Harry as though he was some sort of star. Or some sort of prize. Sydney cops were supposed to be hard and ruthless. They had to battle with crims and villains and felons and two-time losers. You could get your head shot off in a place like Darlo, as it was called, or the 'Loo or the Cross. They'd shown him around the boozers and brothels and clipjoints and the alleys where the deadbeats hung out and the parks where the deals were made, small packets changing hands for stolen money. It had all been an eye-opener for a boy from the bush.

To show him the ropes, they'd cuffed two Lebanese for selling hash, taken them in, protesting. They didn't have anything they claimed. 'Nothin', nothin' bad! Never touch dat shit!' The boys went through their pockets and out popped two small white packets. The Lebs had been amazed. They were really innocent, anyone could see that except Becker. So, they were locked up and left there, yelling for their lawyer. They didn't have one. The poor bastards were still yelling when the shift ended. It was a great joke, everyone grinning. Someone had said, Time for a quick one!

So, they got into their civvies and went down to the Bay Hotel in the 'Loo and had a quick one, then another. They were on the second, Becker's shout, when a big man walked in. Someone said, 'Here's Dickie!' Becker turned, a smile ready. The big man came up to them, grinning in a lazy way, as if he always wore a grin—a kind of mask, behind which he could play any part that suited him. He had a decent paunch and wore braces as well as a thick leather belt with a big brass buckle. Later Becker was to learn he wore the braces to hold his pants up. The belt was for dealing with anyone who gave him a hard time.

Big Dickie Whitford had a red face and small piggish ears, pointy. A pork-pie hat was perched on his head. Even with the hat you could see he was bald. He looked from one to the other, his mouth open, his fat tongue slightly protruding. His small eyes squizzing.

'Who's this, then?'

Someone piped up. 'This's the new bloke, Harry.'

'Harry, eh?'

Becker put out a hand. 'Harry Becker.'

The big man took it, enfolded it with his own two hands. It was a welcoming handshake, like being inducted into some sort of club, a privileged club. Nothing could have been more comforting. Whitford stared at Becker, peering into his eyes, into his body and his brain. Even into his soul. It was at that moment, for the first time in his life, that Becker realised he had a soul. And it was trembling like a leaf.

'Harry Becker? The new bloke, eh?'

'He's been at Hurstville.'

'Hurstville, eh? St George territory, eh?'

'He played for the Saints, he was tellin' us.'

'Oh, just a few games in Reserves,' Becker protested.

'Yeah? The boys treat you all right down there, Harry?'

'Hurstville? Yeah.'

'Before that he was in the bush,' someone said.

'Yeah?'

'Wagga,' Becker said.

'Wagga, eh? Nice town, Wagga. Once did a stint there. Never had any problems in Wagga.'

He said it as if there never could be problems in any town he graced with his presence. Or, if there were, there soon wouldn't be any. He extracted a roll of notes from a trousers pocket and pulled off a rubber band.

'What're we all drinkin'?'

They all said beer, raising their glasses. Whitford made a circling sign to the barman, who didn't even nod. Every time Whitford walked in, you did what he wanted, no questions asked. He peeled off a couple of ten spots from the roll.

'Good day at the races, Dickie?'

'Races? Yeah, every day's a good day at the races, even when they're not runnin'.'

Everyone laughed. Becker was surprised that any man these days carried a roll of notes, in a trouser pocket too. It seemed old-fashioned, straight out of the hard days out west, when no man carried a wallet lest some light-fingered bastard lifted it. You kept your money close to your skin. Either Whitford was naturally old-fashioned or it was all part of an act. You couldn't exactly see how much a man might have in a wallet, but all the world could see a roll—and make a quick calculation. On that day Whitford was carrying a packet, a real packet, three or four hundred. And he didn't care who could see. Of course, this was some time before the royal commission. After that, people were more careful. Secret cameras could be recording every move. Even in a police car or the men's toilet at work.

'Been lookin' after yer, have they, son?'

Whitford was addressing him. 'What? Oh, yeah, shown me the sights.'

'Think you'll be happy here?'

'Sure, happy as Larry.'

They all laughed.

'That's all right then, eh?'

Another man came in. Someone said, 'Here's Vincenzo!'

So Whitford indicated to the barman. Just a flick of one finger. The barman had it half-poured already, because he knew when Whitford was happy, everyone was happy. Someone passed the foaming glass to the newcomer. He was a thin man, trim, lean in the face and mean in the eyes. He had small, dark, unsmiling eyes and curly, black locks and a long, pointed tongue that flicked across his thin lips like a lizard's, testing the air.

Whitford beamed all around. 'We all right? Everyone got one?'

'Yeah,' they all said.
'Happy days, boys!'
'Happy days, Dickie!'

CHAPTER 21

He got out of the car and walked up to the house. It was in darkness, except for a glow from behind the curtains of one room. He guessed it was a bedroom, probably hers. As he approached the porch, outside lights flicked on. Most likely a security camera had snapped him. He rang the doorbell and waited. He was thinking of ringing a third time, when a light came on in the hall. The inner door opened a little. He couldn't see her clearly through the safety screen—just a dark shape with the light behind her, a woman who was both there and not there.

'Evelyn, it's me.'

'Harry? What are you doing here?'

'I've got to see you.'

'Have you? Well, I don't want to see you! I offered you everything, my hopes and my money and my friendship and my body for what it's worth and—'

'You're in trouble.'

'What?'

'The police know all about you.'

'What do you mean?'

'They have you on tape, you and Torrence.'

'Me and Vince? Doing what? In bed? So what? Are you jealous?'

She was angry, no doubt about it.

'Planning it.'

'Planning what?'

'To kill your husband.'

She gasped. 'What are you saying?'

'Let's talk inside.'

'No!'

'You're a lying bitch, Evelyn.'

'How dare you! Go away!'

'You want me to say it out loud? You want the whole street to hear?'

He waited. Her breathing was heavy now, deep and exhaustive. She was afraid, he could sense. Very afraid.

'I was in bed,' she said.

'I know it's late.' It was about eleven o'clock now.

'What has happened?'

'That's what I want to know.'

'If you are going to come in here and harass me—'

She paused. He waited. She was tense and resentful, he knew. He listened for sounds, on the street, anywhere. Not a bird calling, not a car passing.

Then a lock clicked. The screen door opened. He pushed his way past her, so close he could have held her and kissed her or killed her. It did not seem to matter now which. This time she didn't smell so much of perfume as whiskey. Her hair was tousled, and she was wearing a robe over a negligee. The neckline was low and her breasts were almost popping out. Her feet were bare. She snapped at him.

'What exactly do you want?'

'Let's go in here.'

He took her by an arm and tried to propel her into the sitting room, but she resisted.

'Don't push me! Don't even touch me!'

He went into the room, switched on a table lamp. The room was warm, air-conditioned. Probably the whole house too. She followed. 'Why are you here?'

'You'd better sit.'

'Don't tell me what to do in my own house!'

'All right then, stand!'

She was going to argue, perhaps snap and snarl at him, but slowly she sat on the sofa with the air of someone not quite awake. Like that first day he saw her, not quite with it, perhaps affected by drugs or drink or just bad memories. This time she looked a mess—rumpled, worn out and yet still handsome, especially in the soft light. Her eyes were hard, shifty, yet puzzled.

'Have they caught them?'

'Caught who?'

'The people who made Donald do what he did, at the bank?'

'No, I don't think they ever will.'

'Why?'

'Those people are never caught. They have the game sewn up.'

'What is this about Vince?'

He sat beside her. 'He did a little job for you, didn't he? Pretended to be a blackmailer, all for five thousand dollars. That was the deal, wasn't it?'

'So what?'

'It was all a ruse, wasn't it? Not a genuine blackmail attempt at all. It was all cooked up so you could show the letters to your husband. So he'd take fright and jump?'

'Don't speak that way!'

'It's a clever way to murder a man, isn't it? Get him to do the job for you.' He was echoing Palfreyman's words, but that was it in a nutshell.

She put a hand to her breast. She looked alarmed, as though she'd suddenly seen herself in a mirror. And didn't like what she'd seen. 'My God, what are you saying?'

'That's how the police figure it. They've been watching you, Evelyn. Watching and listening for a long time.'

'Watching me? Why should they spy on me?'

'Because of your husband. They knew what he was doing at the bank.'

'Really? If so, why didn't they arrest him?'

'I'd say they wanted to know where the money was going.'

'What money? And what's that got to do with me?'

'Nothing at all.'

'So?'

He stared at her, taking her in, her body and her face and her fear. She was a cheat and a liar who'd known pretty well what had been going on at the bank. Her cousins had told her, and her husband had been sick with fear he'd be caught. So she'd cooked up a little scheme to get rid of him, a man she'd detested. And to bag a lot of money at the same time.

'You set me up, Evelyn.'

'What?'

'You and Torrence schemed to kill him by a clever ruse, didn't you? But there was just one little problem, wasn't there? If you took those letters to him, he'd immediately suspect you were behind them. He knew you detested him. So you needed an independent witness, didn't you? An outsider, who'd swear in court if need be, confirming there was a blackmail attempt.'

'What?'

'And that's where I came in, wasn't it? You played me for a sucker. I was the bunny, the fall guy, as they say. You used me.'

'That's not true!'

'You set me up, just as you set up your husband years ago, with that caper in the local bank in Melbourne. It was easy, wasn't it? All you had to do was flash your tits at him? Like you're doing now.'

'How dare you!'

'You hooked him then and years later you decided to get rid of him. And you did, didn't you? You frightened him to death.'

She was shocked, genuinely shocked. 'No!'

He seized her by a shoulder, raised the other hand as if to hit her. 'Stop lying, Evelyn!'

'Oh, God, what is happening?' She began to squirm. She was trapped. But he had to be careful. A woman like that, a rich widow. All she had to do was make a phone call, and he'd be next.

'Did you promise to share the loot with Vince?'

'What loot?'

'Crowley's money.'

'Of course not. Why would I do that?'

'You wouldn't share it, would you? You wanted the lot, but you feared he'd go on demanding more, time after time. Soon he'd be screwing more than your body. He'd take your money. He'd impoverish you. And you wouldn't be able to do anything about it, would you? You'd be trapped the way you trapped your husband back in Melbourne all those years ago.'

'No, no—'

'So you had him killed!'

'No!'

'That's what the police think.'

'The police? How do you know?'

'They told me, less than half an hour ago.'

'Oh, God, what are you saying?'

'You told your cousins down in Melbourne you had a little problem, didn't you? They sent someone up here to solve it for you—that fat man and some cheap punk. That's how it works in a family like yours, isn't it?'

'No!'

She was shaking her head now, hands to her face, starting to moan.

'Please don't, please don't—'

'Why did you kill that other man, Evelyn?'

'What other man?'

'The one in Melbourne, the lawyer.'

'I didn't kill him.'

'Oh, yeah? You can't take rejection, can you?'

'It was an accident! I forgot where we were!'

'Six storeys up? You knew where you were all right.'

She was rattled. Her hands shook, her eyes quivered, her teeth chattered. She tried again to speak, but whatever it was, it did not come out. She began to break down.

'No, please, please—'

He shook her again. 'You love to be adored, don't you? Crowley decked you out in the finest clothes money could buy. He made you an adornment, not just for his house or even his piss-weak sort of lust, but for his money-grubbing little world, where everything has a price? If you want to fuck my wife, you have to do me a little favour first. That's how he got to the top so fast, isn't it?'

'Stop it! Stop it!'

'But you couldn't bear his touch, could you? What did you call him? A fat, slimy slug crawling over you? Sniffing you like a dog. You had to squash him, didn't you?'

'No, no, please, I've killed no one!'

'No one?'

'You mean Vince? I did not kill him.'

'Then who did?'

'The other people.'

'What other people?'

She shook her head, hands to her face.

'Who are they?'

'I can't tell you.'

'Why can't you?'

'Omertà,' she said, so faintly he did not quite catch it. He leaned close, so close that he could have kissed her. Her breath was coming fast. She was scared, really scared.

'What?'

'Omertà,' she said again.

It was one of the few Italian words he did know. They used to talk about it in the force. If you squeal, you're dead.

Becker watched her. Her head was down, her face screwed up in pain. Perhaps she did not kill Crowley. And maybe it was an accident down in Melbourne. A hot-tempered Italian girl, betrayed, scorned. It could happen to anyone. As for Torrence, he had no hard evidence. Perhaps he was wrong. Maybe someone else had killed that creep, someone much bigger, much more dangerous. What had Buster told him? They'd given Torrence five dollars, then they'd killed him. That didn't sound like family honour. More like business gone wrong.

He waited until she stopped shaking. She had crumpled now, sitting back, crying. Hands to her face, her eyes. She was sure to collapse and beg for pity. They always did in the movies when they were caught out, even the cold-blooded killers. But she was not a cold-blooded killer. She was an impulsive woman, who did stupid things no matter how much she tried to be the perfect wife, the self-possessed woman with nothing to do each day except her nails and her hair and stroll around galleries looking elegantly cool and collected. And picking up men.

He looked around, even at the windows, expecting to see a face. Or at least an eye. He glanced at the ceiling, at the light fittings, the temperature control on the wall by the door. Still, he saw nothing. Nor would he. The bugs would be well hidden. No doubt the tapes were rolling, getting every word she'd said. There could be a knock at the door any minute now, the police. Or someone else?

He did not know what to do with her, so he patted her on the shoulder, more a comfort than a scold. Even so, it took a long time to get her to open up.

'Please believe me, Harry, I had nothing to do with Vince's death.'

'And your husband?'

'I wanted him to go to the police, tell them all about it. But he wouldn't. So I thought if he thought someone else knew what he was doing, he'd give up and confess.'

'Why would he? He could go to jail.'

'Because there was a blackmailer—'

'There was no blackmail!'

'No, but if he believed there was, he'd have to do something about it, wouldn't he?'

'Like jump?'

'No, no, go to the police!'

Becker was not impressed, but he relaxed. The storm was over. He released her, put an arm along the back of the sofa, encircling her shoulders without touching.

'That's a lot of crap, isn't it? It didn't matter what he did. If he jumped he'd be dead, and if he went to the police, he wouldn't get as far as the court. You knew that, didn't you?'

'No, no, please—'

'Whatever he did, he'd be dead.'

'Don't say that!'

'And you'd collect a pile of money, wouldn't you?'

'I did not expect a penny. I thought he hated me.'

'Oh, yeah? You know the law as well as I do, probably better. Even if he left you nothing at all, you could contest the will, and you'd get half. The wife always does. Probably more if there were no other claimants, maybe the lot. The money has to go somewhere, that's the law.'

He studied her. Evelyn Crowley looked a lot older, a crumpled woman, slumped and miserable and finished. She could have been acting, but perhaps she had some sort of soul, some sense of regret.

'Pretty ironic, isn't it? He jumped, just like your boyfriend in Melbourne. This time you were not there to do the pushing. You weren't there to see him hit the pavement. No one could touch you this time.'

'Please don't!'

'It's the truth, isn't it?'

She did not reply.

'Isn't it?'

'Yes!'

He was amazed. She had just confessed to killing her lover, while the police were possibly listening. Possibly they were not. But she didn't seem to care. It was too late to stop her now. What if the police heard? Too bad for her. She'd given him the run-around for too long. He'd lost a lot of sleep over her. He'd tried to help her. Now it was all coming out. She was a bitch, rotten to the core. Let the police have her. Let justice be done.

'So, you set out to get rid of him one way or the other?'

'Yes!'

'Even if that meant killing him?'

'Yes!'

'Now we're getting somewhere. Why did you do it?'

She shook her head. 'I'm sick, Harry, very sick.'

She really was, he knew. There was no need to press her on that point. She too had fallen a long way, six floors with the man she'd pushed years ago. She just hadn't hit the concrete yet. 'What am I to do with you, Evelyn?'

'Just shoot me.'

He pulled her head towards him, intending only to pat her cheek, try to cheer her up, get her talking, letting it all come out. But she collapsed against him, so he had to hold her. She began to cry.

'I'm sorry, Harry. I'm so sorry.'

They remained that way, her head on his shoulder, not moving except for her spasmodic breathing and occasional shudders. Looking down on her, he could see that one breast had slipped out of the negligee. It was a big breast but not too big, not yet pendant. But it would be soon. Just a few more years. He thought of touching it, even kissing it, but to do that would have been to give in. She would soon have him where she wanted.

Suddenly she began to speak. 'Alfredo told me one day—'

'Your cousin in Melbourne?'

'Yes, he told me about the money. They weren't robbing the bank, they were just sending money overseas, a lot of it.'

'Whose money?'

'I don't know. Theirs, I suppose.'

'Theirs or someone else's?'

'I don't know. I just don't know!'

He raised a hand. This was getting dangerous. What if the wrong people were listening? They'd try to kill her. 'Keep your voice down.' Then dropped his own to a whisper. 'He knew how to do it, didn't he?'

'Yes.'

'Where was it going?'

'Nowhere, nowhere at all.'

'What do you mean? Money can't go nowhere. It must end up in an account somewhere. In Italy?' He was guessing, but he wasn't far wrong.

'I think so.'

'Does it go to a bank? What bank?'

'I just don't know!'

He was going to change the subject, but she muttered something. 'What's that?'

'Nebbia.'

'Say again?'

'Nebbia, that's what he said. It means fog.'

'What the hell did he mean?'

'I don't know!'

'Why did he tell you?'

'We were having a drink, and he was laughing and smoking and blowing smoke in my face the way he does, not thinking of anyone else and telling me how clever they were—as if I were one of them, one of the family. And I'm not, and I wish I could get out!'

'Into a fog, he said?'

'Yes, yes. He said it's in a bank and the bank doesn't know it's there.'

'How the hell can they do that?'

'I don't know!'

He looked at her. She seemed to be worn out, finished. Suddenly she spoke.

'It may be in a bank in Sal—'

He slammed a hand over her mouth, hissed into an ear.

'Shut up!'

She gasped under his hand.

'Don't say a word,' he whispered.

He'd made a terrible mistake. If she'd named the bank, she'd soon be dead. And if he got in the way, so would he. Perhaps she'd said too much already. Carefully he withdrew the hand, still whispering.

'The bank people woke up to him, didn't they? They called in the cops, who persuaded them to let him go on as before, hoping they'd find out where it was going? Hoping he'd talk? That's why they've been watching you for months.'

'I suppose so.'

'You are one of them, aren't you?'

'No!'

He raised a hand again. 'Don't lie to me, Evelyn!'

'Please, I tried to get out of it!'

'You're a criminal in a family of criminals.'

'Don't say that!' She was crying now. 'What could I do? If you were Italian, you'd know!'

He watched her with both disgust and pity. Yeah, he knew how it was. Once you're in, you're in. You can never get out. That's how Whitford had sucked him in, along with the others. When you were in the force, you were part of a family. No one went against the family, no one ratted on a mate. If you did, you had no future. If things got out of hand, you might have no life.

She took one of his hands and placed it over the naked breast. At first, he thought it was just another of her tricks. He should have taken it away, but he let it stay there, cupped over the breast, the nipple hard and secret in the palm of his hand. He remembered the incident outside the National Gallery, when they'd shaken hands. She'd touched the palm of his with one finger, very lightly. Had that been an invitation to bed or the subtle setting of the trap? Probably a bit of both.

He whispered in an ear. 'You've got to get out, Evelyn.'

'No, let's just sit here.'

'You can't stay here.'

'What's the point of running?'

'I'll look after you.'

She glanced up, surprised. 'You really do love me?'

'I said you're beautiful, that's all.'

'Even looking like this, an old bag and a lush?'

'You drink a lot?'

'Too much, I'm afraid—too much whiskey and too many pills.'

'How many have you taken?'

'Two, I think.'

'You think?'

'Perhaps three.'

'Why do you do it?'

'Why?' She sighed. 'I'm fed up, Harry. I have no hope now. I thought yesterday for a moment when you came to me, came to eat and drink and talk, that you might—'

'Go to bed with you?'

'No, go away with me for the weekend. But you're afraid of me, aren't you? You despise me, don't you? I wanted you to give me a baby, but you wouldn't, would you? I need a baby, Harry, one I could keep and love and encourage and—'

'Any number of men could have done that for you.'

'No, no, I hated them, because I hated myself.'

He pushed her away. 'Get dressed. We're getting out of this.'

She shrank back. 'Where are we going?'

'I don't know. Get dressed!'

'What? No, you go. I'll wait.'

'I'll look after you.'

'After all I've told you?'

Their whispering had risen. No doubt whoever was listening could not quite hear what was being said, but they'd know the game was up. This man and this woman knew about the bugs—and most likely were getting out. Someone would arrive tonight. He didn't know where he'd take her. His room with the Indians was too well known, and the killers would check every motel. They'd both be dead before dawn.

'Come on, Evelyn, move yourself. Stand up!'

She did so unsteadily. 'Harry, I didn't mean you to get involved in this. I just wanted you to find my daughter. You found her. I've told you everything I know. They'll kill me now. Please go while you can.'

He stared at her, tempted to clear out, leave her to her fate. But he could not. She was something to live for. So he shook her.

'You are going with me. Someone will be here soon.'

She hung on to him. 'No, no, you go. I've taken two or three pills. I was about to take the lot, when you rang the bell.'

'Jesus!'

'I'm getting out in my own way. Quick, you go!'

He didn't know what to do with her, so he lifted her head and kissed her on the lips. They remained that way for some time. Outside, he heard a car passing. It did not stop. The killers wouldn't drive up noisily. They wouldn't hear death coming. Perhaps someone was already outside a window, trying to peep through the curtains. No, that couldn't be right. They'd know about the security systems, the alarms. They'd wait, hoping they would make a run for it. He could drag her out, dash for the car, shooting anyone who tried to stop them. But would the old Webley do the job? What about the ammunition? Would it fire? On the other hand, if the killers had a tie up with Stanton, they could have the alarm turned off. It would not work back at base. Or, if it did, they could ignore it.

'That was nice, kiss me again.'

'Get dressed, Evelyn!'

'I'm sick, Harry. I'm finished. Going back to bed. You can stay and watch me take the lot, if you wish.'

She stumbled a little, yawning. He had to catch her. 'Put me to bed, Harry.'

He tried to get her to the front door. If necessary, he'd carry her as she was to his car, hope for a quick getaway, but it was impossible. She stumbled into the bedroom, where she pulled off the robe, threw it on a chair. He gave up. Perhaps she wasn't worth saving.

She fell on the bed, yawning. There was a whiskey glass, half empty on a table. Beside it was a small bottle, the lid unscrewed. He picked up the bottle, diazepam.

'What about the girl?'

'What girl?'

'Your daughter? Don't you want to see her again?'

'No, no, I can't go anywhere near her. I'd contaminate her.'

'She wants to meet you.'

'Too late, too late.'

'I think you should tell her everything.'

'How I killed her father?'

'She'll miss you. Don't hurt her now she's found you.'

She shrugged. 'I've changed my will and left everything to her.'

He was going to argue, but she had sprawled on the bed.

'You want to do anything, Harry?' He did not answer. 'Want to do me? Better hop on quick, before I drop off. Otherwise—' She stifled another yawn. 'I'll miss all the fun.'

She was taunting him, he knew.

He despised her. She was a criminal, now she was behaving like a slut. And yet he still felt sorry for her. They were two of a kind. She was a woman just past her prime, a ripe peach beginning to rot from the inside out. He, on the other hand, was a loser who never would have a prime.

She lay on the bed, her eyes half closed, watching him under her long, black lashes, her arms behind her head. Then, slowly and deliberately, she opened her legs.

'This is what I do when I'm feeling bad. I'm feeling pretty bad now.'

'Don't talk like that!'

'Come on, Harry, fuck me or I'll take the lot!'

Becker looked down at her with both longing and loathing. She was evil, but she knew it. She wanted to be forgiven, but hadn't the courage to ask. She was a cheat and liar and, in some accidental way, a killer. She was a manipulator and dangerously attractive. In the movies the cheap, chiselling broads always won. This one, however, did not have a hope. Nor did he. Someone was going to kill her. Becker thought about her for a while and about himself. He could have been a good man once. Someone might have loved him. Now all he had for company was a sprawling bitch who had about her the smell of sex and death. If you were a male, you had to have her. There was no way out. Mother Nature saw to that.

He took out the Webley and put it on the bedside table, just within reach. Next, he took off his clothes and got on top of her and did it. She moaned occasionally, even smiled as though she knew what was going on and liked it. She really was a whore, he knew. She'd taken many men, which was not surprising. She and Crowley must have had a perfectly awful marriage, bound together in mutual fear—neither knowing when the other would break.

So, he gave her what she wanted, again and again, at the same time thinking, This is how it ends, on top of a beautiful woman with a bullet in your brain.

CHAPTER 22

When he wakened, the birds were calling. He saw a crack of daylight between the curtains. He looked about, surprised he was not dead. He had to think what day it was. It was Sunday. She was not in the bed. The bottle of pills was still on the side table. So was the pistol. Nothing had been touched. Everything was surprisingly normal. He looked at his watch, just gone eight. He got up, pulled on his clothes and searched around, expecting to see her lying on a floor in the hall, perhaps the living room, strangled or bashed to death. But she wasn't. As he approached the kitchen, he heard her asking questions behind the closed door. No one answered, so she must be on a phone. He listened for a while. She seemed apprehensive.

At last she hung up. He knocked. 'Evelyn?'

'Yes?'

He opened the door. She was leaning against the wall by a phone, a hand to her mouth. She was not yet dressed, wearing the same negligee along with the high-heeled slippers, but not the robe. The place was warm. It was a well-regulated house. The rich always had that kind of house. Everything went like clockwork. If it didn't, something was wrong with the world.

'Good morning.'

At first, she did not reply, still leaning against the wall, the hand still to her mouth, stroking her lower lip with a finger.

'Good morning,' she said. She sounded carefree, nothing at all like the frantic whore of the night before.

'Something wrong?'

'Oh—'

'Bad news?'

She pulled a face, then stepped away from the phone and went to a bench. 'I was just going to bring in a tray for you. Want something?'

'Yes, please.'

He watched as she poured cereal into a bowl.

'How about strawberries and yoghurt?'

'Yes, please.'

'Bacon and eggs?'

'What about you?'

'Just toast and coffee will do me.'

'Me too.'

She was friendly, too friendly. Something was wrong, he sensed.

'It was so quiet I thought you'd gone.'

'Oh, I didn't wish to disturb you.' She looked back over a shoulder. 'You slept well?'

'Like a log.'

'I'm sorry I passed out on you. Did you have a good time?'

'Pretty good.'

'That's good.'

She put two slices in a toaster and brought the bowl of cereal to a small table. 'Please start, I'll be there in a tick.' She went back for the coffee while he began to eat. 'How many times did you do it?'

'Only the once.' He'd woken several times during the night and had lain there with her in his arms, listening. Apart from her gentle breathing, her breath even caressing his neck, he heard nothing unusual. He was surprised. At one stage, he'd reached out and switched on the lamp by the bed. It had worked. He wouldn't have been surprised if it had not worked. Someone out there could have gone to the fuse box and cut the power. That would turn off the alarm system. He'd tried to look at her, to admire her in the dim light, but she'd been too close. He'd even thought of getting on top of her and having her again, sure she would not resist. But he did not. No gentleman would take advantage of a sleeping woman.

'Only once? It seemed to go on and on forever.'

'You were half asleep.'

'Did I say anything?'

'You mumbled now and then.'

'What did I say?'

'Nothing intelligible. You sounded quite contented.'

'Did I?' She was pouring the coffee. The pot was shaking, her shoulders were shaking, the negligee was shaking. She was chuckling with her mouth shut. 'How long?'

'Pardon?'

'How long did it last?'

'Oh, ten minutes, maybe fifteen. I don't know.'

'Fifteen minutes?' She laughed. 'No man can keep it up so long.'

'It takes a bit of practice, but it can be done.'

She laughed aloud, her breasts shaking his time.

Evelyn had a superb body, he could see. Perhaps that was why she was wearing the negligee without the robe—to show him what he'd had. And what he could have again if he were interested. But the change in her was remarkable. Not a suggestion of misery. As bright as a bird. She must have slept well, dead to the world. It was as though she had completely forgotten last night—and her threats to kill herself, if he did not give her what she demanded. Perhaps she was that kind of woman, one who could do horrible things and yet feel no remorse whatever.

'Thank you,' she added. 'I'm very happy, Harry.'

'Yeah?'

'Yes, I really am, so happy I could die.'

'You will if we don't get out of here.'

'Oh, I don't care now. I would willingly die in your arms. Let's take our coffee and go back to bed.'

'We don't have time.'

She was looking out the window, smiling. The toaster popped. Slowly, as she buttered the toast, the good fun faded from her face. It was like watching the sun go down.

'What's happened?' he asked.

She brought the toast to the table, picked up her coffee, took a sip before answering. 'That was Alfredo—on the phone.'

He waited for an explanation.

'Giancarlo is dead.'

'Who?'

'My other cousin. In Melbourne.'

'How?'

'He was just walking along Sydney Road yesterday and a boy on a motor bike—'

'Shot him?'

She nodded.

'A hit?'

She shrugged without replying. She didn't seem to be greatly concerned.

'Did he say anything else?'

'What?'

'Alfredo, anything?'

She sighed without looking at him. 'No, nothing really. He was afraid. They're all afraid.'

'Why?'

She chewed a little toast, swallowed, and took another sip before she answered. At last she looked up. Her eyes had changed. She was anxious, her hands were shaking. Something was seriously wrong.

'I'm not surprised,' she said. 'Those two down in Melbourne, Alfredo and Giancarlo, they were the shame of the family, always the police knocking on the door. When I last heard, they were selling drugs to school children.' She shuddered so violently she had to put down the cup. 'And I'm the worst of them. I'm ashamed of myself, Harry. I did a terrible thing a long time ago. I killed a man and planned to kill another. You must think me a horrible bitch.'

'You're a beautiful bitch, especially in bed.'

'Huh!'

'You are and you know it.'

She was going to say 'Huh!' again, but it did not come out. She sat with elbows on the table, the cup clasped in both hands, looking at him and not at him.

'I was awful last night, wasn't I? I behaved like a whore, didn't I? Did I say things, horrible things? Did I say that word?'

He nodded. 'Uh-huh.'

'Oh, God, how awful. I never say that. I'm a modest woman, I really am. I was brought up that way, a good Catholic girl, obedient, respectful. I just want to love and be loved by someone, a good man. I apologise for all the nasty things I said to you at the door last night.'

'I shouldn't have said he made you do it—with other men, I mean.'

'I deserved that.' She ate toast, watching him. On that first day, she had sat in front of him and he'd been admiring her eyes, when he'd realised with a start that something behind those wide brown eyes was watching him carefully. Now he saw that being again, this time a kind and hopeful creature living inside the body. Some sort of being that wanted to get out. If only someone would show it the way.

'I was hurt,' she said. 'I thought I'd lost you. That's how I am at my worst. I become so angry, and then I am filled with despair. Then I behave badly, with men I mean. I disgust myself. I'm sick, Harry, sick and sorry.'

'You're not sick.'

'Yes, I am, but I think now I may have a chance—'

She put down the cup and took one of his hands.

'Thanks to you, I feel I have a chance. I want to go wherever you go. I want to live with you for the rest of my life. I'll give you whatever you need to set you up in some job you'll enjoy. I want to do it, Harry. Please let me. I need to do some good for someone at last. I want to live.' She tensed, tears welling in her eyes.

'It's all right.' He kissed her fingertips.

'I'm still frightened, Harry. Do you love me? Just a little bit?'

'Love is for people who've never been to hell and back.' He didn't know where those words had come from. They took him by surprise. He must have read them somewhere. He was not a thinking man.

She smiled. Her rich brown eyes glowed. 'And peace is for those who have? Is that it? Is it, Harry? Last night I dreamed a wonderful dream. It went on and on. I was floating down a river—no, upstream. How can one float upstream? I was lying back in a boat and trailing a finger in the lovely green water. Someone was behind me rowing, or was it poling? I did not see who it was. A man, I think. Yes, a man. He was singing softly, just a few words now and then. It was an Italian song, but he was not a gondolier. It was lovely. It may have been my father, although I did not see his face. We were drifting on and on towards a group of trees. They were glowing like gold. And

I was thinking that, if I could only reach those trees, it would be all over. I'd never have to worry again. I would have escaped. Yes, escaped all those years of hell. And here I am. Have I escaped, Harry? Please tell me I have.'

He didn't get a chance to answer. The phone rang again, loud and sudden.

She shook, frightened.

'You want me to take it?'

'No, no—' Unsteadily she rose, wiping at her eyes. He helped her to the phone, a hand on a shoulder. 'Yes?'

A man spoke fast, a stream of words.

'*Si*,' she said.

More hurried speech.

'*Si.*'

She listened again. At last she said, '*Si, io comprendo.*' Then the phone was hung up slowly. She was shaking so much Becker had to do it for her.

'What is it?'

'Alfredo again. Now Uncle Ennio is dead.'

'How?'

'They strangled him—with a garrotte. It's the traditional way. No noise, no blood. Aunt Giulia went into him with a tray and found him, eyes open, mouth open, tongue sticking out, quite dead. They must have crept in during the night. Those people can do that. For a joke, to show how clever they are. They don't need keys.'

Becker was scared. It was coming true. Palfreyman had said, 'Now all she has to do is get rid of Uncle Ennio and his two obnoxious sons.' Two dead and one to go, Alfredo. But it could not be true. Evelyn could not be a cold-blooded killer. She would not destroy her own family, as bad as they were. He began to shake. He was a coward, he knew. No ordinary bloke, who never meant any harm to anyone, should be in a situation like this. It was not fair.

'Anything else?'

'Not much. He just said get out of Canberra—and hung up.'

He grabbed her. 'Let's go, Evelyn.'

'They are going to kill all of us, aren't they?'

'Get dressed!'

'Yes, yes—I'll just jump under the shower.'

'No time for that.'

'I'll be only two minutes. Check the doors and windows,' she said.

He did that, taking the opportunity to inspect the house. It certainly was a rich man's house. Every room was hung with pictures, even in the toilets, but not in the bathrooms, of which there were three. The furnishing was top quality, modern with the occasional antique. But in the study almost everything was electronic and probably the most expensive money could buy, particularly the computer. It sat there on the teak desk like an invitation to crime, something to beat the security systems of the banking world, making money appear and disappear wherever you liked. If you knew how, and Crowley had known how. And what had Evelyn said? It disappeared into nebbia? A fog? What disappeared? The data, a whole stream of data? Why? Because a fog had no form. It could be any shape. You couldn't pin it down. It was money, but it was both there and not there. She'd said she didn't know what Alfredo had meant, but was that true? Perhaps she did, perhaps not. But someone believed she did.

When he returned, Evelyn was out of the shower and running around in her underwear. Already neat piles of clothing lay on the bed. A tidy woman, she'd even made the bed. Quickly, she dressed in much the same clothes as his—shirt, jeans, light sweater, heavy jacket, socks and boots—except that hers were much better. Then, she pulled out a light steel case and was quickly filling it. The case was the lockable type with metal clips. At the same time, she was humming a little tune to herself, perhaps the one the man in her dream had been singing, the Italian song. Even so, she was taking too much time for Becker. He had to signal to her to hurry—and to keep quiet. She seemed too happy to listen, muttering softly as she worked, saying, 'Ah' and 'Good' and 'Yes, yes!' At last she snapped the case shut, the clips too. Anyone listening would know the sound—the target was on the move.

Becker picked up the case and the Webley. She grabbed her handbag, checked for keys, wallet, lipstick, handkerchief, credit cards, tissues, the lot.

Suddenly she ran out of the room. 'Papers,' she called back.

He knew what she meant. If they were to sell the car in Adelaide, she'd need to prove that she owned it. He was amazed. This woman, who, at first meeting, had seemed to be off in a world of her own, was now active, single-minded, highly organised, perhaps for the first time in her life. And full of enthusiasm. When she returned, stuffing documents into her bag, he was at a window, checking. Nothing to see, perfectly normal out there.

'Right?'

She grabbed a comb and ran it through her hair, just two or three strokes. 'Yes, yes.'

They went to the front door. There were two locks, a Yale and a deadlock. She turned the Yale and reached for the other, but he pulled her hand away.

'Let me do it.'

She stepped back, pressing against him, melting into him.

'You know, Harry, each morning, when Papà would open the shop, he'd lift the roller high and there it would be—Sydney Road again, bustling and bumbling, stuffed with trams and shuffling cars and people dashing by—and he'd say, Well, cara, another day, eh? Andiamo!'

She was wasting time. He reached over and turned the deadlock. 'Come on, Evelyn.'

'Si, caro, andiamo!'

Becker opened the door, fully expecting to see a man holding a sawn-off shotgun standing there. At least he would take the blast and automatically his finger would have closed on the Webley's trigger and blasted him back. At least Evelyn would be saved. But there was no one. All clear.

He stepped out, holding the pistol high. It was a clear Sunday morning, blue sky, little wind. Everything looked clear. Evelyn went to the garage and flashed a remote control. A door began to rise. He was right the first time he saw this place. Another BMW was in the garage, a limousine. She pushed another button and her car's doors unlocked. He'd intended to drive, but by the time he'd dumped the case in the boot and shut the lid, she'd sat behind the wheel. So he let her drive. After all, it was her car. Also, he was still holding the Webley. Hard to drive and fight off anyone who might try to jump them. She backed the BMW out slowly, yard by yard, edging it into the street, looking both ways. Nothing seemed to be coming. 'Where to?' she asked.

'North,' he said, hoping the car was not bugged, that she was not bugged. There could be a tracker underneath. It was too late to check.

'Sydney?'

'Wagga,' he said.

'Your hometown?'

'Just for the night.'

'And then where?'

He didn't answer, too busy looking each way, watching for a parked vehicle. He saw none, not close by anyway. They set off along Empire Circuit, heading for Canberra Avenue. She was excited, head up, smiling like a kid going on a picnic.

They'd gone only a few yards when she stopped.

'Look!'

'What?'

'There she is!'

Becker was going to say 'Who?' although he knew already. It was the girl, sitting on the old seat among the oaks. She looked good sitting there. Her reddish hair went with the reddish leaves about her feet and above her. She was beautiful, as beautiful as her mother, Evelyn Crowley. She must have been throwing the ball, for the Irish setter was dancing around her, begging her to throw it again. The girl had seen them. She stood up, the ball ready to throw, her eyes wide. Both surprised and delighted.

'Evelyn, keep going!'

'Oh, how lovely she is, how bright her face, how her hair blazes in the sun. And she's smiling at me. She knows, doesn't she? She knows!'

'We don't have time!'

'I'll just say hello.'

'Just wave to her.'

Already she had opened the door, had begun to get out. He tried to hold her, but she'd forgotten to put the gears in park. The car was rolling, so he pulled on the brake. Now she was out of the car, staring at the girl among the trees across the street.

'Let's go, Evelyn!'

'My own daughter,' she said.

'Now!'

'Just a word—'

The girl looked as though she'd run for her life. But she did not. Instead, she held her ground, waiting. The dog was crouching, barking at her. Becker jumped out, glancing each way. Nothing was coming, he thought. He was wrong. A Mitsubishi off-road vehicle had appeared from behind trees on the left, and a Volvo station wagon was coming from the right. There was no danger; Evelyn was safely across.

She walked up to the girl, who was still holding the ball. Around the other hand, a leash was wound. The dog was whimpering, at the same time eyeing Evelyn as if protesting, Don't look at her, look at me! Throw the ball! The girl did not move, transfixed. Although slowly she lowered the hand holding the ball.

Evelyn was now only five yards away, smiling in the silly way women do when they don't know what to say or do—except to smile in the hope a smile will say everything. For the first time in her life, she was going to hold her only child.

'Are you really my daughter?'

It was a foolish sort of question, so she laughed foolishly. The girl blushed, stuttering words almost too much to bear. She was going weak at the knees, you could see.

'Are you really my mother?'

'Yes, I am.'

'Oh—'

'Your birth mother, darling. I'm going away for a while, but, if your parents would permit me, I would like to write to you now and then.'

'Oh, yes!'

Brakes squealed behind them. At first, Becker thought the two approaching vehicles were about to collide. There was no crash. One had stopped dead. He began to run at Evelyn, to protect her, but it was too late. There was one shot and then another, just two quick ones, bang, bang. The first missed, the second one went straight through the head. The startled dog was dancing around, barking and at the same time whining. It knew something awful had happened.

Becker ran after the Mitsubishi. He raised the Webley, fired three times, trying to hit the driver. One or two shots went through the rear window. The vehicle wobbled and skidded for a moment, then straightened up, went on. Becker tried again. The hammer clicked twice. Nothing happened. Two rounds had misfired. The Volvo had pulled over to one side, the startled driver gaping. On the back window was a sticker: 'Want to lose a million? Buy a horse.' In it were several young girls in riding gear.

The Mitsubishi went on along Empire Circuit, heading towards Melbourne Avenue, then disappeared. Becker tried to get the registration number. It was indistinct, muddy. He made out only the first three letters. It was wasted effort, he knew. It would be a stolen car.

Becker ran to Evelyn Crowley. She was bending over the girl, whose eyes were open, her mouth too. Not a trickle of blood. There never would be. The dog ran up, whining, wagging its tail, crying for her, trying to call her back. She did not move. Evelyn lifted her head, kissed her face, her eyes, even tried to breathe life into her. She clutched the girl to her breast, squeezing her. She looked up at Becker, began to cry.

'My daughter, my beautiful daughter—'

He stood there, helplessly. It should not have happened this way.

'Evelyn?'

'The dog, it jumped at me.'

He stared at her and the girl and the dog and back to the dog. It must have wanted to keep her away, so the girl would throw the ball again.

'Oh, Jesus.'

'Oh, yes, sweet Jesus, what have I done?'

'Evelyn—' He wanted to say he was sorry, but no words came out. He'd failed again.

The man in the Volvo had come up. 'What is it? What happened?'

Becker did not answer. Already he had his mobile out and was calling for an ambulance, although they could do nothing, he knew. Then he called the police. That was a waste of effort too, but he had to go through the formalities. The cops would never trace the killers. There would be two—one driving, the other shooting. The Mitsubishi would be found in the bush burned out, no clues left. But there was something about the killer. It was his arm, stretched out, holding the pistol, a big pistol, long barrelled. It was the left arm, propped up by the right hand. He was a leftie, whoever he was.

The Volvo driver was hanging around helplessly.

'Did you get a good look at them?' Becker asked him.

'What? Oh, two men? In the big red vehicle? You think they did it?'

'Yeah,' Becker said into the phone. 'The driver looked like a bloke named Russo, who works for Stanton Security.' There was a pause. 'No, I didn't get a good look at the other guy. All I saw was a hand and an arm sticking out. And a weapon. Yeah, a pistol. What? Shit, mate, it all happened in two seconds.' He listened for a while. 'Thanks, mate. Tell Palfreyman, will you?'

He hung up.

'There were five shots,' the Volvo man said.

'Yeah, I fired three.'

'You fired?'

'Yeah.'

'You have a gun?'

It was obvious Becker had a gun. He was holding it. 'I'm a cop.' He was not a cop, he knew. He was lying, but in the circumstances, no one was going to complain.

'Oh, God,' the man said. He looked as if he would start crying too. He walked back to the Volvo.

'Don't leave,' Becker said. 'They'll want you for a witness.'

'Oh, my God,' the man said again. He took a few steps before he pulled out a phone too and began chattering, at the same time waving at the girls in the Volvo not to look. They were looking, they couldn't help it. One appeared to be crying. A slight breeze sprang up. A few more leaves came down in the park. Fat, spiky leaves, blood red. Already other vehicles were pulling up. One or two people got out, stood looking— at the man with the gun in hand, at the woman on the ground holding a child. At the dog, still dancing around. It would rush to the girl, try to lick her face, then slink away, whimpering.

In the distance, they could hear a siren screaming its way along Canberra Avenue. There was no need to hurry. It was the gesture that counted. The dog came back once more. It wagged its tail, sniffed at the girl as if checking for any sign of life. Satisfied, it moved a few feet away, squatted on the leaves and grass and stared at her. Then it began to howl along with the siren.

CHAPTER 23

An hour later they were still there. The weather had changed, great clots of grey cloud had come over, like fluffy boulders in the blue sky. The ambulance had been the first to arrive, followed by a police car. Then a police van, forensic people getting out. One of them put up a tape barrier, 'Crime Scene Do Not Cross.' The girl's body still lay on the grass. Another took some photos. Then the Volvo man left with his load of horsey girls. Soon after that, Palfreyman arrived with the young detective, Paesch. Becker sat alone on the seat among the trees. He had taken Evelyn back to the house and left her there, lying on her bed, hands clasped on her chest, and gone into a sort of trance, just staring at the ceiling. It was as though she too were dead, although her eyes were wide open.

Palfreyman got out of his car, spoke to the most senior uniformed man present and then sauntered around, hands in pockets, looking at the grass and everything else except the corpse. Eventually, he gave it a professional glance, nodded and said something. The ambulance men took the girl away. At last he strolled over to Becker, hands still in pockets, sat beside him. His manner couldn't have been more nonchalant.

'Nasty business, Harry.'

'Yeah.'

'Who was the girl?'

'Her daughter.'

'Yeah?'

'They shot her by mistake. They were after Evelyn.'

'Because of what she said? About the bank? Where the money was going?'

'You heard all that?'

'Yeah.'

'The driver was a bloke named Russo.'

'Yeah, I've just heard. A bloke answering his description was found in a Mitsubishi in Melbourne Avenue, slumped against a window. Some off-duty soldier passing by opened the door and he fell out, bleeding like a stuck pig. Hit in the neck, apparently. The soldier stopped the flow and called an ambulance. He's on his way to hospital now, unconscious. Apparently, he's lost a lot of blood. He mightn't make it. They reckon he was hit by two slugs. One went in sideways.'

'Sideways? How could I have done that from behind?'

'Don't know, mate. Maybe his pal did it, to make sure he doesn't talk. You get a good look at him?'

'The hitman? No, he was turned away, leaning out a window, holding the weapon with both hands.'

'See it? The weapon?'

'No, just a blur. It was heavy, long barrelled.'

'How about Mrs Crowley? Any state to talk?'

'She's back at the house. In some sort of trance, probably shock.'

'Yeah, we'll leave her alone for a while.'

'She's got to get out of Canberra. They'll try again.'

'We need a statement first.'

'She knows too much.'

'We can put a guard on her place, night and day.'

'That won't stop 'em, you know that. They could come over the back fence, pretending to be checking power lines.' He was quite right. In Canberra, the powerlines are strung above the back fences. Nothing out front, very tidy streets.

'We've got safe houses.'

'There's no such thing as a safe house, not with those people.'

Palfreyman did not answer. He sat there, hands still in pockets, shuffling his feet on the fallen leaves. 'This bank she mentioned, did she say where it is?'

'No.'

'She said it's a bank in Sal—'

'I don't know what she meant.'

'Salerno? Could that be it?

'I don't know, I said.'

'And what'd she mean by a fog?'

'I don't know that either. You're the genius, you work it out.'

Palfreyman was watching the forensic people at work. They had taken the photographs and scoured the immediate area. They'd found five shells on the road, two from a 9 mm pistol, but nothing to show what make. They'd also found one of the slugs, the one that had gone through the girl's brain. It hadn't gone far after that, hit a tree in fact. But the first one, it was high. That was the one they wanted, hopefully free of impact. A man was sweeping the ground with a metal-detector. As they looked, he held up a hand and the bullet. It had gone some distance across the park but had hit nothing but grass. So it was valuable. Apart from that, they'd found nothing helpful. The dog was still hanging around, whimpering. A policewoman was trying to get it to come to her, accept the leash again.

'You'd better let me have that shooter of yours, Harry.'

'I'm not giving it up.'

'You shouldn't have it.'

'I'm all right.'

'Yeah?'

The forensics team was packing up. A girl took down the police tape.

'Ever heard of the 'Ndrangheta, Harry?'

'The what?'

'The Calabrian mob, very big, very organised. That old piece of yours would be useless against those people.'

Becker did not answer. He did not care now. He was going to get Evelyn out of Canberra today, as soon as possible. They'd go somewhere, probably out west. They'd go on and on, into the sunset until they found a nice place to hide out for a while. Get organised, get clear forever. He did not know yet what he'd do for money. They wouldn't be able to draw money from a bank or an ATM. If the mob had the right contacts in a bank, they could trace them through their withdrawals. So could the police, and he did not trust the police. They'd take her car, sell it somewhere along the way, change their names, buy a couple of tickets to some place out of the country. What would they live on after a few weeks? He did not know, but he would look after her. She was worth it.

Palfreyman was still talking about the 'Ndrangheta, saying something about moving millions, maybe billions, around the world.

'Anyway, those morons in Melbourne had a bright idea. They got in touch with the mob and told them they had a big banker under their thumbs. He could move money around the world without leaving a trace. Next thing Donald Crowley knew, he was working for the mob. In no time flat, they were laundering big bickies through the Royal Bank. We could have arrested Crowley, but we couldn't prove it. On the other hand, the Carabinieri back in Rome was pushing us, wanting to know where it was going. What bank in Italy? We had computer nerds working on the problem, but they couldn't tell us. We were getting nowhere, so we held off, hoping Crowley would break. It was no use. The mob had him trapped. If he didn't do what he was told, they'd kill Evelyn. He had no way out. So he jumped.'

'You could have put him in protective custody. And Evelyn.'

'Yeah, I know.'

'You let him fry until he could take it no more.'

'Yeah, I know.'

Becker was in no mood for excuses. Christine Billings was dead, and Evelyn Crowley was in shock. Probably she was drinking whiskey and looking at the bottle of pills, thinking of killing herself. He had to get back to her.

'Alfredo rang this morning,' he said, 'told her Giancarlo had been shot. Told her to get out of Canberra quick.'

'Yeah, we heard that.'

'Why did they kill Giancarlo?'

'Why? Well, those birdbrains got too big for their boots. They were just a family of peasants from some dump south of Naples, when they started. They'd got into shonky cars, loan sharking, then a bit of insurance fraud, finally a bit of trafficking— you know the story. They were making some dough, no big deal. This ties up with the 'Ndrangheta, it went to their heads. Nobody could touch them, so they thought. Unfortunately for them, they couldn't keep their mouths shut. Apparently, Giancarlo told some joker in a spaghetti joint in Carlton what they were doing. The mob didn't like it. Some kid on a bike popped him in broad daylight walking down the street. Old Ennio went berserk, saying he was gonna get his revenge. Settle things the old way. Just big talk. This morning he woke up dead, strangled.'

'Yeah, I heard that.'

'And they're none too happy Crowley is no longer with us.'

'I suppose not.'

'He was laying the golden eggs for them.'

Becker looked away at the street. It was an ordinary street in a rich part of Canberra. Cars were slowing to have a look at the crime scene. Then they would crawl away, faces at the window, frightened. Word had got around already. Someone had been killed, a lovely girl, a Grammar girl. That kind of thing could drop house prices. You couldn't hold an auction in a street where some goons could kill a Grammar girl in broad daylight.

'They shot Torrence?' he asked.

'Looks like it.'

'Not Alfredo or Giancarlo?'

'They were in Melbourne at the time.'

Becker pulled out the card. 'This is what you want.'

'The one Buster picked up?' Palfreyman studied it, holding it out and squinting. He was long-sighted. 'Jesus, this is serious.'

'You know that guy?'

'Yeah, we know him.' He tapped the card on a thumbnail. 'Did she say where Alfredo is?'

'I don't think she knows.'

'We've got to find him before they do.'

A few more cars went by, slowing to look at the scene. Becker did not look at them. Instead, he sat with his hands in his pockets, thinking and trying not to think.

'Why try to kill her?'

'Evelyn? Well, she was a Scarafini, and she knew a lot. It's as simple as that. You shouldn't have made her run, Harry.'

'You heard that too?'

The policeman patted him on an arm. 'Sorry, mate. She's all right, I guess. Just got born into the wrong family.'

Becker did not answer.

'That her car over there, the Beemer?'

'The keys are still in it.'

'I'll get someone to put it away.'

'I'll look after it.'

He was sick of it all. He was getting out. He was not sure where he would take Evelyn if they did get away—perhaps to Wagga Wagga, where he'd started fifteen years ago. Perhaps further out, some place such as Hay or Mildura. Maybe Adelaide for a start.

Palfreyman got to his feet.

'As soon as she's got her breath back, Harry, bring her in to headquarters.'

'Yeah.'

'Today, if you can. We need a statement from each of you.'

'Yeah.'

'Not thinking of doing a runner, are you? We'll have a car stationed outside her place, to keep an eye on you. If you need any help—'

'For Christ's sake, just piss off, will you?'

'Hang in there, Harry.'

Palfreyman walked off, not as casually as he'd arrived. A few neighbours had stopped and gazed and talked among themselves, even pointed. They soon drifted off, leaving Becker seated under the trees, thinking about everything and nothing at all, except the hesitation in her eyes, the softness of her hand and the silence of the day. Except for the crow flying overhead, cawing.

'Evelyn,' someone said.

Becker looked around, seeing no one. It must have been his own voice, heard as if in a dream. Something touched him on a cheek. He thought at first it was a kiss, but it was rain, just a few drops. Big grey clouds had rolled up from the coast. Big uncertain clouds, shifting this way and that. This was high-plains country, two thousand feet above the sea. Big clouds could appear out of a blue sky, roll around for a while, maybe drop a few drops, then move off somewhere else. As if Canberra was not worth pissing on.

CHAPTER 24

When he returned, she was still lying on her bed dressed the same, except she had kicked off her shoes and had one arm over her forehead. He thought she was still dazed, but her eyes moved as he entered the room. And she was breathing as though relaxed. She watched him, her deep-brown eyes taking him in like the eyes of an Arab woman behind a veil. She wore no makeup and her lids, he noticed, were darker than usual, as if bruised. She came from a long way south in Italy. He'd read that Africa began just south of Rome. There might have been an Arab somewhere in her ancestors. On the other hand, there might not.

'How are you feeling?'

'Rotten.'

He sat on the edge of the bed and took one of her hands. The other was down low, not so much on her belly as on her womb.

'She's gone, hasn't she?' she said. He didn't know what to say, so he just nodded. 'I hurt,' she added.

'I know you do.'

'I hurt down here. Every time I used to think of her, I felt something down here, as though she were still with me. Now my womb is empty. It hurts, it cries for her. My daughter, my lovely daughter.'

He sat there holding her hand and looking at her. He felt inadequate, like a man who has just been born fully grown and knows nothing of suffering. So they remained like that, she supine and he superfluous. Her blinking now and then, and him just breathing for the sake of breathing. For something to do. For several minutes, waiting.

Suddenly she said, 'What happened to the dog?'

'The police took it home.'

'It saved my life.'

'Yeah, I guess so.'

'I wish I had died.'

She stared at him, as if getting right inside him, getting inside his head and his thoughts and his soul. There was something about her, as if she were destined to be this way. Everything going wrong and there was nothing he or she could do about it. He was sorry. She wasn't all bad. There was some hope for her. If only they could get out of this town, try again. Be good to each other. Be honest. Good friends, off to see the world. See what happens.

'I've got to see her, haven't I?' she said.

'They took her to the morgue.'

'I mean, her mother.'

'You are her mother.'

'That's not how she would see it.'

'Mrs Billings? No, I suppose not.'

'And now I've killed her daughter.'

'You didn't kill her, Evelyn.'

She wriggled slowly, stretching, even stretching her stockinged feet. 'Yes, I did. If I'd not been a part of it... If I'd not done such bad things—'

She flinched. He bent down and kissed her on her lips. They were full lips, the bottom one especially, as full as ripe fruit, some exotic fruit, drippingly sweet. He did not know what fruit, but she was exotic. There was a mysterious richness about her. Even without makeup she smelled rich in the way a bazaar or a perfume shop smells rich or a lift smells rich because a woman has just walked out of it.

'You're not bad.'

'Yes, I am. I come from a bad family. And they come from a cruel world, down south. Cruel from our point of view, but not from theirs. They have dreadful poverty, there are no jobs. The government does not look after them, so they must look after themselves. That's what they say. Each family looks after each other family. It's an informal arrangement, it's a them-against-us arrangement. So, they make money any way they can, usually by crime or selling drugs. It's a way of life for them, they see no harm in it. Unless, of course, someone steps out of line. Then someone dies. No question about it. That is the old way—the only way. There is no other form of justice up there in the valleys and gorges and crags and forests of the high country.'

'That's nothing to do with you. You're out of that. You've always been out of that.'

'No, I'm not. They bring it with them, many of them. My family brought it with them.'

'You said your father was a good man.'

'So he was. Good men have to live with bad men if they want to survive.'

'You mean Uncle Ennio?'

She nodded, the arm still lying across her brow, palm upwards, not clenched so much as symbolic. Becker did not know why it was symbolic, it just was. Her whole body was symbolic. Just lying there on a bed within reach was symbolic. She moved his hand, the one holding hers, to her breast. He was not sure what she wanted him to do, so he did nothing, just let it rest there. At first, he thought it was the sexy gesture she'd made last night, when one breast had peeped out of the nightgown, but she was really making him feel her heart. He could not feel any beat, but she was alive all right, sumptuously alive. He realised she was going to tell him something. He could see a story forming in her eyes.

'When I was thirteen or fourteen, we went to a party at Uncle Ennio's place. It was down a side street in Brunswick. We were often there. Everyone was there that day, including Aunt Giulia and Alfredo and his wife and Giancarlo and his girlfriend, who was horrible. She had bad teeth and a snorting sort of laugh and was so greedy she'd eat her own hands if you did not keep them full of food. And there were some children—about a dozen people altogether, counting the kids. It was a happy meal. I think it was Ennio's birthday. Everyone was laughing and telling stories and sometimes singing—and drinking wine, by the bottles full, one after another. Next they got onto grappa, which is very dangerous. I was sitting next to Uncle Ennio and my father was sitting on the other side of me. Someone, I'm not sure who, it may have been Alfredo, said a man he knew had been cut because he had done something bad. I didn't know what, I could not follow it. But I knew he meant cut with a knife. They were making signs and pulling faces and looking at us, the children. I realise now that the man had been punished for kissing someone else's wife—on a dance floor, I think. Well—'

Evelyn wriggled again, stretched again, sighed again, at the same time pressing his hand to her heart.

'Well, what?'

'It's too horrible.'

'Forget it. Come on, we have to go to the police, make statements.'

'Let's go, Harry. We were going to get out. Let's run away now.'

'There's a police car outside. They'll stop us if we try.'

Her lips tightened, her eyes narrowed. 'I can't do it, Harry. I'm such a coward.'

'The woman? You don't have to do it today. She will be grieving.'

'I can't face her.'

'You don't have to. You can write to her from somewhere in a few days.'

'I don't think I could do even that. What would I say?'

He leaned back, freed his hand, tapped her on a shoulder. 'Come on, the police are waiting. They'll give us an escort, then we can clear off. Come on, get up!'

She shook her head. 'I can't move.'

He didn't know what to do with her, so he just sat there watching her.

Her eyes changed. They flickered, like those of a woman watching television or a film or a fire in a grate. Once she trembled, once she gasped. Then she closed her eyes and began again to speak.

'Have you been to Italy?'

'No, never.'

'I have, several times, but never south of Naples. I would not go to Calabria after what I heard.'

'What did you hear?'

'They came from a small town called Santa Vittoria up in the mountains east of Reggio—Papà first, then later, many years later, Ennio and Aunt Giulia and those two brats. It is a hidden place on the edge of a national park covered with pine forests. In fact, it's surrounded on three sides by forest, the only access being a narrow road up a little valley dotted with a few small farms, where they graze nothing but goats and speak a funny language, not quite Italian. More like Sicilian. I hated it. So crude, so common. At school I studied Italian, classical Italian, the language of Dante Alighieri. I read the Commedia right through. I loved it. I loved his love for the divine Beatrice. I wanted to be like Beatrice, pure, divinely pure, but it was not to be, was it?'

Evelyn paused, her eyes wide with memory. Perhaps she was back with the nuns drilling good Italian, and good English, and good manners into her, and the good life to come for a devout Catholic girl. Instead, she'd been double-crossed by a sweet-talking lawyer and then had been hooked up with a smelly little bank clerk who knew how to fiddle books. Now she was telling her story to a failed cop, who didn't know whether she was going to kill him or give him her heart and soul and body and money and everything else he did not deserve. To Becker she seemed to have drawn three short straws, him included. Now, to cap it all off, her one and only child had been killed. Almost in her arms.

She sighed.

'It's a weird place. I've seen pictures of it. They're always dragging out the photographs, boasting and bragging, full of nostalgia. There's a small campanile and an old mill by a stream, a sawmill where the timber was cut. Such nice people, always smiling, at least for the camera, so picturesque, so quaint, so peaceful on the surface, but dreadfully poor. It is a primitive country, ignorant country. They kill people there just for smiling the wrong way.'

'What's this got to do with Uncle Ennio?'

'Well, he was good and truly drunk by this stage. He told a story about a man who raped a young woman, back in the old country as they call it. Except that it was not rape, they just said it was. They were lovers. She was married to the mill owner. He was a young man, a forester on the mountains. Nearly everyone works in the forest, taking out timber, or for the mafia. He'd come down now and then at night and climb in her window and get to work with her, while her husband was sleeping off the wine he'd drunk after work. A bottle a day he drank. One night the old man was not drunk, just asleep. He heard a noise and went to investigate. He opened a door slowly and saw them hard at it. So, after a while, he closed the door very quietly—and let them finish.'

'Considerate of him.' Becker tried to make a joke of it, but Evelyn did not think it funny.

'Next day, he went to the young man's cabin up in the hills, not far out, just a mile or so, with three or four men. They grabbed him, dragged him back to the village and stripped him in front of the local people. They tied him to a post in the mill and tied a garrotte around his testicles—'

'Jesus!'

'And pulled it tight.'

'Jesus, Evelyn.'

'And left him there, half naked, tied to that post in the mill, which was open on one side. He screamed and screamed, day and night. You could hear it all over the village, all over the hills. It went on and on. Until his testicles dropped off.'

'Oh, hell, didn't anyone try to help him?'

'Not a soul.'

'What about the police?'

'There was only one policeman. He was one of the men who'd dragged the poor fellow to town.'

'And what happened to the young fellow?'

'He became the local eunuch, a figure of fun.'

'Why didn't he run away?'

'In that place, that land, there is nowhere to run. They can always find you.'

He stood up, waving his hands. 'Oh, Jesus, Evelyn.'

'And that's the story Uncle Ennio told at that party.'

'You had to listen to a story like that? And you were only a kid. I mean, what did everyone at the table think? Didn't they protest?'

'They all laughed and cheered and clapped their hands, Aunt Giulia most of all.'

'Your father too?'

'He just smiled politely. He was a very polite man.'

'And how did you feel?'

'Sick, I always feel sick when I think of that poor man.'

Becker looked down on her. Her face was flushed with suppressed anger, her eyes flicking as though watching a torture scene in an old Hollywood movie—the kind that goes on forever, because it is too fascinatingly awful.

'Harry,' she said.

He did not answer, but waited. He knew she was going to say something decisive.

'I am going to confess—'

Again, he waited.

'To what I did.'

'In Melbourne? To that man?'

'I will go to the police, tell them what I did.'

He baulked at that. It might be the end for him. The end for the life now blooming with her, as dangerous as it was.

'Don't do that,' he said. 'It's all wrapped up. You said the coroner found he was in trouble at work, hands in the till. He'd jumped of his own accord.'

'I pushed him.'

'Yes, but there's no need to tell anyone.'

'I must confess.'

He could see her point. She was some sort of Catholic, perhaps not a good one, but she had to get it off her chest. Perhaps it would be good for her, good for both of them in the long run.

'You could write to the coroner and say you have further information.'

'That I killed him?'

'No, no, just tell it as it happened. That guy told you he was not going to marry you after all. You were so angry that you pushed him, forgetting he was leaning against a low wall on a balcony. He went over. You were so horrified that you ran away. Now you want to tell your side of the story. That's all you need say.'

'What would he do to me?'

'The coroner? He can't do anything to you. But he can refer the matter to the police if he likes. On the other hand, he might do nothing at all. After all, it was an accident.'

'But I killed him.'

'Forget about that for the time being. Come on, Evelyn, get up.' He slapped her on a thigh. 'Let's get out of here. You can write to the coroner from Perth.'

She was staring at him, wide-eyed now. She had that kind of eyes. Once they fixed on you, they did not let you go.

'But if they arrest me?'

'You can't be arrested on your own information. Come on, we're going to see Mrs Billings.'

Surprisingly, she did not resist. In fact, she seemed to be fortified by the telling. As if stories were the way out, as if talking to God without having Him thundering back at you, telling you that you have sinned, perhaps damned forever.

'Yes,' she said. 'Yes.'

She got off the bed, slipped on her shoes, checked her hair and face, even put on some lipstick. Then they went out and closed the door. A police car was right in front, two uniformed officers—a man and a woman. Becker went to the woman. She had two stripes, the man had one. He looked like a rookie fresh out of school. 'We're going to the Billings place first.'

'All right.'

'You know where it is?'

'We took the dog there.'

'I'll take her car.'

'Better to come with us, a bit safer.'

'All right,' he said.

They went around Collins Park and across to Flinders Way and up Monaro Crescent. Fallen leaves were thick in the gutters each side. The street was an arboreal tunnel, lined with old houses. They stopped outside a flat-roofed house near the top of the street. It had cement-rendered sides and red window-trim. There was no front fence and so no gate. Canberra houses did not have front fences. It didn't look like much of a house. It was neat enough, but the whole place had an air of dignified struggle. To one side was a couple of crepe myrtles and a few nondescript bushes. They could have been azaleas or half-hearted rhododendrons. Nothing was in bloom. Beside the house stood a grey van, and beyond the van a large metal garage. The rain had gone, but not the tears.

CHAPTER 25

The dog uncurled itself from a mat to one side of the verandah. It rose warily, watching them approach. Its hackles were rising. It growled softly, then barked. Becker tried to assure it with a flick of his fingers and a few soft words. The dog did not like them. Possibly it remembered them, blamed them for what had happened. Becker stepped up to the door and used a brass knocker. It was not really brass, just some brass-coloured alloy. In those days, nearly every house in Canberra had that kind of knocker. The dog barked again, not quite so loudly. They heard voices inside, then footsteps. The door opened, a boy stood there, about seven years of age. He had a thin face and blond hair that went in all directions.

'Yes?'

'Hello, is your father at home?'

'Yes.'

'And your mother?'

'Yes.'

'Could we speak to them, please?'

The boy was going to answer when someone inside called. He looked back and said, 'It's a man. And a lady.'

The door opened wide. A man loomed over the boy. He was a tall man with a worn-out sort of face, very bony. He could have been some sort of technician. He wore blue coveralls and on his left breast was a company name. Something about electronics, twenty-four-hour service. His hair was thin and going grey and stood out angrily. His sunken eyes were deep in his sunken cheeks and they were unnaturally blue.

'Yes?' he said.

'My name is Becker, and this is Mrs Crowley.'

'Yes?' He did not seem to know the names. Perhaps the police had not yet told them.

'We've come to say how sorry we are that your daughter, Christine—'

'Christine?'

He didn't seem to know that either.

'She died—I mean she was caught in some crossfire at Collins Park this morning—'

'Are you from the police?'

'No—'

'Is that a police car out there? I can see a police car.'

'They're making enquiries—'

'What do you want?'

'As I said, we would just like to say how sorry we are that your daughter—'

'What name did you say?'

'Becker. There was some shooting. Your dog saved Mrs Crowley's life.'

'The dog?'

There were more footsteps, quick, light steps. A woman said, 'Who is it?'

'It's someone about Christine.'

'Who is it?'

She pulled the door wide open, looked out. Her face was flushed and swollen. Her eyes seemed to have disappeared into her head. She had very small, weepy eyes, inquisitive, hostile.

Evelyn stepped forward. 'Mrs Billings, I just wish to say I'm so sorry Christine was hit. I mean, it was because of me. Some men, you see—'

The woman stepped out, pushing the man and the boy aside.

'It's you?' She glared at Evelyn. 'You're the one? You killed her?'

'No, it was a mistake. They were after me, and Christine happened to be there, and I stopped to talk to her, and—'

'You're her mother? Her biological mother?'

'Yes, you see, I let her go for adoption and—'

'What do you want? You want to take her? You're too late! We've just come from the morgue. We had to identify her. And you come here saying you're sorry because someone shot her. Our little girl? Our lovely child? She told us. She said she'd found her birth mother. Birth mother? What did you ever do for her? You abandoned her. We took her in, we provided for her, we looked after her, we loved her, we sent her to a good school. She won a scholarship, she was so bright—'

Evelyn fell back, shocked.

The man tried to restrain the woman. 'Beth!'

'And now she's dead. And you killed her!'

'Beth—' The man tried to push her back inside the house.

'I hate you!'

Evelyn tried again to speak, but she could not get a word in.

'Get out! I hate you! Hate you!'

Becker pulled her back. There was no point in trying. This woman was beside herself with rage and grief.

'I'm so sorry, Mrs Billings—'

'Get out!'

They fell back, made it to the police car. Becker opened a door, but just as Evelyn was seating herself, the woman rushed down the path. The door was still open. She ran at the car so fast she hit it full on. Her hands flew at it. A watch and some sort of chain on a wrist cracked at the glass. Becker thought she was going to attack Evelyn, possibly try to tear her hair out. But she was not.

'Oh, God,' she said. 'I'm sorry, I'm so sorry—'

She was reaching for Evelyn, but patting her anywhere—on her face, even on her head. Crying, 'I'm sorry, I know you must be—'

She stepped back, wobbling. Becker caught her by an arm. The policewoman had stepped out of her car, but assistance was not required. Mr Billings had come down. He put an arm about his wife, led her back up the path. Evelyn was about to get out of the car to go to her, but Becker waved her back.

'Let her go,' he said. 'Write to her sometime.'

They drove off. The man and the woman went into the house, leaving the boy and the dog on the verandah, watching them depart. The boy had a thumb in his mouth. The dog, for some strange reason, was wagging its tail. Probably glad to see the last of them.

At police headquarters, Palfreyman led them to separate rooms. They made separate statements, which had to be typed up and signed. This took nearly an hour.

Palfreyman saw them out. 'I still say you should go into a safe house, both of you,' he said.

'We're leaving town today.' It was now after lunch. Neither had eaten since breakfast, and Evelyn had had only a slice of toast and a cup of coffee.

'Not wise, mate.'

'They're not going to have another go. We've told you everything we know.'

'Revenge, mate, revenge.'

'Have you heard anything more about Alfredo?'

'Not a thing. He's gone to ground somewhere.'

'Russo?'

'Unconscious, mate, might not wake up.'

'Got a guard on him?'

'Naturally.'

Palfreyman walked with them to the police car. Buses cruised past, traffic lights changed on London Circuit. Another bank of desolate clouds was coming over, so was the crisp air. It was almost the end of May now. Already at night temperatures were dropping below zero. Canberra was a cold place in winter, cold enough some mornings to crack your teeth.

The police driver started the engine.

Palfreyman looked in.

'Hey, we heard from Rome. The Carabinieri checked every bank in Salerno. They couldn't find anything. No unusual accounts, all fair and above board. You're sure you don't know what 'fog' means, Mrs Crowley?'

'I have no idea.'

Palfreyman slapped the roof. 'Mind how you go.'

The car began to move off. In front of the building, a man was watching, hands in pockets and smiling. It was a knowing smile, more a smile with the eyes than the mouth. It was Adams. He'd not been at the interviews. Possibly he'd been behind a glass screen, watching and listening. Becker noticed him, so did Evelyn.

'That man,' she said.

'What about him?'

'He—'

'What?'

'Looks familiar.'

'That's Adams. He's a cop and a pretty nasty one. Loves to see people squirm.'

'I've seen him before.'

'At the interview?'

'No, but he was outside in the corridor, when I came out.'

'Did he speak to you?'

'No, but he watched me and smiled.'

'He just smiled?'

'Yes.'

'So, where have you seen him?'

'I don't know.'

The police car moved off.

'I don't know,' she said again.

Back at the house, they had some cold cuts and talked about what they'd do. They'd go to her bank and withdraw cash. They'd drive to Wagga Wagga and stay the night, then on to Adelaide, where they'd sell the BMW for whatever they could get, fly to Perth. Evelyn would write to her lawyer, instructing her to sell the house and everything in it—and to send a cheque to a post office box number in Perth to be advised. That might take months. In the meantime, they'd have a holiday, relax and get started again. Finally, they'd take off for some distant place where no one would ever find them, perhaps overseas. They were scared, but it was exciting. It would be a big adventure. Off to see the world with lots of lovely cash. It was the kind of life you read about. Sitting on a sidewalk outside a small cafe in a small town on the other side of the world and having a quiet drink and watching the sun go down over the ocean. Or strolling along a beach, barefooted. Or walking through the swishing surf and kicking water at each other and being happy. Not a care in the world. Of course, they'd need passports, but they could fix that in Perth.

She took his hands across the table as she had done at breakfast. But this time she pressed them to her breast.

'Harry, I want to tell you something.'

'What's that?'

She stared at him, her eyes big and soft and sad and fatal. She was going to tell him something pretty bad. He could feel it in the way he could feel the beat of her heart under his hands.

'I killed that man.'

'In Melbourne? I know that. You've told me. It was an accident.'

'No, I killed him deliberately.'

He was shocked. 'Deliberately?'

'Yes.'

'You mean cold-blooded murder?'

'No, hot-blooded murder. When he said he was going back to his wife, I flew at him. I hated him. I deliberately pushed him over.'

His own heart sank. All the weight of living and hoping and disappointment dragged him down, so that his mind seemed to be sucked out of him. As if someone had pulled a plug and it had gone down a drain with his heart and soul and self. He felt washed out. This woman was a killer, possibly unstable. Beautifully unstable and yet beautifully available. She was begging with her eyes. Help me, they seemed to be saying.

'To his death?'

'Yes. For three or four seconds, I really hated him. I wanted him dead. And I did it. I flew at him to beat him, trying to tear his eyes out. I knew he was leaning back. I knew he could fall. I pushed him. He went over. To save himself, he grabbed my arms. But he must have seen that I'd go over too, so he pushed me back.'

'Oh, God, Evelyn.'

'It was an impulsive thing to do, but I did it. I have no excuses. Do you still want to go with me? Take me away? Take your chances with me?'

She stared at him. Her eyes were filled with him.

'I need you, Harry. You must know everything about me. I will never lie to you again, I promise.'

He thought about it. If things went wrong, if he displeased her, if she decided he was an embarrassment, would she push him over too? Or would she do it some other way? He did not know what to do but forced himself to look at her. She was almost weeping. Hungrily, she kissed his fingers, his hands.

'Give me a chance, Harry. Please!'

He thought about it. Or at least he tried to think about it. Tried to weigh it up, the pros and cons, but failed. Someone was going to kill him, so what did it matter if she did the job? He remembered last night, when she'd been moaning in her sleep with her legs wrapped around him and running her hands over his back and kissing his neck and ears and saying, 'Yes, yes, yes...'

'Pack your things.'

'You mean it?'

'Yeah, let's get out of here.'

'Where shall we go?'

'Anywhere. A long way west.'

'To Perth then?'

'Yeah, if you like.'

'Oh, Good.' She stood up. 'I've always wanted to live in Perth—a whole continent away from all this.'

'Maybe not there, too many visitors to a big city.'

She was excited. 'Margaret River!'

'What is that?'

'A lovely little place south of Perth, down in the big timber country and near the sea. Donald and I drove down there one day ten years ago, when he was in Perth on business. Beautiful beach, lots of fishing, lots of wineries and places to eat. We had lunch in a cafe that didn't have tables.'

'How did you eat?'

'We sat at old sewing machines, old Singers and Wertheims and—'

'Come on, Evelyn, let's get going.'

'Yes, yes!'

Evelyn filled another case with clothing, and even found a better shirt for Becker, plus a spare toothbrush. He thought of going back to the Indians' house to pick up some odds and ends, but changed his mind. He'd buy some stuff along the way, except it was a pity not to say goodbye to Leticia. She was a nice kid, a friendly kid. 'Have you caught any baddies today, Mr Harry?'

They had locked up the house and were departing, when the female officer pointed to Becker's car, still parked outside the house. 'Someone will nick it,' she said.

'They're welcome to it.'

'Well, you can't abandon a vehicle in a public street. That's the law.'

'Yeah, okay, I'll do something about it.'

He took Evelyn's keys and opened the garage door. The big BMW was still inside. For a moment, he thought of taking it instead of the small one. It would be worth a lot more—and they were going to need a lot of money, which they could not draw from a bank, not yet anyway. But it was too much trouble to go back inside and find the papers for the limousine. So, he walked to the old Holden, still standing where he'd parked it late last night before he'd walked up to her front door and said, 'It's me, Harry.' And she'd let him in and in and in...

Becker opened the old vehicle. It was nearly thirty years of age, a sturdy machine, reliable, built like a tank. It might have been an oil-dripping clunker, but it had never failed him. He inserted the key, turned it. The engine started. Nothing else happened. It was all right. He put it into gear, let out the clutch. The car began to move.

It blew up. More correctly, it did not blow up, but was blown upwards. It jumped off the ground. The floor came up at a hundred miles an hour. His head hit the roof. He blacked out.

When he woke, he had a headache you couldn't climb over.

He felt sick. His head buzzed and his eyesight was all mixed up. He was propped up in a bed, he knew. His head hurt, his feet hurt. They felt like two bags of hot road gravel. Even his teeth hurt. He moved his jaw, feeling with his tongue. They all seemed to be there, but there was a strange taste, which could have been blood. Perhaps he'd bitten his tongue or his cheek. He tried moving his eyes. Two large female shapes beside him seemed to be waiting for something to happen.

'He's awake,' one of them said.

'Where am I?'

'Canberra Hospital,' she said. 'Emergency Room.'

He couldn't hear. His ears were buzzing, his brain was buzzing. 'Where?'

'Canberra Hospital, Emergency Room,' she repeated.

'What happened?'

'Someone tried to kill you.'

'My head.'

'Don't touch it. The nurses sprayed it with glue. Stops the bleeding. How do you feel?'

'Awful.'

'The morphine wearing off, eh? The ambos gave you a shot on the spot. You must have a tough nut. You're lucky to be alive, isn't he, Stace?'

'Doesn't look alive to me.'

The two women went in and out of focus, in time with his pulse. At first, he thought they were nurses, but they wore leather jackets and skin-tight sweatshirts. One was a brunette, the other a blonde. The blonde had a hand on a hip. No, she had a hand on a Smith and Wesson strapped to a hip, police issue. They were quite attractive if you liked tough-looking sheilas with six-shooters on their hips. He thought he'd seen them somewhere before.

'You're cops?' he tried to say that, but his jaw and mouth did not work too well.

'We're not the tea ladies,' the brunette said.

She flashed an ID at him, so quickly he saw nothing. Even if she'd given him a minute, he wouldn't have seen it. Everything was still a blur. 'I'm Anna Politis and this is Stacey Babchuk. Back at the office we're known as Polly and Chook.'

'Polly Politis?'

'No, Pollyanna, get it? I'm the cheerful one. Stacey's a misery guts, aren't you, Stace?'

'Ah, shut up.'

'How long have I been here?'

'Three hours, dead to the world.'

'What happened?' He knew what had happened. He'd really meant what had happened after that.

'Stun grenade, forensics think.'

'What?'

'A bit deaf, eh? You have a concussion. Your car blew up. The two officers escorting you pulled you out. Risked their lives for you, so we hear.'

'What's that smell?'

'Fire retardant. The young bloke sprayed you. Thought he was doing the right thing.'

'You're just back from x-ray. You've got a bump on your head as big as half an egg. Nothing broken, but. You're lucky.'

'You call this luck?'

'We've seen worse, haven't we, Stace?'

'The other day we had to haul a flash geezer out of a Ferrari on Limestone Avenue. He'd been doing a hundred and thirty in a school zone.'

'He didn't have legs, did he?'

'Nothing you'd want to keep.'

They were like talking twins, each finishing the other's words. The brunette had short, curly hair, and the blonde had a ponytail. Each looked as if she could run a half-marathon without raising a sweat.

'Where—' He glanced around, seeing nurses working at other beds. In the middle of the room was a station, people bent over screens. Against a counter, two surgeons in green were chatting. Paper masks hung around their necks. One was standing cross-legged and leaning on the counter. The other, who was very tall, was standing back, arms folded, and looking down his nose at the other. They seemed to be having a serious discussion. Now and then, the tall one would glance at Becker.

He came over. 'I'm Doctor Katter. How are you feeling?'

'Like hell.'

'You shouldn't be leaving. Not in your condition.'

'He'll be all right, Doc.'

'He has concussion.'

'I've got some pills for him,' the brunette said. She seemed to be the senior officer. At least, she did most of the talking.

'He needs more than pills. He needs rest.'

'Ah, we'll sing him to sleep, won't we, Stacey?'

'No, keep him awake, as long as you can. Wait until the morphine has worn off before you give him that stuff. It's full of codeine.'

'How long?'

'At least six hours from when he was injected. Preferably eight.'

'Okay, Doc.'

'He shouldn't be moved.'

'You want a stiff on your hands?'

'He's not that serious.'

'He will be if certain people find him here.'

The doctor went away, mumbling to himself.

Becker tried again. 'Where is—'

'Your wallet?' The brunette produced it from a pocket in her jacket. 'Your clothes are in that cupboard, but they stink of smoke and flame. We brought you some fresh gear.'

'No, where is—'

'The bird? She's out of harm's way.'

'Where?'

'Uh uh, no telling.'

'Safe house,' the blonde said.

'What?'

'Stop shouting, we're not deaf,' the brunette said. 'I said she's in a safe house.'

'Why did you call her a bird?'

'Bird on a Wire. Didn't you see that show with Mel Gibson and Goldie Hawn?'

'She's not hurt?'

'She wasn't in your car.'

'No—' He remembered now. She was safe. That was all that mattered.

'You took her there?'

'To the safe house? No, the pair guarding you this morning had that honour. They're still there, waiting to clock off.'

'Feel like going for a drive, Harry?' the blonde said.

'With two cool babes?'

'Yeah, I suppose—'

He moved one arm, the other arm, his legs. Then he turned his head. That old spasm went up his neck and straight into his brain like an ice-cold knife. Nothing, however, seemed to have changed, except it was worse. He had to get out, he realised. Anyone could be wandering around a hospital with a syringe.

The brunette said, 'Here, jump into these strides.' She produced a shirt too.

'Where did these come from?'

'The ragbag back at the office. We call it the death in custody bag.'

He began to get off the bed, but lurched.

'Here, pull on these pants. Don't worry, I've got you.'

He realised he wore nothing but a hospital gown. The nurses must have cut his clothes off him. The blonde pulled a curtain around the bed. They had the gown off him in a flash.

'Nice set of knackers,' she said.

'Don't worry, Harry, she's a dyke. She won't grab you.'

'I'm not a dyke.'

'Anyone who rides a bloody great Harley must be a dyke.'

'Ah, shut up,' the blonde said.

They dressed him like nurses, who've seen everything, but a lot rougher. 'Your boots are under that chair,' the brunette said.

They were his best boots. Ever since the day he'd had coffee with Evelyn at Manuka, he'd worn them, hoping to impress her. They hadn't done much for him then. She'd walked off in a bad mood, angry because he'd call her a liar. Last night he'd called her a liar again and look what had happened. He was half deaf and half dead.

He tried to reach for them, but his head felt like broken glass.

'Lift your flamin' feet, Harry.'

The brunette turned about and shoed him like a blacksmith, holding first one leg and then the other between her own.

'Let's go,' she said.

'I hate hospitals,' the blonde said. 'They always make me sneeze.'

'It's all the disinfectant they use.'

One on each side, they walked him out of Emergency to an unmarked car parked under a sign saying, 'Police Vehicles Only' and helped him in. The brunette put a hand on his head as he got into the back. 'Mind your nut,' she said. The blonde got behind the wheel.

'Where are we going?'

'Uh uh!'

'I'm the guy they tried to kill.'

'And they'll try again, if you don't get out of here.'

He gave up asking them and started thinking about it properly for the first time since he'd woken. Why would anyone wire the Holden when he was driving the BMW? But when had they wired it? Maybe last night, expecting he and Evelyn would drive off in his car. It had been parked outside, but they'd got into hers. Just as well. So, the crims had left the Holden in the street all day, hooked up with a grenade fixed to explode. They couldn't disarm it by day, not in an area like Forrest. Someone would notice, perhaps a woman at her window. Or kids kicking a football in the park.

They were going along Adelaide Avenue, towards Parliament House, when he spoke again. 'Where's my car?'

'In the forensics' garage,' Polly said. 'They're still trying to work out why a piece of string was wound around the drive shaft.'

'String?'

'Yeah, the same old trick. You tie one end to the shaft and the other to a grenade in a jam tin taped to the frame underneath. The pin's already been pulled, so when you start to move off, the grenade is yanked out of the tin and—bang! The petrol tank blew up. You were lucky it was nearly empty.'

'Yeah, lucky.'

He was silent for a while. Thinking was difficult, like trying to roll pine logs uphill. His head hurt, his brain hurt. Even thinking hurt. He should stop thinking, but he couldn't.

'Where's my gun?'

'You mean that old howitzer? Palfreyman has it. He points it at everyone and says, 'Pow!'.'

Soon they were crossing the lake. Everything looked flat or, better still, flattened. It could have been a painted town, just a lot of flaps on a movie set. All very interesting, but unbelievable. A picturesque town, where no one lived or worked. They simply acted as though they did.

'Who did it?' he said.

'Tried to kill you? We know nothing, we hear nothing. We just do what we're told, don't we, Chook?'

'Stop calling me Chook.'

'You girls been in the force long?'

'Yeah, too long,' the blonde said.

'What do you do?'

'We used to work in Major Crime,' the brunette said, 'but we were tossed out, weren't we, Stace? Giving too much cheek. Now, as a punishment, we're in Witness Protection, which is as dull as dishwater.'

'Join the cops and die of boredom,' the blonde said.

'Ever get any sleep?'

'Only on the job.'

They went up Northbourne Avenue with the Sunday drivers returning home. It is a long road, the main drag into Canberra, or out of it, depending which way you are going. Every few hundred yards, they had to stop for red lights. He looked around. People in neighbouring cars were passing slowly or slowly dropping back. No one seemed to be agitated or excited or even fully conscious. They just stared ahead like fish, going wherever nature decided. Some were talking, some talking to no one. One or two were singing, some chatting on mobiles. Some seemed half asleep at the wheel, some chewing. One woman wearing a tennis eyeshade was holding a bottle of mineral water high, her eyes closed, sucking it. She looked as though she'd had a bad day on the courts. Anyone who'd pay a thousand times as much as tap water for bottled water would always have a bad day, he thought. The woman had long, dark hair like Evelyn's. Otherwise, she didn't look like Evelyn. No one could look like Evelyn.

'Are you girls Italian, by any chance?'

'Italians? Hell, no. What do you think this wreck is? A mafia staff car? No such luck. No, I'm a Greek and Stacey's a Ukie, aren't you?'

'A what?'

'Ukrainian. You should hear her swear in Russian!'

'You know Palfreyman?' he asked.

'That drongo?'

'You don't like him?'

'Ah, he's the one got us tossed out of major crime, for arguing with him.'

'About what?'

'You of all people.'

'Yeah?'

'Yeah, that bonehead was going to arrest you for killing that bloke found face down in the lake, but we told him you hadn't been anywhere near the lake that night.

'You must've gone to sleep on the job,' he said.

'We didn't lose him for a minute,' we said.

'Well, how come the bullets that killed him came out of his gun?' he said.

'It's a set-up,' we said, 'anyone with half a brain can see that.'

'Hey, you be careful what you say,' he said.

'Ah, get stuffed,' we said. Next thing we know we're hauled up before the divisional super and told disrespect for a senior officer will not be tolerated!'

'So here we are,' the blonde said, 'stuck with you for another eight hours.'

'Both of you?'

'No, one at a time.'

'Glad you stuck with me that night.'

'Ah, that's all right, mate.'

'Why don't you like Palfreyman?'

'Been in the force only eight years. He'd been to college somewhere out in the bush and got himself a degree in criminology, so they made him a sergeant. That peanut's full of himself.'

'All theory and no brains?'

'As thick as two bricks, isn't he, Stace?'

'Couldn't find his own dick on a dark night.'

'Even with a torch.'

'Is he running this investigation?'

'No, he's just doing the surveillance bit. Big Jim Lemon's our DCI. You know Jim?'

'Can't say I do.'

'Big bloke as bald as an egg. Very serious. When you tell him something, he stares at you for five minutes before he makes a decision. A deep thinker is our Jim, isn't he, Stace?'

The blonde did not answer.

They drove on and on. He didn't feel so bad now. Also, he wasn't shouting. His ears were still buzzing, and he had to strain to understand the two women in front, but it was worth it. He liked them. The force needed more like them, gun-toting sheilas with a sense of humour. In fact, he was beginning to relax. He was back in the arms of the police. The Federal police, in fact, the nation's top cops. It was beginning to feel like the old days. He was with friends. These two young women were going to protect him, even if it meant laying down their own lives for a worthless bum like him.

They were honourable women, good women. That's how it should be. Perhaps someday he'd get back into the force. He'd like to be a cop again. In a nice country town, where nothing ever happened. Where the girls were pretty and more than just friendly.

Polly was singing a song, slapping a knee as she went along. It was an old Glen Campbell hit: 'I wake up in the morning with my hair down in my eyes/ And she says hi...'

Polly turned her head. 'You ever go dancing, Harry?'

'Only when the bullets are flying.'

She laughed. 'Only when the bullets are—Hey, Chook, did you hear that?'

'Don't call me Chook.'

'Ah, darling, Polly means no harm. Polly want a cracker—'

'For Christ's sake, shut up.'

There was a long silence until they had just passed Macarthur Avenue, when the blonde spoke up. 'We hear you're one of us, Harry?'

'That was some time ago.'

'Been a naughty boy, eh? Been on the fiddle? Got kicked out?'

'I made a mistake.'

'Took a bullet too, we noticed.'

'Yeah.'

Polly intervened. 'Ah, we all make mistakes now and then. But, it's a good life, don't you think? Being a cop? Except for those all-night stakeouts. I was a cop in Sydney. So was my dad. Still is, back in Bankstown. We were always arguing. After two years we decided Sydney wasn't big enough for us both, so I came up here and joined the feds. Stacey's from Melbourne, aren't you, Stace? She's a kick boxer too, a national champion. You want to give her any cheek, Harry, hang onto your teeth.' She laughed again. 'Your dad a cop?'

'No, army.'

'A soldier boy? Where is he now?'

'Dead.'

'Vietnam?'

'Yeah.'

'Ah, gee. All the good guys end up dead.'

'And all the bad ones live forever,' the blonde said.

'Yeah, but you meet some interesting people, don't you? How did you meet up with the gorgeous Mrs Crowley?'

'I reunited her with her bag. Someone'd nicked it.'

'And things just developed from there?'

'Yeah, from there.'

'Hey, turn right here!'

'I am turning right.'

They'd reached Antill Street. They hadn't gone far up it when Polly said, 'And now left!'

'Look, sister, if you want to drive the bloody thing—'

'I'm sorry, I'm sorry!'

'Jesus, one day, Polly—'

Polly punched her on a shoulder, then patted her fondly. 'I love ya', Stace.'

They drove slowly through Watson. This was an old suburb. Only thirty years ago it had been a new suburb. It looked clean enough now, but the trees looked better than the houses, which all looked the same—a housing commission estate. They pulled up in front of a forlorn brown-brick house. It did not have much garden, just a few small bushes against the old paling fences. A good thing for a safe house. Not enough cover for anyone watching the place.

The lawn was bare in parts. Canberra had had very little good rain for months, mainly light stuff gone in a few minutes, like today. There was a small metal tricycle overturned on the grass and down the back Becker could see a rotary clothesline. A couple of tea towels hung on it. The place looked familiar. On the other hand, it looked like any other house built in Canberra soon after the war. These houses were known as 'govies'. Only the lonely lived there. He thought he might have been here at night. Or he might not. A car with lights and sirens on top was standing in the driveway. Inside were the man and woman who'd been their escorts that morning. The female officer got out, came over.

'Jesus, Polly, we were supposed to knock off an hour ago.'

'Ah, this dopey bastard wouldn't wake up.'

'All right, is he?'

'Still in one piece.'

Stacey was opening a door for Becker.

'Come on, soldier, on your feet.'

Together they got him out, inch by inch.

'Okay, Harry,' Polly said, 'let's meet the folks.'

The house had a tiny concrete porch without a roof. There was a white-painted railing around the concrete, rusty in parts. The front door was almost all glass, rippled. Through the glass, he could just make out a coloured something that could have been left over from last Christmas. After Evelyn's house, everything here was in the worst possible taste, which was no taste at all.

Polly rapped on the door. 'Open up! Armed police!'

The door opened. A large woman with long black hair, too black to be real at her age, and a large red nose stood there, smiling.

'Hello, Harry,' she said.

CHAPTER 26

He walked in, surprised. It was Rita Rawlings, the woman in the credit department at David Jones, the one who'd helped him trace Torrence. He looked around for Evelyn but did not see her. The place was better inside, very tidy, very neat. There was a faint odour of deodoriser, redolent of pine. On the wall were pictures of Scottish lakes. Rita had said she was Scottish, although she did not have much of an accent, just a soft purr. In fact, she didn't look Scottish, more like a Gypsy. He'd met her at P.J. O'Reilly's pub in Alinga Street. They'd each been sitting alone in a corner, and she'd asked him if he were in the police force. He said he wasn't, but she'd said she'd thought he was because of his way of sitting and looking at people, as if memorising every detail, storing it away for future reference. Her husband had been like that. Becker had bought her a drink and later they'd had a pizza and salad together at Mamma's Trattoria, where she told him she looked like a Spaniard because one of her ancestors long ago had been a sailor on a ship in the Armada which had been blown ashore on the Hebrides in a hurricane. He'd survived and married a local woman. So she still had some of his genes. Becker had not believed her, but it was a good story.

'How are you, Rita?'

'All the better for seeing you, Harry.'

'How long—' he tried to ask.

'Have I been running a safe house? Ever since Keith died.'

He looked around stupidly, spotted a framed photograph on a gleaming sideboard. In it was a man in uniform including a hat. He was a sergeant. One day, he'd chased after a joker who'd snatched a woman's bag in the Belconnen Mall. He was too old for that sort of caper. He'd collapsed and died, heart trouble. Becker remembered this place now. He'd brought Rita home after the dinner and she'd offered him a glass of wine. He had politely declined and left, feeling he'd let her down. He was always letting women down. Must have been born that way.

'It helps pay the bills,' she added. 'And anyway, I'd do anything to help the force.'

'Where's—'

'Evelyn? Right behind you.'

He turned and saw her. At least he saw the smile first, then her face and the rest of her formed around it. She was standing first on one foot and then on the other. Her feet were bare. She was dressed as he'd last seen her, but of course without the car coat and the boots.

'Hello, Harry,' she said.

She walked up and put her arms about him. Immediately he knew her scent. It was not perfume or scented soap or any of those things, not even the scent of her clothes but an Evelyn scent. It was not body odour but the natural scent of a woman, warm, clean and intimate.

'You were asleep?'

'Yes. I heard you talking. Are you hurt badly?'

'Just a knock on the head.'

'Concussion,' Polly said. 'Feeling a bit yuckie, aren't you? I've got something for you.' She held out a small packet.

'What's that?'

'Stemetil. Take two now.'

Evelyn was holding him and patting him, even his face. And kissing him, fairy kisses as light as rain. 'I nearly died when I saw you blow up.'

'I was all right.'

'Thank God.' She kissed him on the lips, just as lightly.

Rita chuckled and Polly said, 'Wow!' The blonde had entered. She simply stood, watching them, a hand sitting on her sidearm. She had that kind of stance. Any funny business and you're dead.

'How long are we going to be here?'

Polly said, 'Who knows? Until they can find a nice quiet hidey hole for you both. They tell me Cairns is nice this time of the year.'

'Cairns?'

'Just painting a pretty picture. You'd better get some rest, Harry. It's seven hours since you had that shot of morphine.' She produced another packet. 'These are Panadeine Forte, don't take more than two each eight hours.' She gave them to Evelyn. 'I'm your guardian angel till midnight. Chook will take over till dawn. She's gonna take a break now, going back with that crew out front. Another car will be here soon.'

The blonde nodded and walked out. That was about it.

It was now late afternoon, very late. The sun was down behind the hills.

By the time he'd had a shower, helped by Evelyn, then got into pyjamas, which Rita produced from somewhere, he was worn out, but the pain had gone down. They had an early meal, homemade soup and toast, but Becker could not eat much. He tried to stay awake, but it was difficult. They watched some television, all four of them, until the news came on at six-thirty. There was a brief report on the car explosion, just a shot of the wrecked Holden in the street and a reporter saying someone had tried to kill Mr Becker, a 'retired' policeman, who had been visiting a friend in the street. The friend was not named. Police believed the matter might have been gang related.

Polly went out and patrolled the garden. She seemed to be checking things. Now and then a door or window would rattle. Once Rita looked out and saw her under a streetlight, talking to someone in a patrol car. Inside, her mobile phone would go off and she'd say, 'Yeah, all right.' Or 'Yeah, I know.' Or 'Quiet as the grave.' But on one occasion, 'Go ahead, you creep. Go ahead and report me, you little Dago creep.'

They were surprised, Rita, Becker and Evelyn.

She explained. 'Sorry about that. Gee, that bloke annoys me, he really does.'

'Who was it?'

'Adams.'

Becker sat up. He'd been nodding off. 'Adams?'

'Yeah, you know him?'

'I've seen him around. What did he want?'

'He's going to report me for assault.'

'You assaulted him?'

'Only in self-defence.'

'He attacked you?'

She did not answer at first. They were now watching a bank holdup in Texas. Real Bonnie and Clyde stuff. Got away with four million.

'Well, one night he wandered into the office. This was when we were still with Major Crime. I was minding the shop. Everyone was out on jobs—' She shrugged, half sitting and half lying in a chair, propped up on an elbow. She was really good-looking for a cop. Becker thought she was about thirty.

'I was making myself a cup of coffee. I asked him if he wanted one too. He said he'd have anything I had to offer. He was walking around behind me. I was pouring a cup when he came up and pulled down my panties. Black bikinis, they were. He was rubbing himself against me, the dirty bastard. I had a skirt on that day. We'd been doing some VIP escort stuff and the Arabs don't like women in tight pants.'

Rita had been dozing off, but came to life.

'What'd you do, love?'

'I tried to fight him off with my elbows. I even threw hot coffee over my shoulder but missed the bastard. He just laughed. So I turned and socked him in the mush. He fell back, so I kicked him in the balls.'

'Gee, love!'

'He was dancing around, holding his balls with one hand and his mouth with the other. It was starting to bleed. Finally, he calmed down and said he was sorry.'

'What'd you do?'

'Asked him whether he still wanted coffee?'

'Gee, you were brave.'

'Not brave, just quick.'

'Did he do anything? I mean officially?'

'Mumbled something about reporting me for assault.'

'And did he?'

'That was two months ago, so why is he threatening me now?'

Becker spoke up, 'Why did you call him a Dago?'

'That's what he is.'

Evelyn flinched, Becker could feel it in her body. They were sitting on a couch with iron springs, holding hands and longing to go to bed. It had been a bad day.

'With a name like Adams?'

'George Joseph Adams? I checked him out, just in case he hit me with an assault charge. He was born Giorgio Giuseppe Adamo in Italy thirty-nine years ago.'

Evelyn was sitting up now, frightened.

'Where was he born?'

'Oh, I don't know. Some dump down south, I think.'

'What town?'

'I don't remember, but it was well south. I told Palfreyman. He said to forget it. I was just being racist, calling him a Dago.'

Evelyn tensed. Becker thought it was because of the term 'Dago,' but it wasn't.

'What is it?' he asked her.

'I think he is...' she whispered.

'Is what?' He leaned in to hear her.

Just then the house phone rang. They watched as Rita went to it. 'Hello? Polly? You want to speak to Polly? Just a minute—Hello?'

'Who was that?'

'They wanted to speak to you.'

'But who was it?'

'He didn't say. He just hung up.'

'Jesus—'

'Something wrong, Polly?'

'Yeah, there sure is.'

Polly went to a back room and called on her mobile. No one spoke until she came back. 'I rang Big Jim himself. He's going to station a car outside full time tonight,' she said.

'Why?' Becker said. He couldn't think straight. He knew he should be alarmed, but he felt too sore and old to care. Things seemed to be getting away from him.

'Something doesn't look too good. They've had a phone call.'

'Who from?'

'Some guy with a foreign accent.'

'What did he say?'

'The guy? Jim wouldn't say, but he did say lock up tight and don't go outdoors under any circumstances.'

'Oh, Polly!' Rita said. 'Is it safe?'

'It will be when that car arrives. Put him to bed, Evelyn. He looks half dead.'

She nodded. 'Yes, yes.'

'And another thing, you two will be at the airport at 6 am tomorrow, so get some sleep.'

He took two Panadeine and they went to the bedroom. Rita must have cleared it out for them. Except for the jug of water and two glasses, the dressing table was bare. In one corner a bar radiator glowed warmly. It was a double bed with a doona and four thick pillows. He took one off.

'You don't like two pillows?'

'Gives me a crick in the neck,' he said. 'How about you?'

'Me too,' she said.

Evelyn had a nightgown, but did not use it. She simply stripped off and stood naked in the warmth from the radiator and the subdued streetlight coming through the thick lace curtains.

'So here we are,' she said.

She sounded like young bride on the first night, embarrassed but eager to please.

He did not answer. He went to her and kissed her lips and her breasts and her belly. He didn't know why he did that, except she looked like a fruitful woman. Then he dropped the clothes that had come out of the police ragbag, and they went to bed. He was about to get on top of her, thinking that was what she expected, but she whispered, 'Not tonight, your head might explode. Let's just lie like this.'

'Okay,' he said and held her in both arms.

She snuggled down. 'Hold me tight,' she said. Her body was tense and withdrawn. She sounded tearful. Then he remembered—she had lost her only child that morning. She was grieving. So he held her close. Soon she was breathing deeply, her breath stroking his neck. But she was not asleep, he could tell. Her eyelashes were brushing his cheek.

'Evelyn?'

'Mmm?'

'Why did you recognise Adams?'

'What do you mean?'

'Adams, back at the station when we were being interviewed, you said you thought you knew him. And just then, his name...'

'No, I've never seen him before.'

'Why did you say you did?'

'I didn't recognise him. I recognised his eyes.'

'What do you mean?'

'Oh, the way he was looking at me. He's Calabrian.'

'How do you know?'

'I could see it in his eyes. When a man looks at you that way, he is thinking: I'll have you one day and you'll never do anything about it, because you're one of us.'

'Jesus.'

'No, God. They think God is with them. No one can touch them, no one will talk.'

He thought about Adams. She was right. He did look like her, which meant he looked like just about anyone from down south. She was lying with her head on a shoulder and an arm across his chest. It was his bad shoulder, and it hurt, but that did not matter. Gradually she relaxed. Suddenly her body went soft and welcoming.

'Harry?'

'Yeah?'

'Are you happy?'

'Sure.'

'No regrets?'

'Nope.'

'That's good. How's your old feller? Not hurt, is he?'

She reached down and felt him. He did not answer. They lay that way for a while. Becker was uneasy. He was lying in bed with a strange woman, who was a cheat and liar and, on her own admission, a murderer—a woman who would kill if she were rejected. Or if you became a problem. He felt rotten, he shouldn't be here, but somehow he'd wandered into her world of crime and deception and the old ways, in which you could get yourself killed if you did the wrong thing, such as smiling at a woman who wasn't yours. He had been incorporated, just like Donald Crowley had been all those years ago. He should get out, while he still had a chance. But he couldn't get out. He loved her, for better or worse. Probably worse.

'Harry?'

'Mmm?'

'Do you love me now? Just a little bit?'

'You'll do me for a pissy old mate.'

'What?' She laughed so much against him that pain stabbed through his shoulder. He gasped. 'Oh, God, I'm sorry,' she said.

'It's all right.'

'I'm so sorry, I shouldn't have asked.'

'Go to sleep, Evelyn.'

She was still chuckling. He waited until she settled down again. His head and his brain and his whole person felt bruised. The lump on his head was throbbing. It might burst at any moment.

'Harry?'

'What now?'

'I'm fertile at present. I may be pregnant right now. If I am, I won't do anything about it. Is that all right with you?'

'Yeah, sure.'

She lifted her head and kissed him on a cheek.

'Good night, Harry. And thank you for everything.'

Soon she was breathing deeply, almost panting, fast asleep. He couldn't get to sleep. The codeine was not yet working, or it was not working well enough.

Then he had a vision, something that had been bothering him. It was Adams at the butts. He saw him firing, one shot after another. Five bulls in a row, just like that. The gun was in the left hand, propped up by the right. It had a long barrel, the longer the better. A heavy weapon, almost no kick.

'What's that handgun?' he'd asked a man standing next to him.

'That, mate? That is a Beretta 92FS parabellum. Some say it's the best target pistol in the world and—' The man had leaned closer, dropping his voice. 'Some say it's the assassin's weapon of choice.'

Yes, he thought, that was the weapon. And that was the arm of the man holding it.

He should tell someone. What was her name? He couldn't think straight. Molly? Polly? Yes, Polly. Pretty Polly. Yes, tell her Adams was the one who'd killed... They should check him out, they... At last the codeine began to work, that and the immense tiredness and the shock. His eyes closed. He began to sink, down and down. Sleep closed in. Darkness too. He had to tell Polly something, but it was too late. It was always too late.

CHAPTER 27

The door flew open; the light flicked on. Someone rushed into the room. It was a woman with a gun. She pointed it at Becker. He sat up, dazed. The woman was shouting: 'What happened? Wake up!' She prodded him with the pistol. He sat up, stupefied.

'What?' he said.

'What? Oh, Christ,' she said. 'Oh, Christ!'

'What?' he said again. She was edging around the end of the bed, the revolver still trained on him. He followed her gaze. Or tried to. His vision was blurred. Evelyn was lying beside him, turned away. She must have rolled off his bad shoulder. Her head was down, so he couldn't at first see what Babchuk could see.

'Ah, hell!' she said.

'What?'

'Have a look!'

He leaned over, closer and closer, until he saw it, the blood. It was matted in her hair at the temple, already thick and dark. It must have happened some time ago.

'Oh, God, no, no—' He shook her. 'Evelyn!'

'Don't touch her,' Babchuk said. 'Didn't you hear a bloody thing?'

'No—' He didn't know what to say. It was too horrible.

'How could anyone come in here and you—' She began to howl. 'Oh, Christ, no, no, no!'

'Polly?' he said.

'Dead!'

'What?' He tried to get out of the bed, but swooned and fell back. He tried again. This time he crashed into a wall. It was only then that he realised the acrid smell in the room was the smell you get after an explosion. Like a gunshot.

'Go and look. Polly's lying in the hall.'

'Ah, hell, no, no—'

'How could you sleep through this?'

Babchuk was close to tears. He was sick with guilt. Someone had killed Evelyn as she had lain beside him. And he hadn't heard a thing. And Polly...

Babchuk was on her phone already.

'Get inside here—now!'

At first, he didn't know who she was talking to, until he heard heavy footsteps. Two men in uniform came in.

'Oh, Jesus,' one said.

'Polly's down there, by the back door,' she said.

One of them went down. The other said, 'How the hell?'

'This moron slept through it all, by the look of it.'

'We didn't hear a thing,' he said.

'Didn't you hear me bashing down the door?'

'Must have used a pillow.'

'What?'

'Yeah, look at this.' He held one up. It was scorched by heat and powder burn.

'Jesus.'

The other man came back. 'Gee, poor Polly.'

'Get an ambulance,' she said.

'A bit too late, by the look of it, Chook.'

'And don't call me Chook!'

'Yeah, sure.'

'Search the place, inside and out.'

'Yeah, yeah.'

Becker was leaning against the wall, naked and ashamed. Not because he was naked, but because he'd failed. He'd failed horribly. He was at a dead loss. He'd not been able to save the one woman in the whole world, who'd trusted him to get her out of a mess. No other woman had ever expected him to get anything right, not his wife and not even his own mother.

He was too shocked to think, but not too shocked to feel. He was shaking, as though he'd just stepped out of an icy bath. He was going to vomit, except he did not feel nauseated, just revolted at the sight. Evelyn looked peaceful lying on her side, her nose buried in the pillow, just a smear of blood among her rich brown hair, a few strands lying across her cheek and one lying across an eye. It was closed. At least she had not known what was about to happen. He couldn't see the other eye, but it too would be closed. She seemed marvellously at rest. He fully expected her to stir, turn, sigh, look at him and say, Hello? Why are you looking at me like that?

But she did not.

He could hear Babchuk in the living room talking to someone loudly. Saying what she had found, when she'd smashed the front door glass and walked in. 'Both dead,' she said. 'Him? He's okay, slept through the whole bloody thing. Stoned, by the look of him.'

Becker wrapped a sheet about himself and went out to her.

'Adams,' he said.

'What?'

'She recognised him.'

'What do you mean?'

'She said he was one of them.'

'What'd she mean?'

'Calabrian.'

'So?'

'And I saw him shoot the girl.'

'In the park? You saw his face?'

'No, just his arm and the weapon. It was a Beretta. He has one, a—a—' He couldn't think. '92 something—'

'FS?' one of the cops said.

'Yeah.'

'Jesus!' Babchuk said. 'Did you hear? The weapon was a Beretta 92 FS. Adams has one. What? Yeah, Senior Detective George Adams! He killed the girl in the park. We have a witness!'

Babchuk closed the phone, then went to Polly, lying on her side by the back door. One arm was twisted under her body. She kneeled down and lifted her head.

'Goodbye, Polly,' she said. 'I love you. I've always loved you.'

Rita came out in a heavy dressing gown and slippers, looking stupefied. She was the kind of woman who'd need a pill every night.

'What's happened?'

No one answered. It seemed pretty obvious.

'Not—?'

'Yes,' Babchuk said. 'Both of them.'

It didn't take long to find Adams. He was at home drinking a Bacardi neat and watching soccer on television, when the special operations squad burst in. He'd been thinking he should clear out, but that would make him a certain suspect. He'd shot a young girl and missed the real target. He'd blown up a car, but the woman wasn't in it. He'd shot Russo to shut him up, but he was still alive in hospital under police guard. No one at the office would tell him where the Evelyn was, so he'd had to phone around until he located Polly. So he'd phoned Melbourne. 'The bitch is being moved out,' he'd said.

'Where is she?'

'In some dump out in the sticks. I've been there. They have a car out front and an officer inside. It's three against one.'

'So what?' the man had said. There'd been a long, embarrassing silence. The man was blowing smoke thoughtfully, Adams could hear it. Then he'd said, 'I'll send someone, I'll send the kid. You can expect a call.'

He'd frozen. Now he knew who'd ordered the hit on Ritzi Carbone.

There was a new joker in Melbourne, a young bloke no one knew. He was not Calabrian, not even Italian, but some Albanian or Serb or Pole, who had no connection with any family. It was safer that way. He'd popped that bonehead Giancarlo in Sydney Road. Early in the year he'd walked into Gianelli's Bistro in Lygon Street wearing a full-face helmet. The place was packed, it always was on Fridays, waiters dancing everywhere shouting orders. He'd walked up to Ritzi, who was lunching with some grape growers down from Griffith up in New South Wales, people who'd made a lot of money out of cannabis. Ritzi was called Ritzi because he'd worked, so he said, at the Hotel Ritz in London. He also walked with a cane, inside of which, it was said, was a stiletto. Ritzi had good reason to be happy. He'd stabbed Mario Scotto in broad daylight at the Queen Victoria markets last year. Strangely, no one had seen a thing. He'd been slammed into Barwon supermax, charged with murder. Bail had been refused, and yet now, suddenly, he was out on bail, a man with his reputation. Everyone thought that peculiar. Maybe Ritzi had done a deal with the cops, named a few names.

'Hey,' the kid had said, patting him on a shoulder.

'You the one called Ritzi?'

'Who wants to know?' Ritzi had said.

'You don't need to know, pal,' the kid had said. He'd pulled out a Browning .25, which is a popgun, quite useless unless you hit the brain or the heart. Which the kid must have known, because he'd pushed Ritzi's face down in his plate of zuppa and then shot him straight through the head, so the plate blew apart, scattering soup everywhere. It was pomadoro con pimento, which is very red, so the blood did not show. Well, the kid had just walked out, hopped onto a mountain bike and shot off down the street, singing 'Hi-ho, Silver!' A real psycho, everyone said, and no table manners. But at least he had style. Late that evening, he arrived at Canberra airport on the last plane out of Melbourne. Immediately, he went to a phone and called Adams.

An hour or so later, the kid climbed over the back fence and let himself in with a key that could open any lock. Then he rattled something in the laundry. When Polly had come back to investigate, he'd shot her point blank. Then went from room to room, looking for the Crowley bitch. He had a black and white photo of her. She was in the front bedroom, sound asleep. The creep with her was flat on his back, snoring. So he'd opened the curtain to get a better look. Outside he could see the patrol car. The engine was running, the tailpipe steaming. Two cops sitting in a car and probably listening to the radio, bored stiff. He'd walked right past it, checking out the place according to Adams' details. Then he'd walked right around the block, working out which house in the back street was in line with the target. Now he was looking at the cops from inside. Big joke. He'd picked up a loose pillow, wrapped it around the Browning, held it an inch or two above her temple and pulled the trigger. Hardly any sound, just a sharp whop! like a repressed cough. The creep had stirred but had not woken. At first the kid thought of popping him too, but he had no such instructions. And so he'd walked out the rear door, climbed the back fence and beat it the way he'd come.

The police thought Adams had done the job. They busted into his locker at work and found his service revolver, but it had not been fired lately. They couldn't find the Beretta. Maybe he'd ditched it in the lake or dug a hole in the bush. No great problem.

They had enough on him to hold him on suspicion. A strange man had phoned police operations. A girl working the board had taken the call.

'That fella calls hisself Adams, that policeman,' he was saying, 'his real name he Giorgio Adamo an' he kill that girl in the park, you know? And he kill that fella, Vincenzo, in the lake. An' he put that bomb under that car. You gotta get him. He gonna kill Evelyn, you know? Evalina Crowley.'

'Sir, sir, what is your name, please?' the operator asked.

'That fella policeman, calls hisself George Adams.'

At the same time, she'd been frantically waving. Her supervisor came over, tried to listen in, but it was too late. The caller had hung up.

They couldn't arrest a man on the say-so of an anonymous caller. He seemed to be in the clear. He said he was at home when the job was done. He couldn't prove it, but the police couldn't prove he wasn't. Also, the forensic tests showed that Evelyn was killed with a small-calibre bullet, possibly .25 inch. But Adams did not have such a weapon. It looked like he might never be charged. Then, three days later, his luck ran out. Russo woke up. After thinking about things for a while, he called for the police guard and said he wanted to make a statement. It was curtains for Adams. No way out.

CHAPTER 28

Evelyn was buried next Friday. Only a few turned up. Her Filipina maid was there. So was Stacey Babchuk, whose real name was Anastacia. She'd farewelled Polly at a police funeral on the day before and she wasn't feeling too good, but she wanted to say goodbye. Rita Rawlings was there, and so was a young man in his late twenties, who introduced himself as Troy. He was a trim, fit bloke in a sweatshirt and wearing some sort of medallion on a chain. He had a crew cut and you could see he was tough in a professional way, but he'd probably go to water if you poked a shooter up his snout one dark night. He was her personal trainer, he said. Probably one of her lovers, too. What had Palfreyman said? She likes a bit of rough trade?

'She was a beautiful woman,' he said to Becker.

'Yeah.'

'You knew her well?'

'Only professionally.'

'Oh?' He sounded nervous, as though he did not want to know how professional.

'Nothing personal though.'

'Oh, yeah?'

'I made a few enquiries for her.'

'What sort of enquiries?'

'About some of her friends.'

'Oh?' He blanched, then excused himself.

He was probably the sort of bloke happy to give rich women a good workout, both in the gym and in bed, wherever they wanted it. There was probably a fair sort of living in it for the right sort of bloke. Even in a quiet place such as Canberra.

Evelyn's lawyer came up. She was also her executor, and her name was Sylvia Feinman. She'd arranged the funeral.

'Evelyn had left everything to her daughter,' she said.

'Yeah, I know.'

'But the girl is dead, so there are no beneficiaries, which is like dying intestate.'

Becker said nothing.

'You and she seem to have been close.'

'It was just two nights.'

'You went to bed with her?'

'Yeah.'

'Did she do that willingly?'

'It was her idea.'

'Were there any witnesses?'

'No.'

'And the second night? Of her own free will?'

'Yeah.'

'Any witnesses?'

'Those two over there.' He indicated Rita and Stacey Babchuk chatting.

'It looks as though I shall have to apply for a grant of letters of administration. If the court agrees, all of Evelyn's estate will be vested in me. I will then distribute it according to what I believe would be her wishes.'

'No one knows her wishes.'

'Oh, yes, I do. Evelyn rang me that afternoon, while she was in protective custody. She said she was going away and would write to me in a few days. In the meantime, I was to secure the house, clear out the refrigerator, remove her jewellery and documents to a safe deposit box, dismiss the maid, that sort of thing. I've done all that. She told me where to find a key.'

'What else did she say?'

'That if anything happened to her, you on one hand and Mr and Mrs Billings on the other would share her estate in two equal parts. Of course, with this application I have to attach an estimate of the value of her estate, most of which she inherited from her husband, but his solicitor is handling all that.'

'I don't want anything.'

Becker looked away, no one else was coming. Oddly, there was a strange smell of cigarette, although no one was smoking. The lawyer was a small, dark woman with hair pulled back by a big comb at the back, Spanish style. She wasn't a Spaniard. Her eyes were small and dark and inquisitive, screwed up in the flat grey light. The kind of eyes that didn't miss much.

'I see you are driving her car?'

'Yeah, mine, you see—'

'That's all right. You can drive it until this matter is settled.'

The car, the car she drove. It would be good to keep the car. It smelled of her and had the feel of her. It was like driving with her and in her. She was all around him as he sat behind the wheel. It was the wheel that she had touched, the seat in which she had sat.

'You can do that?'

'Once administration is granted, I will dispose of everything, but that could take months. In the meantime, if you want that particular car, take it.'

An undertaker came up. 'Could we…?' he asked, hands clenched, eyebrows raised, one finger raised.

'Yes,' she said. 'I don't think anyone else will be here.'

She was right. Evelyn knew a lot of people, but had few friends.

There was no priest or celebrant of any kind, just two undertakers. They really were undertakers in this case. She was going down into the deep, dark earth. That's what she'd requested in her will. When it touched bottom, Becker picked up a clod of damp earth and dropped it on the coffin. That's what his mother had done when they'd brought his father's body back from Vietnam and buried it in the Wagga Cemetery. Then she'd nudged him. For a moment, he'd not known what she'd meant, then he'd realised. So, he'd done the same. That was about all Harry Becker knew about burying the dead.

When it was finished, Babchuk came over.

'I owe you an apology,' she said.

'Yeah?'

'I shouldn't have said what I did. I mean, saying you were stoned and—'

'That's all right. I was stoned. I couldn't stay awake.'

'You were suffering a concussion. I was out of line.'

'I'm sorry about Polly,' he said.

'Yeah, so am I. She was the best.' She looked around. 'We failed, didn't we?'

He thought she meant Polly.

'Mrs Crowley,' she explained. 'We let her down, let you down, let the force down.'

'No one was to know he'd come in over the back fence.'

She did not reply.

'What's happened to Adams?'

'He's been charged. With the murder of both Torrence and the girl. Attempted murder of Russo.'

'And Evelyn? And Polly?'

'He didn't do it. He can prove it.'

'Then who did?'

'I don't know, but I'll find out.'

Cars were arriving for another funeral.

'We should have known,' he said. 'We fell short.'

'We all fell short.'

Babchuk stood as a boxer, hands almost clenched. She was not on duty and wore a simple dress and simple shoes. Nothing belligerent about her, but she was ready for a fight with someone, you could see.

'What's happened to Palfreyman?' Becker asked.

'Suspended from duty. He had that piece of shit working for him, a mafioso, would you believe? And didn't wake up to him. No wonder the crims had good intelligence.'

'Yeah.'

Conversation fell flat. She held out a hand. He was surprised, but took it. It was a firm clasp, friendly and sorry. 'Anytime you feel like a drink, Harry—'

'Yeah, sure, thanks.'

'Despite appearances, I'm not a dyke, but Polly was the only person I've ever truly loved. She should have lived forever.'

'Yeah, she should.'

She began to leave but paused.

'That old shooter of yours, if you still want it you can pick it up from the duty sergeant any time.'

He was going to say he didn't want the Webley, just his own Smith and Wesson, but she was already walking away.

The cigarette smoke hit him again. It was old and smelly and probably loaded with nicotine. It reminded him of the smoke he'd noticed when the man in brown was sitting beside him at Manuka. Then he saw a tall, skinny man with jet-black hair and burnt-out eyes standing by a car, a black car. His hair was probably dyed. He had a grey moustache which went with his grey suit and his grey hat, which he was holding respectfully to his chest. It was edged with black and turned up all around like a Homburg. He wore a dark-blue tie, on which was pinned a diamond as small as a chickpea. Also, he had a hooked nose, larger than Evelyn's, but it was the same kind of nose, aquiline. A bird of prey. The stranger was smoking a black Sobranie. The wind was blowing Becker's way, so he went over.

'You're Alfredo, aren't you?'

He did not answer.

'You called the police about Adams?'

Still no answer.

'You were a bit late. Now she's dead.'

The man sucked on the cigarette, squinting. He blew smoke very slowly in a long, fine jet that seemed to go on forever.

'My frien', sometimes is difficult. Some people, they kill my brother an' my father, two good mans. Now they lookin' for me. We used have good life, no troubles. Rich pickings, that what you say? With golden soil and wealth for toil, that what you say? We work hard, we get nowhere. So, we have do little deal here, little deal there. That's what it like in new country. In old country, everybody know what he do. Everyone know him place, womans too. Evalina, she no listen. Many time she say she gonna kill that bastardo she call him. She can't stand him any longer what he do her. She ask me kill him, make some arrangement. Maybe acciden' somewhere, maybe a... what you say? Mugging gone wrong? Anything? I say, no, no, plenty people mad I do that. They kill me. She no listen, she kill him. Now they kill her.'

'She didn't kill him. He would have jumped, no matter what she did.'

The Italian was staring at Becker sideways, still squinting again as if he could not understand a word Becker was saying. At last, he shrugged.

'Evalina, she know rule. You no upset apple cart. That what you say? We say you no kill gold goose. Not in old country, not here, not anywhere. She pay price, yes.'

'She killed another man,' Becker said, 'back in Melbourne.'

The Italian drew on the Sobranie, squinting sideways at Becker. It was the kind of squint that had all the seriousness of death.

'My frien', when a man take good girl an' he say he love her and he do things her and he laugh and run away, you know what happen in my country? We cut him balls out, we fry them, maybe put in some onion and maybe a little tomato, maybe some garlic. You know what I mean? An' then we make him eat it. He don' eat, we have him. You know I mean? We have him with hot iron, what you call poker? So, he know what he done. You un'stand?'

Becker nodded.

'You think that bad? In my country is matter of honour. You take man's daughter, his sister, his wife, you die very bad.'

He did not know what to say.

'That man in Melbourne, he tell her lie, he take her. She cry. She kill him. She did good thing. She know the law, the old law. You no take good girl. You wan' her, you got ask her father. He say Yes, you got marry her. In Australia, everybody got no honour. No respect womans. No respect themself, no respect anything. You know what I mean?'

'Yeah.'

'You love Evelyn?'

'Yeah.'

The Italian studied Becker, still sucking on the cigarette. It was near the end, close to his yellow fingers. He looked the sort of man who'd had a cigarette in his hands most of his waking life. He looked sick, old before his time. He would not last much longer. His grey eyes were full of the ashes of life and his lungs full of nicotine.

He took one last suck on the cigarette.

'She bella donna, the best. We all love her.'

'Now she's dead.'

'She my family. I try save her—'

He let the cigarette fall. Then, with the toe of his shiny black shoe, he rubbed it gently into the cold, unfriendly earth.

'You failed.'

'We alla fail. A woman like that—'

He did not finish the thought. Instead, he extended a hand. Becker was surprised. He looked at the hand with distaste, at the same time trying not to show his distaste. But he accepted. They shook, just one shake. That was all.

'Goodbye, my frien'.'

He got into the car and started it up. It took a long time to move. Eventually it moved off slowly, respectfully. Leaving his stinking smell behind. More cars were arriving, twenty or thirty. Whoever was next to be buried must have been someone important, or had a big family or a lot of friends or held a lot of IOUs. Unlike Evelyn. She'd had nothing on anyone, except that smelly little runt she'd been married to. She was just a memory. Soon she would be forgotten.

That afternoon he went to police headquarters and asked for his Smith and Wesson, but was told he couldn't have it because it was still evidence. He could have the Webley, which was not his. He was going to argue but changed his mind. He might still need something. So he went back to the house in Empire Circuit, walked up to the front door and said to himself: Are you Mrs Crowley? Yes, I am. I think I have something of yours. He stared at the door for a long time, hoping it would open and she would be standing behind the screen. But it did not. And she was not.

He went over to the park and stood among the naked trees, looking at the spot where the dog had saved Evelyn and the girl had died. And thinking about the banality of murder. You did it not because you had to do it, but because it was there to be done. A man like Adams did it because he could do it, kill a woman just because she was a problem. It was a skill some people had, such as playing cards or tennis or balancing a wine glass on your forehead. Or shooting rabbits.

It was getting cold now. Tomorrow would be the first official day of winter.

A leaf fell.

He sat on the seat and thought about things. Today he had buried his wife—not the first one in Sydney, who did not wish to see him, because he was a disgrace to the family and the police force—but Evelyn Crowley. On the first night, he'd slept with her, she'd taken him as her lover. On the second, she'd fallen asleep in his arms, like a wife. Only a loving woman would do that. So, he thought about her like that, like it could have been, despite everything.

'Evelyn,' he said.

'Yes?'

All he could say was, 'I love you.' It was the first time he'd said it to her.

She laughed. 'I love you too. Harry?'

'Yeah?'

'What are you doing out there?'

'Just looking at the stars.'

'And listening to the waves? They are putting me to sleep. We had a lovely day, didn't we? Walking miles and—' She yawned. 'Oh, dear, come to bed.'

She was genuinely tired. They'd walked along a beach, the waves rushing at them and then receding, she was dancing out of the way and laughing. She took no pills now, drank very little, no more than one glass of wine a day, because of the baby. He stood there, looking at the evening star and listening to the sighing of the surf. Out there in the blackness was nothing for several thousand miles, nothing until you hit Africa.

'Harry?'

'Yeah?'

'What will we call her?'

'Whatever you like.'

'Do you have another name? I mean, Harry is just a nickname, isn't it?'

'It's Henry.'

'Henry Becker?' She thought about it. 'How about Henrietta?'

'That's a long name for a girl.'

'Henrietta Becker sounds good, a distinguished name. How about Henrietta Eva?'

'Okay.'

'Henrietta Eva Becker, how about that?'

'Whatever you like.'

'That's settled, then. Thank you.' There was a long pause. 'Come and tell me a story, darling.'

'I'm all out of stories.'

'Just one more, then I'll never ask again.'

He went in and sat on an edge of the bed, held one of her hands. With the other hand, she was patting her belly, as though patting a baby to sleep. She was three months gone now.

'This is not much of a story,' he said.

'Anything,' she said.

'One day I came home from school and found Mum sitting at the kitchen table. There was a cup of tea before her, steaming in the light from the window. She was looking out the window, eyes wide open. At first, I thought she was asleep with her eyes open. "Mum?" I said. She did not answer at first. "Are you all right?"

"What?" she said. I was going to say something, but she got in first. "What am I going to do?" she said.

"What do you mean, Mum?"

"If he gets killed," she said.

"Is he all right?" I asked. There was a letter open on the table. I guessed it was from my father, his first from Vietnam. He'd been a training sergeant at Kapooka army base just out of Wagga.

"What am I going to do?" she said again.

"I'll look after you, Mum," I said. She didn't respond. She just sat there smoking. I watched the cigarette. It was burning near her fingers. "Never mind, Mum," I said. "I'll look after you."'

'How old were you then?'

'I was nine, going on ten. She did not respond. The cigarette was burning closer and closer. She looked awful, as if her whole face had disappeared behind her skin. Her blue-grey eyes were sunken, and her mouth was thin and hard and forlorn.

"Why do they do it?" she said.

"What, Mum?"

"Why do they go off and get themselves killed?"

"Is dad dead?" I asked.

"May as well be," she said, "going to a place like that. All that jungle and all those Asians." She sighed, stubbed out the cigarette in a tin ashtray on the table. She looked so bad I thought I'd better try to cheer her up.

"Mum?" I said, 'I heard a beaut story today."

"Yes?"

"A kid at school told me." She simply breathed out. She breathed out so much I thought she'd never breathe in again, but she did at last.

"Yeah, this big hunter went to Africa and shot two gorillas."

"Gorillas?" she said.

"Yeah, and he brought them home and took them into a taxi man's shop and threw them on the counter and said, I want 'em stuffed. The taxi man said, I assume you want them mounted? Oh, no, said the big hunter. Just holdin' hands will do!" I waited. She did not react at all. Instead, she just went on looking out the window. Now she'd finished the cigarette, she seemed to have nothing whatever to do with her life.

"Why do they do it?" she said again. "Men going off...".'

Evelyn was gazing up at him. 'You poor boy,' she said, squeezing his hand. 'You good boy.'

He sat there holding her hand and looking at her. But as he did, she began to fade and went on fading until she had disappeared altogether.

It was all imagination, of course. There was no ocean and no surf and no evening star over the Indian Ocean, but only the hard, cold wind coming off the Snowy Mountains. And the memory of what might have been.

He ached for her. She had said her womb had ached for Christine. He did not have a womb, but he had a belly and a heart and some sort of soul, and they all ached. Women did not have grief all to themselves.

The last leaf fell.

He took out the Webley, looked at it for a while, then broke it open. He was surprised. There was still one round in the cylinder. He'd expected the police would have removed it, especially for a man like him—a deadbeat cop with a lot on his mind. Then he realised the round might have been left there deliberately. In fact, it might be a brand-new one, something sure to detonate. Maybe someone wanted to get rid of him. He was an embarrassment to the human race. He thought of taking it out, examining it. But he did not. She was gone now, so what did it matter?

He looked about. Two cars went along Empire Circuit, slowly, as if in respect. A lovely schoolgirl had died here, such a waste of life. Then he saw a girl walking along the street towards him, leading a dog. He started, but it was not the same girl and not the same dog. So, he sat there idly turning the cylinder in the Webley, click, click, click, until the one remaining round was lined up. He was smiling to himself. It had been a good life, all in all. He'd had a few ups and downs, but he couldn't complain. Few men had ever met a woman like Evelyn Crowley—Evelyn the elegant, the mysterious, the criminal, the beautiful.

Then, without giving the matter another thought, he put the pistol to his head and pulled the trigger.

CHAPTER 29

She was walking along Baylis Street at lunchtime carrying a handbag and a shopping bag that contained a new sweater, a pair of thick woollen socks and a pair of woollen gloves. It was cool now, well into July, and the mornings very fresh. She stopped at the Gumnut Cafe, thinking of getting a sandwich and a cup of coffee, cappuccino. The Gumnut was a teas and luncheon place, small but cosy, run by a group of women, all middle-aged. They had good food at moderate prices. And everyone was so friendly. In Australia at that time, there seemed to be a Gumnut Cafe in every town.

Robyn Sheldrake was still looking through the glass when her eyes focused on a man.

She could not believe her eyes.

She hesitated, at first thinking she'd duck away before he saw her, but that would have been cowardly. She was pretty hopeless at some things, but not a coward. So she went in, her heart jumping a little, and walked to the table. The man was sitting in a corner, gazing out at the street and the traffic and the people passing by with a faraway look. Obviously, he'd not seen her. He was holding a knife and fork and thoughtfully chewing. In front of him was a chicken and mushroom pie with salad. At his side was a cup of coffee, long black, and a Melting Moment on a tiny dish. She crept up to him.

'Excuse me.'

He did not stir, so she tried again. 'Excuse me, aren't you Harry?'

He looked up, not focusing for a moment. He finished a mouthful, licked his lips, put the knife and fork down and took his time regarding her. His expression was neither welcoming nor hostile. He was trying to think who she was. Of course, he knew who she was. He just didn't wish to look her in the eyes. To do that would have been to acknowledge her.

'Harry Becker?' she persisted.

He finished the last crumb. 'Yeah?'

'Remember me?'

'Oh, yeah. What are you doing in Wagga?'

She laughed, a bit embarrassed. 'I live here. What are you doing in Wagga?'

'Well...' he said, sitting back, trying to take her in, but not enthusiastically. This was the checkout chick, the one in Canberra who'd stood him up. She'd said she'd meet him at the cinema, which he'd thought a bit strange. He would have picked her up at her place, but she'd insisted it would be better if he did not. She was a widow, she'd told him, and when he'd asked whether she had a boyfriend, she'd said 'no' in a way that suggested she did, but one she did not want to talk about. And next day at Woolworths, he'd been told she'd had a fight with him and had quit. No one had known anything more about her. That was months before he'd met Evelyn Crowley.

'Hi,' he said at last.

He was going to let her stand there by the table, looking embarrassed and silly and ashamed of herself. She did, however, have a terrific figure. Not much of a face, but a terrific figure. Her face was covered with brown freckles and her skin was rough, as if it had been out in the sun too much. She was no raving beauty. Just like any girl you might see in the street or in a shop. But her eyes were bright, wide open. Nothing secret about her. She was a country girl, a farm girl, so she'd said back in Canberra. They'd got talking one day at the checkout and, on the spur of the moment, he'd asked her to have coffee and she'd agreed. So they'd had a coffee at Gus Petersilka's Cafe on Bunda Street. Then he'd asked if she'd like to see a film at the Centre Cinema just along the street that night. She'd agreed, but she'd not turned up.

He thought of letting her stand there as a punishment, but he could not. She was begging to be friends again. You could see it in her eyes.

'Would you like coffee—?' He deliberately paused, as if he'd forgotten her name.

'Robyn,' she said, 'Sheldrake. Oh, I... Well, I...' She looked at her watch. 'Oh, yes, I suppose I could. Just five minutes.'

He stood up, or made the effort to stand for a lady, even if she were a rat who had not even contacted him to say she could not make it or had not apologised for not having made it. But she had a certain charm about her, a nervousness mixed with a desperate wish to do the right thing. She had grabbed a chair and plonked her handbag and the shopping bag on the floor before he could stand up straight. So he sat again.

'What'll you have?'

'Oh, er...' She looked about. A woman came over. All the women in the place seemed to wear tartan skirts or slacks and sensible shoes. And had grey hair, or a streak at least. 'Oh, I'll have a cappuccino, thanks, Heather.'

'Something to eat?' he asked.

'Oh, no, no, I...'

He watched her. She was an excitable girl, although not really a girl, probably middle thirties. She had a girl and a boy, she'd said. And her husband had been a truckie who'd died in a road smash on the Hume Highway three years ago. Gone to sleep at the wheel, it was thought. Eleven hours a day staring at bitumen did that to some men. Somehow, she'd ended up in Canberra. She'd never said exactly how, but there seemed to have been a man in it somewhere. They'd never got as far as intimacies over that cup of coffee. They'd eaten orange–syrup cake, which was a speciality at Gus's place then. Strangely, when Becker had suggested they sit outside, she'd preferred to sit inside—out of the wind, she'd said. He'd suspected she meant out of sight. Out of sight of whom? Still, it had been a nice change for him, chatting to a girl only too eager to chat. He'd eaten too much orange cake. She, however, had delicately pecked at hers. Which was why she had a terrific figure and he did not.

'So—' she said, jumping a bit in her chair, hopping forward an inch or two.

'So you live here?' he said.

'Yes, I came home. I mean, I started off here. And now I'm back with Mum and Dad. Why are you here, Harry?'

'My mother's here too,' he said.

'Of course, you said so. You came to see her?'

He nodded. He wasn't looking forward to seeing his mother again. She might not remember him. He'd passed the place when he'd arrived from the east. Had intended to go in and see her, ask her how she was, but he'd not done so. Last time he'd seen her, she had confused him with another boy, a cousin named Barry. She'd told him to go away. She did not like boys who threw stones and smashed windows.

'Where is she?'

'At Kirralee.'

'Kirralee?' She knew what he meant. 'Oh, I'm sorry. Oh, gosh, I...' She shrugged, bit a lip and said a little prayer with her eyes all at the same time. 'So, you came all this way to see her?'

'Not exactly, I'm just passing through.'

'Oh? Where are you going?'

'I haven't decided yet. Maybe somewhere out west.'

'Oh?' She sounded disappointed. She had to get something off her chest, he could see. Her chest, he noted, was still pretty good. She was wearing an Argyle sweater and blue jeans and solid walking shoes. And she had a cheeky sort of smile. That's what had attracted him at the checkout. She'd been bright and bubbly and talkative as she'd dealt with his purchases. She could do it blindfolded—flash the barcode, stack the bag, take his money, give the correct change while chattering away like a sparrow in a treetop.

Her coffee came. 'Oh, thank you.'

She picked it up and began to sip, then remembered sugar. So she took one teaspoonful and tried again, but began to shake.

'Harry, I'm so sorry.'

He shrugged, sipping his long black. He'd forgotten the Melting Moment, but no matter. He was trying to give them up. He had to lose weight. It was now a problem. He was more than a stone overweight.

'I feel so awful, seeing you again. I mean, I did a bad thing, didn't I? I promised to go with you to that film and I didn't turn up. I mean—' She put the cup down and placed her hands together, as if in prayer. Perhaps praying for strength.

'It's okay,' he said.

'It's not okay. I was a mess then. I mean, I really and truly was going to see you at the theatre and... Well, something happened.'

'A man?'

'Yes, a man.'

'An argument?'

'Yes.'

'A fight?'

'A what? Yes, I suppose you could call it a fight. I mean...' She looked about to cry. Her eyes were closed and her mouth bitter. 'He turned up just as I was about to leave. I'd taken the kids in next door. I'd just grabbed my bag when the doorbell rang. I knew it was him. He always rang it like he was trying to waken the dead. I opened it, I had to. I couldn't ignore him, could I? I was going to marry him once. So I let him in. He saw I was dressed—for going out, I mean. He wanted to know where I was going—' She dropped her voice. 'I said I was going to see a picture with someone, a friend.

"What friend?" he said.

"With Helen Sedgwick," I said.

"Helen Sedgwick?" he said. He was staring at me closely, he was tense and I was scared. He was in the army, a Vietnam vet. He was driving a taxi then, so I'd never know when he'd turn up. I'm not a good liar, Harry. 'Who is it this time?' he said.

"I told you," I said, "Helen." He hit me. He slapped my face. I jumped back against the wall. He came at me.

"You bitch," he said. Then, he... he...'

Her head went down, her voice had dropped to a whisper.

He leaned across, held one arm just above the wrist.

'You don't have to tell me.'

'I'm sorry, I'm so sorry—'

'Come on.' He shook her arm.

He waited as she gulped air, head down and ashamed. People were looking. The waitress came forward as if to intervene, but Becker waved her away.

'She's okay,' he said.

The girl sniffled, then took a deep breath and reached for her bag.

'I tried to tell you, but I didn't know your address or number, so next day I packed up and cleared out. I hadn't slept, not really. It was an awful trip. The car broke down twice, but we got here.'

'You and the kids?'

'Um, yes.'

'Where are you staying? With your mother?'

She nodded. 'She's marvellous, she looks after them after school.'

'Where do you work?'

'For a dentist, just along here, only a hop and a step.'

She was referring to Baylis Street. Becker looked out. A parking inspector was eyeing the BMW. He had parked in a one-hour zone and gone for a walk, up one side and down the other, reliving scenes from his childhood. Then, on returning to the car, he'd spotted the Gumnut. It was now more than an hour. He'd probably get a ticket. On the other hand, he might be able to talk his way out. The car had an ACT registration plate, so he could play the ignorant tourist.

She was still shaking a little, blowing her nose on a tissue.

'You don't have to say anything, Robyn.'

It was the first time he'd used her name. She noted that, pleased. She sank a little, the way women do when they think they've made a fool of themselves. And smiled. She was not bad looking. In fact, she had a good sort of face, nothing glamorous but simple and honest, a country girl's face. The kind you could trust.

'You did the right thing,' he said.

She nodded.

'That coffee's cold now.'

'Oh, oh, that's all right.' She picked it up, gulped it down.

'Want another?'

'Oh, no, no, no...' She looked at her watch. 'Gosh, I must run.'

He rose and paid the bill, then they walked out.

'So you work for a dentist?'

'Oh, I'm just the receptionist. I mean, all I do is answer the phone and take the money and make appointments and...' She pulled a funny face.

'That sounds terrific.'

'Terrific? Oh, gosh, no, I mean...'

She rarely finished a sentence, but that was all right. She laughed as though she'd got through a great ordeal. Meeting him again and not being told off.

'Which way?' he asked.

'What? Oh, down here, next corner, just a few steps.' She watched him anxiously. 'You're not mad at me, Harry?'

'Of course not.'

'Oh, I'm so happy, I mean now that we—'

'I'll walk with you. I'm going that way.'

'Are you? Really? Oh, gosh.'

She laughed again, waving her free hand. A couple of cheap bangles and a thin gold chain hung on the wrist. They made a music of their own. She gasped, patted her chest, sighing deeply, at the same time blowing back hair from the corner of her mouth. The freckles on her cheeks were dancing above the warmth of her smile as she bounced along.

'So, Harry,' she said, 'what have you been doing with yourself since, you know...' Again, words failed her.

'Have dinner with me tonight and I'll tell you.'

CHAPTER 30

That afternoon he walked into the offices of Thos. Thomkins & Son, stock and station agents in Fitzmaurice Street. Old Tommy himself was behind the counter, leaning on his knuckles and staring uncertainly at nothing in particular. He looked old, probably more than seventy now. He had false teeth and a smile that was vacant, because all he saw was a shape coming in the door. His eyes were bright little beads, which had once been bright blue and full of the milk of human kindness, but he'd recently had two cataract operations and nothing had been the same since. He wore bifocals, but they weren't much good, so he tended to look over the top. He was wearing an old Akubra hat and an old Harris tweed with leather elbow-patches and looked every bit the perfect country gentleman. The type you could trust with your daughter at a country hop. He'd always been that way.

'Good morning,' he said.

'Good morning,' Becker replied. If old Tommy thought it was morning, that was good enough for him.

'What can I do you for, young feller?'

'I'd like to buy a farm.'

'What kind of farm?'

'About a square mile.'

'But what kind of farm?'

'To run a few sheep and some fat cattle.'

'This ain't sheep country, you know. I mean, it's good sheep country, but nothin' around here's big enough. You ought to go way out west, out past Hay if you want to run sheep and make a quid.'

'Just a few sheep, say a dozen or two.'

'You aren't going to make much money that way.'

'That's all right.'

'And a few fat cattle, you said?'

'Maybe twenty or thirty.'

'Made of money, are yer?'

'Not exactly.'

'Yeah? Where are you going to sell 'em? The local meat works? They've got all the fats they want. Sheep too. Every flamin' hobby farmer in the district tries to sell his stock to the local works, but the works deal with agents like me. Hobby farmer, are yer?'

'Not exactly.'

'Not exactly? After a tax lurk, then?'

'Tax lurk?'

'You know the sort of bloke. Not a doctor, are you? A dentist? A lawyer? An accountant?'

'Nothing like that.'

'Got some money, have you?'

'A few bob.'

'Well, I'm willin' to take your money it off you, son. But don't come cryin' to me later, when you're broke. Did you have any particular property in mind?'

'How about Nil Desperandum?'

'Nil Desperandum?'

'On the highway, out west.'

'I know where it is, son. Why do you want that particular place?'

'I used to go there years ago. As a matter of fact, you used to send me.'

'Did I?'

'You don't remember me, do you, Tommy?'

Tommy Thomkins leaned closer. He had a son, also named Thomas, but he was not there when Becker arrived. There was a granddaughter named Thomasina, who was known as Sina in order to avoid confusion. In fact, the son and granddaughter were running the business, old Tommy being semi-retired.

'We've seen you before, haven't we?'

'Harry Becker.'

'Harry bloody Becker? That cheeky young bugger always tellin' me a pack of lies?'

'That's the one.'

'And went off and joined the police?'

'That's right.'

Old Tommy stood back to get him into better focus. 'My, my, what brings you back?'

'I've retired.'

'Bit young to be retired, aren't you?'

'Yeah, well, you know, I got retired, medically unfit.'

'Yeah? What happened?'

'Someone took a shot at me.'

'Yeah? Didn't kill yer by the look of it.'

'Nothing serious.'

'I see, I see. And you got a lump sum? And now you want to buy a farm? Know anythin' about farmin'?'

'Nothing at all.'

'Just want a tax lurk, eh?'

'I'm just looking for a place to sit on the verandah at the end of the day and watch the sun go down behind the gums.'

'With a whiskey in one hand and a dog at your feet?'

'Something like that.'

'And a nice little wife dancin' attendance on yer? Married, are yer?'

'Not yet.'

Old Tommy studied him. He screwed up his face and rubbed his chin, which always helped him to think. 'Let me see—'

'What about the Hardwick place?'

'They went to Tumbarumba years ago.'

'Yeah, I know.'

'That place has changed hands a few times since then. The feller who's got that place now, he's a dentist.'

'Here in town?'

'On the main street.'

'Why is he selling?'

Tommy dropped his voice, as if the walls were listening. 'Just between you and me, young feller, I reckon the tax people have caught up with him at last.'

'A bit of creative accounting, eh?'

'Yeah, and the word is he has to find a lot of back tax in a hurry.'

'How much does he want for the place?'

'Half a million.'

'What?'

'Yeah, that's what I said when he told me. In my opinion, it is not worth four hundred thousand.'

'How much then?'

'Ah, if you're really interested, I'd say three seventy.'

'Will he come down to that?'

'Nope.'

'What's the condition of the house?'

'Good, very good. The dentist had it done up. Reckons he spent fifty grand on it. A pack of lies, if you ask me, but he's given it a new coat of paint, replaced the roof, got rid of the termites, everything's electric now, even the shaver in the bathroom. New posts and rails everywhere. Even had 'em painted white, so they'd stand out in the moonlight, his wife said.'

Becker thought about it. 'I'll take it.'

'Eh?'

'Offer him three eighty.'

'Three eighty thousand?'

'Yeah, I'm prepared to go to three ninety, but don't tell him that.'

'Strike me pink, son, you haven't even seen it yet.'

'I saw it many times fifteen years ago.'

'Fifteen years?'

'Yeah, you sent me out there.'

'Did I?'

'To get the old bugger to sign a bill of sale.'

'And did he?'

'No, she did.'

'Eh?'

'I didn't have the heart to tell you.'

'By cripes, son—'

'You said don't come back without a signature.'

'Well, I'll be buggered.'

'Got time for a run out there?' Becker said.

'The boy's got the car. He's doin' an auction today and the girl's clerking for him.'

'I have mine.'

'Are you serious?'

'Yeah, I've always wanted to buy that place.'

'No, I mean about young Verity Hardwick signin' for him. I mean, that's criminal, forgin' a signature.'

'That was her name? Verity?'

'Yeah.'

'Some of the nicest people are criminals.'

'Yeah?'

So, old Tommy hung a notice on the glass door saying Gone to Lunch, although it was now after two o'clock, and they went out there. The property was not far out of Wagga, on the left just past a bridge over Kettle's Creek, a pretty stream which meandered all the way to the river. It was named after John Kettle, who arrived with sheep in 1838, following the Faithful overlanding party heading for Port Phillip Bay. Kettle had sat on Crown land without legal tenure and without fences or even a boundary. But a few years later he'd been granted an official lease, 24,000 acres of prime pasture at ten shillings an acre. After the first big war, subdivision for soldier-settlement had whittled it down to next to nothing.

Not long after the second big war, Ted Hardwick bought Nil Desperandum, intending to turn it into mixed farming, which meant wheat and sheep. But he never got the mixture right. Twenty years later he had to give up the wheat and stick with sheep. He hung on, helped by young Verity, who'd come knocking on his door one day during the drought of the early seventies, when graziers were selling sheep for two dollars each. Even at that price, they couldn't sell enough. So they had to dig deep pits, shoot the stock and throw them in. Verity had asked if he had any work. He did, shooting sheep, but he couldn't pay her. All he had to offer were lamb chops for breakfast, dinner and tea. That was all right, she'd said and walked straight in without as much as a by your leave. She was seventeen or eighteen at the time and had run away from home. Ted hadn't asked her where she'd come from or why she'd run away. She stuck with old Ted through thick and thin and a few years later, when she'd turned twenty-one, they were spliced. It turned out to be a pretty good marriage for a couple like that in those days, considering.

When he saw the house again, Becker was surprised. It was the same house in the same spot, but now a show place in perfect condition. The house was bright with paint. Even the galvanised iron roof, rusty in places when he'd last seen it, had been replaced with grey green Colorbond. The front fences were white post and rail. The coolabahs and box gums were grand, the grass cut like lawn. To one side, between the house and the road, stood the same gnarled old pepper tree, magnificent in its ugliness. The creek to the other side was pretty, and the birds sang in the fresh afternoon air, a welcoming chorus. They seemed to be saying: What took you so long, Harry?

'You've got the key?'

'Oh, strewth, son, I forgot it.'

'Never mind.'

Becker took out a credit card and soon had it unlocked. It was smart and fresh inside. There was air-conditioning in the living room and the main bedroom. The kitchen was a dream, so was the bathroom. Old Tommy was right: an electric razor hung from a hook on a wall. The brand-new bathtub was in the ancient style with legs, but the taps were gold plated. Or, if not gold, then a pretty good imitation. Apparently, the dentist's wife fancied herself as an interior designer. Armed with the latest copies of Vogue Living, she and the builder had remodelled the place. The furniture was new, so was the refrigerator. It was nothing like the old one from which Verity Hardwick had taken a beer and said, 'Feel like a quick one?' But the chair, it was there. A sturdy chair. It was built to last. It'd had to last, when he and she were on it, she bouncing up and down on his old feller.

'Yeah,' he said, 'this is the place. Tell him I'll make it three ninety.'

'Three hundred and ninety thousand?'

'If he leaves the chair.'

That night he took Robyn to Romano's, where he was staying. He'd never stayed there before, but he'd often drunk there, leaning on the bar, yarning to Tommy, especially if they'd had a good sale. Or with the football team after they'd won a match. An old-fashioned pub with high ceilings and doubtful plumbing, it had a certain rustic charm. Each had Murray cod with pommes sautés and a side salad containing everything bar the kitchen sink. It was good food. The lights were low, the music was not too loud, and Robyn Sheldrake looked as though she would burst with amazement. She hadn't been to a place like this for a long time. He raised a glass of wine to her. It was a good local, one of the better Riverina reds.

'Gosh, Harry, this is lovely. Can you really afford this?'

'Only on paydays.'

'And when is payday?'

'Just about every day.'

She laughed. 'Wow! I wish I had a payday like that.'

He was not joking. The money was starting to roll in. Sylvia Feinman had been granted administration of Evelyn's estate and, every time she sold something, she deposited it in separate accounts, half for him and half for Mr and Mrs Billings. She was now selling Donald Crowley's stocks and bonds, three million dollars' worth. Also, in her latest letter, she'd said she thought she had a private buyer for the house, which was not yet on the market, although it had been cleared of all furniture, art works, clothing, crockery, wine cellar, the lot.

Robyn was studying him as if she did not quite trust him.

'You're kidding, aren't you?'

'I won the lottery.'

'The lottery?'

'Not the big one, but one of the consolation prizes, big enough.'

'Really?'

'I don't have to work.'

'Oh, gosh!'

'And I'm buying a house.'

'Where?'

'On a farm.'

'Where?'

'Out along the highway, before the turnoff to Lockhart.'

'Oh?'

He watched her. Her face in the candlelight was a lot more attractive, especially when made up. She'd gone to a lot of trouble. Her clothes were not new, except for the red sweater she'd bought that day. The skirt and the shoes were old, he'd noticed, but well cared for. Her mid-brown hair was swept back, held by a simple red band, which went with the sweater. There was a little mascara on her eyelids and a touch of red on her lips. Not too much. She didn't want to look as if she was making a play for him. She was no glamour girl, just pleasant looking in an ordinary way. But that did not matter. She was the kind of woman you immediately took to. She was simple and honest and dedicated to being a good friend, no matter what it took.

'Would you like to see it?'

'Would I? Oh, gosh, wow, I mean...' She grasped her throat, coughed, almost choked. 'Do you mean it?'

They were married four weeks later. By that time Becker had paid out his wife, the one who was not his wife, the one in Sydney. So everything worked out pretty well. Becker did not tell his new wife about Evelyn. Nor did he say he'd been kicked out of the police force for corruption. Best to let sleeping dogs lie.

9 781922 444585